Radio Frontera!

Radio Frontera!

A Novel

James O'Keeffe

iUniverse®

RADIO FRONTERA!
A NOVEL

iUniverse books may be ordered through booksellers or by contacting:

iUniverse
1663 Liberty Drive
Bloomington, IN 47403
www.iuniverse.com
844-349-9409

Because of the dynamic nature of the Internet, any web addresses or links contained in this book may have changed since publication and may no longer be valid. The views expressed in this work are solely those of the author and do not necessarily reflect the views of the publisher, and the publisher hereby disclaims any responsibility for them.

ISBN: 978-1-6632-2869-7 (sc)
ISBN: 978-1-6632-2870-3 (e)

Print information available on the last page.

iUniverse rev. date: 09/27/2021

For Little King

Una flecha en el aire,

cielito lindo, lanzó Cupido,

si la tiró jugando,

cielito lindo, a mí me ha herido.

(An arrow in the air

lovely darling, Cupid launched

if he was playing,

lovely sweetheart, he has wounded me.)

—Traditional

1

Off the train and into the sun.

The diesel motors thrummed at his back while he shifted his guitar-case strap and headphones. Before him was a handsome old red-brick depot whose soaring bell tower cast no shade. Nor did he himself, although he was tall, even for seventeen.

Inside the depot, he found the payphone kiosk and went to it, fumbling briefly in the lining of his acid-wash jacket before coming up with an MCI calling card. A graying, pant-suited woman seated at one of the nearby benches did a double-take at his Mohawk and dagger earring, brought a hand to her cheek, and turned her eyes away with pronounced disgust.

Once outside again, he found his way to the international bridge into Ciudad Juárez, Mexico. As the pedestrian walkway neared its crest, he reached out absently and raked his fingers across the wire-mesh safety guard. Below his feet, the russet waters of the Rio Grande swept along in mindless urgency.

You're making a damned ass out of yourself, young man, Dr. Tune said.

Near the Plaza de Armas, he came to a queue of repainted school buses lining the street. He picked a green and white one with ANAPRA on its destination sign and climbed on. Faces watched him, assessing the dyed shock of raven hair, the earring, the bruised guitar case. He shut his eyes and retreated into the seclusion of his headphones as the bus groaned to life and entered traffic. The boarding stops were frequent—wan-faced young women on their way to and from the outlying factories, vendors touting fresh flowers and fruit, a pair of child buskers in Transformers tank-tops coming on to serenade the aisle with *corridos.* The paved streets gave way quickly to dirt roads, the coarser spots rocking the bus from side to side. Feeling a little seasick, he opened his eyes and took in the foothills, the shanty neighborhoods, the disparately colored makeshift homes made gauzy and indistinct in the perpetual heat-haze and dust. On the nearby mountain someone had written LA BIBLIA ES LA VERDAD LEELA in block chalk-white letters. Not far below that, a vandalized billboard depicted Bill Cosby, grinning and eyeless, as he pointed with satisfaction to a can of New Coke.

¡La Coca-Cola es! the billboard caption said.

You can't cover the sun with a finger, his great-grandfather said.

The road shored up, more than an hour later, at one last colonia. He rose to disembark, finding himself in tow behind a small platoon of those same silent, wary, wan-faced girls who'd boarded along the way. Once off the bus, they formed a loose shoulder-to-shoulder phalanx and started for the shanties. He watched them go, a little offended that none had bothered to flirt with him. A low, hot breeze stirred around him, carrying scents of fried food and urine and—he thought—the faint neighs and nickers of horses.

"Estás perdido, chulito?"

A woman observed him from the window of a tarpaper shack a few yards to his right. A handmade sign over the window said PUESTAS PERSIS. She left the window and came out through the propped-open screen doorway, toting a can of Schaefer with a bendy straw sticking out of it, then sat down in a lawn chair and crossed her legs.

"Cual es la estación de radio?"

She tipped her beer can at him, her eyes branding him an idiot. He turned, looked behind him, and saw the enormous mast tower atop a nearby mesa, jutting mightily from the desert plain like the hilt of a buried stiletto. Then, turning back to thank her, he spotted another landmark that had eluded his awareness at first, as obvious as the transmitter though it lay in the opposite direction.

Cerro de Muleros. The Black Mountain.

He left Madam Beer Straw behind without the thanks and started on the dirt road toward the mesa. He gauged it to be at least a couple of miles on foot, and he could spy no roads going up to the mesa top. When he felt safely out of Madam Beer Straw's sight, he stopped again and unslung his guitar case and barrel bag. He knelt on the white dusty hardpan and rummaged inside the bag, coming up first with an envelope full of assorted pictures. He retrieved one and held it out in the direction of the hill: a photo he had snapped himself five years ago with his mother's instant camera. A teenage girl stood smiling at him in the picture, hand on her hip, clad in a Rams jersey, jean cutoffs, and tortoiseshell shades. Her lopsided grin seemed both to tease and to menace, conjuring for him even now Kristy McNichol's tough-girl grin in *Little Darlings*. Shadows played on her face because of the height difference—he'd been shorter than her at the time—and he recalled as lucidly as life itself, although the shadows concealed it in the photo, the faint port-wine stain that had marred her left cheek. Beyond her left shoulder rose the distant, craggy, black-shale outline of *Cerro de Muleros*, seen from a different angle but unmistakable in its color and shape nonetheless.

Next he brought out a miniature black-and-white photo, this one much older, yet the girl in it appeared close in age to the one in the first when it was taken. A dolled-up cowgirl in some kind of arena outfit waved to the camera from astride a horse, reins in one gloved hand. Again the Cerro loomed distinctly in the background from yet another vantage point.

Handwritten on the back: *A mi querido Mauricio de Hel.*

Back both photos went into the manila envelope, the envelope back inside the bag. Now he retrieved a .45 army service pistol from the bag, carefully loaded a new magazine clip, set the safety, and then stood up and stuffed it into his jeans, taking care to hide the grip under the bottom edge of his jacket. Over his shoulder went the guitar strap, up came the bag, and forward his feet moved, for the tower atop the mesa.

Poco a poco, se anda lejos, Mauricio said.

Little by little, one goes far.

2

Elfa was so far gone—both geographically and emotionally—that she didn't notice the swirling lights bearing down on her until the Border Patrol truck swept around her car and cut her off. Even so, she was prescient enough to recognize Shaw Jepsen's modified '78 Scout once it was in front of her. She switched off the tape deck and got ready to lacerate him with one of her patented tirades for making her late to work. He seemed to anticipate this, taking his everlasting time getting out and unnecessarily fetching his two gorgeous Belgian-shepherd detection dogs from the Scout's rear hatch. He knew her weakness for dogs.

"Hot out here today, isn't it?" Agent Jepsen said. "You know El Paso's only got two seasons, regular summer and summer lite."

"I'm going to slap you," she replied after rolling down her window. "Seriously and truly. I'm going to slap your face."

"Okay. Want to say hello to Willie and Waylon first?"

She got out of the car with a great flabbergasted sigh and propped her sunglasses up over her forehead. Shaw enjoyed this pathetic chase-and-flirt game, probably because his daily existence on patrol out here couldn't be much better than pathetic itself. And because he was in a position to make her life a whole hell of a lot more difficult than it already was, she always played along with as much counterfeit cheer as she could muster. It was just that today's events had already called for more mustering than she could manage.

"Sorry about the drama, but I didn't recognize your car," Agent Jepsen said as Elfa squatted and coaxed the dogs towards her. "Where's that Isuzu you usually drive out here?"

"The pickup was stolen this morning," she said. "And I didn't know you guys cared who's *leaving* the country, only who's coming into it."

"I still like to know who's coming and going in my sector," Jepsen said affably, adjusting his cowboy hat. "Especially since it's my head if anything goes wrong out here. I'm not trying to be a pain in the ass."

"I know," Elfa said, softening a little. "I'm sorry."

The dogs were beautiful. She was partial to Waylon's blue eyes, unusual but not unheard of in shepherds. She stroked their chins and the backs of their ears, and Agent Jepsen gave her some piñon nuts from a Ziploc bag that he kept in the Scout; these vanished from the palm of her hand almost at once. A Union Pacific freight was pushing in off the desert flats to the west. The tracks paralleled the border, and whenever the trains came through, they formed the equivalent of a rolling wall. The clandestine border-crossing that Elfa used to get to the station was just a few yards beyond the tracks, well-hidden in a thicket of chaparral, although there were plenty of others throughout the area—places where the flimsy razor-wire fence had been trammeled flat by migrants and smugglers, and who knew what other sorts of itinerants. For her, crossing here was simply easier than going downtown and waiting in line on one of the bridges only to come back to a place that lay so close to where she lived. She knew Shaw and the other agents who patrolled the area didn't have to allow it, probably *shouldn't* have allowed it, and probably should have arrested her for it long ago. And so the game had to be played, and played with due respect. She stood up and replaced her sunglasses, resigned to being detained here for a few more minutes at the least.

"So did they snatch your truck from outside your house, or was it parked somewhere else?" Shaw asked.

"As a matter of fact, it was parked at UTEP," she said. "I spent half the morning after my philosophy class roaming the parking lot behind Hudspeth Hall like an idiot, and then the other half sitting in the campus police station." She was not inclined to mention how she had also spent the morning sobbing.

"Hell, the campus cops are probably in on it," Shaw said, glancing off at the train. "And it's probably deep into Old Mexico already."

"Thanks, dude. You're just making me feel so much better."

He broke into a grin, the beeswax in his *Magnum, P.I.* mustache nearly cracking apart. "Hey, cheer up. I bet I've got something that *will* make you feel better. Wait right here."

As if there was a choice. The freight train had arrived, its double-stack containers blocking her view of the XAMO transmitter on the distant mesa and, for the moment, cutting off her only means of getting over there. From here, the tracks wound farther back on the American side, skirting the base of the Black Mountain and edging past the Piper estate, home to the station's owner. As always, she couldn't help admiring the hacienda, a handsome pink Spanish-style mansion that looked like something out of old Hollywood. The locals of Nueva Anapra referred to it as Pink Piper.

Agent Jepsen returned from the Scout holding an old-fashioned contoured-glass bottle of Coca-Cola. He pulled a bottle opener from his duty belt and popped it open for her.

"No," said Elfa, accepting it without thinking. "Is this—?"

"Yes," he said, pride in his voice. "The original formula. Bottled in Mexico of course, although I don't know for how much longer. For now it looks like those bigshot executives at Coke are committed to that new donkey piss of theirs. But I've got a lock on some cases of the old stuff, be glad to share them with you when they come in. My compliments."

"You've been listening to the show," she said.

For weeks, Elfa had been railing against New Coke, adapting her seven-to-midnight shift as a radio disc jockey into a handy protest forum. The news that Coca-Loca, as she had liked to call it in her youth, had fallen victim to the obnoxious "New and Improved" trend in American marketing had bothered her ever since Professor Halatyn had first mentioned it during his lecture in Principles of Advertising class. The example happened to fit that day's discussion centering on the three most commonly used words in U.S. ads, which were, according to his research, "Big," "New," and "Free." But it was not until later that she realized why this particular instance of "New" had struck such a nerve somewhere inside, as if she'd thumped an old fracture that never healed right.

The fifth anniversary of her father's death was coming up later in the fall, and because of its suddenness and violence, and because she was still a teenager when it happened, it was never far from her mind anyway. Manny Schultz had been taken from her rudely and without her consent, and so, in a sense, had her youth. Now another remnant of her childhood was being taken—hardly a matter of life and death, but symbolic nonetheless. By definition, the sugary "New" Coke meant that the old Coke was going away forever, and once again, no one had bothered to ask how she felt about it. The symbolism might have been silly, but the untapped well of rage it had sprung—at times its depth startled even her—was certainly not.

Naturally, Elfa refrained from mentioning her father on the air, just as she refrained from saying much of anything about her personal life. Men called in during her show, a lot of them, men from places that she had never even surmised might be listening. XAMO was one of the longest-running border-blasters in North America, and its reach, particularly at night, was still long as well, but the days when it could claim listenership in places like New York and Siberia were over, mainly because the original half-million-watt blowtorch transmitter was itself now just a memory. So it was still a cause for wonder when people phoned in from places like Isla

Clarión and Moose Jaw, Saskatchewan, to request obscure songs by The Monroes and EBN-OZN.

"*Mamas*, you're the sexiest voice I ever knew who lived up to it so splendidly in person," Sammy Hayes, the station's manager and reigning bush-league celebrity, had told her more than once. "I might have a face for radio, but most women in this business have asses for it too." She didn't mind his chauvinist lip since she and everyone else at XAMO knew where Sammy's amatory tastes lay, and his advice, when you could catch him in a serious humor, was usually not to be ignored. "But do take judicious care with what you divulge of yourself to some of these boys calling in to your show, since it's your ass that they're really after. Some of the girls too, I would wager."

"That's Mandy's problem, not mine," Elfa told him, referring to her artificial on-air persona.

"Every night," Agent Jepsen answered her now, his grin a bit too earnest. Yes, he was after her ass. "In fact I just put a new detachable Alpine system in the Scout, installed it all myself. Compact disc, graphic equalizer, three hundred watts per channel. Come check it out. It's not exactly agency-approved, but the beauty of it is, I can swap the whole caboodle out between this and my Datsun whenever I want. I even mailed some pics to *Petersen's 4-Wheel & Off-Road* last month, but I haven't heard back from them yet."

The train had cleared out at last. Elfa consulted the quartz display on her wristwatch with emphasis. "Jiminy Cricket," she said. "I'd love to, but I'm on the air in ninety minutes. Rain check?"

He escorted her back to her mother's car, then held the Coke bottle protectively as she shifted back into her seat and pulled the driver's door shut. "In that case, why don't you play me a request tonight?" he asked, passing the bottle back to her through the window. "I'd consider that as good as a rain check."

"What would you like to hear?"

"'Texas When I Die.' Tanya Tucker."

"Sorry, but that might be a tough one. We don't play much country anymore, not since the *Urban Cowboy* craze sputtered out. I'll do some poking around in the record library, though. Maybe it's still lurking someplace."

"No need for all that trouble. Why don't you pick something out and dedicate it to me, then?"

"I will, Agent Jepsen. Count on it."

"Come on, now, call me Shaw," he said. "You've known me for long enough. And there's just one more thing. See that gas-line marker over there?"

He described an alternate route to the border using a couple of little-known service roads that would be easier on her tires; then he insisted on leading her over them. Agent Jepsen climbed back into the Scout, and she followed him to her secret crossing place, which was clearly not as secret as she had been telling herself. Willie and Waylon watched her steadily from the Scout's open hatch window, ears erect and heads stationary despite the bumps and hiccups of the road. When they reached the border fence, he steered out of her path and waved.

Elfa waved back, tapping the accelerator in relief as she exited the United States of America for the zillionth time. Shaw Jepsen vanished within the dust thrown in her wake. Elfa adjusted her rearview, catching a glimpse of herself, and all the morning's grief and frustration returned, accompanied by fresh tears.

***

"I have a question," said Sammy "The Hitman" Hayes. He leaned forward in his swivel chair, thumped the eraser-end of his pencil on the soundboard in thought, and watched as a 1982 Jetta came barreling across the desert toward the station building, trailing a plume of white dust and exhibiting a certain spirited anger that often indicated the arrival of Elfa Schultz for her evening shift.

"What, exactly, do guilty feet look like? Are they a different shape or size from innocent feet? Is the difference measurable, so that one could theoretically walk into a Payless Shoe Source and be ratted out for some past infraction by one of those medieval foot-clamps they use? And what about feet that have only been indicted—aren't they entitled to a fair trial before we recklessly condemn them as 'guilty feet'? And if it's true that 'guilty feet have got no rhythm,' as George Michael claims in that last ditty, then does this mean that it's possible for one body part to be guilty and all the others to remain pure and unblemished by sin? These are weighty spiritual questions, boys and girls, and I intend to get to the bottom of them for you, because I *am* your Hitman."

He pivoted left and checked the newsroom clock beside the studio door, despite the digital one at eye-level atop the soundboard. "The time is 5:47 at XAMO radio, *el lanzallamas de la frontera*, 1530 on your AM dial, rhymes with *wammo!*, and don't you ever forget it, *chicos y chicas*. Coming up, we've got Paul Harvey at the top of the hour, and don't forget the Party Line here at seven, with XAMO's very own Hipstress of the Night"—here he punched a tape cart, and the voice of Bill Murray's Carl in *Caddyshack* broke in with "Ooh! That was right where you wanted it!"—"yes, the one and only Mandy will be here taking your *every* request. Sta-*ween*-ah!"

Sammy hit PLAY on another cart, and the electronic samplings of a Fairlight synthesizer announced the opening notes of "Naughty, Naughty" by John Parr. He nudged the boom mike away and logged the song title and artist on his clipboard. Then he rose and went across the hall to take a leak. There was the usual moment of existential disgust as he was forced to regard himself—fifty-nine, gloriously bewigged, and rather ingloriously paunchy—in the gold-vein mirror tiles while he pissed. He noted dismally that the pissing required a considerable amount of pushing down below, more than it used to. After washing up, he produced two orange Dexedrine capsules from inside his lambskin vest and belted them down with a splash from the sink faucet.

Elfa was already in the studio when he returned—slumped in the corner, face buried in her hands. Luz Tafoya, the front receptionist, approached cautiously from down the corridor and stood behind him.

"*Estaba llorando cuando entró,*" Luz whispered to him.

"*Está bien,*" he said, waving her off. He proceeded into the studio and changed out John Parr with the new Tears for Fears, then went to over where Elfa sat, shuddering, on the floor. He crouched beside her and took the Colt Mustang that had slipped out of her hastily discarded Bermuda bag, holding it gently by the barrel end, and laid it atop the turntable console. Then he lifted the loose bundle of LPs that she'd brought in and dropped just prior to the meltdown.

"R.E.M.," he read aloud from the first cover, pausing on each letter as if the sound might proclaim something different from what was in his head. "Never heard of them. Hüsker Dü? Lone Justice? I hope these titles are covered in our licensing deal." He paused and scratched his synthetic hair.

"We're a Mexican radio station," Elfa managed through her tears. "Since when do we honor licensing deals?"

"Isn't there a party game called Hüsker Dü?" Sammy asked, skirting this demonstrably truthful remark. "I seem to remember playing it at Scholz Garten in my KTBC days."

"I hate this city," said Elfa after another minute or so. Sammy drew a box of tissues from atop the console and handed it to her.

"Which city would that be?" he asked. "Your nearest choices are El Chuco and Juárez, and you're not technically within either one at the moment."

"Both. All of it. You're the one always calling this place the armpit of Texas."

"A term of endearment, my love. May I presume this has something to do with you bringing your mother's car to work?"

Again, she told her story, all of it this time. A sophomore communications major at her hometown university, this morning Elfa had emerged from class to find her '81 P'up, for which she still owed more than a year's worth of payments, vanished from its parking spot. There was an initial instant of terror followed by the familiar, forehead-slapping realization—*Whoops! Silly me!*—that she'd experienced this before, practically every day in fact, because the lower student parking lot along Sun Bowl Drive was so physically weird—curved and sloped and uneven, like a shard of pork rind. This was, therefore, not the first time that she'd gotten unexpectedly head-spun when returning from class, her mind already ticking away at plans for her evening radio show, causing her to stop and recalculate where the heck she had parked the P'up.

Along with her books and Bermuda bag, Elfa was lugging an inch-thick bundle of LPs on "loan" from the Fine Arts department on her arm. Her prima, Daniela, worked in the Listening Library and had stashed away some of the more interesting new arrivals, which were barred from checkout under normal library policy, for Elfa's private consideration. As per usual for the lower parking lot at ten A.M., the rows were swarming with vultures when she came out—lazy morning students who would rather wait half an hour for a bitchin' parking space than have to spend an extra ten minutes walking to class. Within moments, in fact, a bronze Toronado had fallen in behind her, prowling so closely after her ass that she'd felt like purposely wandering the parking lot until it gave up and left her alone. She'd done it before. Elfa knew she was a prototype passive-aggressive, had even felt oddly vindicated upon learning about it as an official, bona fide personality disorder in freshman Psych, and so she continued to derive satisfaction from tormenting the congenitally stupid any way she could.

But when the space where the P'up was supposed to be slid into view, the Toronado already flashing its turn signal behind her, the P'up simply wasn't there. A Mustang occupied it instead. Elfa stood bewildered a second, then resumed walking, afraid of looking retarded. The only thing worse than dealing with stupid was *looking* stupid. Her brain raced; she tried to reconstruct her arrival earlier that morning—the usual difficulty with her mother, the lack of sleep from getting home at two A.M., the mad scramble to get to UTEP early enough to claim a decent parking space to begin with. She came to the row's end and looped around to the next, marching as purposefully as her nervous system would permit—*no, I'm not lost, I meant to do that, there's a perfectly reasonable explanation for my behavior, mind your own damned business*—and still the Toronado followed, its engine giving off the characteristic whir of a decrepit power-steering system.

Elfa's habit was to park beside one of the generic pillar-shaped light poles, and so she had this morning—she was at least seventy percent sure. But again, she came to the spot where her senses guided her, and yes, there was the light pole, and yes, there was the Mustang—a bumper sticker for KAMA, one of XAMO's market competitors, peeling from its rear, as if for extra spite—and no, there was no blue Isuzu pickup with the *Santa Muerte* decal in the back cab window, and yes, that was when she turned, flung the LPs and the Bermuda bag to the asphalt, and screamed such screams at the Toronado that her throat would be raw for the rest of the day:

"Fuck *you*! Fuck *off*! Get the fuck away from me! *Get! The fuck! Away! From me!*"

There was a cheer somewhere, approving bleats from a few car horns, other choice obscenities yelled out in reply from sundry directions. Behind the Toronado's windshield, a black woman of perhaps sixty-five in a business blazer, bow-tied scarf, and pearl earrings blinked at her from over the wheel, her mouth open in wounded, silent shock.

Elfa might have simply roamed the lot all afternoon, and maybe for all eternity after that. She might have, except that once she'd wandered the last row, she had to collapse abruptly on the curb back by the Fine Arts pedestrian ramp, draw her knees up to her face, and cry. Life was hard. Life was damn hard. Life was never going to be anything but. And judging by the harrowed look on the Toronado woman's face, Elfa had been kidding herself with that "passive-aggressive" bit. She had unleashed full-bore on an innocent bystander, after all, and that suggested another thrilling possibility: maybe Elfa's life in particular was so hard because, in the final analysis, Elfa was not a particularly good person. Maybe she deserved it.

The psychic pity-party continued even as she composed herself enough to find the campus police station and report the theft. While taking her statement, the officer on duty rose unbidden from his desk and bought her a can of New Coke from the vending machine. He was middle-aged, with studio portraits of three children on his desk. When he was through taking Elfa's statement, he brushed a lock of her hair from her eyes and offered to drive her home. She went outside and waited for the city bus.

The telephone request lines were lighting up already. Sammy, who never took requests anymore, swiveled back and punched the closest one.

"XAMO AM. What do you want?"

"Uh—," came a young male voice, the kind that conjured images of acne and National Spelling Bee championships, from the loudspeaker. "Can I talk to Mandy? Can I hear Depeche Mode? Is she taking requests yet?" Sammy thumped the phone again and cut him off.

"That wasn't very nice," said Elfa, daubing her nose.

"They love you here, *mamacita*," said Sammy. "And they always will. Kids and grownups, boys and girls, gringos and wetbacks, virgins and perverts. Try holding onto that."

"Great. Can I have a raise?"

Both knew the answer to that one, but Sammy left her in a better state of mind than when she'd arrived, nevertheless. He waved at her through the studio picture-window as he climbed aboard his vintage British motorcycle outside by the water fountain, and then he sped off for his Juárez apartment. No crossing the border for Sammy; he claimed not to have set foot in the U.S. in over six years.

Before taking the air, Elfa answered each request line once—none of the five would stop flashing until the tail end of her show, around eleven o'clock—and recorded each call on the reel-to-reel, writing down the caller's name and request in her spiral notebook as well. Two of the five noticed the roughness in her voice and asked if she was all right.

"Please try and ignore this nasty little frog in my throat tonight, folks," she said huskily at the top of the show. "He's an uninvited guest. Pay him no mind."

Sunset was imminent, draping a gilded sheen over the Franklin Mountains as they marched away in orderly formation to the north, a sight that never failed to move her. In the foreground, the Black Mountain seemed immune to the sunlight. Its serrated, volcanic textures and gloomy hellscape color-palate intruded on the natural beauty all around it. Drawing somehow on its visual power, Elfa leaned into the orange-foam microphone filter and summoned Mandy's voice…always deeper, more expressive, and more wizened than her own, like some sophisticated older sister, one who hadn't spent her college years slumming at the local state university. Now it had acquired a gravelly Bette Davis rasp as well, thanks to her little explosion hours before.

"The first tune tonight goes out to Shaw, and if you're listening, my friend, thanks for doing me that solid earlier today." She nudged a cart into the Fidelipac machine. The song was "Hard Woman" by Mick Jagger.

***

During the ten o'clock newsfeed from CBS, Elfa slipped out of the studio and made her way to the reception area, holding her gun. The station was a graveyard at night, and it was a lot less scary with the cool weight of her Colt 380 in hand. Everyone who worked at XAMO carried a piece, even Luz.

The front room was bathed in red from the neon wall sign—*XAMO!* in Art Nouveau lettering—and the wall-mounted speakers relayed the radiocast to the room's two empty 1960s vinyl armchairs. Elfa laid the gun on the receptionist's counter and went behind it to the cubbyholes where Luz put everyone's mail and messages. She gathered the small stash inside the one with her last name on it and began chucking things item by item into the wastebasket: new-release fliers; a BMI news bulletin; a postcard invitation to worship from La Paz Ministries, the nearby evangelist church. The fliers she might have ordinarily kept for later; she wrote often to independent record labels, asking to be included in their mailing lists, but given the cluster fuck of a day it had been, her degree of receptiveness right now to come-ons or appeals of any kind was nil.

From the mismatched assortment in her hands, one item slid free and dropped to the floor.

A thick, belated drowsiness now settling over her, Elfa tilted her head to reckon with this orphan, or rather with the momentous decision to kneel and retrieve the thing or leave it there to face Luz's morning push-broom. But once Elfa's eyes had adjusted, they gleaned that it was not a flier, a bulletin, or a postcard. Instead it was an instant-camera photo, not a Polaroid but something akin to one, of a girl standing in front of the Black Mountain on the U.S. side of the border. This Elfa knew because it was the view that still greeted her every day; the vantage point from her neighborhood in Buena Vista, more specifically from the road fronting her parents' old thrift shop. And then there was the date, which she might have guessed at any rate due to the silly sunglasses and L.A. Rams jersey that she'd sported in her more tomboyish days. But she didn't have to guess at all, because somebody had scrawled the exact date in Magic Marker in the white border area at the bottom, in black numerals large enough to be decipherable in the dim red light even from where Elfa stood, unmoving and sleepy, gazing down at it with suddenly fresh eyes.

August 30, 1980.

The day her father was killed.

3

The Lazybones Stables and Trailer Park occupied seventy acres off a narrow two-lane road in Nueva Anapra, New Mexico, bounded by an alfalfa field on one side and a Freemason hall on the other. From the window of his canned-ham trailer he could see the grandstand and pavilion of the Nueva Anapra racetrack glinting in the sun and, further south, El Cerro. Beyond that, the XAMO transmitter. He'd been up for an hour, tooling on his Washburn acoustic and absorbing side two of an unlabeled Memorex cassette on his Walkman. There was a partial box of expired Maruchan in the flea-sized kitchenette, and he'd already boiled a package for breakfast.

After a while, he stood the guitar against the wall and stepped into the hat-closet of a bathroom to wash up. When he subsequently emerged from the trailer, a young redheaded woman in a Union Jack tank-top was fastening a horse to the nearby hot walker.

"Is Tree back already?" she called out to him.

"Huh?" He had to shade his eyes with his hand to make her out. The morning sun was an arc lamp thrown in his face.

"That's Tree Pendleton's trailer," she said. "Did he change his mind about Ruidoso?"

"No, I'm just crashing here a few days. He lent me the key."

"Really?" said the woman, either in disbelief or playfulness; there was no telling which. "I'm Casey, by the way."

"Hi," he said, and moved on.

The office was in a white cinderblock house at the park entrance. An OPEN sign dangled just inside the front door, but when he tried the handle, it was locked.

"Over here, chief," someone called.

Across the road from the trailer park, a short man in a maroon jogging suit and leather cowboy hat stood with a fishing rod in one hand. He raised the other hand and made a beckoning gesture.

The man was angling in a canal lined with tall rabbitfoot and barnyardgrass. He sat down on a partially buried mud-terrain tire and recast his line. The water was a solid cloud, brown and motionless.

"Are you the troubadour?" the man asked him.

"I don't...sorry?"

"Saw you come walking in yesterday evening with that case on your back. Looked like you'd been carrying it a while."

"I was."

"You're staying in number nineteen?"

"Yes, sir."

"That's Tree Pendleton's trailer."

"I know."

He reeled in and recast, startling a family of black-bellied ducks. An F250 barreled past on the road behind them, hauling an empty aluminum horse trailer.

"Something I can do for you?" the man asked.

"Want to know if you're hiring."

The man turned his head and scrutinized him. "Do I look like I need a guitar player?"

"I'm a wrangler and trainer, lots of experience. My family has a boarding stable in Visalia."

"Got a name, pilgrim?"

"Charlie. Charlie Sexton."

"I see," the man said reflectively. "We don't need many wranglers in the off-season. Racing starts in November."

"Okay." He shifted his feet, not sure whether the conversation was over or not.

"I'm kinda wondering why you'd come hoofing it all the way out here to do something you could be doing in Visalia."

"I'm a student. Just looking for part-time work."

"Miner or Aggie?"

He wavered. "Aggie," he lied.

Then the man's line seized and bowed, and they were sudden partners. It took them nearly ten minutes working together to reel and net the eighteen-pound flathead, which had eaten most of the line before it was over.

"*Caldo de bagre*," the man said triumphantly, clutching the captured, squirming creature as if it were a pulsing heart. Then he kissed it and tossed it into a bucket.

"My daughter's the stable manager," he said then. "Redheaded girl. You go present yourself and see if she wants your help. She likes fellas with fucked up hair."

***

A one-story adobe cottage with red barrel-clay roof. Red lightning-motif detailing, frayed and faded but still visible along the outer walls. Images of twin transmitter towers throwing electrical bolts at each other painted above the double-door entrance. Mexican colonial stone water fountain out front.

It sat nearly alone on the mesa, but for the transmitter and one neighbor: an enormous, windowless, hangar-like structure with an ivory masonry sign reading MINISTERIO LA PAZ out front. This other building looked as if it had experienced better fortunes of late, its exterior crisply painted in alternating bands of green and white. Upon seeing it again, his mind's eye replayed what he remembered of the one occasion he'd been inside: the coffin, the velvet painting, his dad yelling at the Rich Lady in front of all those people. The smiling young pastor with his thick hair and pulverizing handshake.

He'd hiked nearly an hour after leaving Madame Beer Straw's hut. He'd found a newly paved access road, the asphalt still black and yielding and glittery with oil, amid the shantytown at the foot of the mesa. The road led him here and appeared to finish up at the church building, if that's what it still was. But he stepped off the asphalt and started on the dirt driveway toward the radio station instead.

The latest Phil Collins dancefloor hit played to a deserted waiting room when he came in. Once his eyes adjusted to the dimness, he went toward the armchairs and unslung his guitar case, grateful for the moment's chance to recuperate from the heat and the long walk. Then a man popped up from behind the receptionist's counter, like a bellboy in some movie-comedy hotel, his back to the entrance doors. He held what looked like a deck of cards and was inserting one in each of the cubbyhole slots behind the counter. A fleshy woman wrapped in floral chiffon and clattering with much cheap jewelry came around the hallway corner and halted in surprise.

"*Válgame, Simón!*" she cried. "*Qué crees que estás haciendo?*"

"I'm assisting you, my lovely Luz," the man replied. "Saving you time and effort, although I admit I sometimes doubt whether you ever distribute these invitations at all."

"*Fuera!*" she snapped, though not unkindly. She scurried around the counter and shooed him out. The man strolled unflappably into the waiting area, a convivial, self-possessed grin at the ready on his face, and met eyes with the young new visitor. He shifted stride immediately, feather-step, and offered his hand in greeting.

"Simon La Paz."

"Mark Knopfler," Asher lied, and recognition seized him in the form of a handshake. He felt his knuckles bunch up in an unnatural and painful cluster as Simon's hand enfolded his. The man's eyes, however, were tranquil, his expression earnest. The wavy hair and mustache from five years ago were gone, replaced by balmy clean-shaven skin and a trim business haircut. A gold ichthus pin gleamed from the upper breast of his oxford shirt.

"You're not from around here," he said in English, the smile unflagging.

An older man in a vest and motorcycle boots appeared from the back hallway and went around the counter, ignoring the both of them.

"How would *you* know?" Asher said, sounding more indignant than he meant to because of the rising pain. Simon released him at last.

"That handsome denim jacket, for starters," he replied. "Let me guess: Jogamoes? Chess King?"

"Am I supposed to dress like you? I'm not selling Amway."

"Easy, *disidente*," Simon said. "I meant no slight against you. But I can deduce at least two more things at face value: one, you arrived here on foot, and two, you're here to meet Mandy, whose voice speaks to your heart, and—you're convinced—to your heart only."

"That tells me she's doing her job," said the man behind the counter, who was fastening the chin-strap of a German-spike helmet underneath his beard. "A good DJ knows that he, or she, and her audience only want the same two things from one other. Speaking of which, you're laying it on a bit thick today, aren't you, Pastor? Leave the poor boy alone."

Simon spared him a perturbed glance. "Our lord and savior laid it on thick on a regular basis," he said, "and rightly so."

"What are the two things?" Asher interjected.

"Why, the very same spiritual tonics that the good Pastor is trying so earnestly to ply you with: love and acceptance. I reckon it chaps his sheepskin that the church of rock 'n' roll might deliver on that promise better than *la Iglesia* does."

"*Perdóname, señor*," continued Simon, by way of dismissing this unwelcome line of conversation. "Whatever the reason may be for your presence here in Anapra, young *disidente*, I would exercise a bit more caution than you seem to be doing with your attire, if you're indeed traveling on foot. There are some around here who would happily knife you for something as inconsequential as a brand-name jacket bought in an American shopping mall."

"I'll remember that."

Simon took Asher's aching hand and placed in it one of the postcard invitations to worship at Ministerio La Paz. "Our business card. Please consider visiting our humble church while you're visiting, even if it's only for the barbacoa tamales. I bring them in myself from El Paso every

29

Tuesday and Sunday. And if true love should blossom between you and Mandy, please bring her with you as well. I've been trying for two years to add that girl to the flock."

He hooked a thumb at the man in the motorcycle helmet, who was making for the front doors. "This one, I don't know. I'd still like to believe in miracles."

"Yes, and I'd still like to believe in Mondale," Hitman Hayes said, and pushed his way outside through the big double casement doors.

Simon excused himself and exited also. Asher examined his throbbing hand and wondered if he would ever be able to play guitar again. Luz set her voluminous Pekingese-fur purse atop the counter in her own preparations to leave. These included digging a silver .38 revolver from the purse's innards, then releasing and turning the cylinder to inspect each chamber for bullets.

"*Me permite usar su baño?*"

Luz turned to him in surprise and eyed him above one of the chamber slots. "*Cuál es su negocio aquí?*"

He explained it.

"No, no, you can't," she said gravely in Spanish, meaning his request to see Mandy/Elfa. She lowered the gun, to his mild relief. "I'm sorry, *mijo*. She is doing her show now, and it's *despues de...*you know, after business hours. Maybe you like to try again tomorrow?"

"Can I at least use your restroom? I've come a long way."

She touched him on the arm. "Are you a good boy?"

Asher thought about it. "Most of the time, sure."

"Oh, good," she said, as if that had settled the matter. She shouldered her hairy purse and led him to the back hall, where she pointed out the restroom door. She beseeched him to please use the facilities quickly, and then to be sure of shutting the front doors firmly behind him when he left the building. She went to the entrance and set the inside lock with her key, and then she was gone.

There was a monitor on the restroom wall, and while he stood washing his hands in front of the gold-vein mirror he listened to Mandy's on-air conversation with a preteen girl wanting to hear "Like a Virgin."

"So why do you love Madonna so much?" Mandy asked. "Talk to me."

"Oh my god, I just *love* Madonna!" the caller gushed.

"Right. Got it. But why?"

"I just love her *music*!"

"I see. Can you tell me why?"

"Because I just love the way she *dances*!"

Asher finished up and crept back out into the deserted hallway, conscious of the door hinge's sharp groan. The station building was the size of a small house. On the wall opposite the restroom was a framed seven-inch record, still in its white paper sleeve. He approached and read the label—"I Fought the Law" on Exeter—then the handwritten note on the bottom sleeve corner: *Sammy, Thanks for your help getting this one off the ground. We couldn't have done it without you—Bobby.*

Another door stood ajar nearby. When he peered within, he found a room where rows of shelves held oblong boxes, and inside the boxes more 45 records sat in upright stacks by the hundreds, maybe thousands. He went to the nearest shelf and flipped through a batch, some in picture sleeves ("I Want Candy" by Bow Wow Wow), some in plain sleeves ("Funkytown" by Lipps Inc.), many marked PROMOTIONAL NOT FOR SALE. There were records going back to the forties, and other shelves held 78s and 33s. One case against the wall was crammed with end-to-end volumes of *American Top 40 with Casey Kasem* on generic, white-label vinyl LPs.

"What if the Rolling Stones re-recorded 'Satisfaction' and took the original one permanently out of circulation in the name of 'New and Improved'?" Mandy was saying on the monitor. "Think of your favorite movie, say *Star Wars*. Imagine them making a new version and taking away the one you grew up with and loved because it stopped making buckets of money. Isn't that just what Coca-Cola is doing? Shouldn't the things we *all* love belong to *all* of us?"

Asher withdrew from the record library and moved on to the last door down the hall, which was the broadcast studio.

She sat before the control panel, her back to him, on the other side of the insulated glass. Her reddish-brown ponytail flitted and danced as she simultaneously monologued into the nickel-plate condenser mike and ran the control board. The bank of phone lights to her left flashed continuously, each winking on again almost as soon as she punched off to the next. He froze there in the hallway shadows and watched, becoming a

32

shadow himself, shrinking back a little each time she turned her head to answer the phone or consult the wall clock.

How do you know my name, you shifty little skitzo creep?

The cold shame from the night when it had all gone so abruptly wrong between her and him descended again like the weight of the world itself. There was still so much to explain. He had envisioned nothing but coming to see her, here at the XAMO studios, all afternoon from his Amtrak coach seat. Believed that his simply appearing here in person would clear everything up from Elfa's (Mandy's) point of view. He would come straight here, make amends with Mandy (Elfa), restart their friendship anew, and then cross the border into Nueva Anapra and set about his *other* business.

But no. The Rich Lady was a different matter, and if he went ahead now, dared show his face to Elfa (Mandy) here, like this, she was just as apt to hate his guts (never mind the loaded *cuete* stuffed down the front of his jeans) before he got two words out. Might even have her own *cuete* and use it on him on sight.

Discouraged—and all too aware that he was behaving very much like the damned ass that Dr. Tune had once dubbed him—Asher went back to the front lobby and located his duffel bag. He took the snapshot picture out and went behind the counter with it, knelt, and searched the cubbyhole slots until he found one whose contents were all addressed ELFA SCHULTZ.

La mayor dicha o desdicha del hombre es la mujer, Mauricio said.

He removed Elfa's mail from its slot, shuffled the photo in with the approximate midpoint of the stack, and returned the whole mismatched jumble to its cubbyhole.

While gathering his belongings, he had a moment to examine the framed sepia-tone portrait on the wall above the two armchairs. A middle-aged man with evenly parted, pomaded hair, round wire-rimmed glasses, and a ducktail goatee and mustache.

"*Hola, tatarabuelo,*" he said to the empty room.

***

The sun lay wasted on the desert's edge. Dreamy shadows lengthened over the badland between Anapra and Nueva Anapra, making it tougher to mind his footing as he negotiated the soft sand, the sudden dry arroyos, and the clumps of chaparral, yucca, and tornillo. He'd discovered a network of makeshift trails, but each petered out abruptly, as if its maker had given up or vanished. Or both. For a time he clung to the trails of litter instead— soda cans, a couple empty plastic milk jugs fixed like ornaments on a dead creosote branch, a lone rubber flip-flop. But the light had dimmed too much.

He thought of Lex, nine years old, who right now was either watching an episode of *He-Man* or conducting a cataclysmic battle with his Castle Grayskull playset. The odds were also strong that he'd been alone all day, eating frosted Pop Tarts for breakfast, lunch, and dinner while Dad was out managing the stables. Lex wasn't interested in horses and didn't like the outdoors.

As the sky darkened, he concentrated on the endpoint: the thin bead of lights coming from Nueva Anapra just ahead. Sure, it would've made more sense to go there first when he got off the train, but the prospect of seeing Mandy in person had eaten at him with such urgency—to the extent that it had stung him a little when Simon La Paz zeroed in on it a little while ago. Asher liked to think of himself as mysterious, not obvious, and yet an obvious phony had read him like a cheap paperback within seconds—

—he slammed into a section of fence, repelled by the chain-link's tension recoil, and fell bass-ackwards in the hardpack dirt. (*Si se tratara de una serpiente habría mordido*, Mauricio had often said.) He stared up at the woven crisscrosses of wires that, to his naked eyes, were visible only now because of the subtle kaleidoscopes that the city lights beyond them made when he shifted his head.

As he retrained his gaze a little further, taking appraisal, he saw that a nearby portion of chain-link had been messily shorn away and contorted with a pair of bolt cutters, no doubt wielded by a very unskilled (or a very hasty) set of hands. Asher gathered himself and his things once more, a few thorny sandburs clinging to him and his clothing, and made way towards it. He unshouldered his guitar case and fed it through first, and then he eased himself sidelong through the gash, stood up, and took in the lights on the Nueva Anapra side of the border as if with new eyes. Weird: so this is what it felt like to enter the United States as an illegal. It wasn't something he had contemplated in coming here, but it was something new and curious to consider.

He pivoted and faced back the way he had come for a moment, since there seemed no particular hurry now that he was stateside once more, and then he scanned the horizon to the south for the XAMO transmitter. The sky was a cloudless canvas, the evening star Venus enthroned by the red afterglow just above the foothills to the west, with whole clusters gathering in the eastern sky to sing her praises. And centered between the two, the XAMO tower seemed to support the whole cosmic tapestry from its place on top of the mesa, its red airplane light winking steadily on and off like the center of the universe itself.

And now here was something else.

A few yards even further away to the right, an entire section of fence was gone completely. No sign of mangled wire, no evidence of desperate vandalism; just a brazen gap of ten or eleven feet, plain as day. It stood there like an unsettling invitation while the whole rest of the fence line said, emphatically, to go away. Like a fake doorway in some screwball cartoon. It was too convenient to exist.

Something else to ponder, then. He lifted the guitar case and went on. The lights drew closer, the sounds of traffic and the hum of machinery. City sounds. And closer than that: horses. Boarding stables. Sounds and odors as recognizable to him as Mandy's voice.

Then: a pair of steely canine jaws snapped shut less than an inch from his face.

36

There were two of them, both dogs alternately leaping toward his throat and face so close and so fast that he dare not move, their barks loud enough that they would rings in his ears for hours afterward. A hatted figure stood at ease and motionless on a rise a few yards in front of him, the charcoal glow of a cigarette hovering near its mouth.

Asher waited for the figure to speak, and when it didn't, he opted for plan B. As slyly as he could, he inched the hand closest to his waist towards his grandfather's gun.

"*Adelante, alegra mi día,*" the figure said. A man's voice, laced somehow with an unseen and unsympathetic smile.

"I'm an American," Asher offered.

"No shit, Scooby," the figure replied, unmoved. "But if you reach for that hog leg again you won't be anything but bones and spare parts. My furry friends here can't smell your nationality."

The dogs' state of frenzy was heightening. Hot-breathed snouts and fierce, bared teeth came closer to Asher's neck, ears, and eyes with each snap, and an unexpected, incipient panic took hold of him. It whispered two things: one, that acting on his fear in front of these dogs and this man who appeared to control them would be the last royal fuck-up of his life; and two, the time, place, and manner of his death would be unknown to anyone who mattered if he perished out here.

The figure tossed his cigarette away, casual to the point of boredom, raised a hand to his mouth, and issued a piercing two-finger whistle. The dogs stopped barking and sat. The man came down from the slope where he'd been standing and strode, at ease, into Asher's view. He wore olive Border Patrol garb and a straw cowboy hat.

"What happened, you get bounced from a Black Flag concert and then teleport yourself here? Got some identification on you, cousin?" he said.

Asher hastened to find his wallet, and the dogs shot back towards him, poised on their haunches.

"Hold it, dummy. I asked if you had any I.D. I didn't tell you to dig it out. Hold your arms out to your sides. Show us your crucifix pose, Arnold Schwarzenegger."

The agent patted him down and found the gun immediately, removing it without comment and checking the ammunition clip before wedging it under the buckle of his utility belt. Then he searched Asher's jean pockets and withdrew once more, holding a Velcro billfold in both hands, which he peeled open and examined under the lens of an aluminum penlight. "Asher Reed," he said, scanning his California driver's license.

"Red-*day*," Asher corrected him. "R-E-D-E."

The agent, named JEPSEN according to the embroidered patch over his uniform breast pocket, tossed his billfold back to him in an underhanded fast-pitch. "Well excuse *moi*, Mr. Red-*day*. Now set the bag and the case on the ground."

Asher complied, proceeding as gradually as possible so as not to provoke the dogs again. Agent Jepsen instructed him to open both and back away, and then he knelt and began poking through the duffel bag with the penlight in hand while Asher stood and watched in apprehension.

"What's this? No goddamn way!" Both dogs turned their heads to Agent Jepsen as if he'd sprouted a third arm. When he rose back to his feet he held a yellow miniature plastic toilet in one hand. He stuck the penlight between his teeth and turned a dial-switch on the ersatz tank. Music erupted from underneath the tiny toilet-bowl lid, ringing out thinly in the unmistakable high-treble peal of AM radio.

"*Shush…keep it down-down…voices carry!*" Agent Jepsen warbled along with the lyrics, off-key and tone-deaf. He feinted a few dance steps, circling away from the duffel bag with the radio speaker up to his ear and then coming back. "I haven't seen one of these Little John radios in about a hundred years. Where'd you get it?"

"Don't know," Ash lied. "I've just had it forever."

"How about that," Jepsen marveled, becoming gushy and boyish seemingly out of nowhere. "I used to work at Spencer Gifts in Scottsdale, where I grew up. You know, with the plastic turds and truck nuts and T-shirts that said 'Fuck Me I'm Irish.' And these things too, except we had them in a different color, sort of an eggshell blue, I think. Mind if I keep it?"

"Yes. Put it back."

The grin faltered. "Alright, cousin. I didn't mean any offense. Why don't you explain to me what you're doing out here?"

"I'm not smuggling anything."

"That's a good thing, since you'd be terrible at it if you were. And that's not what I asked you anyway."

A freight train was threading in from the east, air horn bellowing. Agent Jepsen made a motion indicating for Asher to sit, that it was going to be a while. He went back up the sand rise and disappeared, and Ash, hesitating somewhat, squatted on the ground Indian-style, avoiding the dogs' hardened gazes.

A vehicle engine fired up somewhere, and a set of headlights washed over him as Agent Jepsen returned in a green Border Patrol off-roader and parked it nearby in a spray of dust. He called the dogs to him and had them hop in through the hatchback. Once they were each secured, he waved Ash over and pointed to the passenger door of the Scout.

"Let's go, cousin."

"Am I under arrest?"

"Quit being a dick. Just get in."

The man still had custody of his grandfather's service pistol. Asher obliged, falling reluctantly into the front passenger seat and hoisting his things overhead into the back. The dogs watched vigilantly from behind a web of steel mesh. Jepsen slid behind the wheel and tore out, making easy, familiar use of the same trail system that had confounded Asher. He lowered the two-way radio and reached underneath the dash, where the cube buttons of a handsome tuner/cassette deck glowed like iridescent candy. The sleek, sterile sounds of British New Wave came up on the hidden speakers. The green digital tuner display read 1530 AM.

"You've got a better radio than me."

"Maybe," said Jepsen. "The music is shit, of course. Me, I like country, not this faggoty Boy George stuff. But the girl who spins the records is the love of my goddamn life. Tasty treat, *ese*. You ever fall headlong for a chick at first sight? Or are you a fag also? No offense, again. I just thought because of the hair."

Asher said nothing. They came out of the dirt badland and veered onto a blessedly smooth highway.

"I'm still waiting to hear your story, bro."

"Am I your cousin, your bro, or your *ese*? Make up your mind."

"Going back to your earlier question, this is a detainment, not an arrest. However, we do have a manager's special going today: you can choose to undergo your detainment at the downtown processing center, depending on how stuck you are on this Rebel without a Clue routine you've got going—or you can do it at the DQ over a dose of steak fingers. How do you call it, son?"

The erstwhile Dairy Queen—the owners had not very cleverly altered the road sign to say "Dairy King," as if they'd either changed their minds or forgotten to pay the franchise fee—was located on the same strip of highway, next door to a Taos-style adobe church. A group of teens in shit-kicker boots and Skoal caps called Jepsen's name when he pulled in and Jepsen raised a hand. A handwritten sign on the entrance door announced fresh menudo on Sunday. Inside the restaurant Jepsen ordered for both of them, opting for two Hungr-Busters with fries and lime Dr. Peppers. He brought their drinks, heavy with crushed ice, over to the booth Asher had chosen.

"So, Asher Red-*day*," he said, removing his hat. "You might be interested to know that yonder weed-patch you were out strolling tonight is one of the deadliest on the whole U.S.-Mexico border. Statistically your chances of coming out alive are better in the Bermuda Triangle. In fact, I'll be glad to accept your sincere thanks right now for rescuing you from it—not to mention for this here delicious repast you're also about to enjoy."

"Thanks," said Ash.

"That was beautiful, my friend. I'm all choked up. Really."

A girl in profuse electric-purple eye shadow, visibly pregnant, brought their orders out. After setting the baskets down on the table, she plucked a fry from Jepsen's and ate it as she sauntered back to the kitchen.

"Listen, I get it," Jepsen continued, pulling a hunk of napkins from the table dispenser. "Probably better than you'd ever think. You're a young Turk. You're the kid in *Repo Man*. You're pissed off about something, Mama or Daddy didn't love you, Reagan's an asshole, blah-blah-blah, fine. But whatever your trip is, honcho, you had no rightful or even logical business in that desert out there tonight, and I don't ever want to catch your MTV-watching, Miller's Outpost-wearing amateur's ass out there again."

Asher regarded his burger, which leered up at him greasily from the open end of its checkered wax wrapping paper like a ghoul's mouth. Despite the day's journey, his appetite had fled.

42

"It's complicated," he said.

Jepsen nodded, having somehow already scarfed the contents of his basket. "So's juvenile weapons possession," he said. He nudged his empty food basket aside and took out the confiscated gun, then ran his finger probingly over the grimed U.S. ARMY engraving along the slide.

"Is this Dad's or Grandpa's? Or your uncle's? I tend to doubt you have any older brothers who served this far back. I'll wager the last time this baby was fired was during either the Big One or Korea. Doesn't look like anyone's cleaned it since then, either."

"Can I go to the bathroom?"

"Have you fired it yourself? If there's any corrosion inside, it's guaranteed to jam up on you. These older ones have a basic design flaw in the extractor to begin with."

Asher stood. "I'm going to the bathroom."

"Steer clear of Joey while you're back there," Jepsen called after him. "That's our lovely waitress. She's got a bambino baking already, but you could probably make it twins just by unzipping near her."

Joey was indeed smoking a cigarette in the back hall by the restrooms, leaning against the open door to the kitchen. The red labelmaker tape on her name badge said YOAnNa.

"Do you like Suicidal Tendencies?" she asked without looking at him.

"No, not especially. Why?"

"God, I was just *asking*." She slipped away into the kitchen while studying her fingernail. Asher went into the squalid single-stall men's

43

room and locked the door. For want of something better to do, he filled his hands from the tap and ran them over his face and hair, then stared at the mirror over the sink, lost in himself. Second, third, and fourth thoughts clamored like children in his head: he was found out, and it had taken less than twenty-four hours. No point in going on with it now. Any of it. He tried summoning one of Mauricio's *dichos*, listening hard in his mind à la Luke Skywalker for some whispered blessing or scrap of cosmic guidance. The enraged hiss of a fresh basket of fries hitting hot oil greeted him from the kitchen.

A pair of thuds on the door. "Still alive, slick? Don't hog the facilities, now."

Jepsen handed the pistol back to him butt-first when Ash opened up. "Give me a couple of minutes, and then I'll drive you to wherever you're going, okay? Don't wander off." Then he took possession of the men's room and Ash went back out to the table, where his guitar and bag sat waiting on the bench seat. Beyond the front windows, the shit-kickers appeared to be entertaining, or entertained by, Jepsen's dogs. They were gathered behind the Scout and petting them through the open rear hatch, the same two animals whom, Asher was fairly certain, would have opened his throat on a word from Jepsen not even an hour ago.

Seconds later, Ash had his things and was outside the restaurant. He darted to the building's rear and made for the parking lot of the church next door. There was a row of covered parking stalls on the side-street facing back towards the Dairy Queen; he crept into one and knelt between the front grille of a hoary Nova and the waist-high stucco wall. When he found the nerve to peer over the wall's top edge, Jepsen was outside the DQ, smoking and chatting with the roughnecks. An eighteen-wheeler barreled past on the highway, the very road Asher needed to cross in order to find the Lazybones Stables...if his *bisabuelo*'s spidery hand-drawn diagram of Nueva Anapra was still to be trusted.

He withdrew from the carport and approached what looked like an annex wing of the church, where a set of double doors stood propped open. Glimpsing inside from a safe distance, he found a meeting hall full of Thursday-night Bingoers: a sea of white and balding heads bowed over their playing cards while an ancient *grande dame* called out numbers in Spanish from a giant Plexiglas hopper. Asher fell back and moved on, still ducking like a soldier in combat, along the exterior colonnade to the main church building. The rotunda-style main sanctuary was wide open and deserted. He followed the outermost aisle to the opposite side of the room and then took a seat in one of the concentric pews, feeding his luggage in first to keep it out of sight. On the wall behind the altar, La Virgen de Guadalupe floated in space, head tilted in prayer, her faultless feet resting on a thin sickle moon. A close cousin to this image was inlaid on the back of the Washburn guitar he was carrying.

"Has venido a confesar?"

A youngish priest in a hastily donned stole and chasuble, blue jeans visible beneath, had come into the room. The distinct aroma of a microwave dinner trailed him from the office doorway where he'd emerged.

"No, por favor."

"Puedo ayudarlo?"

"Por favor, no."

This seemed to consternate the priest, which Asher realized wouldn't do under the circumstances. From somewhere outside, he heard a dog barking. *"Habla usted Inglés?"* he ventured.

"I'm originally from New Jersey," said the priest. "Like the salsa commercial. The name's Father Snoddy."

"Neil Peart," Asher lied, accepting the Father's handshake. "What I meant was, I'd like to confess but I was never confirmed. I quit catechism in junior high."

"In that case, you'll have to leave. We don't serve your kind here." Now it was Asher's turn to be consternated.

"Just a little *Star Wars* cantina humor," Father Snoddy added, a grin breaking across his young beard, black as shoe polish. "I don't get to indulge my nerdy side much; people around here find it off-putting." He gestured to a set of herringbone curtains in an alcove near the entrance. "Please be my guest, Mr. Peart."

Asher gathered his things once more, the day's journey suddenly weighing on him in full, and followed the priest into the booth.

He confessed all of it.

4

Asher's first riding horse, Terror, was just that. One day less than a month after Mauricio gifted her to him—on condition that he break her all by himself—Asher lifted his arm while brushing her neck and she sank her incisors, quick as Satan, deep into his left armpit and upper chest. Along with four stitches and the scars that followed, Asher had to live with a permanently misshapen nipple and a new species of embarrassment that he never would've associated with anything so trivial as training a stupid horse.

It didn't enter Ash's mind until much later that maybe that was the point—Ash's secret opinion that the boarding and training of horses was a basically stupid way to make a living. It wasn't as though he'd ever voiced that opinion to Mauricio, or to his own father, or to anyone but (occasionally) his little brother; but then Mauricio was no idiot, and Mauricio knew that Ash was his mother's son.

The Rede stables and homestead occupied eleven acres on Route 99 north halfway between Visalia and Tulare. By the time Asher was born,

Mauricio had ceded the original main house first to his own son, Ivan, who'd come back from Korea with four medals and a dislocated soul; then it went to Asher's parents. As children of both the San Joaquin Valley and of the Sixties, Jared and Timera Rede were two of the worst exemplars for equestrian life that Asher knew. The damning evidence of Jared's first love, muscle cars, still haunted the property as abundantly as his old welding art: the shell of his '64 Ramcharger decomposing amid the weeds beside the south-pasture equipment shed; the 426 Hemi engine block under a tarp in the garage; the greaser photos—so out of place among all the hippie hairstyles—in his high-school yearbooks. It was true that Asher's dad had done a remarkable job, while still in his twenties, of keeping the family business above water after Ivan finally drank himself dead; but weekends still found him tooling on his '76 Cordoba more often than doing flatwork in the exercise pen.

Timera had once loved horses, at least for a little while. All of her loves, ferocious as they often were, came and went on a "for a little while" basis: horses, pageboy bouffants, Joni Mitchell albums, macramé, cottage cheese, aerobics, marriage, motherhood. Her love affair with college had proven slightly more durable than the others; she dabbled in classes at Fresno State all through Ash's childhood, at last bumping into an anthropology degree in 1981. A month after graduating, she moved out.

By then it was evident that Mauricio had suffered his own dislocation somewhere along the way, though no one could surmise exactly how or why. It had happened quietly. Timera had insisted it was an undiagnosed stroke.

"Look at him," she'd said one night just months before electing to relocate her own soul, single and childless and free as the wind, to a new efficiency apartment in El Segundo.

"Look at who?" said Jared.

"Your grandfather—who else?" She planted a bottle of Seven Seas on the dinner table, then hooked a thumb at the kitchen storm-door, through which Mauricio could be seen in the distance about a hundred yards away from the house. He was seated alone on the flatbed-*cum*-deck outside the front door of his green Rollohome.

"He's already got that stupid TV going and it isn't even dark yet. He'll sit out there with it all night—keeping me awake, by the way—and he's not even watching anything."

"He watches Johnny Carson," Jared offered.

"Very funny. And have you noticed he only lives on Big Gulps and candy these days? He's sixty-five going on fourteen, for Pete's sake."

Jared sighed and set aside the *Times-Delta* smog report (the county was on its nineteenth Stage I of the year and it was only April). From this distance, he could just make out his grandfather's white straw hat and the flicker from the little transistor TV he kept at arm's length on the patio table beside him. To a casual observer, the sporadic tilt and nod of the hat might've formed the impression that he was reacting to the TV, but

Jared knew better even without listening to Timera's complaints. The old *mesteñero* was lost in his mind.

Sometimes Tree Pendleton, a seasonal wrangler who worked the racing and county-fair circuits, would join him there on the little makeshift deck, often with a bottle of mescal. It was an odd arrangement, given that Mauricio didn't drink and Tree knew no Spanish, but it appeared to suit both men just fine. Sometimes Jared went out there with a six-pack after dinner and he and Mauricio talked about the stables, or about Jared and Timera's two boys, or about the hostage crisis, or about *conjunto* music. No matter what Timera thought, the old man was still cogent. He was still the de facto stable boss during the day, still rode his favorite paint horse through the neighboring pistachio fields every morning, still knew and grasped—as much as anyone could these days—what was going on in the world. But he'd also stopped taking meals just as Timera claimed, and he seemed to have abandoned the very notion of sleep. Jared further suspected, from the way the straw hat sometimes moved in the distant nighttime flicker of the little TV, that the old man was addressing—at times accusing—someone who wasn't there.

During one of Jared's evening visits, not long after the night in the kitchen and apropos of nothing, Mauricio had downed a long hit from the straw of his Big Gulp and said:

"The *güera* is no longer happy. She will leave you."

Jared was just reaching for another Lowenbrau. He popped the ring tab and leaned back in his lawn chair, suddenly ill at ease. A snort came

50

from one of the pasture pens, probably the old Morgan show-horse whose fickle owners had retired her last month.

"Don't call her that, *Lito*. You're angry at someone else. Don't take it out on the only *nieta* you've got."

The old man was silent awhile. Then:

"Your wife is selfish. She has still the heart of a girl, not the heart of a woman. She will leave you and your sons. She will persuade you that you are to blame for this when you are not."

Jared gave no answer. Whatever was ailing his grandfather, he wasn't going to make it worse by feeding the old man's old bitterness. Besides, it surely wasn't about to happen all over again, what had happened with Jared's mother and Ivan's mother before her. How many wives and mothers could walk out on one family? It was a statistical improbability beyond a certain point.

"You're wrong, *Lito*," he said, getting up to go. "She's had ten years to leave me already. She isn't Katherine and she isn't Helen. Not all women are the same. Good night."

***

Only after the funeral did another layer of possible significance behind Mauricio's gift—a female horse who had immediately maimed him— occur to Ash. Terror had turned into a top-notch saddle horse, winning him several cutting and barrel-riding ribbons once Ash had absorbed that first and most elemental lesson (never trust *any* horse completely), and once he'd sought Mauricio's direct advice. But as time progressed, he began to wonder whether his wily great-grandfather had meant the lesson to extend not only to all horses, but to all females as well.

The old *mesteñero* lingered in the hospital for weeks, felled by pneumonia, before giving up the ghost altogether. His lean body, once taut as a strip of pepper steak, was now a slackened, hollowed, rawboned husk. Asher sat often at his bedside, watching *Hogan's Heroes* reruns on the hospital TV or holding a can of strawberry Ensure up to his *bisabuelo's* lips. The old man's eye sockets were caverns, his voice a barren, papery whisper.

"*Mi novia,*" the voice sometimes sighed, often as the old man drifted like a stray windblown leaf in and out of consciousness. "*Mi novia infiel.*"

My faithless bride.

"He means that rich old lady in El Paso, doesn't he?" Asher asked his father point-blank, one day near the end. They'd gone downstairs for a bite at the hospital cafeteria.

"More than likely," said Jared, feeding a packet of Sweet'n'Low into his coffee with deliberation, as if gauging an hourglass. The divorce was still a fresh memory for both of them; now this. "It wouldn't be anything new. You shouldn't make too much out of the things he says at this point."

"The doctor says that he basically starved himself to death."

"It happens with smokers sometimes. They get to where they can't taste anything and they stop eating. You know he smoked those shitty cigarillos most of his life."

Yet Asher knew also that his father had once taken the old man's sad old tale seriously himself. He remembered that other funeral, just a few short years before. Another grandfather. Hundreds of people. The smiling preacher with the murderous handshake. The handsome lady with the wine-dark hair and hard, loveless eyes.

***

Asher awoke, twelve years old, to the sound of dripping water. He undid the fitful Talon zipper on his sleeping bag and fastened it again around his little brother with the care of a practiced sneak. His parents lay in another sleeping bag, his mom on her left side with arms folded forbiddingly across her chest, black gypsy-cut hair swathed over her eyes. Dad lay prone and open-mouthed, exhausted, his forearm propped against the tire well as if trying to push away some unseen attacker.

The ground was still soaked when he climbed out of the camper shell. The sky had mostly cleared, just puddles and the sound of drip-drop everywhere, the splash of a passing vehicle. The road trip from California to Texas had lasted a punishing eighteen hours, not counting the stop-off in Arizona to see The Thing?, and when they'd arrived in El Paso late last night they'd promptly run into a flash-food downpour and thunderstorm. Then Dad had gotten them lost.

The raw state of things between his parents had been evident all summer, to the point that Asher now had tinnitus in both ears. Jared and Timera were by no means yellers, but whenever he detected one of their hushed late-evening arguments underway in the back bedroom, Asher had taken to utilizing the otherwise forgotten hi-fi system in the den. While Lex had free run of the TV, Ash sat in the big corner armchair with his dad's oversized Koss headphones clamped to his head, listening at first to his *Star Wars* and *Empire Strikes Back* soundtrack LPs. Later, as boredom loomed, he began dipping into the stack of albums leaning against the wall by the chair: It's a Beautiful Day, James Taylor, Chicago Transit Authority, and assorted others.

But Thursday night's argument had lasted longer, seemingly erupting out of nowhere. Jared had come in from the stables that afternoon looking anxious. Seeing his father's face through the front-bedroom window, Asher knew right away that the weekend camping trip to Dinkey Lakes was off. He knew as well that his mother, who, these days, lived for any chance to get the hell away from horseflies, hay, and animal shit-stink for as long as she could, was going to be damn mad upon finding that out.

"El Paso?" she snarled from the kitchen as soon as Jared made his announcement, the exact contents of which Ash was unable to make out. "El Paso, *Texas*? Babe, honey, you need to just stop right there. In fact you might want to turn around, go outside, then come back in and start this conversation over, because nothing you just told me changes the fact that tomorrow's the start of Labor Day weekend, and this family already has *plans* for Labor Day weekend this year, and those plans do not include going anywhere *near* El Paso...fucking...*Texas*."

Something else inaudible from Jared.

"Brilliant. So this came from your grandfather. Naturally. What a surprise."

A longer, more measured response from Dad. Asher slipped down from his top bunk and crept to the bedroom door, easing it ajar by just a few stealthy hairs, which was all he could risk. Today he was restricted to his bedroom for playing hooky from school earlier in the week, no TV or music at all. The junior high in Tulare, where he'd just begun the seventh grade, had proven too big and scary for Asher's taste, and it was all too easy to fake walking out to the school-bus drop-off point on Route 99 in the morning, then double back to the homestead and bivouac in one of numerous hiding places he'd staked out all over the property. Tree Pendleton, for instance, was still up in New Mexico for racing season at Ruidoso Downs, and Asher knew where Tree kept his spare trailer keys.

"I should've known you'd pull a last-minute stunt like this," Timera said, shifting rhetorical gears from sarcasm to satisfied disgust. "You knew how much I needed this break. I barely survived a twelve-hour summer course load, and now I'm facing eighteen when the fall semester kicks off next week. I've got a twelve-year-old son who thinks going to school is optional plus a six-year-old nightly bed-wetter. You knew I was looking forward to spending time with Chaim and Sandra, who were kind enough to invite us up to their cabin in the first place. But you don't like any of my college friends, you resent me for earning a degree in the first place, and now you and that miserable old woman-hater have cooked *this* up. Just admit it, will you?"

Ash withdrew from the doorway and closed it. His father would give Mom her way, as usual, which should have felt good to know because it meant the camping trip was probably still on after all. But the bigger picture wasn't as cheerful. He went to the bedroom window and gazed at the front yard, where the wheel-sized iron peace sign his dad had once welded for Mom as an anniversary gift stood bleeding streaks of rust amidst the desiccated lawn.

But then something even less predictable had happened: Mom went along with Dad's new Labor Day plans. She came into the boys' bedroom in the predawn hours of Friday morning, in freshly laundered road clothes and smelling of Love's Baby Soft, and coaxed them out of their bunks. Their sleeping bag was laid out in the camper shell with extra blankets and pillows, she told them, and they could go right back to sleep.

"We're going to Texas, fellas," she whispered in the dark even though everyone was now awake. "You can sleep all the way there if you want."

"What's Texas?" Ash's brother groaned blearily. By some miracle his lower-bunk mattress overlay was unsoiled.

"Oh, you know, Lexy. That big ugly thorn-shaped thing at the bottom of the U.S. map."

"Is *Lito* coming with us?" Ash asked.

"What a crazy question," said Timera. "*Lito* doesn't go anywhere but Seven-Eleven anymore."

It was many hours getting to the ugly thorn-shaped thing, but through it all his mother remained unnaturally sunny, as if by conceding the camping trip she'd gotten something from his father anyway, some kind of invisible victory. While she held Lex in her lap in the truck passenger seat, fondling his hair and playing clapping games, Jared remained anxious, fiddling with the radio dial and chain-smoking. Near Quartzsite, Arizona, he was pulled over for speeding.

"Are you trying to make the Ayatollah even richer, babe?" Timera chided him after the policeman handed Jared the ticket and left. She was referring to the billboard signs they'd passed outside of Los Angeles, displaying the menacing full-bearded frown of Ayatollah Khomeini accompanied by the message "Fight back...Drive 55!"

"I'm trying to get us there before dark," said Jared, agitated.

"Well that isn't going to happen, you silly man," Timera replied sunnily. "Laws of physics, you know. Maybe you should just ease up and try to enjoy the drive. Aren't we supposed to be having fun? I know how much fun *I'm* having. Are you having fun, boys?"

"Nope," Asher said from the cab window, lifting his chin briefly from the soft comfort of his Adidas foam sweatbands. The view was better from the tailgate, but he'd wanted to watch his dad getting a ticket, so he'd scooted up to the front. For the moment he had the whole camper shell to himself. "But Dad said we were going to a funeral anyway. That shouldn't be considered fun, should it?"

"No, of course not," Timera agreed. "It's always a time to be sad when someone passes away. But we *are* technically on vacation, the only one we're going to get for a good long while, so why can't we have some fun getting to where we're going? There!"—and she pointed to a new series of billboards that had begun appearing as they came closer to Phoenix. "That might be a good place to have some fun: I think we should stop and take a look-see when we get to Dragoon. The sign says it's right there on the interstate, no extra effort at all."

In the meantime, Dad had found a radio station he liked on the AM dial and turned the volume up a few notches. Asher could feel the tension between his mom and dad spiking again, like a gradual increase in room temperature.

"Beach Boys!" Lex exclaimed.

"No, that's what I first thought," Jared said, firing up another Cool from the dash lighter. "It sounds like 'Barbara Ann' but they're singing 'Bomb Iran.' It's a novelty record."

"What's a novelty record?" asked Ash.

"You know, songs like 'Mah Nà Mah Nà' and 'Purple People Eater.' There were a lot of them in the Sixties."

"Do you miss the Sixties, Dad?"

Jared thumped a flurry of cigarette ashes out the window and—only Asher saw it—shot a look of anger at his wife.

"Yeah, sure, I miss the Sixties," he said, returning his attention to the interstate. "Those were good years to be young and stupid, unless you were stupid enough to get drafted. I was born with diabetes, so I got to stay home and play with my cars, cruise the valley, listen to the radio…

pick up the occasional teenybopper in lemon capris and make out with her in the backseat."

"Child molester," Timera added.

A disc jockey broke in at the tail end of the song, urging listeners to take their bashed and beaten-up cars to Ace Body Shop somewhere in El Paso. "That sounds like Sammy Hayes," said Jared, reaching for the volume again.

"That old queer?" Timera replied. "Not a chance."

"Would you please shut up?"

The voice gave way to a succession of commercials in rapid-fire Spanish. Timera made an *Oops! Someone's mad!* silly face at Lex and held a finger up to her mouth. Lex did the same, and the two of them giggled at their shared joke. Ash crept back inside the camper shell and lay face-up on his and Lex's sleeping bag, troubled.

They stopped at The Thing? and bought gas, and as Jared was paying for entrance to the museum, Timera grabbed his lighter and cigarettes from off the sales counter.

"My turn to smoke," she said.

"Where are you going, Mommy?" Lex cried in alarm, turning heads throughout the gift shop.

"Already seen it, handsome. You go on through with Daddy and I'll be waiting next door in the Dairy Queen when you get out. Then I'll buy you a Dilly Bar."

The "museum" was a series of open-air sheds out back. Lex made a fuss of placing his feet in every one of the kitschy yellow footsteps painted on the floor and on the sidewalks between the sheds. Ash was most impressed with the black Rolls-Royce that—according to the placard before it—may once have transported Adolf Hitler. The star attraction, The Thing? itself, lay alone in the last shed, encased in an oblong glass-and-wood box. Jared had to pick Lex up so he could see it. Then the three of them stood there a moment in puzzled wonder, the humdrum sounds of interstate traffic wafting in from the shed's entrance.

"I don't get it," said Ash. "Is it real?"

"I don't think so," Jared replied. "Just a cheap knock-off. Now we know why it only cost a dollar to get in."

"Like a novelty record?"

"Yeah," said Jared, nodding. "Something like that."

"Mom should've told us it was bullshit. Why didn't she?"

Jared gave no answer, not even to admonish Ash's rough language.

A few hours later they were in El Paso, or at least near it. Then the rain hit. Jared explained that they were really looking for a place called Nueva Anapra, a New Mexico town next to El Paso, situated right outside the thorny edge of Texas. Asher took charge of the Rand-McNally from Timera, whose sunny mood had deteriorated almost as rapidly as the weather. But it was only a highway road map, and as the downpour thickened they found themselves lost on a dark, flooded street beside a closed onramp, the CHECK ENGINE light glowing from the dash display and a fender-high backwash cutting off the way they'd just come.

Debes morir de lo que te mata, said Mauricio.

***

Once he was clear of the camper shell, Ash surveyed his surroundings. Then inspiration struck. He climbed onto the tailgate once more and wrestled his mother's Kodak Handle 3 from among her belongings, pulled the neck-strap over his head, and climbed down again. Across the road was an electrical plant, forested with pylons and cables. He snapped a photo of it and watched it develop, enthralled by the miracle of instant photography. His mother had bought the camera for an anthropology project earlier that summer, and after observing how it worked (and maybe because the thing's trade name kind of encouraged it) he'd been unable to keep his hands off it.

He went around to the front end of the pickup truck, the still-wet loose gravel of the parking lot crunching greasily beneath the soles of his sneakers. It appeared they'd washed up last night beside a small, windowless adobe building with the sign ROSA'S CANTINA over the front entrance. He snapped another pic and turned his attention to the nearby mountain, whose distant peak bore a white stone cross that faced into and seemed to draw the blossoming sunrise. A trail zigzagged up the mountainside like a thin line of chalk. Asher centered the cross in the camera's viewfinder, then decided he needed a better angle, so he stuck the first two photos into the front pocket of his windbreaker and began skulking down the puddle-lined road with the camera raised in both hands.

He came to the end of the block, where a barricade of construction sawhorses remained before the freeway entrance. On the opposite corner lay an old adobe gas station, the signage removed and the pump islands long dismantled. The street dead-ended beyond it. He took the picture, and while watching it develop, he realized he was hungry. There was a package of leftover cheese and crackers in the windbreaker's other pocket, from a rest-stop vending machine, their only meal last night. He sat down on the curb to finish them off, then let the plastic wrapper fall into the nearest puddle of water. It landed soundlessly and glided like a skiff a few inches along the surface, then petered out where the asphalt ended in a clump of milkweed.

"Hey."

A girl in her late teens had come up silently behind him, seated astride a ten-speed and watching him with a sunshiny grin much like Timera's, save for the rather unmistakable scorn that it suggested for him.

"Did you really just toss that piece of shit on the ground, kid?" she said. "In front of *my* store? Did I really just watch you do that?"

"Sorry."

"Go get it."

Asher looked again at the thicket of weeds where it had gone. There was no longer any sign of it. He looked back to the girl, a doomed plea on his face.

"That's right, Jiminy Cricket, go fetch it out and put it in the trashcan where it belongs. Didn't you ever see that crying-Indian commercial?"

He blundered around in the weeds for several minutes, first with the camera dangling bulkily from his neck. He stopped to remove it and set it down on the curb before resuming the search. Meanwhile the girl had set the ten-speed on its kickstand and gone inside the gas station, and moments later a bay door rose loudly on its rollers, followed by its counterpart. When Asher returned with the offending wrapper, she was rolling two garment racks out in front of the service bays, each thick with blouses, pants and slacks, T-shirts, and more, all in riotous color and variety.

"Trashcan," she said, spotting him. "*Basura.* Over there."

As he went to the repurposed oil barrel and deposited the wrapper, a spiffy shortbed Chevy pickup pulling a Bobcat trailer came trolling at length up the street and swung in beside the remains of the pump island. Two men in caps and jeans got out. Asher went to where the camera lay abandoned on the pavement and retrieved it, brushing the loose gravel from its bottom casing before donning it once more via the neck strap. He approached the service bays in curiosity, aware his parents had likely awakened and noticed his absence by now. The girl had carried out a sandwich board reading BUENA VISTA EMPORIUM and set it up on the curb corner, and now she was chatting with one of the two men in Spanish. From the snippets he overheard, Ash gleaned this one to be her father.

Within the mechanic bays, he found rows of display bins of a homemade, slapdash, pine-and-particle-board type, all overflowing with stuff: stacks of vintage board games, *Bonkers!* and *Which Witch?* and *Stratego*, even the deluxe electronic *Battleship*. A tabletop of shoes and boots, paired and pointed readily in the same direction like the ghost army in *Bedknobs and Broomsticks*. Heaps of used cookware, pottery, handwoven rugs on the walls, TVs, audio components, and in the corner a giant Kelvinator fridge, a handwritten sign on whose door read in Magic Marker *No entrar*.

He'd just encountered the LP bin with its reams of tattered albums when the girl returned into the shop. The two men had gone back to the truck and left. She paused and observed him from behind as he selected one, lifting it from the stacks between his thumb and forefinger as if it might be tainted and gazing at the front cover—Tanya Tucker holding a microphone cord snuggly and suggestively through the crotch of her skintight black pants—in plain spellbound lust.

"Something I can help you find there, mister?"

The album slipped to the floor, gatefold open, Ms. Tucker posed now in full firehouse-red spandex glory, derrière to the camera, while sparing a tawdry glance over her bare shoulder and licking her lips.

"Do you sell batteries?" It was all he could to say.

"Hmm…guess not." She knelt and reassembled the illicit album cover, then placed it tidily in the LP bin. "This is a secondhand store, so we only

64

sell used things. I don't think a used battery would do you much good."
She pointed at the camera. "Are you talking about batteries for that?"

"Yeah."

"Looks like expensive equipment. Are you a professional photojournalist?"

"I don't think so," he said, flummoxed. Then another inspiration: "I'm going to be an anthropologist."

"Goodness, we don't get many of *those* in here." She threw him another bemusing smile, one with some visible kindness in it. The purple birthmark on her cheek fascinated him. He wanted to take her picture, maybe go off with it somewhere and admire it in secret. "But I might have some things that use the same kind of batteries up front. Come on."

She led him into the cashier's office. Through the storefront windows, he could just glimpse Rosa's a block away and the tail end of the camper shell beyond it. The girl went behind the sales counter and stood in thought, hands on her hips, studying the wall shelves.

"I've only got Polaroids," she said. "That's a Kodak you have, right? What kind of battery does it use?"

"What's the name of that mountain out there?" said Ash. It was better than admitting he didn't know the answer to her question.

She did an amiable about-face and came back out into the lobby. "That's the Black Mountain," she said. "My dad still calls it Cerro de Muleros like the old-timers used to. He's up there right now clearing the trail with my *padrino*."

"Does it take a long time to climb it?"

"Couple of hours on foot, give or take. Speaking of names, do you have one yourself? Doctor Livingstone, maybe?"

She'd nonplussed him again, but he managed to produce his first and last names both.

"Well I'm Elfa Schultz, at your service," she said, shaking his hand with mischievous cordiality. "Let's see the battery in that camera and then maybe you can get some snapshots of the mountain."

They removed the nine-volt battery, still perfectly charged as far as Asher knew, atop the sales counter, and Elfa snapped her fingers in recollection.

"We just got a whole crate of these last week," she said, reaching towards one of the lower shelves behind the register and returning with what appeared to be a miniature toilet, which she set down beside Asher's mother's partially dismantled camera.

"It's a radio, see?" She flicked the on/off/volume dial, and the robotic synthpop of Gary Numan sliced through the morning quiet, though it was muted somewhat by the radio's tinny AM shrillness. She snapped it off and opened the battery compartment, then removed the nine-volt and touched her tongue to the battery terminals, flinching slightly when they tested out at full charge.

"You might as well keep the whole thing, actually," she said then, pushing it all towards him. "Daddy bought these silly things at a TG&Y close-out, don't ask me why. We'll never get rid of the whole box. Enjoy."

Outside the shop, she stood in the center of the deserted street and posed for him in front of the mountain; she explained that having a human subject in the foreground would provide perspective.

She was right.

***

"I want one!" Lex said.

Children not much older than he were weaving through the Mexican port-of-entry lanes, holding blue, pink, and yellow sticks of cotton candy high in the air like fluffy torches. Jared tugged at the knot of his necktie and punched the lighter in frustration.

"Shouldn't you maybe wait till we're all the way through before lighting that?" Timera asked when he yanked out a fresh cigarette by the teeth. "Maybe don't give Mexican customs an excuse to hassle us?"

Jared fired up regardless.

"Mommy, I want cotton candy," Lex repeated with a note of desolation.

"No can do, sugar. Settle for a Chiclet?" She'd curled her hair and had on an elegant black-chiffon dress with a gold sash at her waist. Both Lex and Asher were trussed in dress shirts and neckties as well, though Lex had already gone wretchedly untucked and disheveled from clambering around in the camper shell for the last twenty minutes.

"Are we *there* yet?" he groaned between angry, deprived smackings of his gum/consolation-prize.

They would not get there, it turned out, for nearly another hour. By then Timera's curls had gone lank from the pitiless August heat, and all of them were more or less as disheveled as Lex. Even more disappointing was that "there," once they reached it, didn't seem to be much of anywhere at all. They'd landed on a featureless mesa in the remote western outskirts of Ciudad Juárez. Upon climbing out from the tailgate, Ash realized that they'd come a long way to arrive almost where they'd started— there was the power plant, unmistakable in the near distance; there was the Black Mountain, looming closer and larger from this vantage point. Somewhere beyond was the thrift shop where the stain-faced girl was still peddling blouses and rugs and toilet-shaped radios. Assuming she peddled on Sunday.

When he met Jared getting out of the pickup's driver's side, for an unguarded second his father appeared more than disheveled; he looked alone and defeated and strangely out of sorts, and for the first time during this trip, Ash caught something in his face that appeared to explain their being here in full. Jared had tried, however clumsily, to convey the situation and its meaning to both Ash and Lex during the long trek from California: the man whose funeral they'd come to witness was Jared's great-grandfather and the boys' *tatarabuelo*. (Lex had trouble with the idea in both languages; the thought of so much fathomless age and distance, as huge an abstraction as the expanding universe, seemed to bore him into not caring at all.) Jared wanted them to see the man, or at least his eighty-eight-year-old remains, and maybe even introduce them to their *bisabuela* as well. Ash respected the plan to a point, because he loved and respected his father, although he'd as much have preferred spending the weekend in Dinkey Lakes as Timera.

But the unease Ash saw in his father's eyes just then suggested one thing more—namely, that no one had asked them here. They were uninvited guests, possibly even unwanted guests. That fleeting but strained expression told him that Jared was more than a little concerned about how their presence might be received. For half an instant Ash's young father looked incalculably old and burdened, much like Lito himself.

"How's it hanging, Dad?" It was something to say.

The crowd of mourners, mostly on foot, was filing in from the settlement at the base of the mesa. The last mile or so in the pickup had been particularly slow going while Jared tried, as respectfully as possible, to navigate around them on the single dirt road that led from there to here. He tossed away his cigarette and laid a hand on Ash's shoulder.

"See that transmitter tower?"

Not only was it the most visible landmark for miles, in some ways more imposing than the Black Mountain, but the closer to it they'd come, the more the air itself had begun to feel heavy and…alive. Even the hardpan beneath the soles of his Vans thrummed distinctly.

"That's XAMO," said Jared. "We heard it on the pickup radio coming into town, remember? It used to be one of the greatest rock'n'roll radio stations in America. We cruised to it in Visalia in the fifties and sixties. I first kissed your mother while we were listening to it in the back of my old Dodge. You could pick its signal up as far away as Canada because radio stations in Mexico don't have the same wattage limits as the ones in the U.S. See those?"

He pointed to the more distant range beyond the Black Mountain. "Those are the Franklins, which form the southern tip of the Rockies. By putting this transmitter here on the west side of the Franklins, the people who built XAMO knew they could send a clear signal all the way up the west coast of the United States and beyond—to L.A. and Las Vegas and San Francisco and about half of North America. And that's just what they did." He leaned in close and looked Ash hard in the eye. "That was your *tatarabuelo*. XAMO Radio was his baby; he founded it. So you're looking at a piece of your heritage. We may not own it—I don't know who owns it now, it doesn't matter—but it belongs to us the same way that any place your ancestors once lived in, built with their own hands, belongs to you. It's part of who you are, who *we* are. Do you understand me?"

They were Lito's words, not just Jared's. Mom had been mistaken. The old *mesteñero* might not have accompanied them to the funeral physically, but he'd sent something of himself all the same.

"You could've left out the part about you and Mom *kissing*," Ash said. "Gross."

Timera and Lex came round the other side of the pickup holding hands, minute tentacles of Timera's lank hair now probing the further reaches of space around her head.

All four of them joined hands at Jared's insistence, and they fell in with the rabble, all swarming toward a wide, windowless steel building. A pair of sliding service doors stood parted on the building's oblong side, and here a smiling young man of about thirty, clad in a blue wide-lapel suit, was greeting the entrants by name, bestowing hugs and handshakes and sympathetic shoulder-pats. Ash felt a twitch in Jared's hand—if the blue-suited man knew the local population that intimately, his warm demeanor might just frost over when he failed to recognize them.

"*Bienvenidos,*" he said, laying eyes on Timera first.

He pressed palms with each and every Rede in succession—wife, husband, younger son, older son—and with no less diplomacy than he'd shown all the others, though he'd seemed to dismiss them all in sum even before getting to Asher. By then he'd shifted eyes to the caped and shawled elderly woman next in line (*Ah, Flavia, lo siento mucho pero me alegro de que haya podido venir*) and for an absentminded instant, his hand squashed Ash's knuckles together to the point that Asher all but yelped. Then it was over, they were inside the big windowless building, and Ash could only hold his numb right fingers in front of his eyes in a quick, disbelieving check to verify that they hadn't shattered.

The room within was as stifling with poverty as heat. People sat shoulder to shoulder in loose rows on plank benches, the kind used in locker rooms, and nothing at all seemed to issue from the overhead saucer-shaped air ducts. The stage, inasmuch as it could be considered that, was a platform of conjoined pallets. Atop it rested an open mahogany coffin

71

draped in flowers, and before this an antique desk-podium bearing an open Bible, a glass of water, and an old-fashioned capsule microphone. At stage-right, two boys each comparable in age to Lex and Ash respectively, probably brothers as well, were courageously hollering out "*La Golondrina*" ("The Swallow") without benefit of a PA while a middle-aged gentleman in a black cowboy hat accompanied them from a nearby folding chair, strumming a Mexican-style *vihuela*.

At the foot of the stage was a steel table decked with electronic consoles, from which emanated numerous snakelike cables running in all directions. One led out from the stage area to another microphone stand facing the audience. A lean, goateed technician with half-moon glasses on the end of his nose and wearing big orange-foam headphones sat overlooking the consoles, occasionally adjusting a knob or lever while a toothpick migrated between the corners of his mouth. He sported an ashy braided ponytail, tie-dyed T-shirt, Bermuda shorts, and bare-toed sandals.

Jared raised an arm before his family as they crossed the room together, nodding in wordless signal toward the thing atop the left side of the stage.

A black-velvet painting, vast and garish, was positioned on a display stand at an angle complementary to the coffin but viewable to all. A silver-haired Anglo man of advancing years, in thick-framed eyeglasses and string-tie, standing side-by-side with a white-robed Jesus Christ, each man regarding the other with equal, vaguely smiling esteem. Timera issued a noise resembling a snort and covered her mouth. Jared shot her a warning glare anyway and ushered them forward.

No sooner had he located one of the few remaining unoccupied benches in back of the room, and at last gotten the four of them seated, than a hush fell and the whole homely assemblage rose to its feet. Asher scrambled atop the bench and strained for a better view over the sea of heads, sensing the arrival of something, or someone, not to be missed. He saw a redheaded woman crossing in front of the stage from the entrance doors, flanked by two men, one of whom was the blue-suited hand-crusher. The other man, in wavy, fashionably coiffed flaxen hair and an open-collared three-piece, emitted a definite famous-person electric current even from this distance. But most eyes in the room, particularly Jared's, followed the woman.

She held her shoulders high but her head bowed, acknowledging no one. She wore a handsome, dark, pleated funeral gown and carried a burgundy handbag in the crook of one arm. She went briskly to a pair of reserved chairs in the front row and sat, followed by Mr. Famous at her side, and the crowd took their seats once more consecutively, row by row, each in deference to the one before. The blue-suited man then ascended the stage, and just as Asher had gotten down from the bench, the entire room rose to its feet again.

"Check...check," he heard the blue-suited man say in English. "How are our levels, Jaz?"

Reverting again to Spanish, he told the audience they would soon be on the air and admonished them with chummy firmness to at all times heed the rules of radio etiquette while also remembering they were in a house of worship, however humble.

"They're *broadcasting* this?" Timera whispered, amused. "Lord, it's the Mexican Hour of Power." Heads turned, and Jared stared hotly at the floor. Even Asher felt a shade of embarrassment.

"Is there a question in the back?" the blue-suited man called out from the stage. "Yes? No?"

"Fifteen seconds," a thin adenoidal voice added. Ash guessed it was the ponytailed technician.

Asher mounted the bench again. The guitarist was pacing the stage now, strumming the *vihuela* and singing in his black hat and fancy, embroidered black cowboy shirt, encouraging the crowd to join him and smiling heartily. The lyrics were English.

"*Don't...fence me in!*" cried a woman to Ash's left tearfully, her knobby, arthritic hands high in the air and the fringes of her gray *rebozo* brushing lightly against his cheek. It was the woman from the entrance line.

"*Ahora oremos a Dios,*" said the blue-suited man when the song ended. *Now let us pray to God.* The sea of heads bent forward in obeisance. Ash soon tired of standing on the bench. Lex had his *Dukes of Hazzard* pocket-pinball game out, and Ash reached for his own inside the lining of his blazer. As he shot and manipulated the game's tiny metal spheres around the heads of Ponch and Jon from *"CHiPs"*, his ears inattentively registered the blue-suited man's lengthy praisings in Spanish of *"El Rey de las Ondas,"* though these involved assorted digressions on salvation by justification, on *priístas* and *panístas*, on Jesus and Satan in the wilderness, on the false promise of popery, on miracles and healing.

74

"The voice of God," said the voice speaking from the stage, shifting to English after an emphatic pause, "takes many forms. It finds us all sooner or later, insisting that we hear if not heed, hounding us to the very ends of the Earth if it must. Some may say that's just what Rancho Anapra is: the end of the Earth. A godforsaken place, a *godless* place, a *hopeless* place. Yet hope through the voice of God found its way here, through Donald Eustace Piper.

"We may never have a complete record of all the lands and peoples to whom the Apostle Paul delivered the Gospel, but the Bible hints there were more beyond those which are specifically mentioned. One of the earliest Christian authors tells us that after his first imprisonment in Rome, Paul traveled to the thither-most reaches of the west. And so it was with our own Apostle, Dr. Piper. The voice of God came to Rancho Anapra in 1928, itself perhaps the thither-most—indeed, perhaps the most materially and spiritually impoverished—point in all of *Estado de Chihuahua*, and from this room, from this very spot where I now stand, via the miracle of radio, the voice of God touched the westernmost reaches of an entire continent."

"*Gloria a Dios*," responded the sea of heads.

The long sermon having concluded, people began unbidden to line up at the floor microphone and speak.

"Can we please get the thither out of here now?" said Timera.

Jared was already on his feet. He cast a fatalistic glance at his wife, and she smothered her face in her hands.

"God, Jared, no."

"Boys, come on."

Meanwhile, those two other boys had launched into song once more: a Spanish rendition of "Amazing Grace" ("*Mis Cadenas se Fueron*"). Ash and Lex fell in unenthusiastically with their father at the line for the mike, which had fast swelled to dozens, spilling to beyond the benches at the far end of the room. It shuffled forward in agonizing increments as each and every parishioner at the microphone stand felt the need to expound on Dr. Piper's miracles, on his or her gratitude to God, on the names and life stories of every single member of his or her family and the blessings Dr. Piper's ministry had bestowed on them. The room sweltered more with each testimonial, compounded by the post-summer-storm humidity. Lex had squirmed partway out of his mini-blazer, the Nordstrom tag sticking tongue-like from his back collar.

As the head of the line neared, the redheaded woman in the front row drew gradually again into view, and Ash found himself studying her—in part because he could sense his dad purposely *not* looking at her at all. He could make out her diamond-stud earrings and cameo brooch, could hear Mr. Famous speaking conversationally into her ear, although the conversation seemed a tad one-sided. She nodded at perfunctory intervals, legs crossed and arms folded in her slender lap, and once she tilted her forearm, ever so stealthily, and consulted her wristwatch.

"*Dar su testimonio par nosotros,*" the blue-suited man urged the person in line ahead of Jared—a swarthy, big-bellied fellow in a biker vest and bandana. The redheaded woman lifted the backside of a hand to her face

76

and looked her fingernails over. For a second she met eyes with Asher, saw nothing worth looking at, and went back to inspecting her nails.

Now the microphone stand was vacant. Jared moved towards it weightily, like some movie bit player about to disclose earthshaking news. He drew a breath, close distance with the mike…and said nothing.

The redheaded woman took notice of the pause and lifted an eyebrow. An expression of concern passed over the technician's face, and he craned his neck towards the stage, then returned to his instruments.

"Yes, my brother in Christ?" said the blue-suited man in Spanish. "Do you have testimony to share?"

Jared reached behind himself and pulled Asher and Lex close on either side.

"Yes, brother," he replied, leaning once more into the mike. "As a matter of fact, I do."

5

Elfa woke to music. Not Plimsouls or Simple Minds, but her mother's favorite *ranchera* station. Vikki Carr declaring to the whole world that she's neither a princess nor a slave. The voice and the strident four-four guitar strokes emanated from the kitchen radio, only a few running steps from where Elfa lay in bed in the tiny two-bedroom Schultz house.

Rather than getting up straightaway, she curled onto her side, hugged a pillow, and cast her gaze aimlessly across her unkempt bedroom as her eyes adjusted to the daylight. At length they settled upon the scuffed, third-hand, imitation French-provincial Bassett dresser, a *quince* gift from her aunt and uncle on her mother's side. Waking reality began to reassemble itself, not necessarily a good thing, but there you go. And then her vision found the item she'd stuck into the lower mirror frame a few nights ago and which she had, quite purposely, avoided thinking about in the days since.

The Polaroid. Or whatever it was.

The horrid mixture of feelings that it conjured. The old pain made fresh. She needn't have seen the date in print to know that the photo was taken on the same day when her life had changed so drastically. But someone had written the date anyway, at the bottom, in that rectangle of extra white space unique to instant photographs. And they had left it for her without explanation. Did they have some idea of what that day meant to her? Was it a run-of-the-mill coincidence, or was it an ominous one? Sammy was always warning her of the potential weirdos, ne'er-do-wells, and outright maniacs that a young, female, sultry-voiced disc jockey was likely to attract. It was the reason why he'd suggested inventing Mandy, her alter-ego.

When the photo was taken, she was still a year or three away from becoming a disc jockey herself. She recalled playing XAMO on the radio that afternoon, as was her habit in those days while at the shop. It was right before Art had come in to tell her the news, and the whole world had shattered. She was humming to "My Sharona," probably introduced by Sammy, on one of the Little John novelty radios they'd never gotten rid of, having set it on the floor nearby while she worked.

Think harder. Try to remember.

Even if it stings like a bitch.

And then a mental picture came, triggered by the real one on the dresser top: a dark-haired kid in a yellow windbreaker and Adidas sweatbands— those spongy white wrist and headbands were all the rage in 1980—and an oversized camera dangling from his neck.

If he wasn't a figment of her imagination, the kid would be in his late teens now. Either he or someone who'd come into possession of the photo had delivered it to her at the station personally, with all the logistical effort that implied. And her truck had vanished the same day. Her mind processed this and, in its already sleep-deprived and paranoid state, returned only additional reasons to worry.

A possible psycho who knew where and what hours she worked. What she looked like. Probably even her real name. Someone like "Strummer," that serial caller from California a few months ago. Like a fool, she'd come to welcome his contributions to her nightly show because of their shared musical tastes and because of the funny faux-English accent that he used whenever she put him on the air. But then he'd let it slip that he knew her real name, and then he couldn't (or wouldn't) explain how he'd learned it.

The morning ticked away. On the kitchen radio, "*Querida*" gave way to "*El Noa Noa.*" (The *ranchera* station favored local natives like Juan Gabriel and Carr.) At last Elfa found the will to get out of bed, disdain propelling her limbs and muscles more than anything else. Bad music, New Coke; nothing could fire her up like the things she hated, it seemed. She pattered barefoot to the kitchen and rummaged some bread and *cajeta* from the pantry, got the toaster going, and turned the dial on the old Zenith clock-radio to XAMO.

"Ma!" she called.

Delia was a part-time cook at the racetrack, but Elfa couldn't recall if she was scheduled to work a shift this morning or not. On the radio, Jeremy Santana, XAMO's youngest DJ at seventeen, was spiking his live remote from Thunderbird Lanes in west El Paso with typically inappropriate humor, no doubt lifted from his dog-eared copy of *Truly Tasteless Jokes* ("What do blondes and bowling balls have in common?").

She placed her two slices of toast on a saucer and carried them out to the front porch, where she found her mother's Jetta parked in the driveway below. She chose not to take alarm at this, at least not yet. It was an encouraging sign that the radio had been on in the kitchen when she'd woke. Rather, she took a seat in one of the ancient metal gliders, drew a knee up to her chin, and savored her toast. The morning was bright and cool, the neighborhood dreamily quiet. The majority of its residents were aging retirees from ASARCO, the century-old smelter a mile or so down the road that had once employed practically everyone in the Schultz family, save her mother and she herself. Delia's parents, born and raised in the original Smeltertown or La Esmelda, had even helped settle the neighborhood, erecting the two-bedroom Sears kit house here on Vista Hill themselves in the 1930s. At the far end of the street, the Black Mountain loomed, grim as some feudal overlord's castle, above the tiny foothill colony. The white limestone cross that graced its peak, just like the neighborhood that it allegedly safeguarded, was another legacy of La Esmelda's long-gone first generation. As she finished up her small breakfast, Elfa gazed both at the mountain and, in a certain meditative way, past it, taking strict care not to dwell too much on its manifold presence in her life.

It was at this same end of the street where Delia appeared, a few minutes later, as Elfa laid the saucer aside and rubbed toast crumbs lightly from her fingers. Her mother was clad in a violet-and-green ladies' tracksuit, white tennis shoes, and lemon-colored headband. The sight of her portly mom in such potentially laughable athletic gear might have pained Elfa a little, if Elfa herself hadn't picked it out at Mervyn's and hounded her mom into purchasing it. The extra pounds had accumulated fast, all of them in the years after Manny's death.

Delia reached the house and started up the porch steps. Then she groaned, paused, and bent forward, leaning on the front pillar for support.

"Ma!" Elfa cried, standing in fright.

"No, no, *mija*," her mother replied, making a shooing gesture with her free hand. "It's these shoes. I think we should take them back."

"You're not lacing them right, Ma. You have to do it how the man showed you."

"Ah, *claro*. Did you eat? Let me fix some eggs and *papas*."

"I'm fine, Ma. Danny's picking me up in a little while."

"Oh," her mother said, deflated. "Okay."

"Are you working today, Ma?"

Delia touched the side of her own face in sudden distraction. "No, *mija*. I called in sick." She moved on towards the screen door.

"Why would you do that? You've just been out walking."

"Oh, I thought I was feeling a little sick to my stomach earlier, but now it's alright. You know how it is with old people."

"You're barely fifty, Ma. Don't talk like you're an old maid."

"Do you want to use the car? I don't need it today."

"No, Ma."

"*Bien, bien, pues.*"

Delia slipped waiflike into the house. Experiencing a familiar mixture of irritation and shame—shame because her mother's forlorn, needy kindnesses provoked only raw irritation in her—Elfa decided to set out on her own walk. She had plans to sort out, and she sorted her thoughts best while on her feet and moving. Hanging with her *prima* was probably not the wisest use of her Saturday afternoon, not with a term paper due and finals coming up. But getting out of the house and away from her mother's unrelenting forlornness for at least a couple of hours had lately become just as essential to her continued wellbeing as keeping her grades up. Thus, another reason to go walking instead of joining her mother inside.

But as she neared the far end of the block, Elfa's feet asserted their own agenda. They carried her out of the neighborhood, down the narrow umbilical road leading off the hill, then underneath the Highway 85 overpass, and delivered her a few minutes later to the site of her parents' old defunct thrift store. It was here, not Rosa's, where a certain wavy-haired, ukulele-toting country singer and his associates had once passed an afternoon waiting on a busted-radiator repair job sometime in the late fifties.

Her father and her father's best friend, Art Mercado, had told her the story often, how the black-and-white Imperial came rolling in off the little two-lane blacktop, steam billowing dragon-like from the teeth of its front grille. The two boys were high-school seniors then, working their first jobs as uniformed service attendants before eventually recapitulating their own fathers' careers at the smelter. The car came to a halt in front of the service bay, and three men in rockabilly knit shirts spilled out. Art and Manny had helped push the big white-top sedan into the bay, admiring its gunsight tail lamps and two-tone paint, and after the mechanic went to work on it, they fetched the three men Dr. Peppers from the soda machine, on orders from the station manager.

"These boys were on TV just last week," the manager told them in an excited hush. "I saw them on *Country Style U.S.A.*"

The tallest of the three accepted his drink and wandered outside with it, carrying his spruce-top uke in his spare hand. Manny watched him swallow down his Dr. Pepper, lost in thought, and set the empty bottle in the return tray by the station's front window. He seemed fascinated with the Black Mountain. He strolled away towards it, picking whimsical, freewheeling notes on the little ukulele as he went. Hours later, he reappeared astride a mule, riding behind a man in Border Patrol green fatigues and grinning.

"Suffering Jesus, Marty!" cried the big-eared man who'd been behind the Imperial's front wheel, a cigarette twitching agitatedly from his lips. "Where the hell you been? We dang near called the cops!"

When the three highway travelers drove away sometime close to dusk, the tall one seemed to have worked a melody out on his uke, reprising it over and over. Manny recognized the same cheery Tejano melody at once when it came over the radio a year later. The ukulele man had written a song about El Paso—a grim ballad of love, murder, and vengeance.

Elfa found the spare key, its brass Sky Chief fob still attached, beneath a concrete paver in the back. The hoary odor of Mexican brick, old but adamant, greeted her once inside. She slapped the key down on the dust-coated sales counter and took it all in. Funny how some things persisted without any encouragement at all. She could tell from a certain quality in the air that the pot-party had happened days ago, maybe longer, the tokers long since gone their merry reckless way. She could also visualize just as sharply her father's lifelong friend Art Mercado standing before her in this room, cap in both hands, informing her in trembling, broken tones that Manny had been found shot dead on the Black Mountain, though that savage August afternoon now languished nearly five years in the otherwise dim, dull, pointless past.

With help from Art and other *esmeltianos*, she'd managed to sell off or donate much of the inventory, but quite a bit lingered, particularly the trinket trash here in the front room—the small toys, the drinking glasses, the figurine sets, and the like. All through that shitty first year or so, La Esmelda had coalesced around her and Delia and held them both to its loving, smothering bosom like the vigilant microorganism it was. Delia was eager to absorbe that love, the food, the cash gifts, the incessant *anciana* visits, and the other indulgences like some kind of birthright. Elfa scarcely knew what to do with these people who'd meant far more to her mother and father than they ever had to her. They'd helped square the thrift store away inasmuch as that could be done, they'd arranged the job for Delia at the racetrack, and they'd even scraped together $350 towards Elfa's college education. Yet it took not quite a year for Elfa's unchanneled anger at Manny's erasure from existence to settle, after twisting about in near-space temporarily like an indecisive hurricane, upon the generally decent, unremittingly pious, relentlessly sympathizing, and unforgivably stupid populace of La Esmelda.

We're so very sorry, mija. *Your father was a good and generous man.* ¿Ni modo?

It is very sad, mija. *The Cerro de Muleros is a dangerous mountain. Your father gave his life to keep the path to the holy shrine open and safe for everyone. Be proud of him.*

The bandits have plagued the mountain for many years. They are mostly boys from Anapra and Ciudad Juárez, young and penniless and desperate.

Para olvidar un mal es la mejor venganza.

Worthless observations, useless advice. Blind acceptance of the vileness that went on in the world for no better reason than that's just the way things have always been. *¿Ni modo?* Which was Mexican argot for *Oh, well, shit happens. Why hassle with it?* Yes, she blamed them and their weak-minded customs as much as she blamed the Nueva Anapra police.

Elfa never voiced her feelings, which even she sometimes recognized were as much irrational as they were unkind. But her coldness was noticed. Little by little, the attention paid her and her mother had dissipated. The home visits stopped; the offers to help out with the yard and do small patchwork on the house; the calls to pray for them at Santa Teresita. On her last day in the store, Art and his wife, Carolina, had been here helping to box up some of the trinket trash. Art had found a vintage Tudor electric football game, Raiders versus Chiefs, and was unable to resist setting it up on the sales counter and playing it. Elfa herself was absorbed for the moment in a crate of *Look* magazines that would have to be tossed out. The ads for things like Nora Doone cookies and Dispensomat washers; the advice article by Dick Clark on going steady for teens, had both intrigued her and darkened her mood. Like the after-stench of skunky weed, they evoked only transience, things come and gone. When Art fired up the game, she was brooding on an item about prefab Japanese teahouses, the latest "back-yard fun for the young."

"*O qué la*," exclaimed Art, who was also Elfa's godfather. He grinned and bobbed his head in happy agitation as the plastic miniatures skittered about the vibrating board, the sound like a jar of coins being vigorously shaken. Carolina was setting lunch out on an old vinyl-top card table— ham sandwiches and mango-cucumber salad.

"I forgot how close to the real thing these old electric game boards could be," Art continued, speaking to no one in particular. "This *chapucero* quarterback runs the ball just like Pastorini. He's driving me nuts."

"*Lávate las manos*," Carolina said to both of them. She was a stickler for washing hands before eating. "Lunch is ready. I don't want the sandwiches to dry out."

"Just a minute," said Art. Withdrawing from her magazine, Elfa watched him reset the pieces and run another play, the pleasure in his eyes nearly identical to that of the buzz-cut pubescent boy on the game-box lid. Again the board rattled and spasmed, and Elfa could visualize without getting up to watch the thumbed-sized plastic linemen scattering in every blind, screwball direction imaginable, as she'd played the game once herself. At the time she'd found it funny. Now it cast her mood, like a rudderless boat, adrift in yet darker waters.

"*Yes!* That's more like it!" Art smacked his hands together and leaped in the air, triumphant. He was shorter than Elfa's father had been, with hairy arms and a meaty nose. He had a more antic disposition than Manny, however, and had also prospered more at the smelter. He and Carolina had bought a house in one of El Paso's nicer westside neighborhoods only a few years prior—she still recalled her initial amazement at the cozy sunken fireplace, with its tiered, carpeted seating, in one corner of their new living room—so technically, they were no longer even part of La Esmelda.

"At least you don't have to put up with bad ref calls in electric football. Now if we could just put the team back in the right city, it'd be perfect."

"Get going, Raider Nation," said Carolina, growing perturbed. "Elfa needs to wash up too."

Art left the room, spirits high. He'd undone the past, corrected the course of history—at least NFL history. The sound of splashing tap water came from the teeny gas-station washroom in the back. Elfa stood and dropped the *Look* magazine, Dick Clark's grin forever frozen behind the weathered scratches and discoloring on the front cover, in with the rest. She picked up the plywood shipping crate that held them and walked over to the sales counter, then set it down again. She unplugged the football game and tilted it over the crate, feeding the plastic game pieces into the crate, sending both teams to their deaths. Then she laid the game board on the floor and stomped on it. She paused to observe what effect the stomping had had, found it unsatisfactory, and stomped on it again. Then again, using her other foot. The board framing, also plastic, had begun to fissure, but the board itself looked relatively intact. She bent and repositioned it at a slant against the side of the sales counter, then turned away and shot it a mighty high-velocity donkey-kick. Then another. And another. Something shattered. She turned to face it again and found the frame more-or-less exploded, green-plastic shards littering the general area in perversely Christmas-like color, and the sheet-metal board itself dented beyond its envisioned use. She'd also put a gash in the wood outer side of the sales counter.

"Whew!" she said, plunking the ruined football game in with the moldering mags and slapping her palms together in the universal gesture of a dirty but necessary task having been completed. When she looked up once more, Art had come back into the room, and both he and Carolina were watching her in stunned disbelief.

One day sometime thereafter, Padre Nerón had appeared at the door, himself in blue cross-trainers and Lee jeans, as he liked to roam the streets of Buena Vista often—all eight of them. She observed him coming up the porch steps from her front bedroom, where she lay on her bed propped on her elbow, contemplating the first Pretenders album. She loved "Brass in Pocket," with its ballsy chorus and odd references to "Detroit leaning" and "new skank, so reet," but "Stop Your Sobbing" was her current fixation. Padre Nerón had paid them many visits since her father's murder, and she presumed he was dropping by to check up on Delia, as neither she herself nor Manny had ever had much use for the Church. But he asked to come inside anyway when she answered the door and told him her mom was at the racetrack.

As always, he went first to the living-room shrine, knelt, and crossed himself. As always, Elfa looked askance. She didn't hold his superstitions against him—he'd done much for the neighborhood, and for her and Delia personally, and for a man in his late sixties, he seemed to maintain boundless reserves of energy that she found lacking in herself even at seventeen—but they held no enchantment for her either. She offered him a Coors, which he accepted, and she poured it up for him cold and frothy from the fridge into a *Great Muppet Caper* glass from McDonald's—Miss Piggy riding a motorcycle.

He indulged in just three, maybe four sips of beer in total as he spoke to her. In the strictest sense, really, he spoke to the Miss Piggy glass, as if all too aware that he would see the contempt in Elfa's eyes should he chance to meet them. Not contempt for him, per se, and she could only hope he understood that. Again, Elfa looked away. Padre Nerón spoke. She'd once teased him for him being named after maybe the evilest Roman emperor of them all, and true to his nature, he'd laughed.

"Yes, this is true," he answered, sheepish. His dense white eyebrows, to her somehow suggestive of the Mediterranean, had a way of pulling in towards each other whenever he conceded a point. "But you know what? The word itself isn't evil at all. It's just an old Italian name meaning 'strong.' It's old as creation, going back farther than all the lifetimes of all the Caesars put together. Why let the bad people spoil everything? I'm grateful my mother named me 'Strong.' I like to believe it's kept me that way."

And still Padre Nerón spoke. He spoke of her *ira,* her anger, and its power to destroy all the pleasure in living, forever. He spoke of its power to destroy love, or even the possibility of love. He spoke in the manner of one who'd endured suffering more lasting and profound than she could ever attempt to forget, let alone understand, and in this aspect of his speech, if nowhere else, she found nothing that invited doubt or cynicism—the man was no hypocrite. And yet still she looked away, sometimes to the side window, where the Black Mountain hovered beyond a suddenly dismal beige window-sheer, and sometimes to the shrine in the corner, with its tawdry fake flowers and seven-day candles and cedar Nuestra Señora triptych and, adjacent to this, the framed four-by-six of Manny holding her astride his shoulders during a long-ago rafting trip near Terlingua.

A man is born. He is no one special and neither are his parents. He is nobody at all, really. Like most nobodies, he grows up unreasonably happy,

happy by his own nature and happy to be living, despite the incongruity of growing up, in his particular case, in the callous shadow of a sky-shitting, earth-fouling smelter in an ugly desert in one of the poorest cities in the United States. His smile is a brash and defiant torch, hot as a smelting furnace, fueled with ceaseless delight at being alive. He smiles in every school portrait and catechism-class photo. He smiles just as fiercely in his Texaco attendant's uniform as in his high-school cap and gown. And perhaps unlike most nobodies, his smile doesn't sour with young adulthood or even with middle age. It burns with extra intensity in his wedding photo, but it does the same in a casual on-the-job snapshot taken at the smelter.

This man loves mayonnaise sandwiches. This man does not believe in god, attending mass and devoting his off-hours to church volunteerism out of love for the nobodies who reared him. This man dabbles in amateur black-and-white photography, an accidental passion resulting from his failed engineering studies at Texas Western College. This man is not above asking his young daughter to pull his finger and then chuckling at his own farts. This man is now dead, found one August day face-down in the dirt near the fourth Station of the Cross, robbed of his camera and wallet, while protecting a stupid, unsightly mountain that had never loved him back. Nobody is born, and nobody dies. And practically nobody cares.

And so Padre Nerón spoke, and Elfa listened. She listened and nodded appreciatively and was, nonetheless, wholly unmoved.

The gash in the sales-counter paneling was still there, a permanent leer sewn into the plywood. The building had proven unsellable long before her tantrum, so it hardly seemed to matter. Buying and converting the old Texaco into a secondhand shop had been another of Manny's inspirations, sparked by his promotion to foreman at the smelter and the question of how to use the extra income, slight as that was. Her pop had an independent streak too. Proud as he was to be a machinist like his German-born father, Manny harbored inklings of branching out, of maybe not being a company man his whole life. But his ambitions were soft and tended to collide with his sense of duty. Elfa had loved this about him anyway; other men would have pursued their ambitions to the exclusion of all else, even their families.

It came to her now why her feet had carried her back to Buena Vista Emporium after more than a year away. It was time to resign the DJ gig at XAMO. Both Elfa and her mother were still paying on their respective vehicles. The insurance adjustor had referred her claim to the company's fraud department, not quite accusing Elfa of somehow contriving to steal her own truck. The station was a logistical hassle getting to and from five days a week, even using her illegal shortcut; it paid only a hair above minimum wage; she could make just as much peddling burgers and beer in any of the Barmuda Triangle joints right next-door to UTEP, plus save that much in time and money by cutting the distance between school and work to practically nothing.

And it's just what you deserve, kid. You were incensed at your own mom a few minutes ago for nothing more than offering to make you breakfast. What kind of person thinks that way? Seriously? What kind of selfish, ungrateful, hardhearted.…?

That accusing voice. Will you please just shut the fuck up? I'm giving you what you want, aren't I?

She retreated again, this time flicking hot, errant tears from her eyes. Tears solved nothing, righted nothing. Even the relief they used to bring now felt sterile and false. Like a can of New Coke.

The mind and its torments.

Give Sammy her notice Monday, maybe even collect some restaurant applications today while out with Cousin Danny. The old ten-speed was stowed away in here someplace. She'd thought to sell it after buying the truck, before deciding to close the Emporium for good, so here was one thing that had worked out for the best. She'd rescue the Huffy from its junk-pile fate and do whatever repairs and fine-tuning were needed, which shouldn't be that much, and use it as her primary mode of transport for her last three semesters as an undergraduate. Her broadcasting career would still be there, was bound to reap some fresh opportunities once she had her communication degree.

Easy in theory, yes, but Elfa had not quite crossed the room before the other shoe dropped. She entered the former service bay, where the bicycle was stashed with the heavier junk, and as she went, it came to her that giving Sammy notice wasn't going to be anything like easy. He'd understand and wish her well, but at that moment she was going to fall to pieces. Sammy had been her unwavering friend, her one true *compa*, from the beginning. She would miss those preposterous wigs and that durable, droll advice. She'd miss the station itself, with its roaches and crumbling tile and colorful history almost as long and scandalous as the Black Mountain's. She was going to miss Mandy, whose spirit, something in her blood whispered, couldn't be summoned anywhere beyond the magical, yellowing, asbestos-laced wall panels of XAMO Studio A.

On the other hand, there was the spirit of Mary Jane, whose presence confronted Elfa again when she entered the service bay. The old merchandise bins and tables had been mostly removed, the others pushed up against the walls. In the center of the room someone had erected an indoor campsite, complete with pup tent, tacky velvet floor pillows, Indian rugs and blankets, incense burners, and blackened votive candles. She recognized the chocolate-slag ashtray, an ugly fixture from the old stock, in the center, then knelt and picked out a dead roach—the other kind— from a small mound of them. Together they looked like a bowl of severed fingers. She tossed the one in disgust back with its brethren and stood up again. Then fresh worry tainted her thoughts.

She checked the building's main rooms again to confirm it, then the tiny (and now squalid) bathroom, which was even less of a possibility because of the shoebox-sized window. No sign of forced entry anywhere.

Someone knew about the key.

6

An overstuffed mohair lounger occupied a quaint niche of shade in the levee drainage ditch, the dirty water lapping intimately at its upholstered corners. Ash and Casey passed it on horseback as they negotiated the pallet boards laid across the ditch. Once across, Casey leaned forward in the saddle and spurred her sorrel pony, China, up the levee's slope. Asher followed.

"Stop checking out my ass!" Casey called back.

Atop the levee a rutted dirt utility road stretched away into the distance in both directions. Some forty yards on the other side, the Big River itself was visible between two stands of weeds, streaming placidly from right to left, its brown surface ringlets made gilded and sparkling by the sun's caress.

"Which way, California?" Casey asked.

Asher nodded towards his left. There the levee curled gradually out of sight. Beyond that, the Black Mountain.

Casey had taken to calling him California or "Cal" rather than Charlie. He was in no position to argue since she'd also bestowed him a job.

They set out south at a steady amble. The river remained largely out of sight, concealed by the wild trees and bunchgrass that hugged its banks. He watched the riding track slide past on his own side, marking the westernmost boundary of the Lazybones Stables complex. From the front entrance, the place hadn't appeared to be much more than a trailer park, but now he understood the whole facility easily covered about quadruple the acreage of Rede Stables.

"Looks like you and Fantasia are hitting it off," Casey said, meaning his white palomino.

"She's alright. She doesn't like her name, though."

"And exactly how would you know that?"

"She yawns every time she hears it."

Casey threw him a look. So far she didn't seem to believe much of anything he told her, yet she didn't seem to hold any of it against him, either. He bent over his saddle horn and spoke Fantasia's name. Her head came up in a reflexive motion and he saw a flick of the mare's tongue, heard the distinct exhalation. She repeated it twice.

"You taught her that as a joke," Casey said.

"Would've been hard to do that in only a week," said Ash. "I just think she knows it's a conceited kind of name."

"Well, that fits," said Casey. "The girl who owns her is the reigning Miss Teen El Paso."

They came to the Nueva Anapra Boulevard overpass, and Casey adjusted the bill of her Pirates painter's cap as they awaited a lull in traffic. The main racetrack clubhouse lay alongside the river, the front façade announcing its own glamour and importance with an array of flagpoles, lofty cypress trees, and raised box hedges that spelled out the place's name.

"How far are we going?"

"Good question," said Casey.

"No, I'm serious."

"Yes, I've noticed. I'm thinking...to the power plant and back, maybe?"

"You're the boss."

Beyond the overpass, the vegetation thinned out and the river revealed itself. Here the water was shifting and uneven, interrupted by frequent bends and sandbars. His thoughts turned, unbidden, to the curves of a woman's body—specifically to the curves of Brooke Shields in a *Texas Monthly* jeans ad that he'd come upon that morning in Tree Pendleton's trailer. His eyes fell on Casey in her racerback tank top, only three feet away, and a sort of juvenile, unprovoked shame stung him. He refocused on the approaching power plant and its neighbors, SWIG Cotton and, further off, the ASARCO smokestack, with its alternating bands of red and white.

Casey reined her pony to a halt.

"Here," she said, dismounting. They'd come to a watershed behind the power plant, where another drainage ditch fed into the river. The plant's turbines whined in the near distance.

"Here what?"

"We're going to water our horses at the riverbank just like they did in the old days."

"I don't think the water was that color in the old days."

"Yeah? You were there?"

Both horses took to the earthy water without complaint.

"You've been a big help this week, whoever you are," said Casey, removing her cap and redoing the elastic on her ponytail. "So do you think you'll still be around in the fall? We could use you during racing season."

"What's this 'whoever' stuff?" said Asher, taking the bait. "In that case, my real name is Charlie Manson."

"It might as well be. That's about as believable as 'Charlie Sexton.' Do you think we don't have cable or radio out here?"

"It's a stupid coincidence, is all. I knew a kid in sixth grade named Huey Lewis. I hope he's getting more mileage out of his name now than I am."

"Dude…it's none of my business, and I don't honestly care. But it's clear enough that you're one of us. I mean, you obviously come from this way of life. So don't go treating me like some ignorant rednexican. You're just lucky that Daddy and Ms. Piper still use the wetback payroll system, or you would have had to present some authentic identification days ago. And I better tell you, if living incognito is your thing, the razor-chop haircut is probably a bad idea."

"Thanks. Anything else?"

"Yeah." She finished retying her ponytail and took the saddle once more. "You're it, schmucko," she said.

She spurred China into the Rio Grande at full gallop, spraying beads of water in his face. Asher accepted the challenge. He hopped back astride Miss Teen El Paso's horse, then stood in the saddle and issued a *cloqueo*, the distinct kissing sound Mauricio had taught him ages upon ages ago. He and Fantasia overtook her and China just short of the opposite side.

They ascended the west levee, both half-drenched, and came to a small, weed-addled park with a dilapidated gazebo and playground. Spray-paint graffiti marred some of the waist-high perimeter walls.

"Pine nuts!" Casey exclaimed. She prodded China toward the park's street-side edge, where a heavyset man in a Gilligan-esque bucket hat was seated in a canvas chair beside a GMC van. A poster board reading PIÑON lay propped against the van's windshield.

"You're early this year, Tolf," said Casey, cinching her pony's bridle reins to the street-lamp post.

Ash chose to circle the park on horseback at an easy pace, giving Fantasia a chance to cool. The park lay across a narrow two-lane road from the Black Mountain. A long freight train was trundling through at the mountain's base, its double-stacked container cars even more graffitied over than the park walls. When he came back round to where Casey and the behatted piñon dealer were still catching up, he noticed he'd come to a stone plaque-stand adjacent to the park's entrance. He reined Fantasia to a halt and contemplated the raised bronze lettering:

100

This mark is dedicated to the memory
of Dr. Donald Piper who had a special
love in heart for the communities of
Anapra and Nueva Anapra. Dr. Piper
willingly shared his time and his
resources with the people who live
here. This park is a memorial to his
generosity and service.

We will never forget
DR. PIPER

"Who's Ms. Piper?"

He'd pulled a little ahead of Casey on the ride back so she couldn't accuse him again of checking out her ass. The New Mexican pine nuts, which she'd shared with him out of a Ziploc bag, were a surprising pleasure, with the splintery outer texture of sunflower seeds yet a velvet, butter-flavored inner flesh.

"Just the old thunder-cunt who owns it all," said Casey from somewhere behind. "She owns the stables and half the racetrack and probably half of Anapra, old and new both."

"I thought your dad owned the stables."

"Dad never owned anything that he didn't lose in some moon-headed off-track betting scheme a few months later." Casey's expression turned uncharacteristically rueful. "It's legal now, but Dad was doing it way before then, and he ended up owing money to people like Jimmy Chagra and Sailor Roberts. Ms. Piper loaned him the cash to buy the sharks and bookies off, and she did that for him more than once, so now *she's* the shark. Basically that woman owns him—home, hide, and all. In some ways, I guess that means she owns me too."

She reined up beside him and pointed with one Lycrochet glove to a nearby ridge at the foot of the Black Mountain. "Up yonder's the old miser-bitch's lair," she said, referring to the reddish-pink hacienda that dominated the ridge. "Supposedly Cybill Shepherd was there visiting a few weeks ago. She knows a lot of famous people."

"Who?"

"Give me a break, California, you don't watch *Moonlighting*? I'm pretty sure you watch MTV, at the very least."

"I've heard of it. You seem pretty sure about a lot of things."

"That I am," said Casey, maneuvering around him smartly and taking the lead. "Stop checking out my ass!" she barked back.

But he was still checking out the pink hacienda. A moment or two elapsed, and Fantasia turned her head to the side questioningly. Ash spurred her forward...then reined her to a halt again. On the two-lane road between the levee and the private driveway leading up to the hacienda a familiar green Border Patrol off-roader sat idling. Agent Jepsen held up a hand to him in greeting from behind the wheel, a calculated grin stretching his Tom Selleck mustache out like some dark oily window valance.

Ash kicked his mount into a trot.

"How's Phoenix?" said Jared's voice from nine hundred miles away.

Ash shifted his weight and turned aside from the telephone kiosk, which stood in the middle of the trailer park beside a lantern-bearing lawn jockey. Nearly every mobile home here had a front deck of one variety or another, and something inside him half-expected or half-longed to spot Mauricio seated on one of them with his little TV and his Big Gulp.

"I'm in Tempe, Dad. The school's in Tempe."

"That was just an elbow of Phoenix the last time I saw it. So it's still Phoenix. And still hotter than the surface of the sun out there this time of year, I'll wager."

"It's April."

"Give it a week. Hell, give it ten minutes."

There was a distracted surliness in his voice. The nightly Lowenbrau spiked with Herradura.

"Your mom sent you something. Looks like a graduation card."

"You didn't tell her?"

"She must have figured it out. I don't know why she'd think you were graduating in your junior year. Give me your mailing address out there and I'll forward it."

"Toss it. I don't want it."

"Maybe she sent money."

"She's an adjunct, Dad. She doesn't have money. It's one of her hippy-dippy I-love-you-not-really cards, and I'm not interested. Throw it out."

A contemplative sip-slurping followed. At least Jared had chosen the path of the methodical drunk, not the chugger. Ash could see him slouched there in the same den-corner armchair where the hi-fi and the old LP stacks were. Lex was no doubt in sole possession of the cable TV channel selector. Likely there was a half-eaten pizza or an emptied bag bearing the Golden Arches in the room someplace as well. "'Hippy-dippy I-love-you-not-really'," Jared repeated. "Do those come from Hallmark or American Greetings?"

"I gotta go. I have class in the morning."

"You told me classes don't start until next week."

"Right—I mean orientation. I'll call you Saturday."

A fierce crimson sunset was underway beyond the trailer rows. The smell and hiss of skillet-frying food emanated from the bulky Vindale that neighbored Tree Pendleton's cramped '57 Westerner, making his stomach grumble. He'd never seen the family who inhabited it, but he knew there had to be one from the children's voices that escaped the open window slats and from the toy basketball goal out front. He climbed the steps to Tree's trailer and went inside, where he started up the Kenmore window unit in the stifling heat, then dug out the last remaining pack of ramen and filled the single stovetop saucepan with water.

When he clicked on the Little John's switch-dial, Mandy was reciting the lyrics of "Sunday Bloody Sunday" over the air, with loving precision, word for word. He sat down at the two-chair rose Formica table and listened as the water in the pan began its sluggish journey to boiling point.

"I know you're all itching to hear the new Quiet Riot," she said after finishing the lyrics. "And we'll get to it, don't worry. I just think once in a while we should stop and consider the amazing fact that good music can turn something ugly into something beautiful. People think punk rock is ugly, but there's U2, a punk band, making beauty out of an awful thing that really happened in Ireland about fifteen years ago. And it isn't stupid. *Good music doesn't have to be stupid.* Think about it."

She segued into something by Romeo Void, and Asher consumed the last of his ramen noodles out of the pan in the Spartan light of a Sarfatti table lamp. While he ate, a cricket—he hoped it was a cricket—darted along the confetti-linoleum floor and vanished in the shadow of the baseboard. It was stupid, his coming here. Stupid and beautiful, at least for the moment. He hated lying to Jared, but he liked working with Casey. He liked the Lazybones Stables. He hated the red-haired woman at the sweltering funeral. He loved Mandy. He loved Elfa. He hated the late, legendary, beloved Dr. Piper. He loved his mother and also hoped she someday got the comeuppance she deserved.

You're making a damned ass out of yourself, young man.

Dr. Tune, a high-priced Mooney Boulevard private psychologist, had told him this earlier that same spring. Dr. Tune's analysis was a mandatory element of the dropout paperwork. He was fond of the epithet "damned ass," having used it in passing to describe William Westmoreland, whom

Dr. Tune had known personally in Vietnam, only days before. In spite of himself, Ash came to appreciate Dr. Tune, a defiant humanist who'd overruled the school-district psychologist's urgings to medicate him out of hand. His criticisms directed at Asher were nevertheless blunt, as when Asher had come into the office with his New Wavy new haircut. Asher excused this reaction since Dr. Tune, in his permanent Lawrence Welk time-warp, had probably never glimpsed Iggy Pop or Siouxsie Sioux.

"You control your face a lot," he'd observed of Asher during their first session.

"Pardon me?"

"You seem very intent on controlling the expressions on your face. You're not one of these fashion-model types, are you?"

"I'm no poser," said Ash, affronted.

Dr. Tune's office occupied a fifth-floor corner suite of a bank building overlooking Visalia Mall. Despite the light from the windows the room felt dark because of the wood veneer wall-paneling and Danish teak furniture. A framed invitation to the first Reagan-Bush presidential inauguration hung on the wall near his diploma. Dr. Tune picked a legal pad up from the end table beside his chair and looked it over, scrunching his mouth in thought.

"Your paternal grandfather died recently, is that right?"

"No. He went eight years ago."

Dr. Tune folded over to the next handwritten page and skimmed it a moment. "Your great-grandfather, then. February of last year. Were you close to him?"

"No."

"Your father tells me otherwise."

"Look, do we have to go into this? I didn't really come here for, you know, *therapy*. I just hate it, that's all. I want out."

"Right." The next page went up and over. He detected something and thumped a line of typescript with his pen. "So you can attend audio-engineering school."

"That's right."

Up and over.

"Are all those notes about me? You just met me."

"Quiet, please." His eyes met Ash's over the rims of his thick-rimmed eyeglasses, and he set the legal pad aside weightily.

They regarded each other, doctor and patient. Asher thumped his fingers against the chair arm.

"Yes?" Dr. Tune pressed.

"It feels like I'm in that movie *Ordinary People*. But I didn't try to off myself and I'm not going to. There's nothing whatsoever like that going on here. I'm not depressed or psycho or whatever. I'm not on drugs, and believe me, I could if I wanted to. Half the people at Sequoia High are. I just hate high school, period."

"Has the place that much? I graduated in '43, so I'm a little far removed."

"I don't mean the place."

Dr. Tune clicked his gold ballpoint into retract and laid it aside. "I can sympathize. High school, in general, is not, as we say in our business, a 'well' environment. It's a fundamental design problem. The whole concept should be tossed out, burned to the ground, blown to shards, and replaced with something radically different. The trouble is that no one can agree on what that 'something' should be, exactly, so in the meantime we're stuck with the same old wasteful meat-grinder of a system. Therefore, I can say there's nothing wrong with a young man of seventeen recognizing what he wants to do with his life and getting on with it before the system is through with him…assuming that's actually the case here."

He was still holding his nice (probably monogrammed) chrome pen and watching Ash closely over the frames of his glasses, which were as outdated as his office décor.

"What?"

Dr. Tune steered his eyes upward as if searching for the right thing to say, or the right way to say it. For the first time Ash began to feel uncomfortable.

"Do you fantasize a lot?" he then asked.

"Fantasize? About what?"

"About anything. Battenberg cake. The planet Neptune. Girls. Would you say you're a daydreamer? Would that be a fair way of characterizing you?"

Asher was rubbing the heels of his palms together, realized it, and stopped. "Only during psychology class."

Dr. Tune grunted and reached for the pad again. Up and over—this had to be at least a fifth page of notes that he'd somehow accumulated in the couple of days between Jared making this appointment for him and Ash's actually coming in here.

"I know you're only joking, but then you haven't been to your psychology class in weeks. Or any of your classes. You stopped attending school altogether."

"It's a waste of time. You said that yourself."

"Fair enough. And I also agree that it probably is a waste of *your* time, especially. But I'm still interested in what you did with those hours instead—all those hours when you weren't in class at Sequoia High. What did you do with them? Where did they go?"

"I told you, I'm not into drugs."

"No one is saying you are."

"Then why does it matter?"

"Your dad didn't seek out my services only for the sake of bureaucratic formality. He's worried about you."

"Well, now that you know there's nothing to worry about, can't you tell him that?"

"Sure I can. And as long as I'm acting as messenger, your father would like you to know that he's sorry."

Ash weighed this. "Sorry for what?"

"That he allowed his marriage to your mother to fail. That he's been more consumed with keeping your family business alive than looking after you and your brother. At least those are the things he's sorry for specifically. I get the impression that there's a good deal more."

A siren wailed on the street somewhere below. There was a sense of the world going about its business outside, a sickening and empty sense which he'd begun to carry of late that nothing pertaining to him; indeed, that not a single incident that occurred in Asher's life counted for two shits in the great scheme of things. Except that it did. Dr. Tune seemed to take his silence as validation. He flipped yet another page in his legal pad.

"Your parents' divorce was finalized in 1982," he said, reciting facts now rather than supposition. "Your mother hasn't participated in your life in any meaningful way since."

"*No me importa.*"

"Bear with me," said Dr. Tune. "Allow yourself the treat of hearing out a professional opinion in undiluted terms. In other words, no posing."

Asher willed himself to place either hand on the sculpted armrests of his Scandinavian lounger.

"Your father described a fairly unpleasant home life in the years leading up to the divorce. That means the trouble between your parents extends back into your middle childhood, maybe earlier. Hardly anything unusual in today's society. But like adults, children will tend to seek escape from an unhappy reality. For adults and adolescents, the list of escapes varies depending on one's individual means and inclination, but it includes all the usual suspects: alcohol, drugs, promiscuity, suicide. All readily available options to people above a certain age. The younger a person is, however, the shorter the list becomes...eventually boiling down to just one thing, the only kind of escape that a normal child has the power or the understanding to effect."

"What?"

"An elaborate fantasy life."

Asher's smile faded. "You think there's something wrong with me. You think I'm psycho."

"No, just the opposite. I think you're *normal*. A *normal* child in your circumstances would be *likely* to construct a vivid fantasy life in order to shield himself from commonplace traumas like divorce and death. For more severe traumas like physical abuse and neglect, then yes, this tendency to fantasize can veer into schizophrenia and other, darker disorders—the 'psycho' stuff. But that isn't you. I'm saying there is something *right* with you, not something *wrong* with you."

"Then why'd you drag up all that old junk about my parents? What are we even talking about this for?"

Dr. Tune laid the legal pad aside once more and removed his glasses. It was a very TV kind of gesture, augmented by Dr. Tune's déjà vu-inducing resemblance to some actual TV father-figure—Robert Young or Robert Reed or someone else named Robert, maybe. It was too inexact to place, exactly.

"You're not a child now. You've made an adult decision to drop out of high school and begin your adult life by learning a practical skill. If, indeed, this is a practical decision based in reality, then I commend you.

Godspeed you on your new journey. But if you've conjured this audio-engineer scenario as an escape from the harsh realities of high school, then, months from now, it's probable that you'll dislike the similarly harsh realities of trade school, flunk out, and invent some new fantasy of escape.

"So, young man, I expect an answer to my original question." He leaned forward in his ox-hide chair, brow creased, transitioning from *Father Knows Best* to full-bore *Perry Mason*. "Where were you during those days and hours you weren't in school the past two months?"

Ash sometimes wondered if he could've lied to Dr. Tune and lived with it, let alone gotten away with it. But he'd told the truth that day, because he saw nothing to lose in telling it, and although hearing it deflated Dr. Tune a little, the answer appeared to assuage him. It was just Ash's good fortune that Dr. Tune, like Jared, had simply not known where to look for the lies.

He carried the emptied saucepan to the sink and then searched his jean pockets for an extra dime. Payday was tomorrow. The tuition check in his barrel bag was no good, made out as it was to the Phoenix Music Conservatory. Becoming anxious, he began opening drawers and cabinets in the tiny kitchenette. He wanted to call Mandy.

It took some rummaging, but soon he came upon a pair of ragged size-44 Lees puddled on the floor inside the narrow closet and, tucked within the front watch-pocket, like a gift from the gods, four pennies and one dime. Seizing this, he bounded out of the trailer.

"Well gimme the spread on San Antone and Denver, then!" a toothless white-haired guy of around sixty was spitting into the payphone when Ash came back. The guy's shirt was unbuttoned, his chest bare and trembling with loose, sagging flesh. A hapless beagle was leashed to the lawn jockey beside the phone kiosk. "No...no, no, Shawna, you gotta do me better'n that, now! Come on and help out an old friend here, dammit! How many times I done covered your sorry welfare-cheatin' ass over the years?"

A sporty maroon Mazda entered the park as Ash paced back to the trailer, planning to wait out the old guy's crazy harangue on the front steps. It stopped beside the little landlord's house where Casey lived with her father, its pop-up headlights ducking to a close with motorized efficiency. A tan-blonde Aryan in *Miami Vice* pastels and loafers got out, sporting pointlessly trendy sunglasses in the twilight, and went around the front of the car to the house. Ash transferred his attention to the beagle, an undersized blue-coated thing who, as Asher watched, fell over on his side and began making strange, trembling half-circles in the dirt. The dog was having a seizure.

The old guy lost all patience with Shawna and slammed the phone handset against its cradle a half-dozen times. Meanwhile his dog had stopped seizing and lay motionless. Ash got to his feet, unable to help himself, but before he could start down from the steps the dog came out of its paralysis spontaneously and righted itself, coming back to its original sitting position and resuming its pitiful countenance.

The old guy dug a fresh dime from out of his corduroys and punched in another call. "Chigger? It's Morris. What do you have for me?"

The silhouettes of Casey and her friend emerged from the house together and climbed into the Mazda on either side. Up popped the headlights, and Ash raised his arm in self-defense as they fell square on him before they veered right, whereupon Crockett or Tubbs maneuvered and backed up in order to exit the park.

"California!"

The car braked and Casey stuck her head out the passenger window, her day look jettisoned for teased-out hair and a neon blouse.

"What are you up to tonight? Come to J-town with us, dummy!"

There was a definite grumble of complaint from within the car.

"Lighten up, Aldo," she said, getting out. She came over to the trailer steps and looked Ash up and down, a kind of big-sister pity in her eyes.

"I'm not getting in that thing," he told her. "It's a coupe."

"*I'll* ride in the back. It's tiny, but I can always stick my head out through the sun roof if I get claustrophobic. Besides, I don't want you checking out my ass. Don't try and tell me you have anything better going on."

"What if I do?"

"Lies, all lies. I'm onto you, California. I say you're coming with us."

1

"That is a handsome scarf, by the way," said the young reporter from Mexico City. "Is it Lacoste?"

Sammy put his hibiscus tea on the table and lifted the end of his cheetah-print cashmere scarf from where it had been dangling near his belly, making a face as if he'd never noticed it before. "This thing? I'm sorry to confess I don't remember what it cost. The *mercados* around here are so negligent about price tags."

The young reporter smirked and jotted this in his spiral notebook. Sammy perceived that he was being toyed with, to some extent, by this arrogant little hipster. And what did it matter? The afternoon in general was an agreeable one. The kid had consented to meet at his favorite outdoor café, the traffic on Avenida Juárez wasn't yet so noisy as to smother the conversation, and the patio ceiling fans were effectively dulling the heat for now.

"So you started out at KLBJ in Austin," said the reporter. "Was the 'Hitman' character first born here or there?"

"It's called 'persona' in radio, amigo. Not 'character'."

"*Perdóname*…where was the 'Hitman' *persona* first conceived, then?"

Sammy reached for the beehive jar on the table and topped off his glass with sweet magenta-colored *jamaica*, wishing he'd popped one of the similarly colored pills in his pocket before embarking on this interview.

"To begin with, you're omitting a city or two. I did stints in Corpus and Oklahoma City and Shreveport and a smattering of others before landing here. Country stations, mostly, until Top Forty started to catch on. We played all the white crooners, Elvis, Paul Anka, Bobby Darin. And I dug most of those guys, you know; respected their work. But I also dug Jackie Wilson and Ray Charles. I loved rhythm and blues, and I knew the kids would too, once they'd had a helping, and if only more white station owners would allow it. So, long story short, I came down here because of XAMO's long reach and because I'd have the freedom to spin anything I wanted."

The hipster crossed his legs, one black zipper ankle-boot showing out from under the table. "What do you think of today's Top Forty music as opposed to, say, the same genre in 1965?"

Sammy raised his tumbler and swished the ice in his drink. "It's not so frightfully different, not once you sift beneath the new synthetic puffery. My ears sip from Katrina and the Waves, and my mind's palate returns echoes of Petula Clark. I listen to Eurythmics, I hear shades of Billie Holiday. When the music is good, it's because the fundamentals are still there. When it's bad…well, the occasional shit-pickle managed to float up the charts back then too."

The hipster smirked again and made an extensive show of jotting, as if to remind his subject whose time and amusement were the more valuable.

"One last question, please, Mr. Hayes."

"Sock it to me."

"You were charged with sodomy in McLennan County in 1977, and by all accounts you have not returned to the United States since. You're surely aware that Texas law prescribes a maximum sentence of fifteen years for such offenses. What is the status of these charges? Is this perhaps the real reason why you choose to live in exile?"

The septuagenarian waiter, Huerta, materialized and made his own fuss of replacing the drink pitcher and taking Sammy's lunch order (*pulpo en escabeche*). He ignored the young reporter, who seemed not to mind, with pronounced silence. When Huerta was gone, the reporter picked up his pen and notebook once again and regarded Sammy expectantly.

"Sorry about that, amigo," said Sammy. "They're a little protective of me around here. When he comes back I'll buy you another *horchata*."

"*Ni modo*. No problem."

"The only law keeping me out of Texas these days is the Blue Law. I like cheroots and bourbon on Sunday. I also want the option to go shopping for a tacky scarf if I feel like it."

"Ah. Yet I understand the legislature in Austin is considering a repeal of the Blue Law this year. Would you be swayed at all if that happened? Do you not miss your homeland?"

"Not as much as I miss freeform radio. I don't miss answering to twenty-five-year-old MBAs in pinstripes. That's all U.S. radio is anymore."

"I see. And to whom, may I ask, do you answer now?"

Later, enjoying his octopus alone, Sammy permitted himself the space to dwell on that. He'd spent the morning answering to a twenty-something hipster peckerwood, after all. At the far end of the Strip the logjam of vehicles waiting to cross into El Paso had begun its afternoon buildup, trailing nearly to his curbside seat. A giant Stars and Stripes soared over the bridge-crossing like a floating Smiley Face, vivid and jubilant. Presently Huerta returned with the check and the complementary *mazapan* candies on a tin cash-tray. Sammy pocketed the candy and left Huerta the usual 600-peso tip. Devaluation was a bitch.

At sixteen, he'd once answered to a station owner in Beaumont, fellating him in broad daylight near a railway bridge in said owner's Plymouth. All in all, that was less degrading than some of the later indignities: a dozen firings, the payola lackeys, the mail-order dog-food pitches, the *mordida*, bullets flying in the studio, bankruptcy, jail, lawyers, program directors, failed syndication deals, televised disco. Like the peso, a DJ's existence was subject to steep and sudden devaluation. As Sammy saw it, the only person to whom he'd ever been answerable, then and now, was a scoliotic ten-year-old dancing alone, spinning records, and talking into a hairbrush in his mother's squalid Sabine Pass apartment while she was out waiting tables (and, possibly, fellating her own share of men on the side). This was Hitman Hayes's real birthplace, but he hadn't cared to disclose that to the rude young reporter, who wasn't worthy of such confidences. It became the signature riff, the G7-shuffle of Sammy's teens and all his adult life thus far, that while Samuel Glendower Hayes had taken it up the ass more times, in more ways, and for more years than all the turd records that had ever floated up the charts, the Hitman answered to no one. The question at hand was whether or not the pushing-sixty version of himself still believed that.

The startup roar of his '53 Vincent Black Shadow answered a resounding yes. He scissored through the thick, sleepy traffic back to his condo in Linda Vista, where he chained the bike inside his garage, then chained the garage door and climbed the outside stairs to the residence.

The Message Waiting light on his Radio Shack machine called to him when he entered. He'd left the vertical blinds closed and the red blinking was accentuated by the semidarkness. He turned the dial to Playback and approached the kitchen bar, which doubled as an actual bar, and mixed himself a rum-and-cinnamon. The voice on his answering machine belonged to Elfa Schultz. He was just settling into one of the vintage, crisply reupholstered diner-seat bar stools when her voice began to crack, then shatter. She'd hung up in mid-stammer, but the gist was plain enough.

Sammy polished off his cocktail and then got up and mixed another. He coasted for a while, toying with the flamingo swizzle-stick in his emptied glass. He'd grown much too fond of Elfa in the last two years, it was true. It was even safe to say that he'd fallen in love with the kid. Chaste or not, this love implied a moral obligation, and that was to let lie what he'd seen coming since the afternoon when Elfa had swerved up to the station in her mother's car, trailing her hot, dusty, beautiful fury.

You didn't condemn someone you loved to the fucked-up, loutish life of a radio DJ.

Later, he found himself on the sofa-sectional watching an old Jerry Lewis comedy in Spanish. From here, the English-language TV stations over the river all lay within easy reception range, but he compren-dayed español well enough, and it occurred to him that Jerry Lewis's Buddy Love character was a lot more believable and a lot less jive schmoozing Stella Stevens in Spanish rather than English. Persona again. Maybe Mandy was Elfa's Buddy Love, her G7-shuffle. Maybe his obligation was to Mandy and not Elfa.

The sunlight was slivering through the blinds, which meant that the afternoon had melded into early evening. He regarded his glass, emptied again but for a pebble or two of runny ice. The swizzle-stick had disappeared somewhere inside the sectional underneath him, as his swizzle-sticks were wont to. Gingerly he set the drinking glass atop the *très moderne* tempered-glass endtable to his right and reached for the phone there, balancing it on his lap. He dialed the number from memory—the only United States phone number he knew off the top of his head anymore without having to consult his office rolodex back at the station.

"*Bueno. Hacienda de Piper*," said a woman's voice on the other end of the line. The voice belonged to Idaly Saldivar, his boss's longtime housekeeper.

"Hello, Dolly," he replied, always pleased at having literal occasion to utter those words. "Can I talk to the old battleax? Is she around there today?"

"Hang up the phone, Dolly," broke in the voice of Helen Piper. Her hard, humorless voice sounded nearer somehow, though of course it emanated from somewhere inside the same house. "What is it, you old wig-wearing faggot?"

"Such flattery," said Sammy.

"Yeah? You threw the first punch. Come on, out with it, whatever it is. I'm in a hurry."

"Horse business?"

"None of *your* business, certainly. You sound half in the bag as it is."

"Come to think of it, I have been inside a bag or two over the years. I admit it wasn't as altogether horrid as I thought."

"I'm hanging up."

"I need a raise in pay for one of my DJs. She's the best one we've got and the Arbitrons show it. She gave notice today. I don't want to lose her, and believe me, my love, you don't either."

"You mean that girl who's got the Coca-Cola bottler so hopping mad at us he's about to pull all their advertising? I'd be tickled pink to lose her."

"I'll tell her to cut it out."

"You'll tell her that anyway. And if you want to give her a raise, then fine, fire someone else or cut your own salary. But I'm not laying out one extra penny for that junk-pile radio station or anybody who works there, including you."

His boozy buzz was transitioning to a headache, as seamlessly as the sunlight crawling away behind the vertical blinds.

"Helen...," he began.

"Yes?"

"Your unkindness is showing—again."

That pricked her something good, judging by the brief silence. "I see," she answered evenly. "So it's real insults now, *my love*, not play ones?"

"You know what I meant."

"I'm hanging up."

She hung up.

"That's 'Valotte,' by Julian Lennon," Mandy said. Outside the picture window, some nearby desert scrub or other was giving off dozens of white dandelion-like florets, which scooted busily by in midair against a towering, molten sunset. One nice thing about Daylight Savings Time was that she got to enjoy the dusk's full progression and array of colors through the course of her show for at least half the year; only now did Elfa realize that this was the probable source of Mandy's cosmic Stevie Nicks mysticism.

"In the new *Rolling Stone*, Julian says his dad once promised him that when he died, if he could, he'd let Julian know he was still around and that he'd made it to the other side. He promised to do this by floating a white feather from one end of the room to the other. Julian used to watch for it all the time, until he realized the danger in looking for it too hard. Well, I'm watching about a hundred feathers float by right now. I wonder if John made some new friends on the other side.

"Anywho, I've got two free tickets to Lords of the New Church at El Paso County Coliseum on May 14th to the first caller who tells me which Beatles' song Paul McCartney wrote specifically for Julian."

She turned the potentiometer on her mike down to zero and punched a commercial on the cart machine, then removed her headphones. Carson Jaszkowiak, the station engineer, was poking around at the control console behind her, a Sun Country Cooler bottle in one hand. She hadn't heard him enter the studio.

"Please don't touch that, Jaz. I'm making a reel."

"I left a pack of Newports in here. Seen 'em?"

"Nope."

He came out of his geriatric stoop and surveyed the room at large from where he stood. He wore his beloved nubuck Birkenstocks and a white I Don't Care Bear t-shirt. He drifted off toward the transmitter gauges against the far wall, abandoning his wine cooler on top of a retired Audimax III.

"What do you need a reel for?" he called out. "We got hours of you on tape."

"Didn't anyone tell you?"

The phone lines were all ablaze. Every one of the five people at the other end of those lines gave wildly incorrect answers, including one caller who thought the Beatles recorded "Cat's in the Cradle."

"Tell me what?" asked Jaz after she gave up and went to the latest single by Go West. Jaz had returned from the transmitter cabinets, not with a pack of cigs, but with a baggie of green stuff, probably centuries old. He had hiding places all over the station, mostly cigs and old dope; occasionally candy, expired racing stubs, or yesteryear centerfolds. He seemed to enjoy the act of hiding things from himself no matter how worthless the things themselves.

Elfa explained that her last day was next week. Jaz nodded in thought, leaned against the console, and pried the baggie open, sniffing at its contents.

"*Yolki-palki*," he said. Although he was Polish by descent, Jaz was fond of Russian curse words for no discernible reason.

"Are you grieving over me or over your weed?" Elfa said, returning to her mike.

"Both," replied Jaz. "It's a sin to waste things in their prime."

"I'll take that as a compliment."

"You joining up with those cokeheads over at KRGZ?" He was referring to El Paso's top-rated station, an album-oriented FM powerhouse.

"I told you, I can't afford to work in radio anymore. And I certainly can't afford coke."

"Well, if you do score some, don't be greedy."

"Fuck you. Why are you working so late?"

"ACI problems with the new C-QUAM exciter. Plus Lori evicted my ass again. Spin me some James Taylor tonight, will you?"

"I don't know who that is, Jaz."

He glanced her way in wounded amazement as she adjusted her headphones for the next air-check. "*Yolki-palki*," he muttered again, and wandered at a dejected pace and posture out of the studio.

Assuming Mandy's voice again, Elfa went for what she regarded as a Special-Ed Beatles question ("What's Paul McCartney's middle name?"), and in came another fusillade of wrong answers. She decided to break her own (or Mandy's) self-imposed rules and went back to Line 1 when the others had played out.

"Hello?"

"XAMO. What's your answer?"

"Uh, no, can I make a request? Can you play 'Texas When I Die' by Tanya Tucker?"

"Maybe when *you* die, you cousin-counting brush-ape." Ugly as this comeback was, she couldn't suppress the affection in her voice, not altogether. Shaw did have a way of turning up and making her feel good at the lowest possible moments.

"Now is that any way to greet a loyal listener? Maybe I'll just keep those two cases of the Real Thing I had waiting especially for you."

"Two cases? What did that cost you?"

"Well, for you they were free a minute ago. Now I think they're going to cost you dinner and a movie."

The man was serious. Still kidding around on the surface, yes, but serious not far beneath. Just as she'd always suspected.

"I don't think so, Shaw. I appreciate the gesture. Can I play you something?"

"Yeah. 'Texas When I Die,' by—"

"—by Tanya Tucker, right, I get it. Except I don't have it, Shaw, honestly. I actually went looking for the creaky old thing in our record library last week, believe it or not. But it's like when disco fell apart and we threw out anything in our library with a Casablanca label. The same thing happened with country music about a year and a half ago. I'm really sorry, no bullshit."

"Where does that leave us, then? You're killing me here. Hell, I would've sprung for the dinner and the movie too. All I'm really asking for is a little of your time. Everything else is on me."

He had her dead-to-rights, in his own illogical but insistent way. She agreed to a date on Saturday, with the proviso that they go Dutch apart from the two cases of Mexican Coca-Cola. It also occurred to her as she was agreeing that there was cheap amusement to be had with Jaz by telling him she'd scored some coke after all. For his own part, Shaw's voice turned boyishly jubilant as he wished her a good night, as if amazed his gambit had worked. Smiling to herself, Elfa punched the next line.

"XAMO."

"You have a date Saturday night."

"Yes, I…what? Sammy?"

"Oops," said Sammy's voice, sounding surprised at her being surprised, while in addition sounding rather sloshed. "Did you literally have a date already?"

"I literally don't know what we're talking about."

"Our problems may yet be solved, my love. All is not lost."

"Sammy, I'm back on in fifteen seconds. What's this about?"

"The old barracuda invited me to a party up at the hacienda this Saturday. One of her big society things, celebrating some new prizewinner stud or other she just bought. I assume she meant a stud of the four-legged kind. In any case, I'm invited and I'm allowed to bring a date."

"A date? You mean me?"

"You've never met her, have you?"

"Hold on."

She changed out songs and loaded a commercial or two to follow. The other lines were going dark one by one as the remaining trivia hopefuls gave up. Probably just as well.

"Are you talking about Ms. Piper?" she asked, going back to Sammy.

127

"That's the one," he said. "Joan Collins on the Rio Grande."

"Of course I've met her, several times, but what difference does that make? I'm still just a hired hand. I've never seen her set foot in this building."

"Ah, but—" There was a clink of ice and the splash of something poured. "I was once more than a hired hand, and for all Helen's steel-plated bitchiness, she has real trouble dismissing people who are standing right in front of her. The problem is that I've never introduced the two of you properly. Allow me to correct that error."

"So those lesbian rumors are true?"

"Don't jump to conclusions, my love," he said, chuckling tipsily. "I wouldn't dream of pimping you out to anyone. The causes of Helen's spinsterhood are complex and self-inflicted, verging on the tragic, but they don't involve being a sister of Sappho. I simply mean you're an inherently likable person, and even Helen Genevieve Piper, ice-veined harridan as she might appear to be, is not immune to that. The numbers are already in our favor. We're tenth-place in a thirty-station market, an old AM clunker beating out a dozen FM competitors, and that's mainly because of your primetime audience. Helen knows that. But she's also a Republican Party reptile, so anyone who asks for more money is a de facto threat in her mind."

"Threat? Get real."

"Oh, but mark me, *mija*, that is the fundamental truth which no one understands about the rich. They believe they're *worse* off than the rest of us. They believe they are *more* abused and pushed-around and exploited than anyone else. Perverse, I know."

Elfa heaved a sigh of frustration. "Thank you, Sammy. I wish I hadn't made a date with somebody just, like, minutes ago, but I did. Besides, I don't think her seeing me 'in the flesh' is going to change a thing. I just don't share your faith. The situation is what it is, you know?"

"That it is," Sammy agreed, but then, to her sudden (and at once hopeful) surprise, he didn't relent. "Bring *your* date, then," he said. "So my date will have a date…what the hell. This is the eighties, isn't it? Not quite *Penthouse* Forum, but it's potentially titillating enough to be memorable."

Afterwards Elfa got up to check the newswire, then grabbed her Colt and went out to the restroom. Like Shaw, Sammy had a knack for cheering her up at the proper moment, except Sammy was much better at it and had been doing it much longer. She'd been aware of his slight Svengali crush on her from the beginning back in 1983, but there was little doubt he was standing with her now for the right reasons, and knowing this made her feel better. Emerging from the ladies' room and realizing she had a couple minutes to spare (she'd put on the twelve-inch version of "Don't You (Forget about Me)"), she detoured into the library across the hall. Like Sammy she often fell back on the lie that they no longer had certain songs in stock as a way of dodging oddball requests, but the truth was that XAMO had—again, thanks to Sammy—the most wide-ranging, lovingly curated library she'd ever seen, holding 45s, 78s, LPs, and even Blue Amberol phonograph cylinders from the twenties. She located what she needed quickly and pulled it from the stacks, pleased at herself for finding the generosity to return some of the kindness Shaw had shown her lately; then she left the room with it, taking care to switch the lights off. Jaz had probably been in here before her, poking around for more of his own hidden treasure.

From where he'd been crouching in the back, Ash stood up again and watched her shadow move away down the hall.

Twilight. The scarlet brow of a newborn day slouching against the desert rim, considering, waxing, gathering resolve. The Black Mountain stood sentinel against the strengthening rose-fingered rays of sunlight to the east.

A convoy of amber indicator lights moved in single file on the gloomy playa below.

When it reached the American side, Asher tugged his mount away from the mesa's edge above and started home.

8

A girl is born. Norman, Oklahoma, 1917. When the girl is seven years old, her mother expires on the operating table at the hands of a quack surgeon, who happens to be the girl's father. He is attempting to save his young wife from her Dementia Praecox by removing her ovaries and transplanting in their stead those of a goat.

Four years later, the girl barfs in the backseat of her father's new black-and-burgundy Duesie on the long ride to Texas. The other backseat passenger, a world-famous psychic and medium, had hoped to ease the girl's car-sickness by sharing one of her cocaine-laced nausea pills. The girl's father, riding up front, orders his driver to stop, bringing the two-dozen vehicles caravanning behind them to a halt as well. He gets out of the car—a short beaming man in striped silk shirt, fine wing-tipped oxfords, and pearl-buttoned spats—and directs Zerina Price, the celebrated spiritualist and retired fan-dancer, to take his place in the front seat. Quackery has made him rich, but not so rich or haughty that he's above using his monogrammed hanky to see to his suffering daughter's fresh vomitus.

The caravan files in ant-line formation to the far precipice of west Texas, where, just as the girl thinks there can't possibly be another inch of Texas left to cross, it inches right over the edge, into a lower pocket of New Mexico called Nueva Anapra. The Piper goat-gland and broadcasting empire has come here to begin anew. The Oklahoma City radio station Dr. Piper built specifically to promote his thriving surgical clinic has been silenced of late by meddlers at the Federal Radio Commission, and the clinic itself, he adjudges, might benefit from roomier facilities beyond the legal reach of certain aggrieved former patients.

The girl has never seen real mountains, only pictures, mainly the majestic, pine-carpeted European kind with snow-dusted peaks. Her father promised her real mountains in explaining the move, and strictly speaking, he didn't lie. She is well-accustomed to her father lying, and to his believing his own lies with a benign sincerity that tends to negate the often astounding depth and recklessness of his lies, such as the lie that transplanted animal glands would put an end to her late mother's precocious, suicidal melancholia (again, strictly speaking, he hadn't lied about this either, since his wife's accidental bleeding to death had prevented the treatment from ever taking effect). So the girl does not voice her despair at the sight of their new home, this hot, blighted, alien place of tawdry brown mountains separated by a tawdry brown river.

Her father shows her the abandoned ranch property where he intends to build her a mansion. Across the road, the hotel-style structure that will house his new clinic is already taking shape, designed by Henry Trost and paid for in mint-crisp thousand-dollar bills, which her father carries everywhere as ready evidence of his own legitimacy as well as a matter of pecuniary convenience. In the upstairs rooms of this hotel-clinic he will maintain no fewer than four operating theaters, ready on an hour's notice to receive men eager for rejuvenation in the form of freshly removed and sliced testes (donated by month-old Toggenburgs; the goat-pen will be hidden out back) treated in salt solution for no longer than twenty minutes and then artfully spliced with the inner lining of the patients' own hormone-depleted nut-sacks. These men will enjoy their two-day convalescence (and second adolescence!) in luxury full-service suites with ample bedroom space for those who wish to test their stunning rejuvenation out on the partner of their choice. The lower floors, beyond the opulently appointed lobby and reception area, will house his private offices and mail-order operation, from which Dr. Piper's sixty-some patent-tonics, ointments, and powders will be sold and shipped. The orders for these will be generated, in turn, in response to Dr. Piper's own weekly medical lectures carried across the whole of North America from his new, state-of-the-art Mexican radio station.

The girl loves her father, who loves his lies, because his lies are proof he also loves her. She permits him to spoil her with love and lies, with imported dolls, with designer wardrobes, with enrollment in El Paso's finest girls' school. With the sprawling Piper Hacienda, 17,000 square feet of love (bought with and built out of lies), including fourteen bedrooms, among which she's allowed to rotate her living quarters; plus, for entertainment, an Aeolian pipe organ and electric Darlington dancing fountains brought in from the Chicago World's Fair. All this love and space and beauty very nearly compensate for the constant come-and-go racket of freight and passenger trains on the nearby Southern Pacific tracks, and the peculiar ugliness of the Black Mountain whose shadow the hacienda occupies, and the pervasively charged air due to the twin million-watt radio transmitters on the opposite mesa, hot enough to fell birds in midflight and illuminate unplugged lamps.

With horses. He builds a stable and dressage arena on the arroyo land behind the house; buys her a Shetland and a red-roan quarter horse. The wranglers he retains to look after them teach the girl the fine art of trick-riding and the new sport called barrel-racing. At thirteen she wins Best Horsemanship at the Pecos Rodeo, the judges' decision undoubtedly influenced by her custom-made sequined Annie Oakley outfit. At fourteen she is named among the top dozen barrel riders in the United States. At fifteen, she conceives her first and only child.

A physician in Albuquerque learns of Dr. Piper's surgical practice and publishes a diatribe in one of the national journals, denouncing him as "a vile butcher-quack, perhaps the most singularly dangerous licensed charlatan on this or any continent." Dr. Piper files suit for libel and declares his write-in candidacy for governor of New Mexico.

"'Do not go where the path may lead, go instead where there is no path and leave a trail,'" he declaims, employing Emerson, in his weekly broadcast from the hacienda's front parlor. The large carbon-ring microphone into which he speaks from his wingchair feeds by direct cable-line to XAMO, just over the border and across the desert, less than four miles from the house. Angry at their counterparts in Washington, the authorities in Mexico City have bequeathed the Doctor another kind of license, empowering him to blast through and over the radio "clear channel" usurped by the Americans.

"Why, gentle friends, would a pulmonary physician take such immoderate interest in the work of a humble endocrinologist whose practice lies several hundred miles away from his own, involves no practical relationship to his discipline, and which therefore poses little if any threat to his continued prosperity? Why, indeed? Unless, gentle friends, this humble lone practitioner of Eclectic Medicine represents a philosophical threat to *all* practitioners of Organized Medicine!"

His feud with Dr. Lindenstrauss, director of Lindenstrauss Sanatorium, becomes the campaign's *casus belli* even though the adversary is not, himself, a candidate. Dr. Piper crisscrosses the state in his new Lockheed Electra, stumping away with personal support from his extended cast of XAMO regulars like Zerina, who assures audiences of the netherworld's resounding political endorsement; and Rev. Sterling Smokeweather, preaching the virtues of getting rich—and thus casting votes for self-made richies like the Good Doctor; and the great Temperance champion Arthur Thorncott

Kipness, accusing the Good Doctor's critics of categorical enthrallment to Demon Liquor; and numerous others. The girl accompanies her father on a few of these stumping trips, sometimes introducing him, other times silently gracing the stage in her Dior day-dresses. At a Tucumcari rally she appears in her full riding gear. Before she rises to present her father, she herself is presented to the crowd with considerable fanfare by the editor-in-chief of the Quay County newspaper (the editor is both a rodeo enthusiast and ecstatic beneficiary of Dr. Piper's surgical finesse). She approaches the podium to rousing applause, thanks the editor, and barfs on the double-breasted front of his tweed three-piece.

Prior to this episode, whispers about the girl have already taken wing. They begin predictably enough among the other fifteen-year-olds at Hastings Academy, fueled by the usual jealousies born out of unusual wealth and beauty. They are nurtured and embroidered by certain school faculty, who find her brusque and unbecomingly sure of herself, and by the other schoolgirls' parents, who find her father odiously eccentric—as when he donates a stuffed 800-pound tuna caught off Kona, Hawaii, to garnish the school's front foyer. Not long after Tucumcari, the whispers are investigated by the school nurse, who reports her findings to the administration at once. The girl is expelled.

Her father loses the election in a rout, then again two years later...and yet again two years after that. The libel suit fails in a tumult of damaging publicity. Finally, though he forestalls it long enough to drive his enemies themselves to frothing apoplexy, he is stripped of his medical license.

At the Hotel Geneve in Mexico City, father and daughter are enjoying breakfast amidst the hotel restaurant's stunning vertical gardens when a waiter brings a telephone out to their table. Dr. Piper has just completed arrangements to renew his broadcasting license for XAMO. From the other end of the phone line a panic-stricken engineer informs him that the Mexican army has taken control of the station building and is, at that very moment, demolishing its mighty transmitters. Dr. Piper has failed to pay off the correct authorities. As the girl watches, uncomprehending, the blood flees Dr. Piper's face and he suffers the first of thirty-four heart attacks (ultimately a world record) while still clutching the phone handle.

The empire teeters on ruin. In this moment, the girl who loves her father who loves his lies (and therefore loves her) learns to lie out of love, and thus becomes a woman. She apprehends that the radio station, as their only remaining source of wealth, must be saved first. This woman takes it upon herself to find and bribe the correct authorities, Mexican and American. XAMO, with its vocal coterie of fraud preachers, mail-order mystics, mentalists, crackpots, and obscure musicians, returns to the airwaves. The clinic switches from surgeries to injections and employs new, younger quacks to administer them. The woman learns to divert her father's restored income to corners and crevices of the market well beyond the numerous malpractice judgments against him. She parlays the revenue from the station and clinic into thoroughbred racehorses, eventually founding a prominent derby-hosting racetrack in Nueva Anapra. She also employs her influence to slowly bankrupt, from a discreet distance, the renowned Dr. Lindenstrauss and his heirs.

At sixteen, the girl had once birthed a child and disavowed it. In midlife, the woman is forced to disavow her father, whose lies have at last run afoul of hers. The woman's lies, after all, are the pragmatic kind, born of necessity and the imperative of survival; the father's lies grow progressively childlike and absurd, the wooly, self-stroking concoctions of an incorrigible fantasist. He continues his weekly medical-advice lectures, even though he is a "doctor" now only via self-proclamation...but as another global war runs its course, these broadcasts drift into spiritual and Biblical matters. Dr. Piper, it seems, has found God, having encountered an angel in a suspicious trail encounter in broad daylight somewhere on the Black Mountain, around the time of his dozenth heart attack. And unlike the other huckster evangelists who buy XAMO airtime to peddle Holy Oil and scissor-cut squares of His Garment, her father is convinced of his own bullshit. He declares himself the Reverend Dr. Piper, launches Piper Ministries in the old airplane hangar near the radio station, and attempts to sign wholesale chunks of the Piper fortune away to the local poor. So the woman lies, coaxing him to sign legal instruments that separate him from the very wealth he aspires to throw away, and finally imprisoning him in the latter-day version of a sanatorium until his thirty-fourth heart attack.

The one that finishes him.

Helen blinked at the cursor flashing on her computer screen, baffled. She'd loaded MS-DOS from the hard drive and inserted the Lotus 1-2-3 floppy, then loaded the storage disc which should have contained the payroll spreadsheets for April. Six weeks of adult-education classes taken on the sly that spring had satisfied her that, yes, there *was* hope that foggy old mares like her could conquer this hip new high-tech shit; yet somehow, each and every time she logged onto her office IBM and followed the disc-jockeying procedure she'd learned in class, something different from the last time she'd logged on always resulted.

She swiveled back to her antique executive desk, deciding, just like that, that she'd never given two sincere shits about learning computers and wasn't about to start giving any now. She reached for her Pellegrino and yanked the day's assortment of mail from the desk tray, selecting the new issue of *Blood-Horse* and rejecting the rest of it. Beyond the sloped windows of her skybox office, a rototiller was crawling the racetrack, trailing immaculate furrows in the soft dirt.

Her short junior-college experience had been an eye-opener in other ways. So many young women now were trying to mimic that Madonna person, with the overwrought makeup and layers of gaudy chunk jewelry, that it resembled some kind of contagion, an epidemic of gruesome taste. But most dreadful were the middle-aged ones trying to get in on the act. During a lull at one evening session, Helen was inwardly pitying a preposterous frau the next row over, in a black corset tight enough to accentuate every quivering fold and bulge of Budweiser-fat that ringed her aging waist, when she noticed Sadie Bleiberg seated in the row just beyond.

The Bleibergs, so far as Helen knew, still owned El Paso's oldest TV station. Whether they did or didn't anymore, Helen had laid eyes on the woman indifferently during each night's class for three weeks before it dawned on her whom she was looking at. In fact, recollecting that first night, it seemed now that the woman had smiled at her strangely, as if expecting the same reaction, which Helen had of course not offered. This had to do with Helen's aversion to little old ladies; despite more or less being one of them herself, she disliked their company anyway. One could tolerate just so many conversations about tedious ailments and how many of your common acquaintances were now worm-food.

But returning to the computer lab from a potty-break the following week, Helen had detoured over to Sadie, who was seated at the end of her row near the wall, squinting at her monitor like someone scrutinizing a possible fly in their salad.

"Sadie Kay? Heavens, is that really you?"

Sadie had looked up from her monitor and smiled strangely again, and Helen understood then the real reason why it was strange.

"Yes…have we met?"

The others were filing back in and returning to their assigned computers. The class, which met for two hours every Wednesday night, usually adjourned for a ten-minute break after the first hour. The bald-pated thirtyish instructor was at the front of the room fiddling with his Pocket Protector.

"Oh, well, not for about a hundred years," Helen said, backpedaling. "We went to Hastings Academy together for a little while, for what it's worth. Just thought I'd say howdy."

"How nice," Sadie replied feebly, then skimmed the rest of the room in paranoid distress and added, in a near whisper, "I'm so glad someone my age is here. Do you understand *any* of this? I'm so lost." Her eyes, though pleading, still betrayed not a shred of recognition.

"No, but I wouldn't sweat over it too much, babe," Helen told her, leaning in close and matching her confidential, mousy voice. "There's really no hope for old biddies like us when it comes to this computer stuff, you know. I'm just here to meet some eligible men myself. Good luck."

Quick as she was to dismiss the encounter from her mind during the rest of that evening's class, Helen had to allow later that Sadie's not remembering her, not even bothering to ask her name, had smarted a bit. She recalled a brief time in ninth grade when Sadie and she were the closest of friends, or as close as they could be given Dr. Piper's own aversion to Jews.

"Knock-knock."

Simon La Paz hovered in the doorway. All smiles, as always.

"Too late, Pastor," she said, returning to the earnings-index pages in *Blood-Horse*. "I sold my wretched soul to MasterCard years ago."

"It would grieve me to hear that," said Simon, approaching her desk with hand outstretched—something else he always did, knowing full well she would ignore the offer of another too-hearty handshake—"if I didn't know you were kidding," he finished. "In fact, it's kind of funny that you should be the one to bring up the subject of buying and selling first."

An additional man had trailed him into the room. He approached her with an outstretched hand as well, and this too, she ignored.

"What a pleasure. What can I possibly do for you boys?"

"May we sit?"

They each took an accent chair, and Helen removed her reading glasses and mentally girded her loins for a tiresome religious testimonial. Simon was the youngest (and best-looking) in the series of burning-bushers who'd taken the helm at her late father's old ministry, but he was also the most ideological. Given a choice between computer shit and Jesus shit, the first was still the more preferable torment, in her estimation.

"This is Tommy Cereceres, my brother in Christ—," Simon began, adding swiftly, "—and in business."

"Convenient," replied Helen. "I guess that saves you both an extra Christmas card every year, huh?"

The other guy, a short business-suited fellow with a pair of orange-and-silver Swatch Shields perched upright on his glossy bald dome, chuckled appreciatively at this. Helen concluded in his chuckle that Simon had coached him for this encounter. Her estimation of Simon rose a notch.

Simon nodded to his bald friend, who reached into his blazer and brought out a sealed white envelope, which he placed with both hands, and slightly unctuous diplomacy, on Helen's desk. Helen retrieved her glasses and regarded it from afar, making no move to accept it. The words MINISTERIO LA PAZ, in professional letterhead accompanied by a stylish sunrise logo, ornamented the envelope's upper right corner.

"A love-letter?" she said, returning to her magazine. "You're chock-full of surprises today, aren't you, Pastor?"

"Only a humble business offer, I'm afraid," said Simon. "We'd like to buy your radio station."

She gave this a moment's pause.

"In that case, I appreciate the offer, Simon, but I'm afraid it's too low. I'll have to pass."

Flipping the next page of *Blood-Horse*, she observed Simon and his friend exchange disquieted looks through her excellent peripheral vision.

"Ah…aren't you even going to open it?" he inquired, his gracious good humor now straining.

"That won't be necessary."

Outside, the rototiller snailed round the far end of the racetrack. Helen wrinkled her nose unconsciously at the detestable whiff of cigarette smoke she occasionally caught up here, no matter how many floors and walls lay between her office and the closed-circuit-TV betting areas below.

Simon laughed softly—another surprise—and folded his hands in his lap.

"I see," he said.

"Do you? What do you see, Simon?"

"That it's no use, trying to blow smoke up your ass."

Helen nearly snorted her Pellegrino in mid-sip. Simon had said a dirty word. The pastor himself seemed pleased with the reaction he'd provoked.

"Good golly, Simon, what next?" she said, reaching for a tissue. "Are you going to pull out a pint of Ancient Age and try to grab my breasts later?"

"*Es tentador, no?*" Simon said to his friend, who chuckled again.

"But I'm glad we're speaking to each other in honest terms, at last," he continued in English. "I admit it's probably my fault we never have before. It's just that you've always presented a unique problem for me. Around some of my parishioners I can be as plainspoken and downright vulgar as need be—in Spanish, of course. But my training in English is largely formal, and then you have the cultural strictures owing to my background. So when addressing certain classes of people, namely rich Anglo women, I tend to comport myself a bit...stuffily...out of respect. Even with sassy, no-bullshit cowgirls like you."

"You were smart to keep 'old' out of that last sentence," Helen said. "Can I offer you or your brother-in-whatever something cold to sip, by the way?"

"Not necessary, thank you."

"So then," she continued, "now that we're talking business, maybe we can both comport ourselves with a little less—as you say—bullshit." She said this not without some affection. "Let me clarify what I meant, in business-speak, by refusing earlier. I *will* gladly sell you XAMO for your current offer, increased by twenty percent."

"But you don't know what the current offer is."

"*No son nuestras culturas que nos separan,*" said Helen. "*Tampoco se trata de nuestras lenguas, ni nuestro nivel de riqueza.* It's our level of faith that separates us. I don't generally deal in faith, because I generally see next to no value in it. But I have faith in you and your basic decency, Simon; I always did. And so I have faith that the next offer you bring me will be twenty percent higher than whatever the figure is inside that envelope.

"On the other hand, if you actually came in here with your top offer, then I'm granting you the opportunity to withdraw without embarrassment. Call it Christian charity. I hope your...uh...I hope Mr. Cereceres has explained something about the art of business negotiation to you. Now that you boys have entered negotiations with me, you've come to Rome, so to speak. You've gone from sacred to secular. And the first thing you should know about negotiating with me is that no matter what it says in that envelope, I'm going to demand twenty percent more."

The two men exchanged another look. Mr. Cereceres leaned forward, took the envelope up again gently, and returned it to the inside pocket of his blazer.

"Hail, Caesar," Simon said, smiling.

"What gives, anyway?" Helen said, closing her magazine. She rose from her desk and glided over to the wet bar in search of something livelier than Pellegrino. "Why the radio business all of a sudden?"

"No suddenness at all," said Simon. "The ministry is thriving, thanks in part to the donations we receive through the Sunday broadcasts on XAMO, and in part to Tommy's investing savoir-faire. We believe the next step is manifest. We would like to make XAMO into the full-time voice of God, and we believe that voice should speak mainly Spanish. We believe your father would have approved."

"This was Daddy's favorite drink, you know," said Helen, holding her lowball glass up for them to see. "Prickly-pear mojito. Savoir-faire on high-octane. Sure I can't tempt either of you?"

Both men's grins tightened. Helen carried the drink back to her desk, the crisscross points of her tufted-crystal glass throwing off winks of sunlight as she neared the windows.

"There were a couple of extra items inside the envelope apart from the dollar-figure," Simon ventured then.

"The love-letter? Don't tell me I blew my big chance."

Simon crossed a leg casually over one knee. All the pretense—and obsequious hopes of schmoozing her—had left his body. Her estimation rose another notch.

"Despite your frequent protests to the contrary, you are and always have been Ministerio La Paz's kindest benefactor," he said.

"Tax write-off," she rejoined, poking through the mail again.

"In the beginning, no doubt," said Simon. "Yet I accuse you of caring nonetheless. You continue to provide us the free airtime and technical support on Sundays. You donated the airplane hangar and helped us finance its refurbishment. You signed over all rights and ownership of the ministry to me with no consideration at all for your own fortune."

"I *considered* it one less thorn in my side, Simon. Don't kid yourself."

"Very well. But on the rare chance that I'm right, and just supposing that your position right now reflects an unspoken sentimental concern, let's say, for certain staff members at the radio station, I want to assure you that our offer includes specific provisions for their continued employment."

Mr. Cereceres's eyes had drifted to the old rodeo picture of her on the far wall. She registered now that his cheek sported three tattooed dots just below the corner of his right eye, too symmetrical to pass for birthmarks.

"Much obliged, Simon," she answered, following another appropriately noncommittal pause. "Why don't you boys come up to the house Saturday night and bring your revised offer. Some associates and I are toasting a new thoroughbred. If you don't mind all the sinful drinking and gambling-talk, maybe we can sit down together and haggle a little more. I might even open the envelope this time, once I've had a few. You'll have me at a disadvantage.

"Simon, old pal?" she called out once he and Tommy had bade her good day and were mostly out the door. Simon swung back to face her from the outer corridor, agile as a ballroom gigolo—he was one slick, sexy burning-busher, all right.

"Yes, of course," he said—all smiles even still, everlasting patience even still, at least for all outward appearances. "Anything."

"Welcome to Rome."

9

Tolf Denetclaw was marooned in the Koran, having crashed and burned not far into the second chapter, the one titled "The Cow." The Marie Callendar's takeout bag at the foot of his lawn chair contained an assorted glut of used paperbacks, and he was already contemplating forsaking the Koran for one of John Gardner's James Bond-revival novels. What with the daily carnage out of the Mideast these days, the attempt to educate himself about Islam had seemed a magnanimous gesture on his part, even if no one else on Earth was ever going to know or care that he'd done it.

He glanced up from his book, grateful for a distraction, as a green Border Patrol vehicle turned off of the highway across the river and came to a stop on the bank opposite his, shifting twin trails of flattened weeds etched behind it. Shaw Jepsen got out and waved to Tolf from across the Rio Grande, then ambled over to a black Maxima that had parked there a little earlier. The driver's side window slid down, and Agent Jepsen bent and rested his folded arms atop the door's interior, crossing his ankles in a leisurely let's-shoot-the-shit posture.

Tolf returned his eyes to the page before him once more prior to closing the book.

He knoweth that which is in front of them and that which is behind them,
While they encompass nothing of His knowledge save what He will.

Then he heaved his nearly three-hundred pounds up out of the chair and went to the open rear doors of his van for some refreshment. A couple dozen Ziploc bags of New Mexican cocoa-colored pine nuts, his main stock-in-trade, were arrayed on the van's rear floorboard. He reached past these and tugged an Igloo cooler towards him, opened it, and examined its treasures. The van was also his home.

He returned with a Bartles & Jaymes Fuzzy Navel, not his first of the day. Only a couple of hours ago his old friend Helen Piper had ridden by astride a magnificent chestnut filly and had accepted his offer of a wine cooler, gratis, with her purchase of two Ziploc bags. Then she'd removed her chocolate-felt cowgirl hat and joined him for a moment, occupying the spare lawn chair that he kept in honor of his late wife.

"That's my new winner, Tolfy," she said. The horse was sniffing at the limp wild grass that lined the river. She seemed to think better of snacking on it.

"A fine-looking animal," he replied. "What's her name?"

"'Winner,' of course."

"Very good," he said. "I suppose there's not much room for humility in the horseracing game, is there? Sort of like wrestling?"

"Hmm. Come to think of it, that's not a bad analogy."

Tolf ignored the implied insult to his intelligence. Attendant to the price of Helen's company—and he enjoyed her company very much—was a tacit acknowledgment of her ultimate superiority as a human being. In Helen's case, it was probably the honest truth anyway.

"There's a certain amount of necessary bravado in horseracing, for sure," she mused. "A typical thoroughbred depends on her reputation just as much as your typical pro wrestler does. You need the handicappers and the sporting press talking about you—for the right reasons—long before that starting bell. You want the competition running scared. And I'd gladly stack my girl's style up against Hulk Hogan's any day of the week."

What, exactly, Helen was doing riding her high-dollar investment unaccompanied along a remote and historically lawless length of U.S.-Mexico border was a question that might've occurred to somebody else. For one thing, Tolf understood well enough, she'd lived on and raised her horses on this same lawless land all her life. The northern face of her rose-colored mansion was just visible atop the ridge beyond the river. For another, like him, she was surely packing heat of some kind, probably in the handsome russet pommel bags that adorned her saddle. And for a third, well...just like the blueblood aristocrats of old, Lady Helen did whatever the hell she pleased, whenever the hell she pleased. Just *did*.

"Something special going on at the house?" Tolf asked. At last count, a half-dozen delivery trucks had come and gone through the mansion's front gates that morning. The latest, probably a catering van, was now lumbering up the slender strip of road that connected the property to the nearby two-lane highway.

"Just a little necessary bravado," Helen said, as if it were something she regretted already. She gestured to the open paperback tented on the arm of his chair. "What do you think of that one? I was a little disappointed."

He was just drawing the same conclusion about the latest Jean Auel epic himself when Helen and her horse had come upon him. Both the Marie Callendar's bag and the van itself were overrun with paperbacks culled from exchange shops and flea-markets all over lower New Mexico. Nina, his late wife, had started him reading; at some point her compulsion had become his. Mostly genre fiction, a lot of romance and mystery, then sci-fi and horror, with the odd Wouk or Michener tossed in here and there. They'd often swapped, finishing one title and trading it for the one the other had just finished. They went their separate ways on New Age (he couldn't get enough Castañeda and Shirley MacLaine and had read *Dianetics* four times) and westerns (she loved Kelton and adored L'Amour). He kept Nina's lawn chair out, aside from the hospitable gesture to regular customers like Helen, because he liked to imagine Nina's continued presence there beside him when he read.

They chatted about V.C. Andrews; about the recent collaboration between Stephen King and Peter Straub (the paperback wasn't out yet, but Helen, who could afford hardcovers, felt the two authors' wildly incongruent styles had clashed to the point of embarrassing results); about Pat Conroy.

"Give *The Great Santini* a try, if you find the time," she said, rising. "The movie doesn't quite do it justice."

He accepted her emptied bottle while she took her purchases and tucked them snugly inside each of the two pommel bags, leaving room for little else, to his observation. Surely, Tolf thought, the woman wasn't so heedless as to ride the river alone and unarmed *both*. Living in and doing business exclusively out of the van, he himself lived with a firearm always in easy reach—the Beretta 70 in his flak jacket, the Smith & Wesson revolver underneath the van's driver seat. He was most vulnerable when asleep, obviously, but daylight holdups were still an unfortunate fact of life in his line of work. So were unprovoked attacks by the young and pathologically bored, like the pack of feral teens in Rio Rancho who'd once tried to roast him alive. He'd opened his eyes one night—the only available reason was still pure, shit-stupid luck—to a drunken, spiky-haired jackal face watching him through the van's rear window and the sound of others scurrying around outside, their muffled, murderous, barely controlled laughter like something out of *Clockwork Orange*. On instinct Tolf had seized the revolver from under the seat and pointed it at the jackal's face. The face's owner fled and so, Tolf finally concluded, did his companions. Only the next morning did Tolf discover the stench of gasoline on and around the van, dried streaks of it visible on the hood and side panels. The spouted canister the little limp-dicks had used to pour it was discarded in the weeds a few yards off.

Agent Jepsen had concluded his tête-à-tête with the sketchy figure inside the Maxima. He moseyed back to his Scout with the satisfied swagger of someone who'd just mopped up in a winning hand of poker as the Maxima's driver made a three-point turn back up to the highway and sped off. Tolf expelled a sigh and set aside *Licence Renewed.* Sure enough, Shaw had leaped into his Scout and was now flooring it across the adjacent bridge to Tolf's side of the river.

"What's the good news, Hoss?" he exclaimed, his boots hitting the ground again less than a minute later. "Got any more of those roasted piñons for me?"

"I thought you might be the one with good news," Tolf replied, addressing the first question. "You're grinning big enough." Shaw disregarded this in breezy fashion and went straight to the rear of the van, poking through the merchandise.

"No more roasted for a while, I'm afraid," Tolf added in response to the second question. He picked up his book and resumed his place. "Sold the last of them to Ms. Piper this morning."

"Fuck," said Shaw, head lost inside the van. "It ain't enough for that old *bruja* that she owns half of creation. She has to go and hog all the pine nuts."

"You can roast them yourself, you know. All you need's an oven and a cookie sheet."

"The only oven I know how to turn on is the microwave."

He returned with a single bag and chucked it onto the vacant lawn chair for the moment in order to locate his billfold. This he parted with both hands and peered into studiously, making a comical miser's face, as if weighing whether or not he could genuinely afford such a reckless extravagance. Behind him the Scout rocked visibly as his two detection dogs sensed the nearness of Tolf and, thus, pine nuts.

"Keep the change there, Hoss," he said, holding out a tented five and sporting his usual self-satisfied grin. He knew well enough that five dollars was the going rate.

"Have you seen anyone else on horseback out here today?" Shaw asked then, retrieving his purchase.

"Like who, pray-tell?"

"Forget it." As if Tolf wasn't aware of his long-concluded romance with the Barefoot girl, who ran the Lazybones Stables for her father. "Listen, is it true you've got a college degree, Tolf?"

A curve-ball.

"I hold a Bachelor of Science from New Mexico Tech. Class of '52."

"Why?"

"Why what?"

"I don't know. I mean why'd you even bother? Who goes to all that hassle getting a Bachelor of Science degree just to sit in a lawn chair by the river selling goddamn pine nuts?"

"Well, that isn't exactly what happened. The one didn't necessarily follow the other. I won't burden you with the details."

"*Details*. Right." He said this as if he and Tolf held some dreadful, misunderstood affliction in common. Then his eyes wandered off toward the Piper hacienda, as if the cause—or cure—for that affliction lay there.

"Go easy on the *asada* tacos tonight, Dad," Casey reminded her father. The extra firmness in her voice suggested she wasn't referring strictly to food.

Lou grunted a faint acknowledgment. The hacienda filled the pickup truck's windshield as he downshifted and made a left onto the road of fine bare caliche that led up to the main gate. The road was lined with cross-ties, and a Southern Pacific freight was rounding the curve just above the house where the tracks skirted the Black Mountain. The road leveled off at the gate entrance. They passed between the pair of soaring iron swing-gates, each bearing the shape of a rearing stallion, and an unexpected sweep of plush, manicured lawn came into view, at its center a tiled lily pool and three-tiered black-granite fountain.

"It's like a cherry on a turd, isn't it?" Casey remarked, nudging Ash. "All this big, beautiful house in the middle of all this big, horrible ugly."

"Pity the old bat who lives there," said Lou.

"Hey, you hush up. That old bat's been good to you."

They came to a circular driveway around the back, where a couple of teenage valets in bowties and ill-fitting burgundy service jackets waited

155

to take possession of the truck. One of them approached the passenger-side door, reached for the handle, and stopped. It took Asher a beat to comprehend his challenging look—he was waiting for Ash to remove his elbow from the open window.

A village of white canopy tents was erected in the courtyard behind the house. The scent of smoking beef ribs mingled with the airy sounds of snare brushes and jaunty jazz saxophone. No tacos were in evidence.

"That's Mayor Rogers," Casey observed as a tall business-suited man strode importantly past. "I think we're a little underdressed."

"Aw, hell," said Lou. "Why'd she bother inviting the hired help, then? That's all we are. You want to go home, then go home. Take the truck. I'm getting some food." And he marched off, defiant, in the general direction of barbecue smoke.

"I thought this was one of her regular-people parties," Casey explained, apologetic. "She throws them for the racetrack staff and us every so often."

"Those look kind of like regular people," Asher offered. The nearest tent was occupied by jeans-wearing civilians, one of whom, a lean gentleman in a silver-haired ponytail, had his sandaled feet up on the plate-littered catering table while he tipped a bottle of Hoegaarden merrily at passersby.

"God, it's the radio station," Casey concluded, all trepidation swept from her voice. "I guess anything goes tonight if she invited *that* bunch of pervs and stoners.

"I hope Elfa's not with them," she added with hushed significance.

The evening's star celebrities were gathered beside another placid, elegantly gurgling fountain, a close cousin to its tiered counterpart out front. Here stood *La Ganadora*, Helen Piper's new star filly, flanked by rider, trainer, and the owner herself in a yellow Donna Karan skirt-suit. A photographer was busy clicking away at them with a heavily augmented Nikon.

"Come on, pout, baby! Pout!" the photographer teased.

"Exactly which animal are you speaking to, Mr. Urquidi?" Helen inquired, deadpan. That drew an appreciative chuckle from the large ring of spectators. Then owner and trainer moved aside for the jockey—himself all gushing smiles in his black-and-salmon silks with embroidered cowboy-shirt accents—who stood for more winning poses alongside his mount.

"*Disidente*," someone said.

Ash noticed the man standing to his left.

"Pastor," he replied.

"Señora Piper," said Simon La Paz, bowing obsequiously.

"Simon," said Helen. She'd appeared from the other direction in almost the same instant, emerging like a fine willowy mist from the crowd. "Casey, hon, how've you been?"

"Oh, you know," said Casey.

"Is that dad of yours around?"

"Guess so…he bolted right for the food tent."

"Well, I wouldn't hold that against him, dear. That's why it's there, after all. If you would, though, please tell him I'd like to chat about something real quick before he leaves? And who's this?"

"This is Charlie, the new hire. Chuck, Ms. Piper."

"Hello, Charlie." She accepted Asher's hand and shook once, firm and cordial, looked him graciously in the eye, and saw nothing at all worth noting.

"So where's your brother-in-whatever, Simon? I thought we'd go inside for our pow-wow."

"He was detained, I'm sorry to say," replied Simon, though his eyes lingered on Asher just a moment too long. The name thing, Ash realized. "But I'm empowered to speak for him, if that's agreeable to you."

"Babe, talking about money is always agreeable."

"Ms. Piper?" said Casey as they started away.

"Yep?"

"Alright if I show Charlie around the old casa? He's never seen the place."

She took Ash's arm and they trailed Helen and Simon into the house, the gothic Honduran-cedar front door held open for them by another red-jacketed youth. Simon paused to greet the boy in Spanish, in low and familiar tones, before joining Helen on the other side.

The main foyer boasted a magnificent iron-and-adobe grand staircase and parquet floor, a wrought-iron chandelier suspended from thick black chains above it all, big as a jet turbine. Ash had never seen anything like it.

"Home sweet home," Helen said.

"It always takes my breath," said Simon.

"That's just what Daddy intended," Helen replied, a touch of boredom in her voice. She led Simon away towards the vacant dining room. There were voices and laughter coming from the other direction, so Ash and Casey wandered that way, into an enormous high-beamed great-room opposite the stairs. Here several people were seated idly about, while a man in a dark blazer and tiger-stripe silk scarf stood holding court in front of the fireplace. It was Sammy Hayes.

"Yes, it's a treat to see Tina finally getting her due recognition," he was saying. "She deserves it. I knew Ike and Tina pretty well in the old days, and I experienced firsthand glimpses of Ike's extramarital antics once or twice, let me tell you. There was this one afternoon in Hollywood when I heard he was rehearsing in a studio just a couple of blocks away from mine, so I walked in on him, figured I'd surprise him with a little belated birthday visit. Ike's facing the studio door, very absorbed in his piano playing, not looking up. Now Ike could sizzle to be sure, but it seemed to me he was *really* into it just then, and I just had to kind of stop and watch."

He paused to sip the mixed drink he was holding.

"So he ends the song, and I cross around the side of the piano and stop, because that's when I notice someone underneath, a bouffant-haired white woman, and I guess she was finishing up her own little number on Ike. Neither one of them notices me at all for an awkward minute or so, until Ike, smiling this beatific smile of a man recently and profoundly satisfied, looks up from the keyboard and says, 'Hey, Sammy! Whasappenin, man?'"

Everyone laughed. Ash spotted Elfa Schultz at the back of the room, seated with her back to an enormous antique-organ console, nursing a beer can wrapped in a napkin.

"Christ, come on," Casey whisper-hissed in his ear, noticing Elfa too. She tugged his arm.

"What's the matter?" he responded a bit too loudly, and a few heads turned.

She led him out and up the grand staircase, halting when they'd reached the second-floor landing.

"Well my stars, looky who's here?" she said.

Elfa had slipped into reverie while Sam monologued. She knew all his showbiz tales—the long ones, the short ones, and the tall ones—and in her opinion there were better tales to tell, not that it took so much to impress El Paso's limited jet-set. Ignorant Texican though she might've been herself, even she could see that his efforts were wasted on these bush-league aristocrats—a prominent local eye surgeon, a litigator, a charbroiled-chicken restaurateur and his wife, and the mayor himself. But her date had wandered off, and it was still something of a marvel to her, the way that Sammy continued to thrive on his own small-time celebrity. It touched and saddened her that he craved the approval of people who were so fundamentally beneath him. The litigator, for instance, had already offered to touch her in an entirely different and repulsive way earlier in the beverage tent outside.

She was nonetheless contemplating an excursion back there to swap her warm half-can of Dos Equis for something harder when Helen Piper materialized with a plate of peppery brisket, sausage, and slaw, and nudged her to scoot over on the organ bench.

"How's your mother doing, sweetie?" she asked. Elfa accepted the plate, presuming Helen meant for her to hold it while she seated herself, but when Elfa tried handing it back Helen produced a set of plastic ware bound in a napkin and held it out to her as well, as if to say *That's for you, stupid.*

"Alright, I suppose," said Elfa, seeking a parking space for her beer; Helen took this and placed it behind her on the walnut console wing beneath the rows of toggle switches. The faint irritableness in this gesture was nothing new.

"You know," Helen said moments later, in the tone of someone with an agenda and making little effort to conceal it, "I've got some business friends in Atlanta. They tell me the Coca-Cola people are absolutely committed."

"Then they're backing the wrong horse, aren't they?" Elfa stabbed into her brisket, surprised at her own sudden appetite.

"I was just making conversation, hon."

"Sorry." *It's just that 'hon' and 'sweetie' aren't in your usual vocabulary,* she wanted to add, but this seemed a tad combative. "Does this beast still work?" she asked instead, in her own effort at small-talk.

"Beast?"

Helen turned sideways and regarded the pipe organ like some excruciating eyesore for a second, but the timbre in her reply when she turned back was more introspective than Elfa would've surmised. "They were status symbols back in the twenties, these old organs. You can still find them in certain neighborhoods in Beverly Hills, Grosse Pointe, Long Island. Did you happen to read *The Great Gatsby* in high school?"

"No. I read it on my own, in junior high."

Helen smiled as if acknowledging a crafty opponent. "In any case, Daddy ordered this from the same company that showed it at the World's Fair in Chicago. It used to be linked to the lighted fountain out on the front lawn. Except Daddy and I couldn't play it, so he hired his version of Klipspringer, a Belgian organist named Goossens, to live with us, entertaining us and the crowds who used to gather on the road out front each night to watch the lights. Goose was a handsome gent, had the Valentino hair and the narrow mustache. Played the Tower Ballroom in London, worked for the Du Ponts, even made a few records. But instead of prowling after me he was usually after one of the stable hands. Truth is, I was already at an age then where I might not have minded being prowled after, especially by a sweet-smelling European with a continental lilt in his step and in his voice."

She paused, examining the tip of her suede ankle boot. "Goose was my first lesson in disappointment concerning men."

"Klipspringer...," said Elfa. "Isn't he the one who asked for his shoes back?"

"Exactly. See what I mean?" Helen gave another appraising little nod—whether in acknowledgment of Elfa's question or of Elfa herself wasn't altogether clear. Perhaps both.

Elfa's white compartment plate had emptied rapidly, and Helen rose then and took it from her as unceremoniously as she'd offered it.

"Sammy and I spoke earlier," she remarked in afterthought. "You've got your raise. Two-fifty more an hour, provided you keep those ratings up and drop it with all that New Coke bullshit. Agreed?" She strode away, the answer a foregone conclusion in her mind, it seemed.

"Thanks?" said Elfa.

Shaw had been studying a piece of modern art that garnished the second-floor landing, wondering if he'd stumbled into that far-out gallery in *Beverly Hills Cop*. Or maybe his old gig at Spencer Gifts. The rest of the house, at least what he'd seen of it, featured southwest art by the usual names—the landscapes of Tom Lea, the quarter horses of Orren Mixer, the beckoning female crotch-blossoms Georgia O'Keeffe. But here was a screaming blowup photo of Howdy Doody's face, sectioned into three red-border boxes, overlaid with the legend WHEN I HEAR THE WORD CULTURE I TAKE OUT MY CHECKBOOK in ransom-letter newsprint.

The sound of ascending footsteps on the grand staircase came as a welcome interruption, at least until he discovered to whom those footsteps belonged.

"Well my stars, looky who's here?" Casey Barefoot was eyeing him in sullen delight, hands on her hips. Next to her was the kid, Red-Day, wearing the sudden stricken look of someone in abrupt need to be elsewhere fast.

"What's new, Case? How's your bod?"

"Eat your heart out." She glanced at Asher, registering his discomfort. "What? What're you looking at, Jepsen? Do you two know each other?"

"Sorta kinda."

Asher pivoted away in embarrassment, and Casey reached out with her index finger and placed it underneath his chin.

"Don't tell me you came wading across the river, Cal. Is that your big secret?"

"Robbing the cradle these days, Case?"

Casey's expression changed.

"Hey, only kidding." Shaw threw his hands up in a gesture of truce. "I already verified the kid's citizenship, if that helps. The rest of it's beyond my jurisdiction. You've got no legal problem with *me*."

"What is he talking about?" Casey asked, watching Asher closely.

"Oops…my date is here," said Shaw. Elfa was making her way up the stairs, slowing when she spotted Shaw and his two acquaintances. Ash blinked at her dolled-up look, in her Nagel-wave bubblegum top, rouge, and high-top basketball sneakers, but then it occurred to him that she was in character. The port-wine birthmark was still there underneath the rouge, and so, upon a second look, was the girl he'd met in that dim dusty thrift shop five years ago. "Let's make it a foursome, then. What do you say?" Shaw held out an arm.

"Don't make me puke," Casey replied. "No offense, Elfa. It's just that I'm not actually on a date."

"I guess that makes two of us," said Elfa, shooing away Shaw's extended arm.

"Ladies! The night is young. Does everybody know everybody?"

All eyes fell on Asher.

"I thought we were going to check out the terrace."

Yet another youth was wiping down a portable minibar just outside the back terrace's open double doors. On the bar's edge were three remaining cups of green Jell-O shots and a bucket of watery ice containing one last longneck. The sunlight had turned in its notice, streaks of red marbling the sky as the party below wound down. The jazz trio had ceased playing and the catering staff had begun collapsing the tents. Across the lonesome *despoblado*, the XAMO transmitter light pulsated against the dark sky to the south.

Shaw helped himself to the longneck. On the way out, Elfa and Casey had fallen to chitchatting. They'd gone to the same high school, Ash gathered, as had their parents. Casey's earlier, unexplained fear of running into her had somehow evaporated.

"I was trying to introduce you back there," Shaw commented, taking in the view.

"Who?"

Shaw set his beer on the stucco balustrade. Casey and Elfa had moved further down the terrace. Elfa had produced an open pack of cigarettes and held it out to Casey, the filtered ends jutting out.

"Is there some reason you're not telling people your real name? Why did Casey call you 'Cal' a minute ago?"

"That's just her little joke. She knows I'm from California."

"You're up to some peculiar cloak-and-dagger hijinks, Hoss. Sneaking around in the desert like Obi-Wan Fucking Kenobi. Shining me on at the Dairy King that night when I was only trying to help you out."

"Yeah, sorry about that."

"I can see you're into older women as well. I'd ask you if you're banging Case, but now something tells me I've been misconstruing things just a little. You were up at the radio station that night, weren't you? What gives?"

Asher's eyes had drifted in guilt back to the three Jell-O shooters— which the kid behind the minibar must have taken for longing, because he picked one up between his thumb and forefinger and set it back down before Ash with emphasis, as if to say *Have at it, dummy. What makes you think I care?* Ash checked back with Shaw, who'd turned his back to the balustrade and was leaning against it now comfortably, feet crossed and smiling in amusement. Ash took the shot cup and threw the lump of gelatin back, wincing at the sour Hornitos.

"Good show, Hoss," Shaw said, grin broadening. "Now finish those other two and I'll introduce you to the love of your goddamn life… and mine."

The alcohol hit him fast, detonating in his stomach and igniting his whole nervous system from head to toe. He accompanied Shaw to the terrace's far corner, where the girls were smoking and catching up, the tips of their cigarettes tracing twin firefly figures in the deepening dusk.

"S'cuse us, ladies."

"Okay. You're s'cused," said Casey, both scorn and flirtation in her voice.

"Fair enough," said Shaw. "I just thought *Mandy* should know there's an admirer who's come a long way here to see her."

"What are you talking about?"

But Elfa had surmised the situation. "Hi, nice to meet you," she told Ash, holding her hand out in greeting, old-pro style.

"Hi," said Ash, accepting.

"Great," said Elfa. "I don't mean to be rude." She flashed Shaw a look whose implied reproach, even in the dark, carried the force of words.

"I'm Strummer," Ash added.

"You're who?" said Casey.

"His name's Asher," said Shaw, as if no one else had spoken. "Asher Red-Day."

"Yeah, but I'm also Strummer."

Now Elfa's face had changed.

"I'm *so* confused," said Casey.

10

Shaw kept all his junior-high and high-school yearbooks on the top shelf of a barrister bookcase in his apartment. Coronado Dons, Scottsdale, Arizona, Class of '74. The bookcase was as much a point of pride as its contents.

His father, Theron, was a general carpenter who'd helped build the German P.O.W. camp at Papago Park during the war and, much later, television and movie sets at the studio complex in nearby Carefree. In high school by then, Shaw assisted his father on some of these jobs, meeting Dick Van Dyke, Bob Hope, and Bill Cosby, among others. An aspiring arriviste all his life, Theron finally sold a patent on a special tool belt that he'd invented in the sixties and used the proceeds to open a craft woodwork shop in Old Town Scottsdale. Here he bided his time building coffee tables and bar stools and other modest utilitarian pieces, mainly from Ponderosa Pine and Indian Rosewood, while he awaited the inevitable flood of patent royalties. The flood never came. The anonymous buyer of his patent buried it in favor of their own design, to which Theron's had posed a competitive threat. Then the property owners who controlled his shop space canceled Theron's lease, citing the "appropriate commercial aesthetics" clause. Theron's furniture was too plain and workmanlike for the area's touristy, boutique-minded clientele. The owners then granted the same space to a family of Lebanese tile-makers.

"Mormon sons of bitches," complained Theron. "It's not enough that they control all of Mesa and Gilbert and half of Chandler, oh Jesus Harry Christ no. They have to have Scottsdale. They have to have *all* of it. What is it with Mormons and Arabs always owning the goddamn deserts?"

Shaw's mother had divorced Theron well before this, claiming half the patent money and fleeing with Shaw's future deceased stepfather to the faraway land of Tucson. Yet even a hundred miles apart, destiny had somehow steered both of Shaw's parents into more or less the same fate: each now lived in a trailer park entering his/her golden years on the lido deck of the good ship *Afternoon Drunk*.

In the fifth grade Shaw had briefly taken up amateur pornography. Inspired by his father's garage *Playboy* collection and by the Polaroid Swinger he'd received for his eleventh birthday, Shaw talked three different girls into showing him their breasts inside the section of concrete sewer pipe on the school playground near the blacktop. Only two of these girls had any breasts to speak of, a fact that young Shaw used in his own defense when the teacher discovered this enterprise and marched him and the confiscated photographs to the principal's office.

By high school he had discovered something about himself—or about the whole world *apart* from himself, depending on how you looked at it. In all his early confrontations with authority, he was always smarter than the person who held the position of authority over him. Or the world had a way of putting universally stupid people universally in charge, which amounted to the same thing. That wasn't to say that he won every confrontation; far from it. The topless-pictures episode in elementary school, for example, had bought him not only a three-day suspension but also a battery of psyche tests administered by a chubby district psychologist who, for all her education and brains and double-breasted scarf-suits, seemed insensible to the chocolate-colored caterpillar living on her lip and who, in addition, toted a satchel crammed with ink blots and Teachy Keen dolls everywhere she went, a de rigueur facet of her duties. As far as Shaw knew, no one had checked out the three girls who'd said yes for any loose marbles in *their* heads. As the lyrics in the John Cougar Mellencamp song suggested, authority always wins, whether it ought to or not.

Mormons and Arabs. Arabs and Mormons.

So he learned to kiss ass. Learned to prosper by it, as a matter of fact. There was no dignity to lose in kissing up to idiots, because dignity couldn't exist in a world where idiots called all the shots. You had to be worse than an idiot not to recognize that. Indeed, if you lived your whole life in sheep-like obedience to the rules of idiots (or Arabs or Mormons) and you ended up holding the short end of the stick, well...you kind of deserved whatever you got.

Being no idiot himself, Shaw recognized that the proper dictionary term for this attitude, i.e. the general tendency to expect the worst of people, was cynicism. And so it was quite the lucky irony—yes, "irony," a theme on which he'd once authored a legitimately kickass essay in Honors English, one of the two or three gems that he hadn't paid others to write for him during senior year—that Shaw happened to love people as much as he did. Fascinating creatures, human beings were, no matter how thickly, Heinz-ketchup gullible they also tended to be. It was true: he loved people, and people loved him, and so it wasn't so much cynicism as plain practical reality if he sometimes sought and exploited that love to his own ends. The yearbooks, strewn with messages of friendship and approval on nearly every page, were proof-positive how many of his schoolmates had loved him back, including the three stupid girls who'd shown him their tits at such a tender age and in later years wished him love and a great summer.

The same was true of the framed Border Patrol commendation on the next shelf below.

Arabs and Mormons.

A soft knock at the door: the old "Shave and a Haircut." He closed *Iacocca*, grateful for the interruption. Shaw liked to use his few evenings off as opportunities for self-education and/or inspiration vis-à-vis his plan to start a new woodworking and carpentry business—a way of honoring his father's dreams without repeating his own gullible fuckups. But sometimes, instead of actually reading, he just stared at the open pages of whatever motivational tome he'd picked up at B. Dalton, sipped his beer, and dreamed separate dreams about the girl whose husky voice kept him going so many lonely days and nights on that empty, ugly section of *despoblado* that he patrolled.

He rose from the loveseat, turned down Mandy's show on the hi-fi, and unbolted the door. Moments later, as he lay bleeding to death on the carpet, he had the chance to savor Mandy's voice on the radio one last time. The love of his goddamn life.

Should have told her, he thought. In his mind's eye he was already standing judgment before the glorious throne of Jesus Harry Christ, hastily defending himself. A United States flag waved in the sunshiny heavens behind the divine court, and in a ceremonial chair to Jesus's immediate right was none other than President Reagan. But, on second glance, Jesus looked an awful lot like that chubby woman psychologist back in Scottsdale. He appeared to be wearing the same caterpillar lip and frumpy scarf-suit, at any rate.

You know why I couldn't tell her the truth, Lord! Shaw shouted at Him/Her. *You know because I prayed to you on it! I'd have had to tell her everything! The whole stinking mess! And I couldn't have stopped what happened from happening anyway!*

President Reagan bent forward in his chair and lifted something from the glistening bed of cloud at his feet: a gilded white doctor's satchel, which he raised to the throne in offering, the clasp handles held apart to reveal its contents. Jesus reached inside it with one hand and retrieved a blonde Teachy Keen doll, holding it out to Shaw in accusation.

Defeated, Shaw mouthed his confession—the name of the man who'd wasted Elfa's father—feebly with his own dying lips.

11

Asher had never phoned in to a radio station before. There were dozens in and around the San Joaquin Valley, and on the AM band you could still pick up the old powerhouses out of L.A. and San Diego, though these seemed to be jumping one-by-one into the turgid killjoy waters of round-the-clock news and politics.

His mother was gone, flown on the wings of her mighty anthropology degree to El Segundo. The old *mesteñero* was dead and buried. The FOR SALE sign out on Route 99, its "Price Reduced" rider flapping crazily in the windswept wakes of all those barreling semis on their way up to Fresno, had stood there all summer and attracted few offers, none worth considering. Jared had elected to give the local real estate market a try—out of growing financial pressure, true, but also because he'd drawn the conclusion that neither of his sons could be reasonably expected to continue the family business in the future, should there even be one left to inherit. Lex, now eight, had taken up playing with dolls. And Ash, who'd learned at his great-grandfather's side and won eight riding championships between the ages of twelve and fifteen, had disconnected.

The final breakdown between him and Jared would come later. In the waning days of that summer in 1984, each remnant of the Rede family had more or less retreated to his separate corner. Asher found his in the old *mesteñero*'s trailer home, where he contemplated the past, tried to make sense of it, and gave up. He mind-melded with his Walkman and decided to be a musician, not a horseman. Having exhausted his parents' LP's, or rather the ones that Timera hadn't absconded with, all he had left was the radio. He absorbed Top Forty and Album-Oriented Rock and college radio and even bland Adult Contemporary. He listened to the Spanish stations. He meditated on Prince and Springsteen, the two heaviest hitters on the airwaves that summer. He deliberated to Cyndi Lauper and ZZ Top. He pondered "Sister Christian" and "Lights Out," mulled over "Hot for Teacher" and "The Heart of Rock & Roll" and "Round and Round," and also over "The Glamorous Life" and "Let the Music Play" and "What's Love Got to Do with It." He had little idea what the faces behind the voices who'd made these records looked like, there being no affordable cable service yet in rural Tulare County and thus no MTV. So he imagined the faces for himself, at times captivated with what he saw in his mind's eye, and at other times unmoved.

While listening, he sometimes tinkered with his great-grandfather's guitar, the one with Mexico's famed star-cloaked *mestiza* inlaid on the back. Sometimes he watched the horses playing in the east pens through the Rollohome's picture window. Sometimes he smoked Swisher Sweets.

Sometimes he grew bored and frustrated and searched the dial for something, anything else.

He knew, or rather sensed, that what naturally followed this kind of boredom was anger. His boredom was dry and combustible, like wild chaparral, the kindling the sheer stupidity of it all, the stupidity of *people*. His stupid parents. Hippie rednexicans who'd sported the long hair and mouthed the sayings and worshipped the symbols and then just as quickly forgot them because they never meant anything in the first place. His stupid grandfather Ivan, taken in by Uncle Sam and ruined by a stupid war when he could've (and probably should've) run away to Mexico, where he might've reclaimed his heritage and his destiny and headed off the wreckage later wrought by his own stupid son. And his stupid great-grandfather, the old *mesteñero*—so wise and still so stupid, who by his own admission had brought upon his clan the generational curse of stupid wives and mothers who so stupidly walked out on their men. All of them, in the end, so spectacularly stupid. Ash contemplated them all and smoldered in his boredom.

He first tripped over Mandy's voice during a particularly jaded back-and-forth circuit-session through the AM band, the kind where he just kept turning the thumb-dial on his Walkman, not so much searching anymore as giving himself up to the noise like a defeated fugitive. The frenzied static, the overlapping voices, the general chaos on AM reminded him at times of the commotion within himself.

Then a miracle, sort of. Maybe not even sort of. Maybe even for real. He knew this voice.

"I have one word for you people," the voice said. "*Basura!*"

This was actually the third or fourth time that he'd located the voice, having hit upon it repeatedly before, only to lose it each time he went back.

"That was Quiet Riot with 'Mama Weer All Crazee Now.' Because, you know, why write your own hit songs when you can just keep recycling hits by better bands? It especially helps if those better bands are from England and never made it big in the U.S.A. so your audience has no idea what a poser you are. And you know, I get that it's an accepted thing to do. I get that Van Halen started out by covering The Kinks. But they didn't *keep* doing it like nobody would notice. So what you actually just heard was 'Mama Weer All Crazee Now' by *Slade*, not Quiet Riot.

"Listen to this: 'To me, it's not really interesting unless it's part of everybody living a life. I'm not really interested to build it into a fantasy world like heavy metal groups do with swords and sorcery, you know, a fantasy landscape. I don't really like to be in that landscape, you know, I like to be part of the whole world.'

"That was Joe Strummer of The Clash. And now here's The Clash, another English band, covering an American song without ripping it off. See if you can tell the difference when a band covers a song for the right reasons."

And she played "I Fought the Law," by The Clash.

He loved the song. And he knew beyond doubt that he knew her voice, had encountered it somewhere, somehow, in person.

"*Basura!*" she repeated on another occasion, this time in reference to the current hit by Scandal Featuring Patty Smyth.

"*Basura!*" she said of Frankie Goes to Hollywood.

"*Basura!*" of the new David Bowie. Of the Michael Jackson/Mick Jagger duet. Of Corey Hart. Of Madonna after her writhing-on-the-floor stunt at the first MTV Video Music Awards. Of music videos in general. Of Ronald Reagan and Walter Mondale. Of "We Are the World." And finally, of New Coke.

By then, she and he were regular phone correspondents, both on the air and off. By then, he was also certain that she was the girl he'd met in the thrift shop when he was twelve: the girl who'd sold him the Little John radio.

It had to mean something, his encountering her twice across such distances in time and space, and under such crazy, blind, dumb-fucking-luck conditions. But what did it mean, exactly? Was the whole business of life nothing but a slot machine or a horserace? And if so, was it random or was it rigged? Why did both possibilities depress him just as much?

Not everything was "*Basura!*" of course. For each item or event that Mandy—he guessed the name to be some kind of DJ alter ego—found objectionable, she presented an enlightened (or at least reasonably digestible) alternative. Asher could tell that she was trying to educate her young and mostly clueless listeners, no matter how discouraging a prospect that was—no matter how often they called in begging for more Quiet Riot and Madonna, for more Wham! and Frankie Goes to Hollywood. She told them about Julian Lennon, who was just beginning to chart nationally, and what his sudden appearance on the music scene meant to so many olders who were devastated by the father's death only four years before. She spun older hits by The Clash, by Bowie in his glam-rock heyday, by the newer bands like U2 and Suicidal Tendencies and The Smiths in between all the obligatory Top Forty dreck. What did it mean to have good taste? What did it mean to think for yourself? That's what she was trying to teach in between all the records and commercials and station identifications and weather bulletins. That's why she talked to her audience.

"Where you calling me from, Strummer?" she asked, the first time he phoned the XAMO request line, a long-distance number. He wanted to hear "I Fought the Law" again, and the name "Strummer" had jumped from his lips spontaneously, the impulse to concoct his own alter ego taking him by surprise. He had zigged without meaning to.

Do you fantasize a lot? Dr. Tune asked.

"Visalia," he allowed, zagging back to the truth.

"Earthquake country, huh?"

"I wish. Nothing that exciting happens around here."

"No? Aren't you near that famous fault line, the what's-it? San something."

"San Andreas."

"That's it. So are you on the safe side, or on the falling-in side? You know, if California ever drops into the ocean? Hold on a minute."

She let him brood over that while she did a station-break, leaving the line active instead of putting him on hold. There was the sound of someone switching out tape cartridges and pressing buttons.

"Yeah, so you're bored," she said, returning to him. "Me too. I'm bored with summer, Strummer. Bored watching the Olympics. Bored, bored, bored. You in school, Strummer?"

"Sure." He hadn't yet made the decision to quit.

"I'm so-o-o ready to go back. What's your favorite subject? Mine's always changing. The trouble with school is there are too many options. It's like going to the mall. So many ways to spend your time and money. I want to own *everything* I see. In the case of school, I want to know *everything* there is to know. I can't help it. What was it you wanted to hear again?"

"'I Fought—'"

"Wait."

She held him through three commercial breaks in that way, using him somehow to keep herself going, which he was pleased to do. After all, he couldn't possibly be the only one calling in. She'd chosen him somehow, attached to him, if only for the duration of that first call. Maybe she was having a bad night. Maybe he was just lucky. Either way, it was a thrill.

And, oh, he definitely knew that voice.

After over an hour of this, she played his song. She introduced it for him on the air. "This is The Clash's version of 'I Fought the Law,' going out to Strummer, all the way out in Visalia, California." (The long distance bill for this call alone would be six dollars and change.)

"Can I ask you something?" he said when the record was over. "What's your real name?"

"You're kidding, right? It's been groovy chatting with you, Strummer. Let's not spoil it by talking reality. Don't ask me mine, and I won't ask you yours. Ring me again sometime."

He believed he knew her name anyway, but belief and knowledge weren't the same. If it was her—Elfa, the girl at the thrift shop, the girl with the faint port-wine stain on her cheek and the voice like warm elixir—then there was reason to believe in *believing*.

It occurred to him then that there might be proof. Proof in the form of old Polaroids. His mother's sociology project that summer; the Kodak. Jared had relocated most of Timera's possessions, the ones she hadn't taken with her, to the long shed near the east pens. A feeble act of vengeance, as if moving some suddenly detested loved-one's things into storage wasn't the same as holding onto them forever.

Boxes, crates, and bags galore, scores of them, not so much stacked as thrusted atop one other, shoved this way and that as needed to form paths of access. He'd rarely set foot in the shed, an L-shaped building of corrugated tin and alternating clear fiberglass panels on the roof, the only sources of light. It adjoined the row of carports where the Cordoba and the blue-and-white Glasspar Sunliner outboard sat dormant and decaying underneath moldy hay tarps. As he poked through the nearest open box a stripe-tailed scorpion stung his hand twice. He managed to fling it against the opposite wall, where it fell behind a pile of quilts and disappeared, before flailing backwards into another pillar of junk himself. A wig box fell open onto the concrete floor, the foam stand rolling away. What was the fucking point of this stuff, anyway? Maybe he wasn't the only fool in the family who kept clutching to the past while also loathing it.

As fortune had it, his mother's college paraphernalia was the most recent junk that Jared had stowed away. Rather than becoming a sociologist, Timera had found her professional and spiritual calling as senior manager of the VIP lounge for Air New Zealand at LAX. Jared hadn't even boxed up the spiral notebooks, three-ring binders, textbooks, and other whatnots she'd left behind from her Fresno State days, tossing them instead into a chewed-up Rubbermaid laundry basket.

Inside the basket he found the Polaroids he'd taken during that summer of the long drive to the thorny edge of Texas, the summer of the Piper funeral. Timera had chastised him for wasting the film she needed for her photo-essay on the oil shock and how it affected people's behavior in those ceaseless gas-station lines. It was still there in a red-Naugahyde photo album, the snapshots of all those bumper-to-bumper thyroidal Cutlasses, Crown Victorias, LTDs, and Continentals at a total standstill, of people standing in those same lines with their gas cans and lawnmowers, of one guy she'd spotted tying his horse to an Exxon service pump. Ash remembered fibbing on the spot, off the top of his head, something about the thrift shop being a converted gas station—how maybe that had something to do with the gas shortage, and how it might be something that his mom could use for her big assignment.

"Ah-ha," Timera said then, catching on. "Who's the girl?"

The question embarrassed him. Later Ash would recollect this as the last conversation in which his mother intuited anything that mattered to him—a skill she'd once been exceptional at. She kept the pictures he'd taken, going along with his claim that he was only trying to assist her. That was when she'd explained to him the importance of writing the date on each photo in black Sharpie for the sake of archiving. She included the Polaroids in her final project, on which she'd received an A-minus, and left it afterwards on the family-room coffee table, where she knew he could access it any time he wanted to and admire it.

Who's the girl?

Of course he knew. Of course he *didn't* know. On a certain level, "knowing" wasn't the imperative thing. Mandy/Elfa, Elfa/Mandy. She lived in his mind now.

He called her again.

"What's up, Strummer?"

"Nothing." Now he felt a little bit like an asshole.

"Nothing at all? Still no earthquakes?"

He was gazing out the picture window again. There the old *mesteñero* sat on the deck, white hat brim tilting up and down, drinking his Big Gulp and watching his transistor TV in the gathering dark. And there he wasn't.

The story of life itself: here, not here. Dust to dust. And a lot of groping, stumbling, pointless nothing in between. In the end, darkness.

"No, just smog. And horse flies."

"You sound bummed. Want to help do my show?"

That knocked him for a loop. "How would that work?"

"Easy. You introduce the next song."

"Over the phone?"

"Uh-huh. 'Sunglasses at Night.'"

"A song you hate. *Basura*."

"Exactly. I still have to spin it, though. By order of high command, which means station management. You'll be doing me a favor." She slipped into a faux-Corey Hart voice: "*Don't masquerade with the guy in shades, oh no!* 'Oh no' is right. Classic poser *Tiger Beat* crap. Gag me."

"What should I say?"

"I don't know, dude, but you're on in about ten seconds. Better think fast."

A Spanish-language ad was playing in the background: the Plaza de Toros in Juárez. The Sunday headliner, some retiring has-been on his *despedida*.

"Ready?" she said. The commercial played out. "Go."

Silence.

No quakes that summer, but oodles of rain beginning in late August. The green-brown haze in the sky gave way to brown-green puddles on the ground. Peculiar weather: winter was the normal rainy time in the valley. The FOR SALE sign was gone for the time being, but the wrought-iron peace sign out on Route 99, long rusted over already, began to slump sideways in the sodden earth where it was planted. In the lots out back the drinking troughs spilled over and the muddy pens gave some of the horses thrush and rain rot. Jared needed extra help moving the hay bales inside and keeping the horses groomed. The paid stable hands, of whom there were fewer because of the slower business, began griping about the unreasonable amount of work. One of them quit.

Asher worked his usual twenty hours a week but knew his father needed more. Jared refrained from asking because school had started up again—Ash's senior year. Except that by then Ash had stopped going. He hid out on the stable property during the day, alternating between the old *mesteñero's* trailer home and Tree Pendleton's. On the weekends when he wasn't working, he borrowed Jared's pickup and drove into Visalia, where he found a couple of sleepy independent record stores—no malls, no Hastings or Sam Goody, where there were too many real-life posers his own age—and picked through the remaindered 99-cent cassette bins. The plastic cases had holes drilled in their spines, marking them as rejects. He bought whole shopping-bagsful. He began reading *Circus* and *Spin* and *Rolling Stone*—just as quickly disregarding these journals as the work of posers. He took the tapes home and sat for hours, spinning out images in his head while the music played, absorbing the words, smoldering in his silent anger.

He's in love with rock'n'roll, woah…

He's in love with Janie Jones, woah…

He lived, for the most part, inside of his own head. Imagining how he would someday beat the system. Conjuring how he would escape the stupidity of his parents and grandparents. Hitting all too many dead ends, even in his boldest fantasies. There was no escape, not really. Not if Mauricio had been right: if the Rede men were all cursed. And not if the world was run by posers. There was no way out, no transcending the stupidity and the futility. No way not to be small and insignificant and pointless himself. At such moments he smoldered again in his boredom— and anger. When the anger threatened to take over he thought of Elfa. Of Mandy. His Janie Jones.

She forgave him for going mute on the air. Sort of.

"Dude, you really cramped my style there. Dead air is, like, the deadliest sin in radio. We're both lucky I have an understanding boss."

"Was he really in *American Graffiti*?"

"Who?"

"Hitman Hayes. Isn't he your boss?"

"That was Wolfman Jack, bud."

After hanging up last time, Asher had grabbed his headphones and put them back on in a state of guilt, wondering what sort of damage he'd wrought. To his wonder the Spanish bullfight ad was still going, and when it ended there was a barely perceptible pause before the song started up. When he'd held the phone to his lips and found he couldn't speak, it had seemed like much longer.

"It's called a dump button, my friend. There's a delay of a few seconds between the studio and the transmitter. Someone says one of the seven dirty words on the air and we can block it. It's like White Out for the radio."

"That's pretty cool."

"Yeah, except I have to log it every time it happens, and the computer can only do it so many times an hour."

"I didn't say any dirty words," Ash pointed out.

"True enough. So I guess you're out of the penalty box for now. Want to try again?"

"What song?"

"You tell me."

He chose "Train in Vain." She complimented him on his taste and cued it up a few minutes later.

When the moment came he zigged once more without meaning to. A mock-cockney accent came unbidden out of his mouth. He introduced himself as "Stroom-mah" and the song as The Clash's answer to "Stand by Your Man," which, lyrically, it was.

"Well…that was something," Mandy said afterward. "You're a real gas, Strummer. I'll have to make you a regular on the show."

"Thanks," he said, zagging back to himself.

A routine was born. Ash began haunting the video stores in search of bootleg tapes, anything that featured interviews or spoken-word segments with British punk musicians, The Clash and Joe Strummer especially but not exclusively. He sought out attitudes and opinions as well as accents. Mandy, still the greater musical expert by far, recommended also studying New Wave artists like Elvis Costello, Squeeze, and even Boy George ("his speaking voice is deeper than mine, believe it or not").

The Strummer character became an on-air hit. At first Mandy used him to introduce some of the newer undergroundier stuff that she wanted her teeny-bop audience to hear, both European and American: songs by R.E.M., The Waterboys, Tears for Fears. She briefed him on each new band and every new song, more or less scripting out what she wanted him to say, though he soon learned to embellish and improvise on top of her material. In response, some listeners began calling—in English and in Spanish—to request "Radio Free Europe" and similarly left-of-center titles rather than, say, "Like a Virgin." The novelty of an authentic (in their minds) British person guesting on a Mexican border-blaster from all the way over in jolly old England, thus taking an interest in their part of the world, thus acknowledging its very existence—thus legitimizing *their own* existence, however remotely—seemed to enthrall them. Did it matter that most of those kids probably couldn't locate England on a world map even if it were colored with pink polka dots? No, it didn't matter. These young callers soon formed a small but vital minority, a miniature cult large enough to encourage Mandy to keep the gag going. After a few such shows, some began calling in not to request particular songs but to hear from Strummer himself.

"Here he is, ladies and gents, live by long-distance from Surrey, England," she told them on the air. "The one and only Strummer. What's new and exciting across the pond, mate?

"Tell me your life story, Strummer," she said to him one night between her broadcast monologues. Again Asher was thrown. She wasn't a half-bad zigger herself.

"There isn't much to tell yet. I was born in 1967—"

"No, not *your* life story, doofus. Tell me *Strummer's* life story. For practice. We need to work up his backstory, and you need to work on that accent some more. You still sound too much like a smarter-than-average Yankee teenager just aping an English accent. We need to establish how Mandy and Strummer know each other for the act to work. Plus we don't want the real Joe Strummer's people to get wind of this; or at least if they do we have to convince them that you're not impersonating him. You have to be a *different* Strummer."

"That isn't fair, though. I can't think of how Mandy and Strummer know each other if I don't know who Mandy is. You should go first. You tell me *Mandy's* life story, then I'll tell you Strummer's."

Strangely enough, this half of the equation had never occurred to her.

"Hmm," she said after hesitating. "That's a good one, Strummer, I grant you. Who exactly is Mandy?"

Who's the girl?

"Let's take turns, starting off with the simple things. It's the simplest things that tell you the most about a person…they're what determines everything else."

"Like what?"

"Like, I don't know. Favorite foods. Mandy's favorite food…let's see."

"Shouldn't favorite color be first?" Asher was reminded uncomfortably of the psyche inventory Dr. Tune had once given him.

"We'll get to that. Or we won't. It's not a whole catalogue; just enough defining traits to build a story around. An outline, like stars in a zodiac sign."

"So," said Ash, prodding her, "what food?" She's enjoying this game, he thought.

"It's a secret!" she exclaimed, suddenly pleased with herself. "The one thing she'll never tell anyone, even her husband if she had one, but she doesn't. *Especially* her husband, in fact. See, she believes that big secrets are dangerous. They hurt people—they've hurt *her* a time or two. So she doesn't keep any. Instead she believes in keeping a few ordinary things complete secrets. Things that if somebody discovered them, they couldn't use them to hurt you. Things that someone who loves you should be able to figure out for themselves anyway."

"That's very complicated."

"That's Mandy," said Mandy. "Simple yet complicated, just like the name, which is short for Amanda, you know. Now, what's Strummer's favorite food?"

"Easy," he said. "Tacos. Puffy-shell beef-and-cheese tacos with red salsa."

189

"Strummer is English, remember?" said Mandy, bristling. "I really don't buy how tacos count as English cuisine, bud. Try again."

"But that's the point," Ash countered. "Strummer is complicated too. He's an Englishman obsessed with Tex-Mex, even though he's never been anywhere near here. Tex-Mex music, food, culture, all of it. That's why he likes talking to Mandy. It's the closest he'll probably ever get to actually seeing this part of the world. See, he's a cripple. Paraplegic."

He was warming up to the game now himself. They kept going at it for almost a week. In the end they developed elaborate backstories for each of their characters—so elaborate that it was hard to imagine what good any of it would do on the radio. Mandy was originally from Duluth, Minnesota, just like Bob Dylan. Strummer had a PhD in parapsychology. Mandy quit high school for a year to follow the Grateful Dead on a European tour, only to come down with hepatitis in Dijon, France, where she was stranded for two months. Strummer sang in a disco duo in the late seventies with his then-girlfriend, who was black. Their career and romance ended when he lost his legs in a horrific Vespa accident—no, a horrific double-decker bus accident—no, wait, scratch that—a terrorist bombing by fanatical Norwegian country-western anti-disco neo-Nazi, neo-pagan anarchists. Or something like that. Both Mandy and Strummer were Geminis, and both had gotten into radio after failing at a long list of other things. They had corresponded by phone for years but had yet to ever meet each other face to face.

"Well, well," Mandy sighed when at last they couldn't think of any more bogus details, both their imaginations spent. "Nice to know you, Strummer."

"*Stroom*-mah," he corrected her.

The first big phone bill dropped in October. Jared stomped out of the house one Saturday morning, in boxer shorts and hastily buttoned flannel chamois shirt, clutching a sheaf of tri-folded pages. Asher sat near the hot-walker firing blank rounds into the air using his grandfather's service pistol. Inside the walker-pen a couple of geldings ambled along, heads swathed in green mesh fly masks, while Jerry, their pied Alpine goat, trotted merrily between them for fun. The blanks were a way of conditioning the horses to gunfire.

"I thought you were saving up to buy a car?" Jared said, approaching him.

Asher lowered the gun and set it aside. "Yeah. So?"

Jared threw the pages in his face. They scattered like petals, little blue Ma Bell logos littering the ground.

"I'm listening," Jared said, the epitome of composed outrage.

At that moment Asher saw three men standing over him. Something about the bald and accentuated temples, the hint of cobwebbed skin near the eyes, the whisper of collapse near the jowls. The salted mustache. A breeze lifted his thinning black hair, like an invisible hand revealing the truth behind the sideshow magic. *We all become our parents, kid*, that breeze seemed to say. *What, you thought you were special? Fooled ya, didn't we?*

"I was going to tell you," Asher said.

"New Mexico?" his father added as if Ash hadn't spoken. "Who are you talking to in *New Mexico*, for Christ's sake? This is what you do in Lito's trailer every night? You couldn't go into Visalia and find a girl locally? You had to go and do this? Who is she?"

"It doesn't matter."

"You're right about that," said Jared. "It doesn't matter who she is, what she is, it doesn't matter to me one bit. What matters is who's going to pay for it. That's the only thing that matters here. We're on the verge of bankruptcy. Fifty years of blood and sweat and hard work about to blow away like a fart in the wind, but who cares? At least you got your kicks talking to some phone-sex twat in a New Mexico housing project. She probably has six kids and weighs two hundred pounds. But that's alright. At least you got what *you* wanted, you selfish ungrateful snot-nosed little shit-stain. My whole life, your grandfather's whole life, Lito's, what's left of this family, and it just doesn't make any difference to you, does it?"

"No."

Asher meant it. He sat looking at the mud-soiled phone bill pages at his feet, some buried yet vital part of him glad to have it out there at last, the Rede family legacy, the whole foolish fucked-up feckless enterprise exposed for the wasted effort that it was. Then he looked up and faced Jared with the resolve in his eyes that he felt in his soul.

"No," he repeated. "I couldn't care less. I never did."

Bullseye. Something in Jared's body—not just his eyes and face but his entire physical frame—gave way. Even that airborne black strand of hair fell lifeless onto his brow, its wind literally taken.

"Thanks," he replied. "That's just what I was waiting to hear."

Reagan swept the election and was re-inaugurated that January. Mikhail Gorbachev became leader of the Soviet Union. The images of starving, round-bellied children in east Africa dominated the news, prompting charity efforts by musicians on both sides of the Atlantic. Mandy and Strummer debated the relative merits of Band Aid, the English pop-star collaborative, versus USA for Africa, on the air.

"Sorry, mate, the song is *basura*," Mandy said, meaning the latter of the two. "The lyrics are boring and so is the production. The chorus puts me to sleep. You don't write a song about a humanitarian crisis and turn it into a lullaby. You need a march like 'Do They Know It's Christmas?' You want people sitting up and paying attention. You want a shot of tequila, not a glass of warm milk, know what I'm saying?"

"You're too hard on your own countrymen, love," countered Strummer. It was a chore bending every vowel-plus-r combination into a double-u, but he was growing more confident at it. "Lionel Richie is your best balladeer and Michael Jackson is your best R&B tenor after Smokey Robinson, so 'We Are the World' is just what we should expect when you put the two of them together. You have to go with your strengths." (He didn't believe a word of this, just riffing as usual off Mandy's tutelage.)

He assisted with the promotional games and giveaways, reciting clues to the mystery song or lyric of the week, often guessing the answers himself though he was ineligible to play. The female listeners wanted to know what Strummer looked like. Did he have a girlfriend? How old was he? He thrilled them with his English-accented Spanish.

"*Soy lo suficientemente mayor para saber mejor,*" he'd tell them.

"Don't overdo it, *mujeriego,*" Mandy commented later.

And there were days when she brushed him off. He could tell just listening to the show that she was going through the motions, wearing the radio disc jockey's equivalent of a smiley-face button; that whatever it was which she sometimes used him to overcome was eating away at her more persistently than usual. He knew that calling in on such days was an exercise in futility, but he often did it anyway. Just because.

"I'm kinda busy today, Strummer," she'd tell him, often cutting him off before he'd finished saying hello. The flatness in her voice suggested she wasn't busy—or that even if she was, that it wasn't the immediate problem. Another male would have no-doubt surmised it to be that most obvious of unspoken problems, the kind that showed up every thirty days or so, but Asher had learned too much from observing his mother in the final year or two before the breakup. Timera had expressed her dissatisfaction loudly and often, sure, yet she'd also tried at times to hide it, which was somehow a more painful thing to watch. The pointed silences, the reassuring grins at odds with eyes whose remoteness and distraction were hidden in plain sight. He could sense also that whatever explanation lay at

194

the center of Elfa/Mandy's unhappiness, and no matter how different its cause compared with Timera's unhappiness, it was still nothing to trifle with. Yet he'd gone and pushed his luck anyway. Just because.

"Try me again Thursday, alright?" she'd told him the last time they'd spoken over the XAMO request line. "Now's not a good time."

"Wait. Can I just ask you something?"

"What? *Andale.*"

Nothing. He had nothing. It was complicated.

Looking back, there was no reason not to ask the question that was really on his mind, the question that had moved him from the very start: whether or not she was the girl he'd met in that thrift store who'd sold him the Little John radio. Yet it seemed then just as obvious, just as insulting to him and her both, as asking her if she was on her period. It was unmentionable. And the answer might have cost him as much as it might've cost her. So instead he asked:

"Should I drop out?"

That one knocked *her* for a loop. He could tell.

"Drop out," she repeated. "Are you in high school? Wait. Never mind. I think I kind of knew that already. What are you asking me for?"

"Because I—"

Silence.

"Hello?"

There was the palpable sound, or perhaps rather the palpable *weight*, of all that instrumentation around her: lights and buttons and machines once capable of blasting two million billion ding-dong-dillion watts of radio gaga halfway up the ionosphere, halfway across the globe, into outer space, maybe even to the throne of the godhead itself. The weight of it all kept her anchored, he knew, in some inexplicable way. But sometimes even that wasn't enough. All that power wasn't enough. He knew this and he understood.

"Strummer. Listen. I'd like to help you, but I can't. I think maybe you and I have let this thing go a little too far. It's not your fault. But I can't help you. Please don't call me again."

"Elfa, wait. I won't do it again. I promise."

Weightier silence.

"What did you just call me?" she said.

"I mean Mandy. Mandy, I, wait, just a second, I—"

"How do you know my name?"

"No, I didn't mean to—I was going to tell you—"

"Bollocks! How do you know my name, you shifty little skitzo creep? Why did you even befriend me in the first place?"

"Mandy—"

"What other private, personal details about *my* private, personal life have you dug up? What kind of con are you playing, *Stroom*-mah?"

"Elfa—"

Unyielding silence. She was gone.

12

Sunrise, and someone was knocking loudly on the trailer door. Ash rose from the twin bed in search of his jeans.

It was Casey. She came in, sat down at the cluttered table, and buried her face in her hands, crying. Ash stood over her, shirtless and wondering what to do.

"Shaw's dead," she said quietly.

He took the chair across the table from her. He'd thought at first maybe he'd overslept and she was mad at him. They were supposed to start breaking in a new colt today. A problem horse, according to the owner.

"How? When?"

"In his apartment last night. Someone stabbed him."

Ash looked out the window, shocked but unsure how to feel. He'd never known anyone who'd been murdered before. He pictured Shaw's cocksure grin, the hat and sunglasses, the pampered mustache. There was no picturing him dead; for that matter there was no picturing him ever being born. Guys like Shaw Jepsen didn't proceed through the normal stages of birth, childhood, adolescence, and the rest. No beginning, no end. They just existed.

Casey was quiet for a long while, eyes tearing, weeping soundlessly. Then she noticed the items on his table.

"Is this what you live on, you idiot?"

He was out of ramen and had moved on to peanut butter and crackers from the convenience store near the racetrack. She pulled the open brick of Saltines towards her and shuttered at the sight of it, the same for the empty bottle of Big Red.

"Get some clothes on and come to the house," she told him, getting up. "I'm making us breakfast."

Lou was already fishing in the canal across the road. Inside the tiny Barefoot home, Casey had sausage and eggs going in a cast-iron skillet within the few minutes that it took Asher to dress and join her.

"Do you ever get tired of fish?" he asked her, opening the screen door and stepping inside.

"I don't eat that shit he catches," she remarked from the kitchenette, the act of cooking having restored her composure to some degree. "God help you, what those canals are probably swarming with. The toaster's over there, by the way."

The eggs came hard-scrambled, the sausage patties fried to the size of checkerboard pieces. Asher sliced the toast into diagonals and stacked it on a saucer, which he placed between them on the table. Then he ended up eating all of it himself. Casey picked at her food and lit a cigarette, observing him with still-swollen eyes.

"So, Asher *Red*-day," she said, mimicking Shaw's pronunciation of the name. "Nice to meet you. I'm going to miss Cal, though."

"I'll still be Cal if you want," he said between bites. "It doesn't matter to me."

"I gather that." She tapped her ashes into the rim of her plate. "How did Shaw know your real name?"

"He caught me walking into town from Anapra a few weeks ago, when I first came to work here. He checked my ID and let me go."

"And that was that, huh?"

"Yeah. That was that."

"How do you know Elfa Schultz?"

He claimed the last diagonal of toast from the saucer. "Is there any milk?"

She smothered her cigarette and went to the cabinet for a glass. Asher was nearly through with his plate as it was. She set the milk down in front of him just as he stabbed and ate the last pellet of egg. He grabbed the milk, drank, and grimaced.

"Buttermilk," said Casey with a wry laugh. "Dad loves it. You know how old people are."

They both fell silent. A box-stall freightliner rolled by outside, the traffic on the little road that paralleled the irrigation canal swelling in a steady crescendo lately as racing season approached. Any day now Tree

Pendleton was likely to show up, and odds were quite high that he was going to have a question or two to ask when he discovered Ash flopping in his trailer without his knowledge or permission.

"You and Shaw were..." he began, sensing she had more to say.

"Yes," said Casey. "We were. It's been over for a couple of years, but we were. You're pretty sharp, there, Asher Red-day."

"What do you think happened?"

Another cheerless laugh. "I don't think," she said. "I *know*. He knocked me up and I had to get rid of it."

He'd meant the murder, of course. But at least now her reaction when Shaw had teased her about robbing the cradle the other night made a bit more sense. The age difference between Casey and Shaw had to be appreciable, about ten years' worth, Asher would've guessed.

"I was still in high school," Casey said, as if reading his mind. "He likes them young. Or *liked*. Whatever. He was a jerk."

The puzzlement must have shown on Asher's face.

"Yeah, he was *that* kind of jerk," she explained. "The kind you could still feel sorry for. The kind that *I'm* always falling for. He wasn't half as clever as he thought he was, as I'm sure you noticed. You could see him coming from about ninety miles away, he was so obvious. He was the smooth older guy with the cool car when I first met him, and that was the angle he used to bag me, for sure. But he was also like a junior-high kid who's trying too hard. It was all an act, but it was lovable anyway. Know what I mean?"

Asher shrugged.

"You remind me of him that way," she added.

"So…what do you think happened?" he repeated.

"Oh, right," she said, drawing the connection from earlier. She rose and took their plates to the sink. Then she lit a fresh cigarette. "Well, he was a con artist, after all. And not even a very good one. These Border Patrol guys around here, I'm not saying they're all crooks, but they've got so many options available, so many crooked roads they can go down if they decide to. Plenty of temptation. I can't see Shaw ever intentionally hurting anybody, not for real. But I can totally see him getting crossways with people who would hurt *him*. Hell, I remember wanting to kill the stupid, smiling, gorgeous shit-head a time or two myself. He was so overconfident, so sure he could outsmart anybody, that I know for a fact he never would've seen me coming at him with a knife. Not until the very last second. Not until it was way too fucking late."

More laughter, this time salted with more tears, all of it raw and real and bottomless. "I can just see the dumb surprised look on his face," said Casey, her cheeks and hair melding wildly as she tried, trembling, to wipe away her tears and hold onto her cigarette at the same time. "Is that horrible, or what? The thought of him still makes me crazy. Goddamn you, Shaw Fucking Jepsen."

The lonesome *despoblado*. Not a bad song title, Asher thought. Someone should record it, take it to Number One with a bullet. He'd come to think of these three miles of borderland between the two-lane highway in Nueva Anapra and the XAMO transmitter as the physical embodiment of a song: verse-chorus, verse-chorus, and bridge-chorus. The verses and bridge were the low-lying-brush areas, where you had to choose from any number of thin openings through the sage and ocotillo. The choruses were the clearings that occurred about every three hundred feet, where all the brush paths seemed to converge. The choruses were all the same, the verses all different. But who's the songwriter? he wondered.

Fantasia knew the song well now. They'd ridden the *despoblado* together four times, twice by day and twice by night. He'd also taken to calling her Asia, and the yawning had soon stopped, which he considered a good sign.

Minutes ago he'd spotted a Border Patrol truck, a different vehicle from Shaw's, crawling west along the fence line; but it was moving away now and appeared not to have noticed him. Who'd taken possession of Shaw's modified Scout—and the dogs—following his death? How did that work? In Ash's experience most horses adapted fairly easily to the sudden absence of their masters, as disheartening as that seemed, but it also made sense: horses mourned their own kind. Dogs were different. Ferocious as Willie and Waylon had been towards the strangers who'd dared to cross into Shaw's patrol sector, they must have felt at least the same fierce degree of loyalty for the leader of their pack. Had they already been reassigned, or were they in a kennel somewhere mourning their dead master?

Another horse and rider had materialized in the distance, coming towards him from old Anapra.

When he introduced himself as Strummer at the party, Elfa had said nothing at first. But the look on her face was more devastating than silence. She recognized him, of course; recognized the name, the voice. But her face and eyes told him she found no comfort in that recognition—in fact, she was calculating about a zillion reasons why he might be there and finding none of them good. Whatever had been bothering her before, the mysterious whatever that once had nothing to do with him...the same whatever that she'd used him and the Strummer character to shield herself from...he'd now exacerbated by showing up in person. Now *he* was the whatever.

Let it go, Dr. Tune would've advised. *Did it ever occur to you that she might be afraid?*

Yes, it did occur to him; he just couldn't live with it. No way was he the problem. No way.

So he said: "What's the matter, love? Cat got your tongue?" in the old mock-cockney accent.

Shaw laughed at that, and so did Casey. And so, at last, did Elfa, breaking into a smile and—to his own everlasting shock—stepping forward and hugging him warmly.

"I see you've grown your legs back, Strummer," she said. "Must be a miracle of science. Welcome to America. How was the Concorde?"

The memory of that hug, still fresh in Asher's mind, galvanized him. He coaxed Asia quickly through the next clearing—the third chorus, if he was counting right—and still the rider from the Mexican side approached. They were zigzagging towards each other now, each negotiating a verse of thicket, but still basically headed for convergence at some point. Whether deliberate or arbitrary there was no way to determine. Only as they both entered the next clearing, the one nearest the border fence (and the one he considered the musical bridge in his imaginary song) did he recognize the shape and face of Helen Piper, riding astride her new big-ticket racehorse.

"*Buenas tardes,*" she called to him in a guarded tone, keeping her distance.

"Hi there," he replied. He raised a hand in greeting, and she halted, regarding him.

"You work for Lou Barefoot?" she asked.

"Yes, ma'am," said Asher.

That seemed to put her more at ease, if only slightly. "Then I suppose you work for me. Whose filly is that?"

She thinks I'm stealing, he thought, amused and insulted. He explained that it was the local beauty queen's personal riding horse.

"*Muchacho,* am I going cross-eyed?" Helen said then, nudging her mount a few paces closer and pushing her sunglasses down the end of her nose. "Or are you teaching that horse two-rein?"

Asher shrugged. "Why not? It's the style I grew up with, and it's better for the horse."

204

"Maybe. But I don't think the girl who rides her is going to be roping many cows. Are you planning to teach her two-rein style too? Is this your way of trying to land a date?"

"Sure." The thought hadn't occurred to him.

"It's been a long time since I saw any of that old vaquero stuff. Where did you grow up?"

"California. Visalia. My *tatarabuelo* used to work for you too."

"You don't say."

"Maybe you remember him," Asher added, going for broke. "He taught you how to ride, is what he used to tell me."

Something in the air, or in the sunlight—or in Helen—shifted.

"My goodness," she said thoughtfully. Her mount, *La Ganadora*, turned its head and sniffed in Helen's direction as if to verify there was still a rider in the saddle. "I used to have a memory like flypaper," said Helen. "But now there are just too many flies stuck to it. You'll have to remind me of his name. And yours while we're at it."

"Asher Rede." No more zigzagging, not this time. "His name was Mauricio."

Helen lifted her refined square-shaped jaw towards the sunlight and flicked the reins from side to side in her gloved hands, weighing this information. "Nope, doesn't ring any bells. I do hope you're not planning to ride Miss Teen Whoever's pretty new horse beyond that border fence, Asher Rede. People over there aren't always as respectful of personal property as we are."

"Didn't I just see you come from that direction?"

"I had business there, yes. And I'm also carrying traveler's insurance." She gestured to her pommel bag, trusting that she needn't explain to him that she was armed.

"Yeah, me too," he said. The service pistol was tucked into his nylon horn bag. *Your dead son's service pistol*, he thought in a sudden inner spate of rage. *Want to see it?*

"I was just taking Asia up to your radio station," he continued instead, keeping it cool. "She likes the ride, and Elfa invited me to come visit today. I won't let anything happen to the horse, I promise."

"It isn't my radio station anymore," Helen said, repositioning her sunglasses and starting away. "Pleasure talking to you, Asher Rede. Say hello to your great-grandfather for me."

"He's dead," Asher replied, but she was gone in a fine blaze of hot dust.

***

That bitch, Elfa thought.

She was seated in the studio, waiting for Sammy to wrap up his show and meanwhile thinking over the news that he'd just shared with her, just trying to absorb it.

"Of *course* she promised me a raise," she said out loud. "She won't have to pay for it, so why not? What does she care? God, she's a piece of work."

"*Fait accompli*, my love," Sammy commented. He was right, but she still felt like crying. Shaw was dead. Ms. Piper was selling XAMO to a

206

bunch of holy rollers. Her truck was still stolen. And Sammy, for his own part, was looking pale and listless of late.

"Hey, are you feeling alright?" she asked, placing a hand on his arm. Maybe it was the general brutality of the last few weeks, but it came to her now that he was looking less and less like himself. Maybe it was because he still looked *exactly* like himself: the mullet wig, the pot belly, the outrageous flamingos-having-sex Hawaiian shirt. But the pot belly belied the loose skin in his arms and neck, the haggard cheeks.

"Tell me that old story again," Elfa said when he didn't answer. "Tell me why you loved her."

The Hitman swiveled in his chair to fetch a 45 single by Katrina and the Waves, which he pulled from its paper sleeve and loaded onto one of the two McMartin turntables.

"Stay in the present tense, my love," he reminded her.

"Sorry."

"I believe there's a better-than-snowball-in-hell's chance that Helen still loves the both of us," said Sammy once the record was cued. "Or she wouldn't have stipulated that Simon keep the two of us on when she sold him the station. So there's that."

"That isn't the story I was talking about."

"And I do know *this*," said Sammy, raising his index finger by way of changing the subject. Then he swiveled again, raising an arm in one of his favorite operatic gestures—the kind that no listener would ever see over the airwaves but which he, like all the great disc jockeys, understood as sacred to summoning the almighty Spirit of the On-Air Persona—and swept it around to the studio's picture window.

"I found true love here, once," he said. "I found it, and it found me. Right here in the hot, hoary, interlocked triple armpits of exactly one *estado de Tejas* and two *estados de Mejico*. It didn't last long, granted, but in some ways, maybe in the only way that matters, it lasted a lifetime. But you, my darling girl, will never find true love in this hot hoary place. Because it isn't here, not for you. You must go and find it elsewhere."

"I'm working on it."

"You can work on it better somewhere else. There are other universities, other radio markets. You've kidded yourself about those two things long enough. Go and find love, Elfa. Leave Mandy here if you like. I would agree that Mandy belongs here. But it's time for Elfa to move on."

Now she was crying for real. He opened his frail, liver-spotted, operatic arms and she collapsed into them, shuttering. Behind them, beyond the picture window, Asher/Strummer came riding at an easy canter up to the station astride his borrowed horse. Elfa let go and Sammy handed her some tissues.

"You are so full of jive bullshit," she told Sammy.

"I have a treat for all of you," Mandy said on the air an hour later. "He's *here*, live in my studio, for the first time ever. Say hello, *Stroom*-mah."

She pulled the articulated mike arm towards him. Ash looked around the room. This was real. This was where it originated. The music. The voices. *Her* voice. Novelty records like "Bomb Iran" and "Mah Nà Mah Nà." The magic in his head. Radio.

"Hello, love," he said.

13

They were calling it "Live Aid." Two concerts, two cities. One mammoth worldwide broadcast. The famine in Ethiopia had spurred an unlikely confederation of the world's pop musicians. Elfa wanted XAMO to carry the radio simulcast, scheduled for July 13.

La Paz Ministries took possession of the station on June 1. Or rather, La Paz Comunicaciones de Medios took possession, as Mexican law technically forbade churches from owning and operating broadcast outlets. But when Simon parked his black Maxima outside the station and began handing out ichthus pins to all the employees inside, it became clear that not only was XAMO Radio under new management, but that the new program director—if Pastor La Paz was to be believed—also amounted to the ultimate figurehead.

"But seriously, folks…" Sammy deadpanned at a working lunch one day not long after the sale went through.

"Ever and always," said Simon, his smile steadfastly genial. He had invited the whole station staff to Sammy's favorite Avenida Juárez café—including Sammy himself, Elfa, Jeremy Santana, Jaz, Luz, and even Asher, who was as yet not a paid employee, or any kind of employee at all. Simon continued to address him as "*disidente*."

There would be no immediate format changes, he assured them, but yes, he expected that XAMO would be a Spanish-only radio station by September 1987. The famous former border-blaster once heard as far north as Fairbanks was going to redirect its still-considerable energies—both physical and spiritual—to the south. This would necessitate building a new transmitter, for which he intended to raise funds via solicitations during his Sunday-morning Spanish broadcasts and new daily bilingual mini-sermons, to be prerecorded and aired during morning and afternoon drive-time throughout the regular workweek. Presiding over that hastily assembled row of sidewalk tables, in the dappled sunlight of a blossoming desert willow, he indeed looked beatific, a bona fide lifetime member of the Sainted Multitude, whose every thought, word, and deed bore the official heavenly stamp of divine providence. It was all a bit much for Asher.

"He's like an Amway salesman," he told Elfa as the two of them walked the pedestrian bridge back over into El Paso, where she'd parked her mother's Jetta. "I can't stand it. He keeps calling me *disidente* like it's a pat on the head or something. But you know what? I think he hates troublemakers. He watches out for them, and once he decides that's what you are, he adds you to a little list that he keeps in his head." He thought again of the bone-crushing handshake years back.

"Keep talking that way," said Elfa. "We're trying to get you hired on as a disc jockey, remember? I know you don't like posers, but you'd better get used to them if you want to break into the business. They're kind of all over the place."

"So you agree that he's a poser?"

"Anyway, back to Live Aid," she said. Asher looked at her. It still bowled him over to be walking next to her, talking to her in person, working with her. Even though it wasn't officially work in the paying sense. The reality of her was what mattered. But watching her now, even in profile with her hair in her eyes, it was evident that the *other* reality was just as much there—the one that drove her to distraction, made her seize on things like fighting the displacement of Old Coke by New Coke or co-crafting radio personas with him or getting him hired at XAMO so they could keep working together. Now it was Live Aid. Soon it would be something else. Because that other thing, that whatever-it-was, must never be allowed access to the forefront of her mind.

By way of demonstrating some good faith to his new employees up front, Simon had agreed to carry the Live Aid simulcast all day, setting aside the usual Saturday programming. One of the FM stations in El Paso was doing the same, but then, as Elfa had argued, XAMO still had the advantage of geographic reach. The old million-watt transmitter—the one that had once burned up the entire western seaboard and Kentucky-fried whole flocks of birds in midflight for miles in all directions—was long gone, and the new one was yet to be built, but Jaz had kept the current

1959 RCA BTH-250A jalopy in fine working order. It would be an honest-to-god regional exclusive, and she was going to produce it, if only locally.

When he came to the station that first night to join Elfa on the air, Ash showed her the Little John radio she'd sold him when he was twelve. (He didn't tell her about the other two nights that he'd snuck into the building to watch her doing the show, seeing no good reason to stoke her mistrust of him any further.) She held it in her hands, looking it over, as if weighing both it and his story explaining how he'd known her real identity.

"Yep, I think this is the only one of these things we ever sold," she said finally. "The box is probably still sitting there. You can have the whole thing if you want."

"Did you get the Polaroid too?" he asked. "I left it with the receptionist—Luz?"

"So that was you also, huh?" said Elfa, handing the little Stellarsonic back. "Yes, I got it. I can't believe I was ever that skinny. Spinning records for a living really puts the fat on your ass after a while."

"You still look good to me," he offered.

"Yeah, well."

"Is the shop still there? Who's running it now?"

"It closed."

No offer to elaborate. Also no further interest in who *he* really was, beyond his once being a kid who'd bought some silly novelty item from her at Buena Vista Emporium. She still enjoyed Strummer but showed zero curiosity about Asher. It wasn't as though he used the English accent anytime except on the air; it seemed she was prepared to allow him his own identity to that extent, at least. No comment on his blurting out that he loved her that night over the phone—admittedly a dopy move on his part, but even so. No interest even in why he rode a horse into Anapra when he came to do the show every night; that alone seemed like the kind of detail you'd have to work at ignoring. In some ways it was as though he'd never left California.

She looped her arm around his as they strolled down the El Paso side of the Del Norte bridge. An unconscious move on her part. Whether friendly or romantic, it gave him hope. She was still chattering about Live Aid. There were calls to make, legwork to be done, and fast.

"Can I ask you something?" he said as they neared the car and she let go of his arm to locate her keys.

"Shoot."

"Were you and Shaw in love?"

She made a sour face. "God, no."

"Do you miss him?"

"That's two somethings, not one." They climbed into the car, which was an oven after two hours in the parking lot under the July sun. Every surface was afire to the touch. She started the engine and the A/C, then cranked her window down until the air coming from the dash vents had a chance to cool, which typically took a while. She then reached over him and did the same with the passenger-side window.

"Jesus H. Christ, *que calor*," she exclaimed. She leaned back behind the wheel, then seemed to go limp from the heat, just gazing out the front windshield. The bridge itself was a parking lot, all lanes at a virtual standstill, as was common this time of day.

"See, it kind of hurts to talk about Shaw," Elfa said finally. "He was just a friend. Not even a close one. But he's also the second person I've known who was murdered. I'm a little afraid it's becoming a…what. I don't know. A riff. A theme in my life. Like that song you hear in the supermarket or somewhere and just can't get out of your head. Not the song you love, the song you hate."

"Who was the first one you knew? The other murder?"

"The air's working now. Roll your window up."

Ash was having Sunday dinner with Casey and Lou when the five o'clock news came on, its lead story the arrest of Shaw's killer by Nueva Anapra authorities.

Casey was frying breaded catfish fillets. Store-bought, she assured Asher. Safeway.

"Nothing wrong with the ones I catch," Lou groused while doing nothing at all to help. Asher had at least set the dinner table and poured the iced tea before joining Casey's father in the adjoining TV room to wait. Every so often he looked at Asher from his Archie Bunker wingchair, marveling at Asher's hair, or rather the lack of it. Ash had gone into town the day before and gotten a trim on his Joe Strummer mohawk.

"How much you pay for a haircut like that?" he finally asked.

"Leave him alone, Dad," Casey admonished from the kitchenette.

Then the news. An arrest mugshot appeared on the screen while the anchor recapped the details of Shaw's murder: stabbed in the lower back and the throat, no sign of forced entry in Shaw's apartment, as if he'd let the killer inside and turned his back before the attack. The suspect was a girl. And Ash had seen her before.

"Josana Briseño, eighteen, was arrested and charged with First Degree…."

Joey, the pregnant purple-eyeshadow girl at the Dairy Queen/King. Had she had the baby yet, he couldn't help wondering? You couldn't tell from the mugshot, naturally. He turned to look at Casey, who was standing in the archway between the kitchenette and TV room, hugging herself with one arm while clutching a spatula in the other. She wore a gag-shop apron with the caption WHAT THE… followed by a cartoonish image of a fork just below. She wasn't smiling.

"It's funny," he remarked at the tiny dinner table a little later. There was hardly room enough for three people. "I just kind of assumed that it had something to with the Border Patrol, whatever happened to Shaw. I always got the feeling that he was into something…underhanded."

"He *was*," snorted Lou. "And it looks to me like he finally put his hands under the wrong one."

Casey smoked in silence, her mint eyes darker than normal, the fine if no-nonsense food she'd prepared so efficiently herself going once again to senseless waste. A single fly was going to town on her square of Jiffy instant-recipe cornbread.

Afterwards, Ash helped her with the dishes while Lou went out for his Sunday night six-pack.

"How's it going with the lady of the night?" she asked him.

"Who? Oh."

"Yeah. 'Oh.'"

"There's nothing going on *with* her, if that's what you mean. I don't think she likes me like that."

"But you like *her* like that, don't you?"

He shrugged.

"You mean to tell me that you and she are up there at that radio station alone, at night, for hours on end, and all you're doing is playing records and answering the phone. That's *it*."

"We're not alone," he replied. "There's this engineer guy around, somewhere. I mean you never see him, but he's supposedly there."

"You're a virgin, aren't you?"

He opened his mouth to protest, but nothing came out. She plopped her towel on an upside-down glass in the dish rack and took his hand.

"Come on. Let's go to your trailer."

"Why?"

"Shut up."

In the moment, as it was happening, it was easy enough to gauge who was doing whom the favor. She showed him where and how to put his hands on her. She acted the patient teacher, putting up with his awkwardness, prompting him, shifting tactics as needed with an expert's clean, keen sense of timing. No nonsense. And then it was done.

Only afterwards did things get fuzzy. Maybe it was the literal dark outside, the lingering July sunset. In the gloom he could tell she wanted his arm around her, so he tried putting it there and she pushed it away, gentle but firm.

"Elfa's still a virgin too, I'd bet my life on it," Casey said after a while, resuming their earlier conversation. She rose from the mattress, tossed her hair and began picking out her clothes, which had gotten mixed up with his. "She's a Catholic, of course, but I don't think that's why. She had boyfriends in junior and ninth grade. She changed when her father died. Nobody liked her much after that, me included. The worst part was she didn't even notice that people had stopped liking her."

Asher sat up on the edge of the bed. "I'm a little confused about what's going on here."

Casey was picking some floor lint from her blouse before pulling it back on. She looked at him over her shoulder. "Yes, it's still there. That clueless lamb-to-the-slaughter look on your face. I guess I thought I could hump it out of you."

"I'm not clueless. You're still upset about Shaw. That's why you did this."

They dressed and he walked her back across the trailer park to the house. It seemed like the thing to do. Lou was watching *Trapper John, M.D.* with a tall open can of Rolling Rock beside him on the lamp table.

The stoical expression on his face said he knew perfectly well what had just occurred between the two of them but also had brains enough not to comment on this one. Casey pulled some orange-sherbet popsicles from the freezer and she and Asher took them out on the porch and sat.

Lightning flashed to the southeast, filling the sky like a sheet and revealing an anvil cloud moving in from old Mexico.

"Elfa's father was murdered," Ash said aloud, though he hadn't intended to say it. He'd just now figured out the connection.

"Is that a question or a comment?" said Casey. She raised a foot and turned it so that the sandal she was wearing fell to the porch floorboards, and then she nudged his leg with her bare toes kiddingly. "Now I can see those wheels in your head turning. You only look that way when you're working with horses. The rest of the time you look lost."

Another lightning discharge. For an instant the Black Mountain appeared in outline, the crucifix monument at its peak like a tiny but emphatic punctuation mark.

"I'm not lost," he said.

14

It was still the most beautiful place he'd ever seen. Even on its worst days. Even on his. Glimpsing it for the first time from behind the wheel of his MG Roadster in 1953, the sunrise at his back after an all-night gin-fueled trek from Fayetteville, Sammy knew he'd come home.

So the trees were few if any. He could live without trees. The piney woods in Arkansas and Louisiana and east Texas—he could live without those trees in particular. Trees obscured things, masked reality, hid the truth. Sometimes they harbored out-and-out evil. Not the becharmed, fairytale, magic-and-menace Brothers Grimm kind, but rather the brutish and all-too-corporeal kind that walked the night in white robes and pointed hoods. The kind that had firebombed the nightclub in Bossier City where he'd lost his hair. The third-degree burns that ranged up his arm and torso and scalp were permanent reminders to him of the sorts of people who often dwelled in pretty places with trees.

So he'd learned to appreciate beauty in all its other forms. Beauty mingled with ugliness: that was truth. The crude, the unsightly, the rough and unadorned—there was beauty in such things. Beauty in "The Huckle-Buck" and the Bo Diddley beat. Beauty in black, brown, and white. Beauty in men as well as women. Beauty in the forsaken desert.

And what strange beautiful wonders the desert yielded. A tabletop mesa sprouting a miserable scattering of weeds, a Quonset hangar, and a single adobe cottage. A triad of soaring pylon-shaped scaffold towers linked across their tops with thick cables, themselves tethered to the ground by fanned webs of guy-wires. Together the towers formed a V whose vertex pointed due south and whose opposing ends faced north like a set of open jaws. As he forced the MG up the caliche road to the mesa's top, a procession of pilgrims from the Mexican town below moved aside for him without complaint. The penniless poor arrayed in their Sunday best. He'd arrived just in time for church.

Within the hangar sat an ancient bespectacled man, emaciated, covered in liver spots and clad in string-tie, tattered charcoal frock, and high-crown felt sombrero, seated in an elaborate carved throne-like rocking chair complete with a foot paddle extending from the front, on which rested his bare spotted feet. He was attempting feebly to light a calabash pipe as the penniless poor filed in. A trio of musicians in red bandanas stood to his right, singing and strumming ukuleles, the song a vigorous Spanish rework of "Joy Like a River." To the old man's left, a radio engineer sat behind a long table layered with broadcast-transmission equipment. At some point the old man motioned vaguely with his pipe and the service began.

The ukulele trio launched into "Under His Feet," this time in English. The old man set his pipe on a nearby table alongside a fat gilt-edge Bible and Musical Jolly Chimp toy, then pushed himself with visible exertion from the rocker, stood at length, and approached a microphone stand, arms raised high. His congregation rose from their plank benches and joined in singing. The Spirit swept the room.

"Sta *ween*-ah!" cried the old man when the song ended. "He lives!"

"*El vive!*" his flock cried in response.

"I said He lives, halle-holy-lujah!" the old man repeated with emphasis.

"*El vive para siempre!*" cried the penniless poor.

Then the old surgeon-cum-preacher stood bent forward at the mike Speaking in Tongues for several long minutes. The room went wild. The glossolalia flowed from his trembling mouth, unbroken, a song in itself—a dizzying profuse skewbald scat well-worthy of Fitzgerald and Calloway, Sammy thought. Many in the crowd threw off their weary faces and postures and joined in this new music, hopping and waving madly, spurting their own gibberish, the whole place at once united in a bona fide grand universal tongue—the spittle-spraying language of shared hysteria and mystical nonsense.

Returning at last to something resembling English, Dr. Piper spoke then of his Great Task and the enemies who'd so long thwarted it. He denounced the pope in Rome. He denounced the Communists. He denounced with singular fury the United States government and its legion of meddling bureaucrats. At this point he took the monkey toy from the little table and set it on the stage at his bare feet. He snapped a switch in its back and set it in motion bashing the toy symbols in its furry hands together eagerly, relentlessly.

"Look at him go!" cried Dr. Piper. "Listen to his mindless jingle-jangle! You love making that racket, don't you, Mr. Government Man? You're nothing but a silly noise! You're nothing but Satan's cling-clanging dancing monkey! Well we're not afraid of you here, you rascal! You keep on cling-clanging til the cows come home! Nobody here's gonna dance to your tune anymore! Get thee behind me, Satan! Go on, you brainless wonder! Go! Sta *ween*-ah!"

A dancing spirit had infected the old man, a sort of happy, twitching, desperate tremor that took root in his feet and worked its way north, the earlier fit of glossolalia gripping his whole frame, vocalizing through limbs and joints rather than tongue. An unseemly striptease commenced onstage. First went the sombrero, falling away to reveal the remaining tufts and mutinous lone strands of crazy white cobweb hair. Next he sidled out of the frock coat and let it drop. Next the string tie, which he yanked away like some accursed fetter and flung into the crowd before him. The trio launched into a waltz called "*Mi Plegaria*," and the whole room wailed in sweet sadness as the Reverend Doctor tore away his suspenders and at last opened his banker-stripe dress shirt, revealing an angry lurid crucifix-shaped rash across his pale doughy chest.

Having witnessed many such cornpone acts in the country churches of his youth, only later did Sammy pause to consider what he *hadn't* heard in Dr. Piper's: there were no pleas for money. Not one. A pair of offering plates had changed hands, true enough, moving back and forth among the aisles without fanfare sometime between the Speaking in Tongues and the monkey. Each platter bore a generous heap of assorted well-traveled bills and coins, both Mexican and American currency. And when he reflected on it, hadn't he noticed as many hands *taking* from those plates as contributing? Really, hadn't both pewters looked noticeably *lighter* after they'd made the rounds? It was hard to say. His own mind and body were under the lingering sway of a different sort of spirit at the time.

That night—at 12:30 AM, his head having yet to touch a pillow since he'd lit out of Arkansas—he signed onto Dr. Piper's radio station as Hitman Hayes. The first record he spun, pulled from one of the Falstaff beer crates that had accompanied him in the Roadster, was "Tipitina." Rock 'n' roll had come to XAMO.

"I honestly thought you were black," Helen later told him as they lay in her bed together. "So did Daddy. He would've thrown you off the air if he could. You nearly gave him another heart attack."

But the station was in receivership then, and there was nothing the Reverend Doctor could do about that coarse Negro's voice coming out of the radio. A man named Guzmán was in charge, a local union heavy and *interventor* appointed by the authorities down in Mexico City, where the political quicksands had again shifted.

When had Helen and he first laid eyes on each other? Sammy no longer remembered. He was no believer in love at first sight. (A radio man couldn't afford to be.) Besides, there was love and then there was love. In two years he was gone to New York City. Helen had her racetrack and her championship horses. The both of them loved what they loved, and loving each other was never the point.

He returned nine years later in a custom '62 Starfire convertible, a man of reputation now, a man of means. Opal and fire-ruby rings on his fingers. Still no trees. He could live without trees.

She was living in semi-seclusion with her father, now seventy-two, his long, sporadic mental voyage to the shores of all-out dementia and full-time nudism at last ended in permanent shipwreck. Idahly admitted Sam when he arrived at Pink Piper, kissing him in silence on the cheek and taking his suitcase. Later that evening, over a home-cooked dinner of flat iron steak and beet salad, Helen proposed.

"Why me?" Sam asked.

"Don't be stupid."

He regarded his glass of Bordeaux, which had emptied fast. "Is there any bourbon?"

He helped her put the old man away, deducing this to be the real reason she'd summoned him. They drove Dr. Piper to Las Vegas, New Mexico, in Helen's black Continental, whose tinted windows and rear-hinged coach doors made it easier to confine the old man and his unflappable nudism.

"Sta *ween*-ah!" cried Dr. Piper at odd intervals from the backseat. He rode with arms splayed across the seat tops, the angry raw rash that intersected his torso standing out like fresh blood against a canvas of white, curded old man's skin. "Sta *ween*-ah!" he exclaimed, smiling. The pain pleased him. A God-sent scourge, an authentic affliction, branding him for the scoundrel and fraud that he was before the whole world. "Sta *ween*-ah!" he exclaimed again.

After depositing him in the psychiatric hospital, neither of them was in a terrible rush to return to Nueva Anapra. Sam joshed that they should light out west on Route 66 just for yucks—and to his amazement, Helen took him up on it. They stayed at the Painted Desert Inn the first night, sipping mescal Negronis on the patio at sunset. The next morning they toured the Petrified Forest on foot. An excited young ranger led them through the park, having recognized Sam from his appearances on *House Party* and *To Tell the Truth*. Helen trailed the two men through most of the walking tour, her face demure and mostly hidden underneath her sunglasses and yellow headscarf. When they reached the heap of displaced rocks near the park's south entrance, she asked why they'd been moved, since the pile was obviously manmade.

"That's the Conscience Pile," said the ranger. "People steal rocks from the park and then send them back to us by mail, parcel post, whatnot. Folks say they're cursed."

"Who?" asked Helen. "The people or the rocks?"

"Both, I guess, ma'am," said the ranger.

They chased Route 66 to its very end, to the neon archway at the Santa Monica Pier. The trip from New Mexico had taken three days.

"I wish we'd brought a convertible," Helen said.

"You can buy one here and drive it back," Sammy told her. "You're a rich woman. Or hadn't you heard?"

They got out and walked the pier, enjoying another sunset. Sammy took her hand in his, something he'd not done once on the whole trip.

"Do you know what I wish?" Helen had asked him then.

"I can't begin to imagine. Are you about to ask me to marry you again?"

"Don't be stupid. I wish life were like that pile of rocks we saw in Arizona. I wish it was always as straightforward as sending your mistakes back with an apology letter. The people who stole those rocks weren't *cursed*, they were *lucky*. Imagine if every wrong thing you've ever done could be undone that effortlessly."

He'd thought it was her father who'd inspired these thoughts. The sight of him there in the backseat, the rash of guilt on his chest.

"You're not to blame, sweetie," he assured her.

"For what?"

"For any of it."

She looked at him, pain in her eyes. He loved her then, of course.

"Marry me, Sam."

"Don't be stupid."

People shuffled past, walking pairs of dogs on twin leashes, wearing strange clothes and long hair, baring more skin than would have been tolerated only five or six years ago. How savagely the times had changed. Helen looked beautiful and desolate, a forgotten starlet shown up for the wrong premiere. It was her story, and he was only a bit player. Sam would never love her more.

"Why me?" he asked again. No need to protest that he loved her and that it wouldn't work.

"Because I trust you."

"Ah," he said, his gaze shifting to the violet sunset. The Pacific was putting on its usual hoary, voluptuous, irresistible sundown show. "I see the problem. You're confusing trust with love. I've loved many whom I didn't trust, and vice-versa. Don't you go making the same mistake now. You're too smart."

"No, you've *lusted* more than you've loved," Helen replied. "And you're right, I'm a damned sight smarter than you, so you'd better take me seriously. I won't ask again."

"Good," he said, taking her into his arms. It was the finest of kisses. Somewhere close a group of teenagers broke into raucous applause, and then a flashbulb went off.

Sam rose from his sofa, head throbbing. Lightning flitted beyond the patio doors. Summer storms afoot. The sliding glass was open at a slit, the synthetic bleat and pulse from the neighboring discothèque compounding his discomfort. The odor of urine from the disco's back-alley *pissotière* stung his nostrils. Still the most beautiful place he'd ever seen, yes, you bet your sweet ass.

He went to his vintage pink-and-yellow bubbler juke and punched Number 24. A 78 disc slid onto the turntable and the chrome clamshell tone arm dropped, channeling a long gone sublime doo-wop by The Elegants. He stood over the Wurlitzer's mighty glow, eyes closed, gripping its sides like a man in chains, and at last admitted what was happening to him—confessed it. Just a whisper in the mind, and it was done. Then he wandered down the narrow hallway to his toilet and vomited, then vomited again. And again.

When his eyes opened next, it was to the ferocious glare of sunlight through the custom brick glass of his bathroom. His first cogent thought was *Now what?*—he'd expected to wake up dead.

"*Sammy!*"

The apartment door. Insistent thudding. Then the scuffed toe of a neon-laced high-top, signed by Charlie Harper, an inch or so from his face.

"Jiminy Cricket...I'd know those clodhoppers anywhere," Sammy rasped.

Behind Elfa was an unfamiliar kid bearing a tousled mohawk; this, it seemed reasonable to presume, was the illustrious Strummer. They each took hold of Sammy's arms and bore him across the hallway to the master bedroom.

"How do you dial an ambulance in Juárez?" said Elfa, going for the phone.

"Zero-six-six," replied the kid.

"Not necessary, *mamas*," Sammy said. He pressed backwards, in vain, against the shifting tides of his Pacifica waterbed with his elbows. Now the bathroom floor seemed a preferable surface. "Just light me a *veladora* and let me float away."

"Shut your mouth," said Elfa. "You're not even Catholic."

"My Van Heflin…please." Sammy was gesturing to the bureau. Asher looked, and there was an array of toupees on a family of Styrofoam wig stands.

They were forced to drive him to the hospital themselves. Ash took the Jetta's wheel while Elfa sat with Sammy in the backseat. Afternoon rush hour was underway, and the streets, already too narrow and poorly marked, were clotted and nearly as paralyzed as the bridges.

"Sta *ween*-ah!" Sammy blurted out of the blue as they idled at an intersection near Avenida Tecnológica, the line some ten vehicles thick.

"Is he delirious?" Ash asked, peering at the rearview.

"I'm perfectly sensate, thank you," Sammy replied. "Just stumbled down memory lane for a moment."

"You missed your show today," Elfa told him.

"So I gathered," Sammy said, eyes closed in weary acknowledgment. "I never missed an aircheck in my life. Not once in thirty-two years. *Je suis désolé.*"

"Dear god."

Elfa's voice and face had gone slack.

"My truck."

A blue Isuzu pickup was idling in front of them. In the rear cab window a *Santa Muerte* decal stood plain in the daylight, the *dama's* skull radiating black halo lines and her bony fingers gripping her scale and scythe. The window itself, like much of the pickup's body, was covered in dried mud splotches. The line pressed forward and the truck swung right at the intersection, disappearing.

"Go after it," Sam said—eyes still closed, head back against the rear dash.

"No. Forget it. Just get us to the hospital."

"Wait—are you sure?" Asher made mental note of the street and direction where the Isuzu had gone.

"What are you going to do, take them on? Get into a shootout?"

"The truck is salvageable," said Sam, opening his eyes now and taking her hand into his. "The odds on me are much, much worse. Don't squander your efforts on the wrong broken-down wreck."

"Shut your goddamn mouth. I mean it."

"*Yo también te amo, mamas,*" Sammy groaned.

"And don't give them any of your refried Spanglo-French at the hospital. You'll only confuse them."

His hairpiece fell off in the emergency room waiting area, once the desultory staff got around to claiming him. Ash went and fetched it off the floor as the nurse and orderly wheeled Sam away on a stretcher. Holding the thing in his hands, Ash recalled his first horse, Terror, whose mane he'd used to grasp in fear for his own life.

"We're on the air in an hour," said Elfa. "Better get back." She made no other sign of intent to leave. Her voice was far away, like Mandy's on her bad radio days. She'd gone to one of the backless cushion seats near the front windows and settled there, crumpling into abrupt gloom. Across the street outside, a pubescent schoolgirl in a tartan skirt, knee-high socks, and red hair bow sat alone on the curb, dangling a severed tree limb into the street, looking as though she had nowhere to be and less reason to care. Elfa looked about as despondent.

"So he's still awake and talking," Ash told her. The comment came out more question than assurance. He crossed the room and came as close as he dared before taking a seat with a spare cushion between them. "He'll be all right, don't you think? Maybe it's food poisoning or something."

Elfa turned to the window, hands cupped together in her lap, shoulders lifted in a kind of infinite shrug. "Sure. He ate a bad octopus. That's probably it."

"But you don't believe it."

"No, I don't."

Her portwine stain. He wanted to caress her cheek with the side of his hand. He wanted to take her in his arms, the way some hunky movie boyfriend would do at such moments, and comfort her. He wanted to throw himself through the plate-glass window and into the oncoming traffic outside. What was he even doing here?

"Then let's go find your truck. I know where they went. There's nothing we can do for Sam by waiting around here."

She didn't move. "Don't be a plonker, mate."

"I saw them turn down a dead-end street. They're probably still there."

She was watching him closely now, dark amber eyes full and alert. "The truck was a ghost. I'm sick of ghosts. Sick of losing people and things that matter to me. I'd like for them just not to matter anymore. Can you help me with that?"

A noisy family had barged in led by a portly woman with big red hair and loud purple pants. The ring of children around her swarmed and then separated to explore the room, leaving only the one whose face and neck were bleeding standing alone at the woman's side. The child, a girl, appeared oblivious to her own wounds.

"You're looking at me funny, Strummer."

"Sorry."

Elfa took his hand into hers, enclosing it. "I know you still have some kind of crush on me. But you know now that I'm not Mandy, right?"

"I know. And I'm not Strummer, either."

She released him and averted her own eyes, the meaning within them before she did so clear as day: she had not the slightest desire to know who *he* really was, not now, not ever. The callousness of it seared him.

"You're not the first one to come to the station in person looking for her, you know," Elfa went on. "Sammy told me once that in the old days, the picture window outside Studio A had this two-way intercom and a couple of bar stools. Listeners would walk right into the station off of the desert, sit down and watch him do the show live, people who'd driven hundreds of miles to see Hitman Hayes. They could push the intercom button outside the studio window and make requests. Sam says he finally had to put a stop to it because too many people found out he wasn't black, and the word started getting around. He never worked at sounding like a black man on the radio, you understand; it just happened naturally. But after a while his career depended on the illusion.

"Mandy's been good to me—I guess she's been good to the both of us. But I need a break from her, and now's as good a time as any. No more illusions. Why don't you go and do the show by yourself tonight. I'm staying here until Sam pulls through or until they know what's wrong with him. I'll call Jaz and tell him to set up for you."

"What should I do with this?"

He was still holding Sam's toupee.

Ash arrived near sunset, the titanic western sky behind the little adobe cottage ablaze with reds—with crimson and candy-apple and ruby and vermilion, plus an admixture of fandango pink and cadmium orange and Indian yellow and even African violet. Fantasia, the beauty-queen's horse, stood tethered just inside the perimeter chain-link fence.

You're making a damned ass out of yourself, young man, Dr. Tune said.

Ash went inside.

15

XAMO! 1530 AM

La mejor música en
el estado de
Chihuahua, México.

Registro por hora de la emisión

8 de July 19 85

Hora	Contenido	Notas
20:04	Muh Nuh Muh Nuh	
07	aircheck	
18	I Fought the Law	
21	Tx When I Die	
33	Wild Horses	
37	Don't Fence Me In (aired)	
45	We Are the World?	
49	Ves Carry	
21:	I Don't Care Anymore	Bollocks!!!!
	Anarchy in the U.K. !!!	Noddy
	Midnight Rider	

Firmado por el empleado(a) de turno:

Astur Rede

RTC

Dirección General de Radio,
Televisión y Cinematografía

16

Lou Barefoot was on the phone.

"He stole her horse."

"Who?"

"The new wrangler. That Charlie Sexton punk. It looks like he lit out with Roene Baffert's nine-thousand-dollar white palomino either late last night or early this morning."

Helen still wasn't registering any of this. Donny Semko, her lawyer, was holding on the other line. Her workday and her first cup of Café Vienna weren't yet five minutes old. Now two additional lines were flashing, and Yvette, her dingbat assistant worthy of Carol Burnett's Mrs. Wiggins character, wouldn't be at her desk to field calls until nine.

"Well then you'd better call the authorities."

"Her folks went and did that already. Fighting mad and ready to sue the hell out of us. I told them the kid usually takes her for a ride mornings, evenings too, and that just made them all the madder—"

"Wait, which kid and which her? You're losing me, Lou. Are the girl and the kid the same person?"

Elfa Schultz had appeared in the office doorway, raising a hand involuntarily to shield her eyes—the sunrise was slicing in through the window blinds, which probably accounted for her standing there frozen when Helen motioned for her to have a seat.

"The kid is the horse thief. Charlie Sexton. You've met him. Fucked up hair. Was staying in Tree Pendleton's trailer, but now it looks like he's packed his shit and beat out of here for good, except for a worthless guitar. Never would've hired him if Casey hadn't talked me into it."

"Hold on a minute." Helen punched the first line. "Sorry, Donny. Is it urgent? I've got someone on the other line."

"Urgent? You called me, remember? Although it's funny you did because I was just about to—"

"Yep, that's right, I forgot. Just stay with me another sec, then." She covered the phone mouthpiece with her palm. "You want to sit down, babe?" she told Elfa. "This might take a minute or ten."

Elfa obliged, still shielding her eyes, which were puffy and bloodshot. So it was a rude daybreak for the both of them. Helen returned to Lou first, instructing him to call her back when the police arrived.

"Still there, Donny?"

"That's what retainers are for."

She bumped him over to the loudspeaker and replaced the headset in its cradle. "I need to talk to you about Sam Hayes. He's in the hospital over in Juárez. I want to get him back on this side of the river sans any cowboy-sheriff bullshit."

"Right, I'm confident we can do that. But first, have you gotten any calls from the media?"

Helen's blood froze, her risk-assessor's mind tallying the sudden significance of those other flashing lines. "Not just yet," she ventured.

"So you haven't heard?"

He sketched it out in broad strokes first: a disc jockey, some bizarre on-air stunt last night on the radio station. Helen shot another look to Elfa, still shielding her eyes though she'd sat with her back to the window blinds.

Then Donny related the excruciating details, all based on some hastily scribbled notes that he'd taken at his desk, these based on a conversation minutes ago with a couple of young female paralegals. As it happened, they were both regular fans of XAMO's nightly *Party Line with Mandy* program. It seemed that Mandy's fill-in last night, a mysterious English DJ who sometimes co-hosted the program and had a particular way of charming young, female, paralegal callers most especially, had decided all at once, about ninety minutes into the broadcast, to stop being English. From there the program had taken a sharp turn for the weird, concluding in several hours of XAMO going completely off the air.

"He, uh...let's just say he went into storytelling mode," said Donny. "And it was quite a humdinger of a tale. Something right out of Charles Dickens or *Dynasty*, depending on which one you favor."

"Hold tight, Don," said Helen. She punched the next flashing line. A reporter for the *El Paso Sun* asked if she'd heard the broadcast and cared to comment. She told him no, she hadn't, but that she would look into it and call the editor-in-chief—her good friend—right back. The next call, from McLean, Virginia, wasn't so easy to dispatch. A reporter from *USA Today*.

Helen danced around this one as best she could, telling the woman at the other end that the radio station in question was no longer hers. "Yes, but even so," the woman pressed…a certain assiduous snark in her voice. All at once, in her mind, Helen was talking to Sadie Bleiberg. "Even so," this harridan pressed. The woman was gloating now. "Even so." At last Helen hung up on her.

And still a fifth line blinked at the end of that long row of translucent buttons. Her Café Vienna was beyond all hope now. Elfa had taken a place on the sofa but abandoned it just as quickly, as if she'd done enough sitting and waiting. "There's coffee, sweetie," Helen told her, motioning to the saloon-knockoff wet bar. "Don't be shy about spiking it if you need to. I might be hitting the sauce soon myself if the morning keeps going like this."

She punched the last lit button on her phone.

"Ms. Piper?" said a man on the far end.

"Yep. Make it quick, please, whoever you are."

"My name is Jared Rede. I'm Asher Rede's father."

"I don't know who—" Helen began, impatient, before catching herself. Elfa paused at the bar, having poured a glass of Smirnoff straight.

"Right," Helen finished. "Hang on." She punched HOLD and tapped a lacquered nail against her leather desk pad in thought. Elfa eased onto a bar stool, observing.

"Sorry, Don," Helen said, punching line one again. "Give me the rest of it."

After dumping the Englishman bit, the kid had reintroduced himself to his audience as Ash, or Asher, Something-or-Other. Helen visibly winced at the name. From there this Asher So-and-So had launched into a sort of musical pastiche-history of XAMO itself, of the Rede family... and of Helen.

"He claimed you had a baby back in the thirties and disowned it," reported Don. "Claimed that baby was his grandfather—now deceased, I gather."

Line five continued to flash. "Well, now," said Helen, marveling at her own composure. "I don't entirely see what that has to do with the price of rice in China. Except it sounds like *someone* should tell Simon to keep his employees on a shorter leash now that the station belongs to him. Or else *somebody* might just decide to sue the holy-rolling shit out of him."

"Uh, yes...about that."

"Yes? What now?"

Donny made that uncomfortable clearing-of-the-throat noise that lawyers make. "It's possible that I'm proceeding in the wrong order here, Helen. The embarrassing personal details, true or not, are actually the least of this. The kid told a lot of tales during his show, and while I haven't had nearly the chance to check all of them out, I can reasonably say that the other allegations ought to at least concern us, especially given that…you might still own XAMO Radio after all, at least in the eyes of the Mexican government."

And on he talked. The La Paz organization was a sophisticated smuggling ring—of people as well as things—Donny said the kid had said. Whole busloads of migrants driven regularly across the open *despoblado*, the term he'd used for those few flat miles of scrub brush behind Helen's mansion. Border Patrol agents like Shaw Jepsen paid to look the other way and sometimes lend a hand. Girls. Prostitutes. Drugs. The same dirt-poor labor force that drove the *maquiladoras* in and around Juárez being marketed, sold at auction, to fuel other seemingly legit enterprises north of the border—including the racetrack. All right under Helen's nose. And possible blessing.

Line five. Still flashing.

And now someone's *primo de un primo* in Mexico City had pushed back on the XAMO sale in the thirteenth hour, no doubt because that someone's *palanca* hadn't been greased.

"So, back to Sam," Helen said. Enough already.

"Of course, I'll get right on it," said Donny. "But listen, if you were thinking of visiting Sam while he's hospitalized over there, I advise against it. We don't know yet how seriously the Mexican authorities are taking this…this incident. But I do know that Simon, the Asher kid, and the station engineer have all gone missing, and they're all wanted for questioning. The PJF might detain you, given half a chance and any half-assed excuse."

Silence fell in the office once the call ended. Helen lifted the waiting cup and saucer to her lips, only to confirm that their contents had achieved room temperature. Line five flashed away steadily. Helen sipped her instant coffee and turned her eyes askance.

"How'd he look when you left him?" she asked Elfa. "Was he awake?"

"He says he'd rather be in Philadelphia." Elfa regarded the glass in her hand and set it aside. Helen rose and carried her cup and saucer over to the bar.

"I've got some Sunny D. back here if you'd like a mixer for that."

"Did you know?"

Helen abandoned the coffee altogether and reached for the globe decanter containing her preferred brand of eighteen-year-old scotch.

"I only know that Simon's check cleared weeks ago, and I'll be a monkey's drunk uncle before I ever give it back," said Helen.

"No...I mean did you know Sammy was sick?"

Helen brought her own glass around the bar and slid onto the stool beside Elfa.

"I'll tell you a little story, sis," she said. "I know it isn't what you want to hear right this split second, but the truth is there are all kinds of sick. My daddy used to call himself a doctor and he was the sickest man I ever knew. You could say that being sick was what really made him happy, kept him going nearly a whole century.

"Daddy hated blacks all his life, and he hated rock 'n' roll and Sam Hayes both because they reminded him of niggers. No good reason for any of it, of course. Daddy was just a poor ignorant Okie long before he was anything else, and he brought the nigger-hating with him from Oklahoma. Me, on the other hand, I've never had the time or the justification for any kind of prejudice. When Sam first arrived down here back in the fifties, I liked him immediately. He put XAMO back on the map by sounding black and by playing rock 'n' roll. Right away the revenues increased and kept increasing, and I wasn't about to give that up. So I brought Sammy up to the house to meet my father. Sam was and is every kind of Prince Charisma when he really gets rolling, as you know, and he and Daddy hit it right off in person. They were both southerners, after all. Both radio men. Both extraordinarily talented con men too, lest we forget. The evening was a brilliant success. And then what do you suppose was the first thing Daddy said the very next day when he heard Hitman Hayes on the radio? *'Get that dirty nigger off of my station.'*

"That same stupefying, maddening, willful ignorance drove most everything Daddy ever did, good and bad. I watched it make him rich. I watched it kill my mother. You get to wondering whether unreasonable people like my father are sick because they're sick or because they're unreasonable. The chicken or the egg. Is any of this making sense, hon?"

"I don't know," Elfa admitted.

Helen shrugged and threw back her glass of scotch, reaching again for the decanter.

"I'm saying that Sammy and my father really are no different. They loved doing and saying and believing things that made them sick. In the end those things might've killed them—might kill you or me—but when they also keep you going long enough, who's to say they were ever sick at all?"

Elfa looked disappointed. *That's it? That's all you've got to say?* were the questions scrawled on her face, but Helen gave her credit for not uttering them. Because the only available answer was yes. Helen touched her hand.

"You're going to have to be our go-between for now," she said. "You just convey to Sam that I'm doing everything I can for him. I'll have him transferred back over here as soon as it can be arranged and see that he gets the best possible care. I know you must want that as much as I do. Did the doctors give you any clue what might be wrong?"

The girl's eyes said enough.

"Well never you mind about that for now. Don Semko's the best fixer I know at these border pinches. He'll keep the politicos out of our hair, and we'll have Sam moved to a decent hospital stateside in no time."

"But what if Sam doesn't want that?"

Helen had emptied her second glass of scotch, only then remembering the face-to-face with her bloodstock agent scheduled at nine-thirty. Time for a breath mint.

"Beg pardon?" she asked Elfa, returning to her desk.

"I'm pretty sure he's happy right where he is," said Elfa.

"Then I'm either a might confused or a might intoxicated. Isn't that why you came to see me?"

"I suppose it's partly why, yes. But mainly I just wanted to apologize for what Strummer—I mean what Asher—did last night. I'm the reason he got on the air in the first place. I was worried about Sam, so I stayed at the hospital and sent him back to the station to do the show by himself."

The telephone had ceased flashing.

"You knew this joker well, then," said Helen. "How do you suppose he came up with all that crazy nonsense? How much of it did he tell you before this happened?"

"None of it," Elfa said solemnly. "He was a fan. He used to call me from California to make song requests. And then suddenly he was here. I liked him. He was like a kid brother.

He was smart and goofy and funny, he had good taste in records, and we had fun working together. The rest of it…I just didn't know about. I should've asked more questions."

"I guess you should've, hon," said Helen, enjoying a brief moment of spite.

"Are you going to call his father back?" Elfa added, suddenly eager. "I'd like to know his side of the story, wouldn't you?

"I'm sorry, never mind, it's none of my business," she corrected herself in haste. She approached Helen's desk, her hand out in offering. Helen accepted, and they shook.

"Thank you for all you've done for me. And for Sam." She hesitated. "I admire you." And then she retreated, leaving Helen alone, dumbfounded, at her desk.

Are you going to call his father back?

Only then it clicked. But of course: the DJ and the horse thief were one and the same person.

And that person was her own great-grandson.

17

At daybreak a set of sealed-beam halogen headlights appeared at the far end of Asombro Road from the general direction of the Nueva Anapra racetrack and approached in a sort of sluggish, uncertain amble, then paused as if in thought. The maroon Apache four-by-four's headlamps went dark, and then the vehicle inched forward and swung at a ginger pace off of the road into the Lazybones Stables and Mobile Home Park front entrance, stopping at the row of mailboxes near the gate. The driver's door popped open and Tree Pendleton—all five feet, two inches of him—hopped out. Behind him the radio blared something by Santana.

"Switch that noise off!" came a woman's shrill voice from within the nearest trailer. "It's too early in the mornin' for that beaner shit! You goddamn Mexicans don't know when to quit!"

Tree studied the direction from which the voice had come, the locks of his carrot-colored Ziggy Stardust mullet flicking this way and that. "Fuck you, Ma!" he shouted. His mother was nineteen years in her grave. He went to his mailbox, banged and rusted and bearing a rain-washed

Justice Brothers decal under the doorlatch. Waiting inside were a water bill, a belated birthday card from his half-sister in Farmington, a free sample of Prell, a *Sun Shopper* weekly circular, and an envelope from Columbia House. These last two were addressed to someone named Charlie Sexton. Tree scratched his whiskered cheek.

He tossed the sheaf of mail onto the pickup's passenger seat and climbed back in behind the wheel, adjusting the radio volume as the music had ceased, displaced by some silly churchy happy-crappy. "*Y ahora por tu afirmación diaria del pastor Simón,*" an announcer declared in obsequious tones. "*Este mensaje ha sido grabado previamente.*" Tree thumped the Apache into gear and moseyed onward around to the park's west corner. He'd been away some three months, working the rodeos in Fort Worth and Merkel, then the stables at Ruidoso Downs. Now he was bound back to California and the San Joaquin County Fair. Probably.

An open brick of crackers lay on the kitchenette table when he entered his trailer. He ate a couple and chucked his shaving kit and wardrobe bag onto the bed, noticing then the Washburn leaning against the bedframe. *That* wasn't there before.

He set it aside and napped a little bit. The weariness of the road—and the weight of his thirty-nine years—tugged at him with abrupt urgency. He dreamed of Kalen, the girl who'd jilted him in the fifth grade. His girlfriend for a day, until she opted for Mike Bonilla the very next. His first lesson in impetuous women, or impetuous fate, or both. Freckled face and green eyes, orange-sherbet shift dresses. Turlock Elementary, 1957. "Kiss me," she'd said at recess, in the lunch line, in reading group. She'd hold her wrist out coquettishly and he was required to kiss it in front of everyone. Just once he refused in embarrassment. And that was that: *c'est dommage*.

An hour later Tree woke, washed up, and happily discovered an old beloved bangora hat of his hiding on the closet shelf, which eased somewhat the discomfiting blue feeling that his catnap dream had left on him. Then he strode out to the stables with it, puzzling once more over that Washburn guitar. Where had he seen it before? He reached the stables building and perused the regular stalls one by one, halting at the one that held Budweiser, a twelve-year-old gelding and one of his favorite quarter horses in the Lazybones stock. He offered him a few knuckle-touches and pats on the whither before electing to saddle him up, after which he climbed on and guided Budweiser out towards the riding arena.

Casey Barefoot was leading another quarter horse, a young sorrel mare, back inside the building on foot when he exited out the main doors. She walked right past him, head down underneath her bullhide hat.

"Had a good nap, did you?" she said behind him.

"*Bueno* to you, too," said Tree. "Some welcome back I get. You ain't even seen me in three months."

"You didn't hear us come in," said Casey, proceeding to the stalls. "We knocked and knocked. Daddy finally had to use his key."

Tree scratched his cheek. "You come in when I was sleeping?"

"We weren't expecting to find *you* in there," she said. "We were afraid that…never mind."

"You had to see my truck outside. Who in the hell did you think I was?"

"It would take too long to explain."

"I've got all morning."

Casey closed and latched the stall door between herself and her sorrel, then gave him a look over her shoulder. "It's four in the afternoon, Tree."

He glanced at the sky and scratched his cheek again. "Huh," Tree said.

She left him there and headed in a weary saunter out through the trailer park back toward the house. The day had been long and upsetting, and it was far from over yet. First the Bafferts had come and screamed at her and Lou for a big chunk of the morning, their daughter Roene squeezed between them on the living room sofa, a portrait of stylish *YM* heartbreak in her pink acid-wash jeans and whale-spout pony tail. Then the police, and then Helen Piper herself. The grim calmness on Helen's face portended more terrifying wrath than anything the police said or did. When they left, Helen remained in the living room sipping Sanka from an OLD FART coffee mug, one of Lou's favorite vintage novelties.

"Case, hon," she said. "Tell me more about this kid. Cal? Was that his name? Tell me everything you remember about him."

"That isn't his real name," Casey replied.

"So I gathered." She patted the sofa cushion to her left. "Come talk to me."

Lou was in the kitchen, bent in puzzlement over the open dishwasher with a yolk-soiled plate in his hand. The drama had disrupted his breakfast, and he'd had to toss the remainder of his food out cold. Both dishwasher racks were at capacity as it was.

"Just leave that in the sink, Daddy," Casey told him. "It needs to soak anyway."

Lou stared at her, Mason pendant swinging loose at his waist. He was still in his V-neck undershirt.

"More coffee, Mrs. Piper?" she said, returning her attention to Helen.

"I'm good," Helen said, setting the OLD FART cup aside on a chintz Lilies of the Valley coaster. "I'm also not married," she added.

"Pardon?"

"I believe you said 'Mrs.'"

"Oh. Oops." She took a seat on the opposite end of the sofa from Helen. "Why is that, by the way? If you don't mind my asking."

"Why is what?" The mid-morning sunlight seeping through the upturned front blinds had shifted, casting Helen's redoubtably handsome face in something of an unflattering hue. All that money, Casey thought. All the pricey potions of Estée Lauder and Alexandra de Markoff, all the visits to Red Door and Cooper Spa. Lou had told her stories. And still there was no shielding yourself from the cold cruel claws of old age. If old age was indeed to blame. Maybe it was only the light.

"Does she *mind*?" said Lou, wandering back through the living room en route to the hallway. "Hell yeah she *minds*. The woman minds *everything*. If you have to ask, then don't."

He drifted out, and it was just the two women.

"Maybe that's why," said Helen. "You probably recall that your father and I had a dalliance once. And you can see what I got for my trouble."

"Daddy's been a good friend to you."

"And I to him. It's not a zero-sum game, sweetie. But if a man's involved, you can bet your bippy there's always a game of *some* kind afoot. *That's* why I never married. Is this Cal person your main squish?"

"My what?"

"Isn't that what they're calling it nowadays?"

"'Main squeeze,' you mean. No, he isn't. And his real name is Asher."

Helen rose from the sofa and crossed the room. "How long have you known that?"

"Is there some reason why it matters? I knew he didn't want anybody else around here to know who he was. Look, I don't know who half the people in this trailer park are. They're all seasonals, and some of them are pretty shady. I thought we weren't supposed to ask too many questions. Daddy always said it's bad for business. He said you're the one who told him that."

"Did he tell you to give the shady ones jobs?" Helen was glaring at her. "I understand that he hired this kid on your recommendation. Let's just be honest with each other. What was the deal between the two of you?"

"I don't like where this is going." Casey got up herself, folding her arms in withdrawal.

"One more thing then. You know Elfa Schultz, up at the station?"

"I knew Elfa back in high school. What's she got to with any of this?"

"You heard what happened last night. You heard what that kid said about me, about my family, to the whole world."

"No, I didn't. What kid?"

"Cut the shit, will you? You can't be this ignorant!"

"Get lost, Helen." Lou had returned in his jogging suit. Casey, crying, turned to him. "I mean it. Get out."

Helen went to her leather clutch on the sofa and produced a packet of tissue, handing it out to Casey, who accepted it.

"Two whip-smart girls," she said. "And this kid, this what's-his-name from who-the-hell-knows, played the both of you for total dupes. That's the way it looks to me. And now I've got a stolen horse and a shattered reputation because *I* believed the two of you were so smart. You really showed me what's what, didn't you?"

"Enough." Lou took Helen firm by the arm and led her to the door. She permitted this to a point, then halted and flung him off.

"Where is he now?"

Casey had collapsed on the sofa, head in her hands. "How should I know? And what should I care?"

"Right," said Helen. "Naturally you don't care. That's how we got here, isn't it? Do *you* care, Lou? I was just wondering."

"Helen…please." He had deflated suddenly.

"Right," she repeated, and was gone, marching out past the twin black-boy lawn jockeys to her burgundy Lincoln. Tolf Denetclaw was fishing in the canal across the road. Lou had latched the storm door and watched

Helen drive away, exchanging waves with Tolf and standing vigil long after Helen had disappeared up the street towards her racetrack and casino, towards her mansion, towards her privileged and wretched life. Then he had resigned, hands limp at his sides, and faced his daughter.

18

"Get out of my house!"

Daylight. The world had jumped a track somewhere, skipped a beat. In his dream he'd been racing for his very life—riding a white horse in the dead of night at the foot of a Black Mountain, pursued by Shaw Jepsen's two dogs, Willie and Waylon, all too aware that he'd brought the whole situation onto himself—though he couldn't exactly say how he'd done so. At least, at present, he was winning the race. His white horse was beautiful and strong and true, and beauty, truth, and strength always won. And then in the next second he was the frightened, dirty, nameless denizen in the final scene of *The Day After*. A ravaged and delusional Jason Robards loomed unsteady above him, in a trembling rage, his face and scalp a pallid sore-pocked canvas laid waste by radiation sickness, and the world beyond him a ruined, smoking panorama of ash and rubble.

"Get out of my house!"

Except that this Jason Robards spoke Spanish.

"¡Thal de mi catha!"

Ash was slumped against a jagged pile of rock. Sweat on his face, pooling in his eyes and along his upper lip, seeping into his mouth. Skin burning, lips desiccated and cracked. Pain in his legs and arms.

"*Ereth un ladrón de caballoth. ¡Dije que te vayath!*" *You're a horse thief. I said get out!*

A pair of eyes was locked on him, scrutinizing. Were his own eyes closed or open? How long had they been that way? The other eyes were buried in dunes, whole Sahara deserts of wrinkles. The head they belonged to pulled back, revealing an ancient face and upper body clad in a dirty indigo rebozo and neon Bugle Boy breakdancer hat.

"*Thta ween-ah*," said the face.

"Eulalia," said Ash.

The eyes, buried in a sea of dunes, blinked. The woman broke into a toothless smile. For a woman indeed she was—definitely not Jason Robards. Lalia backed away, and beside her appeared a blue-eyed chamoisée LaMancha goat, the nubbin wattles at her throat like dainty beads of candlewax.

Ash recollected collapsing in a ditch. Before that, the chase. Before that….

The old woman turned away and retreated underneath a sheet of flatbed tarp strung across the ditch walls. Behind her, he now saw, Fantasia was slumped against one side of the ditch. He started up in alarm, and a shooting pain down the back of his leg yanked him back. Lalia emerged from the shadows holding out a *Dastardly and Muttley* Slurpee cup filled with something warm, foamy, and brownish. She thrust it in his face.

"*Thta ween-ah,*" she said again, this time in command. He accepted, noting the dirt on the cup and on the old woman's knotted hands. Lifting it reluctantly to his lips, he strained to make out Fantasia's condition from where he sat. Horses could and often did nap on their feet, but they were known to lie down on their sides much like humans when in need of deeper sleep. The question was whether Fantasia was lying down for that reason or because of something else.

"*Ella tiene una pierna mala, pero the curará,*" Lalia told him, reading his thoughts perfectly. *She has a bad leg, but it will heal.*

"*Ereth un ladrón torpe,*" she added, returning to her hut. *You are a clumsy thief.*

"I didn't steal her," he protested in Spanish. "It's not what you think."

"*Creo que tú también ereth un mentirotho torpe,*" the old crone chuckled. "*Cállate y bebe tu medithina.*"

He obeyed. Marzipan and cane alcohol mixed in raw goat milk. In the shadows underneath the tarp he could make out scattered heaps of open cardboard boxes and plastic crates, brand names like Tandy, Soundesign, and Pierre Cardin declaring themselves here and there. Lalia left him and went to a palette laden with beach towels, where she slipped off her orthotic Japanese sandals and sat down Indian style, producing a palofierro tobacco pipe from someplace within her shifting layers of clothing and lighting up. Her eyes gleamed at him in the dark. The LaMancha approached one of the open boxes and dunked its head inside, withdrawing with a striped rayon necktie in its teeth, which it proceeded to eat happily.

Asher finished his drink and made a second attempt at getting up, managing to at least pull himself upright against the slope of black slag at his back. In doing so he discovered his grandfather's service pistol lying in the dirt beneath his right leg. Yes: there had been a long chase, and there had been shooting. And there had been death, for which he was unquestionably responsible.

He returned Lalia's gaze, wondering how much she remembered, how much she could tell him. If anything.

"*Mi bisabuelo fue Mauricio.*" *My great-grandfather was Mauricio.*

"*Ethtáth hablando de ti mithmo,*" replied the hoary crone at once. "*¿Dónde ethtá tu bella novia? Nethethito bendethirla.*"

Crazy. Of course she was bats-in-the-belfry crazy. Ash had feared as much or he would've come looking for her much sooner.

The ground had started to tremble beneath him rhythmically. Asher found his feet at last and scrambled up in time to glimpse a Southern Pacific lead diesel in Kodachrome paint-scheme barrel past atop the slag heap, followed by an almost interminable cargo of double-stacked shipping containers. Fantasia, startled awake, found her legs as well and nearly bolted before he intercepted her with outstretched arms. Eulalia laughed.

"*¡Un ladrón torpe, pero un bailarín agrathiado! ¡Thta ween-ah!*"

The last car rolled out of sight. Now the exact place on Earth where he'd fetched up with Fantasia was revealed. The Black Mountain, *Cerro de*

Muleros, loomed close and disquieting in the daylight, the pilgrims' trail etched up its side standing out sharply like scratched vinyl.

Eulalia approached the horse, arms raised, issuing a strange series of adroit kissing and cooing sounds mixed with pidgin. Fantasia went to her at once. The old woman led her to an inflatable child's wading pool underneath the tarpaulin and bade her drank. It entered his head to ask her how the hell she'd found water up here, and then he wisely dismissed the question. He joined her and the horse in the shade, stroking Fantasia's withers while she drank.

"I have to take her home," he said, more an externalized thought than a communication. But the old woman rebuked him anyway.

"*Te ethtan buthcando. Elloth te matarán.*"

They are looking for you. They will kill you.

The room, the mike, and the turntables were all his. Ash thought of the afternoons he'd spent playing DJ on Tree Pendleton's hi-fi back home in Visalia. He'd had his parents' outdated albums, plus a Ronco collection called *Disco Super Hits*, an Eddie Rabbitt LP, and a Steve Martin album, the one with "King Tut." A smattering of 45's. "Hot Child in the City," ABBA, a local band's state-fair rendition of "The Night the Lights Went Out in Georgia." He hadn't known what DJ-ing actually looked like, whether you sat or stood, what gadgets were involved, the physical layout of the studio. None of which mattered. He paced the trailer like a fevered scientist while the records played, holding one of Tree's 4-H trophies and talking into it between each song, doing his own lead-ins and lead-outs, improvising monologues, repeating jokes he'd picked up from the stable hands, at least the clean ones. He learned to switch out and cue up records singlehanded. Lost in the music, lost in himself.

Do you fantasize a lot? Dr. Tune had asked.

Not a fantasy now. He was really here in Hitman Hayes's chair, in Mandy's chair, spinning the same records, speaking into the same mike… the voice of God. All at once it hit him: the funeral, Simon's words, and the ugly scene that had followed. The truth that had brought him here in the first place. And because it was all so real there was no real choice. There was no Strummer here, there was only Asher Rede. Son of Jared, grandson of Ivan, great-grandson of Mauricio Rede and Helen Piper; great-great grandson of Reverend Doctor Donald Eustace Piper. Rightful heir to the throne. So he harnessed the mighty voice and he spoke the truth.

And then Jaz, the station engineer, was in the studio with him. Asher hadn't known he was even on the premises.

"*Now* you've gone and done it," he said entering the broadcast booth, Birkenstocks clapping on the floor tile. He pulled the boom mike away from Asher and gestured for him to get up out of the chair. "I don't know which I liked better, the part where you burned Helen Piper or the part where you burned Simon. It was all beautiful, man. Never thought I'd see anyone stroll in here and hang both those fascist hypocrites out to dry using their own goddamn radio station. And now—you have to run."

"Run?"

"They're right outside. They'll be *inside* in about half a hot minute. I locked and bolted the front doors, but that only gives you an extra few seconds. I'll distract them, make it look like you ran out the back towards the church. You can take the attic stairs and climb out from the roof down that dead boxelder out front. I've done it myself."

There was a crash from the direction of the front desk.

"Better haul ass, *disidente*." He was grinning. It would be the last time Asher saw him alive.

"Right. Thanks, Jaz." Asher snatched his barrel bag from the floor and darted out of the room. There was cursing and commotion at the far end of the hallway. He slipped into the dark record library just as someone, or a couple of someones, rushed past towards the studio and began shouting obscenities at Jaz in Spanish. He sidled along the wall's old beadboard wainscoting until he reached the attic stairs, which were permanently extended for ready access to the transmission lines. Then he shouldered his bag crossways and climbed up.

At the top of the stairs he heard a gunshot and froze. The attic was pitch-dark. This was all too real.

You can't cover the sun with a finger.

Asher squeezed his eyes shut and waited. The voices below barked, footsteps succeeded, and then the barking was further in the distance. Jaz's diversion had worked.

When he opened them again his eyes had adjusted. Now the attic was bathed in blood, pulsing with it, and a demon shape hovered before him. Its body exoskeletal, bent and obscene with wrong geometry, its eyes throbbing with that same venomous crimson light.

El diablo sabe más por viejo que por diablo.

He seized it in both hands, ready to murder it, have it out once and for all right here, wrestle the vicious, smothering, hectoring s.o.b. to both their deaths. His fingers were greeted with the touch of cold metal and cobwebs. The weight of the thing surprised him and it toppled, clanking raucously to the floor. He bounded away from it in a clumsy pirouette and crashed into a stack of crates. He was back in the Rede family shed, and the punishing sting of a striped-tailed scorpion was next. But instead a bottle of pills tumbled into his hand. *Flor...ex*, it said on the moldering label in the blood-red pulsing light. *He...cho...en...Mex...ico*. He flung the loathsome fat bottle away just as if it had stung him and it exploded somewhere in the dark, spitting glass and pellet-like pills in every direction. Now an apparition appeared across the room. Hitman Hayes, clad in cape and cravat and wayfarer sunglasses, cringing and leering in mock surprise. A life-size giveaway glow-poster.

The bloody light throbbed with greater intensity, a soundless heartbeat, alive and adamant. Ash trained his eyes upward and beheld its source. A hatch door in the roof was propped open, a dubious old Lattistep wooden ladder at the ready just beneath. Outside, the cloudless night sky, a speckling of stars, and the XAMO transmitter mast tower flashing its red aircraft beacon.

Time to run.

He unshouldered his barrel bag and located the .45, his hands shaking. What had that gunshot down there meant? And who was running the booth? Crazily he imagined Elfa's profound disappointment in him when she learned he'd let the station go to dead air. *It's, like, the deadliest sin in radio.* The cold mistrust he'd worked so hard to thaw returning to her eyes immediately, now with a hot vengeance. What the Christ had he done?

¡Corre, maldita sea!

It was the thought of Fantasia that set him in motion. Maybe they'd taken her already. Like Elfa she was likely to never trust him again. He tucked the gun into the waist of his jeans and re-shouldered the bag.

A length of paracord had been strung from inside the hatch door to the sloped edge of the roof, right where the dead boxelder stood. Ash took it and stood up on the rooftop with his back to the edge, intuiting that Jaz had installed the cord there as a sort of rappelling line to avoid slipping on the clay tiles—no time to dwell on why Jaz himself had ever needed such a setup at all.

He reached the roof's edge and dropped himself into the crotch between two perfectly situated limbs. On an underbranch to his left lay an alligator roach clip, an unfinished spliff caught in its jaws.

Now he could see Fantasia near the water fountain. Simon La Paz stood beside her in a white linen suit, stroking her face and whispering sweet nothings in Spanish. He was otherwise alone. Ash slid out of the tree and drew the pistol, raising it as he approached, training the gunsight on Simon's broad, bronzed forehead and gripping the .45 just as his grandfather Ivan had taught him on their winter boar hunts. The wild thudding in his chest and throat belied the newfound steadiness of his hands. When he was sure Simon knew he was there, he stopped.

"This is very unwise of you, *disidente*." Simon offered his upraised palms in surrender. "Unwise and uncalled-for. *Que malo. Que vergonzoso.*"

"Get away from her."

"Having said that, I'm not angry with you, *disidente*. Your resentment at the Pipers is to be understood. And the slanders you made tonight against me and my ministry are also to be forgiven under the circumstances."

Simon's eyes were still on Fantasia.

"Your taste in music leaves much to be desired, of course. As long as we're being honest with each other."

Now he was looking at Asher directly, open-mouthed smile affirming his essential calmness much as the jest had affirmed his smarmy, imperturbable confidence. Yes, it was all really real, and these people really meant to kill him.

"You won't make it across tonight, you or your beautiful horse." Simon tilted his head towards the black stretch of *despoblado* to the north. The lights of Nueva Anapra glittered in a thin, beckoning razor line against the interposing pocket of darkness.

"Fuck you," said Asher as the first bullet sliced the air near his chin. He fired the pistol in reaction and Simon jumped, cursing. There were shouts from the others returning from their search expedition at Ministerio La Paz. Fantasia recoiled and Asher chased her, fearing that in her panic she'd step on the blue cotton rope he'd used as a tether and hurt herself. He caught her and took the saddle as another bullet whizzed by. A head wearing red-trim Swatch sunglasses popped up from behind Simon's Maxima, parked at the station's front entrance. The man the head belonged to raised his gun, and Ash fired one-handed while yet distractedly trying to free Fantasia from the tether. The Maxima's rear windshield exploded.

Simon had landed in the water fountain. Struggling to stand and sopping wet, he had produced a Glock from somewhere inside his linen suit. He aimed it at Asher once he made it to his feet, the imperturbable smirk at last satisfactorily banished from his face, only to discover the Glock's slide-stop was jammed.

Ash reached the fence and tugged loose the quick-release knot that he'd tied there. He gathered as much of the slack as he could and spurred Fantasia out through the open gate. The moonless night might've been an advantage if not for his white horse, but even so he was mindful enough in his frenzy and terror to curse the moon and not the horse.

Moments later he was cursing himself. In only seconds they'd come to the dirt road leading down off of the mesa and he still hadn't managed to retrieve the remainder of the lead rope. Now it caught between Fantasia's hind legs and they were both skidding and then tumbling, horse and rider, ass over teakettle, first together and then separately, over the road's unlined edge and down the sharp rocky incline to the desert floor below.

To her credit, Fantasia found her hooves sooner than he found his feet. When he came to she was nuzzling his shoulder, with an occasional lick against his neck. The sky was a fierce menagerie of stars overhead. The Milky Way arched above him. *I'm really sorry about all this*, Ash thought as her slick eel-like tongue tasted his ear.

A splash of headlights somewhere overhead shattered the spell, and he heard what had to be the four-stroke engine in Simon's Maxima screeching in high holy dudgeon down the sloped road above. In pursuit of him, no doubt. Since he wasn't dead it seemed like a good time to get up and keep running. But run where? The engine sped away in the same direction he'd been planning to flee, which meant they'd have caught up with him already if he'd actually gone that way. Simon was right: there was no crossing the *despoblado*, at least for now.

The Black Mountain.

A freight train was moving in fast from the east along the foothills at the mountain's base. What the railroaders used to call a hotshot, gauging by its velocity.

Little by little, one goes far.

He'd come this far, hadn't he?

As he swung back into the saddle a whistling sound pierced the night somewhere close by. Fantasia lifted her head. Then a familiar voice, echoing in the distance: "*Estás perdido, gaucho?*"

He kicked Fantasia into a hard gallop, guiding her towards the moving train's headlamp. Then another pair of car headlights came into view on the opposite side of the tracks—and another, this one sporting an extra set of flood lamps. They were waiting for him…but with any luck, hadn't yet spotted him. He had to put the train between himself and them while making a run for the mountain. After that he wasn't sure. He would need the old *mesteñero*'s help.

More crazy thoughts as he crossed the desert. Lex's Mantenna toy. Ash's little brother tended to leave his *He-Man and She-Ra* paraphernalia all over the goddamn house—you could run into those demented nightmarish mutant figures just about anywhere, but Mantenna had a way of turning up most often: between sofa cushions, buried in the laundry hamper under the stinky skid-marked whites, and once even in the fridge crisper. Repugnant bat-eared thing with bloodshot eyeballs on extendable plastic stalks. You picked it up, it was like a reminder of everything out there that hated you. Then, once, Asher had caught an episode of *She-Ra* while Lex sat rapt with it on the den floor one Saturday morning. Turns out that Mantenna is a figure of comic relief. The real baddie, Hordak, dumps Mantenna down a trap door every episode, usually moments before Mantenna begs him not to. You could actually feel sorry for the dimwitted hapless motherfucker.

Max Headroom. Another mutant; another poser. "Catch the wave!" Elfa had pinned the character's picture, cut from a full-page ad in *Rolling Stone*, to the studio bulletin board, devil's horns and pitchfork craftily doodled onto it in black Sharpie. She was an excellent hate-doodler. The *Like a Virgin* LP cover where she'd transformed Madonna into an aging prostitute, haggard and wrinkled, a half-wasted cigarette jutting from her lips. The spider webs, black eyes, and thick drooping tongues she drew on trade magazines. Her scorching hatred for New Coke. Opposing posers was her true and singular passion; music came in a close second. Until today he'd believed that mutual hatred of fake people and things had brought him and Elfa together and would naturally keep them together, but it had only done so for Mandy and Strummer. Elfa and Asher were still total strangers.

In his peripheral vision he saw the two sets of car headlights change direction and speed. They'd sighted him. He cut the distance with the train until the lead engine sped by so close he could see a startled brakeman's face in the cab window. When he thought he'd put enough of the train between him and the two cars he eased up on Fantasia and turned her around, assessing. The train's air horn sounded just as a pickup, the one with the floodlights, leapt the tracks and landed in a swirl of dust.

Asher kicked his horse into a renewed gallop. No, she was never going to trust him again after this. Who could blame her?

The twin track lines began to diverge as they entered the curve rounding the Black Mountain. The westbound line branched off and hugged the mountain base while the eastbound continued at a steeper grade onto the mountain itself. He chose the steep one in the hopes that it would be narrower, too narrow for a pickup truck. He looked back again to catch sight of the pickup trailing him and another train already approaching from the opposite direction. As the tracks fell away to his left the Piper mansion shifted into view. Crisscrossing bullet lights traced elegant figures up the pink stucco walls, accenting the tiled window overhangs and the arcade piers along the east wing. A pair of geese loitered near the champagne-lit spray fountain. He could imagine himself riding Fantasia down there, scattering the geese and leading the murderous assholes behind him right to Helen's doorstep—tragically disturbing her evening—if not for the iron fence all around the place.

Mi novia infiel.

He checked again over his shoulder. The pickup had stopped where the west tracks split away and the eastbound line began its ascent. Ash lightly tugged Fantasia's right rein, cueing her to slow down. The barrel bag's shoulder strap had migrated up into his neck muscles, slicing into them, and the gun was threatening to tumble from the waist of his jeans. Still he kept Fantasia going until the tracks bent a little further around the mountain and the pickup truck had slid out of sight. Sweat in his eyes, in his crotch. It was a stifling June night, the vintage Palmer dial-thermometer back in the XAMO studio having rested at close to eighty even near midnight. The oncoming train sounded its horn somewhere behind him. At last he brought Fantasia to a halt and dismounted, pausing to stroke her face and neck in gratitude before straightening up his own disheveled self.

"I'm really sorry about all this," he told her out loud this time. "Everything is just so fucked. Have you ever noticed that? Or am I the only one?"

A sound close by, something like a woman's laughter, and he half-expected Persis to appear from the shadows behind the next mountain crag and come on to him again. But he'd left her behind in Anapra, so it had to be his imagination. Again the train's air horn sounded, closer now. He removed the pistol from his jeans and decided to set the safety before replacing it there. This whole caper would really be all for naught if he accidentally shot his own dick off and lay here bleeding to death on the mountainside.

And then he heard them.

The second train's headlamp appeared in the distance, moving up the eastbound track. In the shadows between it and the mountain slope two small figures, low to the ground and light as wraiths, flew toward him alongside it. Underneath the air horn's declamatory howl he could hear the two figures barking.

Willie and Waylon? How the fuck—?

Fantasia started, hind legs stiffening as if she wanted to bolt. Ash held her just long enough to remount, after which she needed no spurring.

Strummer had found his lost legs—because they'd never been lost. The terrorist bit was a lie, as was his degree in parapsychology. All a quaint fabrication. Strummer's real name was Phil Sumner, and he'd begun his career as a rant poet before shifting to journalism at London's *Melody Maker* and *New Musical Express*. He met Fantille in a Munich nightclub and formed their disco-duo union that same night. Fantille's real name was Casey—no, Connie—Schultz. On their first tour together they'd concocted alter egos for each other to enthrall the press and amuse themselves. Like Ziggy Stardust, Sgt. Pepper, Alice Cooper, and Bob

Dylan, Fantille and Strummer had sprung to life as a matter of convenience as much as art.

El que nace pa' tamal, del cielo le caen las hojas.

The dogs were gaining, the light staccato of their paws on the loose rocks as distinct and relentless as the diesel's thrum or the beat of Fantasia's hooves. Meanwhile the tracks and the mountainside to which they clung bent sharply away into deepening darkness. Now it was his turn to trust Fantasia, who seemed to anticipate the path ahead without seeing it, leaning into the curve with no guidance from the reins.

Something snatched the leg of his jeans and let go, then snatched again, taking a fresh sliver of skin from his calf with it. There was no reason to look. Asher pulled the gun from his jeans and fired blindly just above his lower leg; the thing released him with an anguished cry. The distance ahead illuminated now as the eastbound hotshot's headlamp drew close from behind. Here where the railroaders had once blasted into the mountainside, exposing the layer of andesite beneath, the rock turned white—a white scar on the black mountain. The world before him in monochrome negative. Reality raw and exposed. His faithless mother in her Pond's night mask. Mauricio lying dead in his coffin. So too the old man, the "doctor," *tatarabuelo*, his embalmed face collapsed and blanched—then hideously rouged and dolled and lying in sainted repose among crisp folds of satin, in the kind of ultimate mockery of all justice that only rotten money could buy. Helen Piper screaming at his father to get out, Simon La Paz intervening.

The other dog had closed in on the right, stealing into the narrow space between Fantasia and the mountain wall. Ash switched the pistol to his other hand, and true to Shaw Jepsen's prediction, when he pulled the trigger this time it jammed. The freight train's horn wailed as the engineer had likely seen him—no doubt in dumbfounded shock. The dog leapt for Asher's forearm and he clouted it with the gun. This time an enraged snarl rather than a cry of pain.

My turn, he thought, directing this at Fantasia. *You're the best friend I've made out here. Trust me one last time and I'll ask nothing more of you.*

And trust him she did. Together they leapt in front of the oncoming train and into the ditch beyond it.

The witch Lalia had to be eighty years old at the very least. The way Mauricio told it, she'd already achieved cronehood fifty years ago, so ninety was a better guess. One hundred wasn't out of the question either. She and her goat disappeared that afternoon while Ash and Fantasia rested. Ash woke for the second time in the shade of the tarp, this time feeling somewhat less worse-for-the-wear. The old witch's magic drink had done the trick. Fantasia was on her feet and sniffing at a Hawaiian Tropic crate. It came to him then that he'd journeyed to Nueva Anapra, in effect, to find a horse. A faithful female at last—just not the one he'd hoped for.

The shadow cast by the tarp had changed direction, lengthening away to the east. Asher stood up and went out into the sunlight, pausing to exchange greetings with Fantasia. While rubbing her neck he stared once more up at the Black Mountain, at the trail his *bisabuelo* helped build. While living on the Piper estate, Mauricio had befriended the people of La Esmelda and volunteered what spare hours he had—when not tending to the Pipers' horses or, later, to Helen herself—moving rocks and hauling dirt and erecting the fourteen Stations of the Cross at strategic points along the more than two miles of winding trail. In those days, Mauricio said, the monument at the very top had been a simple wooden cross. Only later, back in California, did he learn that the *esmeltianos* had cobbled together the funds to hire a renowned Catalan sculptor to craft a permanent limestone cross. Recalling this had clearly made him a little blue.

"*Me gustaría haber vista eso,*" he said.

So would I, thought Asher. There it shone above him in the brilliant daylight, though from here it was hardly more than a white speck.

The sound of an off-road vehicle approaching. As if by sorcery Lalia and her goat popped into sudden view on a ridge some hundred yards away, near the first of the mountain trail's several zigzag turns. Her garish neon hat was cocked askew on her head. She made an impatient movement with her arm, a warning to him. Taking the hint, Ash returned underneath the shelter, tugging the end of Fantasia's halter as he went and leading her out of sight. The vehicle came to a stop by the railroad tracks just above the tarp, the engine idling. A door swung open and footsteps crunched the dirt along the tarp's edge mere inches from Fantasia's raised head.

"*¡Oye!*" cried the old hag from her perch further up the mountain. "*¿Qué quiereth, éthtupido? ¡Aléjate de mi catha!*"

273

"*Con permiso, Lalia,*" returned a man's voice. "*¿Has visto algún extraño en el barrio?*"

A spate of shrill, improbably melodic cackling erupted at this; every nearby crevice, slope, and outcropping seemed to laugh in agreement with Lalia. Must be how she got her name, Asher thought.

"*¡Fuithte un extraño aquí una veth, pendejo! ¡Yo tambien! ¡Athí fuimoth todoth nothotroth!*"

"*Perdóneme, señora,*" the man answered in plain exasperation. The vehicle's suspension groaned as he climbed back in behind the wheel and swung the door shut.

"*¡Etho eth theñorita, cretino! ¡Todavía no thoy una theñora!*"

It seemed only moments from the time the visitor drove off that Lalia and her goat came in leisurely fashion around the ditch's curve and back inside the makeshift tent. The untethered goat seemed content to follow her anywhere. She approached Asher and from the shifting rags that wrapped her body appeared two packages of yellow cheese and crackers and a cold bottle of Big Red.

"*Llévate.*"

He accepted the repast, a hunger like he'd never imagined roused immediately in his gut as he tore the wrapping from the crackers. Lalia took her place on the palette, brought her pipe out once more, and watched him devour the meal she'd consecrated in secret before he could lay hands on it.

"Debeth ir a la thima de la montaña," she said. *You must go to the mountaintop.*

He'd been thinking the same himself, but only because of Mauricio's late words, which she couldn't have known anything about.

"Why?" he asked her.

Lalia said nothing.

19

The Cortinas family ranch in tiny Canutillo, Texas, had found an unlikely way to thrive in those early Depression years. The *charreadas* had returned to Old Mexico, and north of the border the same appetite for the old ways (confined as they were now to arena theatrics) was almost as strong.

The young *mestenero* arrived on a peach truck from Tulare, his whole earthly fortune amounting to no more than the worthless Tagus Ranch scrip in his dungaree pockets. The Cortinases needed experienced hands for their horses, not for picking fruit, and better still they paid cash. By summer's end he was not only their most trusted stable hand, but he was also a star in each Sunday's rodeo. His specialty event was the *Paso de la Muerte*, in which he leaped from his own mount to an unbridled and untamed mustang mare.

It was during one such afternoon pageant when Mauricio first glimpsed the doctor and his beautiful daughter watching from the whitewashed stone risers. The doctor in his spectacles, goatee, and white summer suit; the redheaded girl, fourteen, in lace dress and feathered headband. They were there again the Sunday that followed, and again each Sunday after that, often accompanied by a third spectator—like the chubby lady soothsayer, or Goossens, the tall *maricon*. The girl rarely smiled or exhibited reaction of any kind to the dangerous feats on display before her, her congenital pout accentuated by thin, pencil-drawn Dietrich eyebrows and Carmine lipstick. A face as placid and unreadable as still sea waters. Until he fell during the Pass of Death.

Something in her impassive, uncaring, achingly beautiful face had done it: taunted Mauricio to the point of near-suicide. He'd just managed the leap, taking the bucking white-faced *grulla* as the three *charros* behind him held formation, pinning her into the thinnest possible lane along the arena wall. He gripped the enraged *grulla*'s mane while she thrusted and contorted her every available muscle against him, and he steeled himself for the last *suerte*, the final trick: dismounting her, still on his feet, before she could throw him. All this in a matter of seconds. The other *charros* drew away, allowing him room. The young *mesteñero*'s mind ticked through the same fluid, instantaneous calculations that it had so many hundreds of times before, and then Mauricio permitted himself a moment's recklessness: he looked up into the arena and sought the girl's face. Today she sported a summer cloche, the gold-ochre sisal enclosing her wan features with a delicate French ringlet escaping on either side. A single arrow-shaped ribbon jutted from the cloche's brim. He met her eyes and held them—or had she held his?

His body still in motion, the young *mesteñero*'s spurs hit the arena dirt too soon; his heels lodged at an angle, only for a fraction of a second, but it was all the invitation the mare needed. Next she was dragging him by the arm, his saddle whip momentarily caught, and then he slammed face-first into the hot sunbaked loam and she was trampling him with extra spite. He had dislocated his arm.

Moises, the rancher's eldest son, helped him out of the arena before a roaringly appreciative crowd, and after coaxing him to swallow a few hits of mescal on a bench behind the horse stalls, he used an old *sobador*'s trick to pop the bone back into place. When Mauricio found his senses he was lying on his back on the same bench, and the rich white doctor was staring down at him, smiling. The man's daughter stood poised and aloof just behind, her porcelain face as inscrutable as it was in the arena.

"By god, boy, you're a sight to behold," the doctor told him in adequate if unwieldy Spanish. "It looks as though you finally ran out of Luck today. Fortuna's Wheel has betrayed us both. My Helen here and I had a bet riding on you, and now I've lost a silver dollar as a result. I believe you owe me a favor."

At last, Helen smiled.

The favor entailed Mauricio agreeing to train and look after the señorita's five horses and two ponies, an appointment that also necessitated his coming to live full-time on the Piper estate. So one day in early September he rode his own Cerbat bay, a parting gift of honor from the

Cortinases, ten miles south to Nueva Anapra along a road named for a battle in the war with Mexico. The road came to an end at the foot of the Black Mountain, in whose shadow a turnoff led to the red-brick neoclassic hospital building, and on a hill beyond it, to the pink Piper mansion.

As he neared the mountain Mauricio felt the air change somehow, becoming denser, a living presence. Paloma, his mount, lifted her head high and snorted, ears twitching as if she sensed danger. He bent forward in the saddle to pat her neck and yanked his hand away when a shock detonated against the end of his finger as if he'd touched a bare lamp socket. Withdrawing his arm, he observed filaments of Paloma's black mane floating upright, a sight so strange that his blood went still and his mouth went dry.

The girl Helena met him astride an overo paint horse near the mansion gates and led him down to the stables. She looked emphatically Plain Jane, for once, in a simple gingham blouse and jodhpurs.

"It isn't the mountain," she answered Mauricio in Spanish when he told her about the electric shock. "Don't you know where you are?"

With one calfskin-gloved hand she pointed to a mesa in the distance, where the massive directional antenna for her father's radio station dominated the horizon.

The utility bungalow behind the stables contained a small living quarters with a single bunk and wash basin. He unpacked his few belongings and went out to the stables, where he introduced himself to his new wards, all of them magnificent, tastefully chosen beasts. Later that night he dined on smoked ox tongue in champagne sauce, a guest of Helena and her father along with Zerina Price and Goossens, the four of them waited upon by a Chinese butler named Seong. After dinner Goossens, resplendent in his satin-lined cape and beret, regaled them in the magnificent great-room with a Passacaglia and Fugue by Bach, followed by a recent Tin Pan Alley tune called "Stars in My Eyes," on the Aeolian. At the song's peak, Helena, seated in the chair beside him, touched his hand. He turned to her in question, but the young woman's unreadable mantis-colored eyes were fixed on Goossens.

El que nace pa' tamal, del cielo le caen las hojas. This oft-repeated assurance from his mother Beatriz occurred to Mauricio then. The girl Helena wanted him here—this daughter of the rich white *curandero* of men's testicles—but why him exactly? Moises had told him the stories. The girl's mother dead by way of her father's clumsy scalpel, or so the rumors went. The doctor's reputation as a quack belying his popularity among the people of Anapra, whom he lavished with charity. And the girl's reputation, at least outside the rodeo arena, as a *consentida*, spoiled and wanton and pitiless. The two of them could surely have lured a pricier and more pedigreed trainer from one of the famous ranches, had they—had *she*—wanted to do so. Mauricio was skilled and experienced with horses but he had no name. On some of the nights that followed, often on the edge of sleep in his new (if slender) bed, Mauricio permitted himself to relive his moment's recklessness that day during the Pass of Death, when she'd held his gaze, for that moment had now changed his life. Did he dare to imagine what else the beautiful girl's gaze, and her subsequent decision that *he* be caretaker of her beloved horses, might signify? Her touching his hand that first night seemed a ready answer.

Yet he was not invited back up to the house for dinner on any of those ensuing nights, nor, indeed, was he invited to set foot in the majestic main house ever again. The girl Helena's aspect and manner toward him in the weeks thereafter was firm, distant, and businesslike. Gradually Mauricio came to understand that he had misunderstood, and gradually he came to find solace in his own folly. The prospect of coupling with the girl made for pleasant fantasy, but that was all it could ever be. A world in which such an improbable coupling occurred, after all, would be a world that made little sense to him from that point forward.

He concentrated on his work. The girl's favorite was Wahnfried, the thoroughbred descended from Captain Byerley's famous black stallion. Then there was Parfait, the mare paint horse; the doctor's white appaloosa, named Chantilly; and Gordo, the mixed-breed; plus the two ponies. The organist Goossens also fancied himself an equestrian and came to the stables frequently during the day, if the doctor had no chauffeuring for him to do. One afternoon Mauricio was grooming Wahnfried in his stall when he reached behind him for the flick brush and touched a human leg instead. It was Goossens, who stood watching him with one arm hooked over the stall board, his wavy black hair fallen over the side of his face and his glazed bloodshot eyes revealing him to be drunk. Dr. Piper kept a plenteous liquor cabinet.

"She adores that German stud, doesn't she?"

"*¿Mande?*" said Mauricio, his hand shrinking back. Goossens smiled and nodded unsteadily.

"*Mis disculpas*," he offered, loosening his herring scarf with one absent hand. "*Ella simplemente adora a…uh…*" He looked momentarily confused.

"My English is good," said Mauricio, standing.

"Ah, so it is." He removed his arm from the board and ran his languid fingers through that loose flap of hair. "What part of Mexico are you from, anyway? Jalisco? Sinaloa? I once toured the central states during my Peabody Institute days. Mexico City is one of my favorite places on Earth."

"I come from California," Mauricio replied. "I have never once seen Mexico."

Goossens made a long comical face. "Pity, that. Perhaps you'll let me show you a good time in Ciudad Juárez then. I know a couple of swell jolly-up joints, a little out of the way but worth it."

A distant explosion disturbed the afternoon quiet beyond the stables. Both men paused to take in the plume of chalky white smoke that had sprouted on the Black Mountain.

"Those Smeltertowners are really going to the races today with that confounded dynamite," Goossens observed. "Celebrating their legal victory, no doubt. Maybe now isn't the best time for a ride after all." He winked at Mauricio. "Timing is so very vital an element in so many of life's endeavors, isn't it?" Then he half-swaggered, half-staggered off in the general direction of the main house.

The jarring periodic explosions had troubled Mauricio as well, mainly because they troubled the horses. Unlike him, they seemed to have made their peace with the electrified air, but the activity on the mountain was clearly something new and unusual to them. When Helena emerged from the house for her predawn ride the next morning, he decided to ask her whom Goossens had meant by "Smeltertowners." Her routine included a leisurely, meditative ride each daybreak before school, followed by rigorous barrel-racing practice sessions in the afternoons. By the doctor's edict Mauricio accompanied her on the early-morning rides, maintaining a respectful distance as the girl roamed the foothill trails behind the house in silence.

Outfitted already in her maroon schoolgirl jersey and sateen necktie for the day ahead, Helena chose a different trail on each morning ride. There were more of them in the area than Mauricio had first expected. Sometimes she led him north along the dusty banks of the Rio Grande, letting her horse stop to sniff through the saltgrass and thistle; others across the scrub-brush basin into Anapra, where they ascended the mesa on the Mexican side and paused underneath the great radio-station towers and took in the sunrise. The dangerous power hummed overhead and in the very ground beneath, and fine strands of the girl's red hair danced in the morning glow, her eyes afire. At such moments Mauricio could gather nothing of her thoughts or mood. Or indeed at any moment. But right or wrong, in private he also wanted her as he'd never wanted any woman before in his life. For without a doubt, she was no girl at such moments but a grown woman. After holding for a bit, this wily, willful young woman would then turn her horse away and lead him back to the house.

But today it was she who broke the silence. Mauricio had been working up the nerve to inquire about the Black Mountain.

"Do you know what I really want right now?" she said.

"Pardon?"

Helen looked him in the eyes for the first time since that day in the arena. The emotions at play on her face just then were a study in contradiction, all that youthful innocence mingled with some terrible calamitous knowledge. Which, taken together, was a vast improvement over the nothingness that had been there before. At last the waters were stirring.

"*Cajeta*," she said. "I want *cajeta* for breakfast. Come on."

She led him down off the mesa and into the Hooverville-style colonia at the bottom, where, outside a tarpaper shack, a white-haired grandmother with a colony of moles invading one side of her face cooked them *panqueques de dulce de leche* over an open fire. The sun now stood well above the horizon.

"You will be late for school, Miss," said Mauricio. Helena removed her necktie, draping it on the copper frame of her wobbly high-back chair. Mauricio was squatted uncomfortably on an old shoe-shiner's stool.

"There's no school today—see?" She cocked her head toward some shirtless children playing Shanghai with a broken broomstick. The old woman handed Mauricio and Helena each a hot, sticky fried tortilla in a red clay *cazuela* bowl. Scrawny chickens pecked the ground at their feet while they ate.

"Oh, balls," Helen said after dropping the last bit of tortilla hungrily into her mouth, her eyes fixed on the mesa from where they'd just come. Mauricio looked, and a figure on horseback stood poised at the mesa's edge, then sprung to life, the horse dashing down the dirt road leading to the colonia.

"Oh no you don't, nancy-boy!" Helena cried, seizing Mauricio's arm.

"Who is that?"

"Why, who do you think? It's Goose, that beastly fruit fly. He's supposed to drive me to school, but he's not going to today. Come on."

In a heartbeat she'd swung onto her ride and sped off. Mauricio made a hasty apology to the grandmother and followed suit. He took the saddle just as Goossens, in his mackinaw waistcoat and German top hat, reached the colonia outskirts astride Chantilly, Dr. Piper's own prized appaloosa. It also became immediately clear that Goossens had lost control of his horse. He fell to one side, hat tumbling off, and hugged his mount by the neck. He tended to ride the same way he sat at the organ console—knees pinched together, hands flat—and like as not, three sheets to the wind; so even under normal circumstances his rides seldom ended well. Mauricio was torn. Stay and assist Goossens or catch up to Helena? The both of them propended towards trouble. Fortunately a pot-bellied man near the settlement's edge, face lathered for shaving, appeared from behind a clothesline and waved the white appaloosa down.

He spurred Paloma in the opposite direction, just catching sight of Helena's red ponytail flitting as she maneuvered her horse between two shanties at the settlement's far end. Her fine riding posture, her seasoned barrel-racer's keenness, was the living anathema to Goossens's slovenly antics.

After clearing the Anapra settlement Helena looked back only once, and Mauricio understood that the chase wasn't over yet: she required *him* to chase her. Except now the pursuit implied an invitation, not an escape. Would he pursue her no matter which way she went, or how far? Was his only care seeing her off to school, like Goossens? If not, what did he mean to do with her when—and if—he caught up? All this she telegraphed to him simply by way of the deft dancelike movements she coaxed from Wahnfried.

For a crazy moment or two he thought she might actually light out for Juárez, vanishing for good into old Mexico, perhaps forming her own band of *soldaderas*. But instead Helena veered left toward the Black Mountain and its neighboring hills. At long last he found her standing idle beside her horse, as though she'd been waiting there patiently for hours, on a sage-speckled bajada overlooking the copper smelter on the American side of the river. An 800-foot chimney soared over the smelter grounds, and a Southern Pacific freighter was steaming in over a trellis bridge towards it.

"'Snails...*that* took you long enough," she told him.

"Miss, your father will be angry with us. Why are we here?"

Helena pouted and leaned up close against her horse, her back to the saddle, pressing herself into Wahnfried's protective, muscular frame. In less than an instant she'd transformed from brash, strong-willed woman to craven, fickle-hearted child.

"I swear I have not the feeblest inkling what you're talking about," she replied in singsong coyness. "And besides that, whatever are *you* doing here, young man? You didn't have to come following me over the hills and far away, but you did, didn't you? Why on earth would you care what happens to little old me? Just go ahead and explain yourself. I've got all day."

She bit her lower lip and eyed him closely. The obvious answer—on the tip of his tongue an instant ago—was that her father had commanded Mauricio to stay with her on her morning rides. But the obvious answer would mean nothing to her. Neither, it seemed, did it mean a thing to him anymore as well.

"*El gato tiene tu lengua, ya veo,*" said Helena.

To his credit, Goossens pursued them steadfast all morning and well into the afternoon. The white appaloosa materialized once again on the desert floor when Helena and Mauricio stood in each other's arms on the bajada above. So they reluctantly ended their embrace, and Mauricio led the two horses on foot while Helena, out in front, navigated a rocky path down the other side to the Rio Grande. At the river's edge they stopped and climbed back onto their horses. The river waters were impassible, swollen with runoff from the late summer rains. On the far side before the smelter lay a village of tightly arrayed adobe and brick houses, modest in appearance but more permanent in nature than the homes in the Anapra settlement. Smeltertown.

They turned their horses north, following the riverbank with Helena in the lead.

"Have you ever been to New York City?" she called out to him over her shoulder, apropos of nothing. "We can stay at the Astor, see the Follies, take in the races at Belmont. You'll love the Follies—the beautiful costumes, the tableaux vivants."

An explosion high above pierced the relative calm. They had passed underneath the railroad bridge, and the Black Mountain's prominent steeple-like pinnacle shifted into view, overlooking the smelter and the two cities beyond it. A trail lined with human figures etched its way about two-thirds of the distance up the mountain face. The back-and-forth movements along the trail suggested a chain-gang furiously at work. Another plume of white smoke hovered near the spot where the trail terminated, no doubt marking the source of the latest explosion. Helena halted and Mauricio pulled up alongside her. A strange, remote, puzzled look had come over her face.

"Look at them," she said reflectively. Her eyes followed the trail of chain-gang workers on the mountain. "Slaving away for nothing, placing their own lives at risk just so they can put a silly cross up at the top. Daddy tried to buy the mountain from them last year. He wanted to put a new transmitter tower up there, something called television. Radio with pictures, if you can believe that. The funny thing is he would've used it to do his preaching, and he would've reached more people all over the world with it than that silly cross ever will."

"Perhaps this is the way that God wants it to be," Mauricio observed.

"Well that's all wet. Why would God be so stupid?"

To this Mauricio could summon no answer. She didn't seem to notice, moving her head sharply a moment later as if detecting something out of the corner of her eye—which, of course, she had.

"My, poor Goose is quite determined this time," she said in mild wonder. "He's never pursued me this far before. Let's see if he's willing to go the distance."

And they were off again, hugging the river as it sidled north into the farm valley of lower Nuevo Mexico. The rows of dark-green chile-pepper plants lay ready for harvest; the mature stalks in the corn fields stood desiccated and drab, skeletal platoons on a forgotten battlefield. Monarchs and orange ladybugs flitted and danced in the golden sunlight. Meanwhile the white appaloosa continued trailing them. Whenever Helena decided Goossens was closing in, she and Mauricio would spur their horses up onto the levee road and switch to full gallops, Helena laughing in delight at the organist's foolish persistence.

Still tracking the river, they approached a pecan grove with trees that stretched away indefinitely on either side of each bank. Mauricio eyed the sun, adjudging the time to be about noon.

"We should be going back now, *mi amor*," he suggested. "The horses will be fatigued."

Helena shot a sudden, overjoyed grin his way upon hearing the new term of endearment. "You're right, yes. But let's rest a little in the shade first."

They came down from the levee side-by-side and crept into the dim flooded orchard, the horses' hooves splashing in the freshly released irrigation water. The pecan trees were well-grown and thickly canopied. Rather than resting, they chased one other on horseback, playing hide-and-seek among the trees. Mauricio finally caught her near the head canal, and while kissing each other they fell from their horses and tumbled together into the water, ending up beside a deserted thresher with her astride his waist.

"*Estoy tan feliz,*" she said.

"*Yo también,*" he replied.

Her pale naked body. Her silken Botticelli hair-braid tickling his face. The mingled scents of moist earth, human sweat, and Shalamar. And cruelest of all: "*Te quiero mucho.*" They both whispered it.

Then:

"*Ta-da!*" snarled Goossens.

ALL LIFE-ENERGY IS SEX-ENERGY read a framed lithograph in Dr. Piper's office. Among the other wall ornaments hung his diplomas and various certificates, most of them bearing the rod-and-serpent seal of the Eclectic Medical College of Oklahoma. In the wire pen outside the office window a dozen or so Toggenburgs sat dozing or stood chomping alfalfa hay.

A dish of fancy white-sprinkle nonpareils sat on the doctor's Victorian kidney desk. Helena took one and ate it, then, not satisfied, snatched another.

"These two love-birds," Goossens said, pacing the room, his right eye blackened and swollen from the recent encounter with Mauricio's fist. "It would be too elegant, you know—an outright *kindness*—to say that I caught them in *flagrante delicto*, but you could say it that way if you wish. Another way of saying it is that I caught them rutting in the mud like barnyard swine."

"Is this indeed true, Melon Pie?" the doctor asked gently. He was still dressed in his capacious surgical gown and cap, and also looking somewhat lost in his own hospital office.

Helena, eating her second nonpareil, said nothing. The begrimed state of her face, hair, and clothing (like Mauricio's) rendered the question irrelevant, if not outright laughable. Then again, Goossens's waistcoat and breeches were hardly in better condition.

"I am sorry," Mauricio muttered.

"I spoke with Mrs. Hatley on the telephone earlier," Dr. Piper continued, addressing Helena. "I told her your grandmother came unexpectedly to visit."

"So you told her it was my time of the month," Helena corrected him. "Do you think she's stupid? She knows when my period is—I've used that one on her before."

"I had no other choice. She wants to expel you."

"That's aces with me. That's the best news I've heard all year."

"Excuse me, Doctor?" Nurse Braaten, the doctor's portly chief assistant, had appeared in the doorway. "The congressman is prepared and waiting upstairs. Shall I administer the tropocaine myself?"

"Yes, yes, I'll be along shortly." The doctor looked increasingly frantic. He beheld his daughter with pleading eyes.

"Helen, Melon Pie...."

"Hello?" Goossens threw his arms in the air. "I would like to know if there's going to be any reckoning *at all* for the physical assault on my person? Yes?"

"Oh, stuff it, Goose." Having finished her treat, Helen folded her arms and regarded her fingernail.

The organist burst into tears. "Why are you so awful? You're the cruelest woman I have ever known."

"That's quite enough of that, Arnd," said Dr. Piper uncomfortably. At last his attention turned to Mauricio. "You are dismissed from my employ, young man. This should of course go without saying. Please return to my stables, gather your personals, and go back to wherever it was you came from. Or go to Hades. It is all one and the same to me."

"Daddy, don't you dare send him away!" Helena cried, bolting to her feet. She pointed to Goossens. "He lies! *That's* the man who has dishonored me, standing right over there! Molested me in my own bed, in *his* own bed, in the pantry, in the stables, indoors and out! *That's* why I was running away, to get clear of this fiend, this *wolf* who you insisted on bringing to live with us! Mauricio was a perfect gentleman with me today! My loyal guard and protector! My *only* protector!"

"In his bed...*and* yours?" Dr. Piper said, befuddled.

"You fantastic, perfidious, little snot-nosed harpy!" Goossens hissed, boiling over, at Helena. He turned to the doctor, runny eyes and cheeks now flushed with rage. "Sir, I tell you, anything untoward that may have occurred was entirely her instigation!" He returned to Helena and his eyes became slits. "Indeed, this innocent of yours is acquainted with the most vulgar, unhygienic acts and practices...I will spare you the heinous particulars."

"You grubby faggot," Helena told him calmly. "You're fired. Now get lost."

Goossens laughed and started out of the room, then paused to throw out one final retort—this one a speculation on the true nature of Helena's interest in horses. Mauricio leapt from his chair, chased him out into the corridor, and hit him square in the jaw, dislocating it.

Mauricio stayed; Goossens went, head still bandaged, on a train bound for St. Louis by way of Fort Worth, never to be heard from in Nueva Anapra again.

The explosions on the mountain continued into November. By and by, a white cross made of welded steel crossbeams appeared at the summit, and the following Sunday a pilgrimage of hundreds was evident. Drawn by the spectacle of it, Mauricio opted for a rare day off and rode his horse to the trail gate, tied her to a yucca tree and fell in with the line of pilgrims. The new trail was marked with the fourteen stations of the Via Dolorosa, small numbered crosses representing the path of Jesus Christ through Jerusalem on his way to the crucifixion. Clusters of people stopped and prayed before each of the small crosses on the way up. Some were making the climb on their knees. A few of the younger men carried makeshift crosses on their shoulders. Mauricio was reminded of Santa Rita's, the tiny mission-style church that his mother had once belonged to in Tulare. On Good Friday she would take him to each of the church's clay Via Dolorosa shrines and they would pray together. Now she was sharing a one-room workers' cabin with three other women and picking nectarines during the day; rarely could she make the Sunday trip into Tulare anymore. The Depression had claimed the Rede family home.

He reached the trail summit to find a large outdoor mass underway. A canopy and portable altar had been erected beneath the new forty-foot cross, and a mitered bishop stood in the canopy's shadow, a gold chalice in his raised hands. The crowd filled the narrow mountaintop cavity that constituted the sanctuary from end to end. The *esmeltianos* had scaled the mountain arrayed in their Sunday best, the women in their cotton home-sewn dresses and flowered hats, the men in their brown fedoras and chino slacks. The sky was a brilliant autumn blue, as unblemished and fathomless as still lake water.

When the procession for Eucharist began Mauricio removed his straw hat and again took his place in line, inwardly fumbling to remember the last time he'd taken the Host. He reached the altar, bowed, and accepted the wafer on his tongue from one of the two assisting deacons. When he turned away a hand fell on his shoulder.

"Those are tears of joy, I am hoping. *Sind sie nicht?*"

A short older gentleman in wool cap and bowtie had caught him. Mauricio raised a hand to his own face and found it wet.

"Yes," he lied. In truth he didn't know why he was weeping, or even that he'd been weeping at all. The gentleman looked doubtful.

"You are not from Esmelda," he said kindly. "You have come from Mexico, then?"

A woman who'd had her back to the gentleman now turned and chided him, in Spanish, for being too nosey. She was about the gentleman's age, if her crows' feet and gray temples were any guide, and in her arms she held a newborn child swaddled in a colorful crochet blanket. Mauricio recovered himself and explained his leaving California to work first for the Cortinases and now for the Pipers.

"The Doctor!" the gentleman exclaimed happily. At the same time the woman's embarrassment appeared to suddenly magnify. "You must tell him what has happened! This," and he pulled the woman to him, placing his other hand on the baby, "this is the result of his masterful work! Our son, born after those other *Quacksalber* doctors said we could have no children! Tell him Carsden and Magda are forever grateful!"

Mauricio politely asked why they couldn't tell this to the Doctor themselves. The gentleman made a sound of dismissal mixed with weary sadness.

"He has a disagreement with us," said Carsden. "The Doctor had other wishes for the mountain, but we have been seeking to place this sanctuary here since long before he came to Nueva Anapra. We were forced to go before the magistrates to settle it, and so the magistrates did. But the Doctor's displeasure with us is…not yet settled."

She came to him that night, as had become her custom, her pleated shorts and sailor blouse gracing the wooden floorboards and her flawless, nubile body gliding onto his wobbly bunk bed in what seemed a single catlike movement. The electric shock, also customary, detonated in a sweet, painful, thorn-shaped spark before their lips even touched. The flash captured her face as she mounted him, and Mauricio glimpsed again the indifferent porcelain beauty that had nearly tempted him to his death in the Cortinas arena.

"*Cásate conmigo*," he whispered in her ear when it was over.

Helena said nothing. On the radio a string band was performing a song about a man crossing a river with shackles on his feet. The green Air King radio, with its male and female Egyptian figures reaching out to one another, was a gift, a souvenir from Helena's last visit to Fort Worth.

"Daddy's running for governor again next year," she replied finally, tracing invisible cryptic lines on his chest. "I can't."

He pulled her arms away from him, gentle but firm, and held her face in his hands.

"We are going to have a child. This...what we have been doing...soon you must conceive."

She smiled, her eyes pitying him as either deranged or hopelessly ignorant. "No, my love, that is not going to happen. Modern women don't conceive unless and until they want to."

"But what if God wants it to be? It is God who decides such things, not women or men."

Helena chuckled and rose from the bed. "It's okay," she said, picking her clothes off the floor. "You're not acquainted with the New Thought. How could you be? But, really, you needn't trouble yourself over such nonsense. I assure you."

But he was, in fact, growing more troubled by the day, in part because they both knew and spoke each other's languages (her Spanish was considerably better, more nuanced, than the Doctor's), yet still she seemed not to understand him, and vice-versa. Their lovemaking remained fierce and pleasurable, her desire often outpacing his. Such passion could only be the will of God.

The following afternoon he rode his horse back to La Esmelda and located the tiny Catholic church, which stood just outside the smelter gates. When he entered the building a single priest, Padre Ruben, was seated in one of the back pews reading a newspaper. Mauricio approached him and requested confession.

After receiving his penance (ten Our Fathers, fifteen Hail Marys, and one Stations of the Cross), he emerged from the church and stared up at the Black Mountain in desolation. Padre Ruben had said that his first journey up the mountain didn't count because Mauricio had not stopped and prayed at every station.

"Consider why God brought you to this place," the Padre had said through the confessional screen. "Perhaps it was the mountain and not the girl which compelled you here. Perhaps your salvation depends on something other than what you wish for yourself. Was it not the same with Our Lord and Savior?"

Mauricio had never felt more lost. For one thing, he had detected the priest's bourbon-spiked breath through the cloverleaf latticework of the confessional screen. The newspaper in his hands when Mauricio first walked in was camouflage for a bottle or flask—of this he felt sure. But the Padre's counsel rang true. Since coming to the Piper estate, Mauricio now recognized, he had been living poised on a knife's edge between elation and confused anguish, never quite tipping over into one or the other. Helena's wanton attentions had exacerbated this problem, this state of tension. She loved him but would not have him. She fondled him, caressed him, made vigorous love to him with the attentions of a wife yet refused him for a husband. And somehow her body devoured his seed (*¡Y tanto de eso! Y tantas veces!*) while yielding it no purchase.

Again he steered Paloma to the trail gate and tethered her to the same yucca. The advancing afternoon sun lay behind the mountain, casting the white cross high above him in stark black silhouette. He started up the deserted trail, soon arriving at the first station in the narrow V-shaped canyon at the mountain base. The small plain cross, a Roman-numeral one at its intersection, stood on the canyon slope among the rocks and prickly pear. Mauricio stopped, kneeled, and made his first silent prayer. Standing up again, he found the trail wasn't deserted after all.

The second station occupied a ridge where the trail turned and curled sharply as it rose. Atop this ridge, underneath the station cross, a woman in a colorful petticoat skirt and tall black bowler hat appeared to be dancing all alone. Her raised arms gyrated while her body spun, the voluminous green skirt ballooning outward from her waist in a bell shape, her hands brandishing what appeared to be a stick and a pair of bolas. He lost sight of her as the trail led him around and behind the second station, and when he reached it, she had gone.

This became the pattern for the whole of Mauricio's journey up the mountain, until he began to feel a participant in some kind of game. Again she appeared at the next station in front of him and vanished—completely, it seemed, for while the mountain obscured the trail ahead at some points, at others there was plainly no living soul between him and the next station—when he caught up. If the dancer was aware of his presence on the mountain, however, she allowed no indication of it.

The mountaintop sanctuary, overflowing with pilgrims the day before, was likewise deserted. After finishing his prayer at the fourteenth station Mauricio approached the large cross at the very top, even though he had no devotionals left to perform. It was sacrilege to pray the fifteenth station, the Resurrection, at any time but Easter. For her own part, the dancing woman was nowhere to be seen. Had his mind conjured her in its distraction?

Compelled by nothing, by the acute lack of inspiration that his penance had done him, Mauricio climbed the final few steps of carved rocks to the monument itself and stood taking in the famous Pass of the North, that place where the river turned between the Juárez and Franklin mountains on its journey to the Gulf of Mexico. Then, inspiration striking at last, he turned and knelt in the lengthening shadow of the steel cross, a new prayer flowing from his lips.

"Amen," he said in a loud voice when it was done, and then he crossed himself and got to his feet, ready to start the long hike back down. And there beside the cross stood the dancing woman, her bowler cocked to one side, watching him with a bemused, toothless smile. Her face, so thoroughly parched and cragged and otherwise shaped by the elements, might have been as old as the mountain itself.

"*Thta ween-ah, mijo*," said the face.

"*All is vanity*," Helen repeated bitterly, mocking her own reflection in the mirror above her vanity table. Ragdoll, Helen's white Turkish cat, perked up her head and fixed her striking eyes—one blue, one yellow—upon her (at times) perplexing young mistress. Those eyes followed Helen's hand in detached curiosity as she tore another disposable handkerchief from the box on the table's edge and daubed her smeared face with it.

Vanity was the leitmotif of Dr. Piper's evening radio address, underway right now on Helen's bedroom Philco. Her father had recorded it that afternoon in the great-room downstairs, as he did six days a week. "You remember the adage that I've said to you," he was expounding, "about the young man traveling along the road and coming aside the elderly man who said to him, 'Remember, man, as you pass by, as you are now, so once was I. As I am now, so you must be. So prepare to follow me.'"

Her father's logic was unassailable. We are all, every one of us, going to be worm food someday; that day is probably sooner than any of us suspects, so why compound the tragedy by delaying the glorious rejuvenation to be experienced by way of Dr. Piper's surgical skill? The patent-medicine man's *memento mori*. Helen had read the death meditations of the great, nameless Anglo-Saxon poets in her prep-school English class—actually read them, as opposed to cribbing notes from Beryl Galbraith, the class show-off—and at the moment she was certainly inclined to agree with half of her father's thesis. The pagan Teutons had called it "weird," their word for "fate." Life was weird, it was harsh, and it was ultimately futile. All is vanity, yes, ain't that the cotton-pickin' truth. That her childish father could manage so deftly to exploit the one vanity by solemnly evoking the other was indeed a testament to his infinite, deluded genius.

Still wearing her dinner dress and beaded ostrich-feather headband, Helen had fallen prey to unusually low spirits, to the point of collapsing into a rare sob, precisely because of the spiritual events that had occurred after dinner that evening. At least once a month, at the Doctor's request, Zerina Price led a séance so as to facilitate regular communion between father, daughter, and Helen's late mother. The precise method of contact varied from one session to the next, be it planchette, slate, trumpet, or spirit box. Tonight it was the box, a mahogany chest wrought with vaguely oriental exterior carvings and revealing within its velvet-lined enclosure a pewter bell suspended by a silk ribbon.

To her credit, Madame was in rare form tonight. In her pearls, floral devoré capelet, magenta crystal-brooch turban, and black opera gloves, Zerina might have shamed Coco Chanel herself for sheer presence. In wake of Goossens's recent dismissal, the butler Seong had consented to round out the number of participants, if only because of the strain it presented for three to maintain an unbroken union of hands across the séance table. Seong, ever the Shanghai-trained professional, looked as though he were enduring necessary humiliation.

Eyes closed, Zerina led them in the requisite opening chant in her cloying sparrow-throated voice. The woody aroma of frankincense extended its tentacles from the bohemian copper censer, and the flickering candles launched shadows aloft, sprinting like cats up and down the magnificent great-room's lime-stucco walls. Then she bade the spirit of Alanthia Piper to move among them and speak through them.

The bell rang once.

"Lanthie?" The Doctor shot his eyes to the heavens in sudden, sincere, trembling expectation, a sight that never failed to rend Helen's heart. As if there was any doubt that Zerina would ring the bell again in affirmation. Helen had long ago sussed out the string mechanism that Madame employed (the noiseless catgut line ran underneath the tablecloth and hooked onto her shoe), but try telling that to a man so eager to guzzle any and every fanciful brand of gimcrack swill—including his own. Which to detest more, the drink or the drunkard? The drunkard or the drink?

"Lanthie, my Sweet Sunshine?" the Doctor pressed. "My Everlasting?"

Ring-a-ling.

"O luminous spirit!" cried Zerina. "O denizen of the ephemeral! Do tarry! Fear not this mortal realm!" She stifled a hiccup. Madame had exceeded her fair share of amontillado at dinner, as per usual. In addition Helen thought she might have farted her smothered pheasant, which the frankincense was mercifully acting to mitigate.

"I dream of you still, my Lanthie." The firelight danced along the Doctor's quavering blue lips, which always assumed that color following his nightly injection of paregoric. "As I made known to you oft during our too-short life together, I believe I saw your face in those thunderclouds at Soissons, before I ever knew you. I envisaged your face on that blood-soaked battlefield, in that German machine-gun nest where my own life nearly ended, and I saw the home we would share one day on Chautauqua Avenue, in Norman, after we were joined in marriage. The home where I delivered our exquisite daughter, who is seated here at this table right now. Do you remember, Lanthie? Do you remember the Queen Anne?"

Ring-a-ling.

"Do you have a greeting for our Helen? Isn't she radiant this evening? Is Heaven not jealous of Our Daughter, now grown to the very cynosure of Young Womanhood?"

Ring-a-ling.

"Hello, Mama."

"A decorated Equestrian, Lanthie, can you fathom it? The sweetheart of the rodeo! Annie Oakley reborn! But with such more feminine charm, a worthy successor to your own timeless beauty...with a modest admixture of, dare I add, my irascible Stick-to-It-Tiveness!"

Seong's hand twitched in hers, giving her cause to wonder if this extra chore wasn't more of an imposition on his Buddhist faith than he let on. His face remained impassive.

"And yet I must disclose, Lanthie...the constancy of our happiness on this side of the ectenic membrane trembles in doubt. My Enemies conspire against me as never before. That abominable Jew tuberculist in Albuquerque has now sullied my name, perhaps irretrievably, in the medical trades. A woman in Duluth has made baseless charge of tortfeasor against me, *res ipsa loquitur*, in the name of her late husband. What to do, Lanthie? What shall become of us?"

A peculiar, insufferably contrived groan had commenced somewhere within the dankest fumy recesses of Madame's throat. How Helen detested her, this gaudy, grossly perfumed, illiterate sideshow soubrette. Zerina arched her powdered neck and turned her face to the high imaginary heavens above, eyelids squeezed into hard puckered curdles, plump double chin jutting forward like the business end of a ripe butternut squash.

"Is that you, Donald?" Her eyes flew wide in supreme, perfectly timed melodrama. For a moment Helen actually wished she could vomit at will.

"Yes, oh my Lanthie!" the Doctor cried.

"Donnie, my dear darling cabbage! How I wish you could join me on the blissful nether-plain! Come to me, Donnie!"

"Then you forgive me? Do you indeed forgive my gross incompetence on that fateful day of your passing? Oh, Lanthie, I have so bitterly regretted my error! No matter how many I save from the cruelty of old age and the desolation of loveless marriage, no matter how many men and women continue to bombard me with their praise and gratitude for the priceless rejuvenation I bequeathed them…in the secret chambers of my heart, I fear I will never be free of the burden! The guilt! I beat my breast still at the thought of it! Oh, Lanthie! How many years of earthly joy did that instant of frail maladroitness rob from the both of us! Would that I were not so irredeemably human!"

"*Stop!*" Zerina's voice had dropped in timbre, shifting from feminine to masculine. Eyes closed once more, she brought her head forward and lifted her chest and shoulders, face assuming the stern countenance of a reproving parent. "Cease this stubborn, unseemly melancholy at once, my wayward child! No more!"

"Who...who is this?" The Doctor leaned forward in his chair as if peering closely into an open window or perhaps a book with fine print, though his own eyes were closed. "*You're* not Lanthie."

"No." Zerina took in a long studied breath, relishing the moment. Some new gambit was afoot. "I Am," she said at last.

"No, you're not," the Doctor protested, more befuddled than defiant. "This is certainly not the voice of my beloved Lanthie! Identify yourself, trespasser!"

"I Am...that I Am."

The Doctor gasped, and Seong's hand twitched once more. Helen glanced at him again and noticed a drop of perspiration sliding down his right temple. The poor man was in plain, mounting discomfort.

"But why?" the Doctor all but whispered. "I'm not worthy of your Holy Presence. This must be...oh, no, but I fear it. The moment of Reckoning! How I've dreaded it and longed for it! Have you come to condemn my soul at last?"

"*Fear not!*" Zerina bellowed. "Your Alanthia is safe with me, and you will join her in due course. She shall welcome you inside the gates of paradise at the appointed time. But that day is not today."

The Doctor nodded his head. "Then I am to suffer, yes," he said. "I will gladly endure this cruel purgatory knowing that Lanthie waits for me at the gates."

"No! You are to *triumph*! In my name you shall pursue the governorship once more, and in my name, this time you will capture the state!"

"Oh, for shit's sake, Daddy!" Helen shoved Zerina's gloved hand away and got to her feet. "Why do we have to go through this every time? You don't need this cheap floozy's blessing to do anything! And now she expects us to believe she's the voice of God? Well that wasn't the Holy Ghost I heard singing out of her ass a few minutes ago, I'll testify to that! I've heard enough!"

"Helen?" The Doctor had yet to open his eyes.

"Yes, it's me, Daddy—I'm not dead yet, remember?"

Zerina rolled her head as if in a swoon. "Where am I?" she cried. "Oh, what on earth? Something, someone, must have shattered the psychic connection! How long was I immersed in the transcendental state?"

"You're still *immersed*," Helen returned, "judging by your breath."

"Now, Helen, Melon Pie...this outburst is most undignified," the Doctor pleaded. "You've no cause to attack Madame Zerina so cruelly. For Heaven's sake, she's been like, like...."

"Like a mother to me?" Helen was unable to restrain her disgust, much as the look on her father's face stung. He was gazing up at her, still in his chair, like a child whose birthday-cake candles had been dashed out all at once by a sudden arrant gust of wind. Or by another mean-spirited child. "Is that what you were going to say? I'm afraid not, Daddy. If anything she's been a mother to *you*."

Her father's mouth, first agape in flabbergasted horror, shut itself, then opened again. Then shut.

"*Get it off of me! Oh! Oh!*" Zerina clambered out of her chair, tipping it over, swatting at her forearm. Once free of the chair she howled in pain, refreshingly, in her own unmistakable voice.

"*Xiānshēng,*" Seong interjected then with a raised index finger, addressing the Doctor. "If I may." He lowered his hand to his lap and sat in fixed, peaceable deference, awaiting.

"Answer him, Daddy!"

Zerina had proceeded to dance around the room yowling, close to hysterics. Helen walked around the table coolly and raised her palm, readying to slap her father's face, as was often necessary when his paregoric overcame him. But she halted upon catching sight of the fresh welt standing out in angry bright-pink relief on his cheek.

"Daddy, you are bitten!"

"Not precisely," Seong amended. "He is stung. I noticed, after we sat down, a wasp nest," and he pointed to one of the high casement windows, where a brown egg-shaped growth hung from one of the upper corners. As he pointed, Helen saw that his hand had grown grotesquely waxy and swollen, the wasp sting no doubt the reason for his strange twitching earlier. He withdrew his hand underneath the table. "I did not wish to interrupt the proceedings," he explained by way of apology. "But I see that I was mistaken in not doing so. I believe the *mogusa* smoke has disturbed their sleep."

Only later did it occur to Helen that the wasps hadn't dared touch her. The others, including her father, had ended up nursing multiple stings apiece. Yet being so miraculously spared moved Helen not at all. Her "weird," her fate, it seemed, was the curse of relentlessly good fortune, so relentless that it was impossible to take pleasure in it. The new goddess Psyche, bloodless and immaculate, an earthbound immortal destined to walk forever between the raindrops, for rain and wasps and men would eschew her forever in fear of her beauty: that was her curse. She beheld her sterling silver manicure set and picked up the trimming knife, wondering who or what would intervene if, on some heedless impulse, she elected to open her wrists with it. For surely someone or something would.

The "Doctor Piper Healing Hour" had segued to the Picanniny Jug Band, and after relinquishing the trimming knife to its mirror tray she rose at length and snapped the Philco off. Ragdoll stretched, yawned, and took up Helen's former spot on the vanity table chair. Moving to the French rococo bed, Helen stopped short in uncertainty, for the music had continued. A chorus of guitars and male voices came from somewhere outside.

"Despierta, dulce amor de mi vida…con esta canción te vengo a entregar el alma."

A goddamn, full-blown, old-timey serenade. She proceeded to the bed and collapsed slump-shouldered on the mattress edge, hands in her lap, listening. Mauricio. Needless to say, proposing marriage again. And he had brought others with him this time from the sound of it.

As she sat there Helen's spirit absorbed the words against her mind's wishes, and her quiet sobbing resumed. All is vanity. Of course he would never understand. And she well knew the serenade tradition in Mexico. If she went to the window and allowed herself to be seen then it was the same as accepting his entreaty, and *that* was entirely out of the question.

The song ended, and she rose to give Mauricio a firm answer in the form of a darkened bedroom window. She went to the hurricane lamp beside her bed and reached for the key-switch. Then another song began.

> *I never really knew what love could do*
> *Until the day I laid my eyes on you*
> *'Cause love was something I could never see*
> *It has been a mystery*
> *I never thought that you could be so sweet*
> *It seems that fate arranged that we should meet*

They were singing in English. It was her favorite song, and thus a consistent number on XAMO Radio between the revival preachers, snake oilers, and her own father: the Boswell Sisters' "Gee, But I'd Like to Make You Happy."

> *I've got a ring, just look at it shine*
> *And I know a finger where this ring oughta linger*
> *Won't you say you'll be mine*

And next she was at the window in spite of herself. Below were Mauricio and three of the Cortinas brothers, all in their fine studded *charro* outfits

310

and sombreros, all wielding guitars. Mauricio stood out in front, eyes meeting hers at once—and so fate had achieved its will.

Her answer was yes.

The "wedding" was performed in secret that very night. She rode pillion with Mauricio, hugging his waist tightly, on the long trail up the Black Mountain. The sanctuary at the top was alight with candles. A crazy, witchy old hag bade them drink a bitter tea mixture from a Clabber Girl can. Then they knelt before her while she sang and waved a desiccated animal fetus about.

"*Thta-ween-ah!*" she cried.

Thus, Señor y Señora Rede. Husband and wife.

Para siempre.

20

Elfa was seated alone in a booth at Trygg's ice cream parlor, apricot Gherardinis propped back behind her forehead, tapping cigarette ashes into her uneaten banana boat. An Alan Parsons tune droned thinly from the ceiling drop-in speakers. The place was mostly deserted this time of day, one reason why Josiah, the manager, looked the other way at her smoking there. Another was that he and Elfa had at one time been a couple. Sort of.

She laid aside the textbook she was reading, tenting it upside down on the faux Victorian-walnut tabletop. Her brain was threatening to pop like a distended egg yolk. Not because Gerbner's cultivation theory was so very thrilling, but because the totality of input over the last few days, the sheer catastrophic weight of it, had rendered her more or less shell-shocked. Dazed and confused. Crazy from the heat. Su-Su-Sudioed.

At least now you know my real name.

As if she hadn't always known. And as if she'd ever cared.

The storefront door squealed as her cousin Danny entered. She strode to Elfa's table and dropped her things in the opposite booth seat.

"I just pissed my giraffe Maidenforms thanks to you," she announced.

"You're welcome," Elfa replied.

Danny turned sideways and maneuvered her eight-months-pregnant body onto the booth seat. Her thrift-store maternity blouse clashed brilliantly with her mod bangle bracelets and French-wrapped hair. Josiah emerged from the back in his orange-striped shirt, bowtie, and apron.

"How was Family Planning class?"

"Wonderful. I get to keep a mucus diary now. I think I'll get one of those gold-leaf writing journals they sell at Hallmark."

Josiah set a glass of iced Tab, a straw, and a saucer of lime slices before her on the table, then backed away in prudent silence and returned to the kitchen.

"So thank you again for dumping that boy in junior high and leaving him free to knock me up."

"That was eight years ago, sweetie," Elfa said.

"Lame excuse. What did you think of that Waterboys LP?"

Elfa returned to her book. "Haven't gotten around to it yet. Been a little busy."

"Give me a break. You're never too busy for music. Boys and fun, maybe, but never music."

"I was at the hospital in Juárez all morning with Sam. He won't let us move him over here."

"Do they know what's the matter with him yet?"

"Yes."

Elfa left it there. Danny sipped a little from her straw, watching Elfa's face, then released the straw as the realization came. She set her soda glass down.

"No. Oh, no. Not *that*."

Elfa flicked to the next page in her book as if she were actually reading it. "Want the rest of my banana boat?" she offered, by way of changing the subject. Then Danny snatched the book from her hands, shut it, and laid it aside.

"Hey, I'm really sorry. I know he's, like, your closest friend."

A tear slid from Elfa's eye and she rubbed it away, frustrated. Then she reached into her purse for a fresh cigarette. "Yeah, well. I guess he has a point about staying put. It's not like they can do much more for him here in El Paso."

"Listen, don't take this the wrong way," Danny said, and Elfa stopped to process that. Her fearless, brassy cousin had grown suddenly tentative. "But now that you know what he has…like, you don't hug him or anything during these visits, do you? I mean, you don't touch him in any way?"

"What if I do?"

Danny bit her lower lip and looked away. "Never mind."

Elfa pulled her sunglasses down over her eyes and began to gather her things.

"Where are you going?" Danny asked, alarmed. "Please don't. I'm sorry I said anything."

"It isn't that. I'm just not getting anywhere with this yucky textbook and I have a midterm tomorrow. And there's still the pesky matter of finding another job."

"Didn't they offer you a job at Z98?"

Elfa shrugged. "No more DJ-ing for a while. Mandy's all pooped out for now."

"Well that sucks eggs. I'm going to miss her like hell. Come on, just sit a little longer with me. Josiah's off in a few minutes and we can all leave together."

Elfa relented. "You know, I do believe your delicate condition is making you maudlin lately. I admit it's kind of cute. When did you take to wearing giraffe underwear, anyway?"

Josiah emerged once more from the back, this time carrying a tray of salt and pepper shakers. His gangly build caused his uniform to sag and migrate in numerous funny ways as he bent over the tables, switching out shakers.

"Oh, that's nothing new," Danny said, smacking her lips as she finished off a wedge of lime. "There's so much you don't know about me, *prima*. I always had my precious side, even when I was wearing razorblade necklaces. You have to keep that part of yourself intact as you get older. Or else that basket-case girl in *The Breakfast Club* is right."

"I haven't seen *The Breakfast Club*."

"'When you grow up, your heart dies,' she says. It's my favorite line in the whole movie."

"God, you *have* gone maudlin on me. Remind me never to get pregnant."

"Which reminds me!" Danny exclaimed, following a sudden unprovoked gasp. She leaned in close to Elfa and lowered her voice, though the only other soul in the room was her boyfriend/roommate/common-law spouse. "I haven't even told you who else is in my NFP class now."

"Hey, Danny, why do you want to bring that up?" said spouse spoke up from nearby. For a moment Josie rose to his full height from where he'd been bent over a table, and standing at full height always made him look even more sheepish. Even in junior high school his nickname was Gentle Giant.

"What's it to you, beanstalk?" Danny snapped back, her irritableness having returned in a flash. "We're having a private conversation over here, buddy. *Girl* talk. *Comprende?*"

Josie, who knew no Spanish, resumed his work.

"Sheesh," Danny said. "Where was I?"

"Family Planning. Somebody new."

"Right." Danny took another lime wedge, sucked the last flavorful fiber out of it, then dropped the desiccated rind into her soda. "You know, I'm still perturbed at my mother for making me go to these numskull classes after she found out about the little bambino, but there's something to be said for Catholic paranoia. They have a way of educating you

316

unintentionally while trying to scare the living shit out of you. Did you know that before the pill, women used to douche themselves with Lysol, like, for the purpose of birth control? And I don't mean as some crazy backwoods home remedy—I mean the Lysol people actually *pitched* it that way to girls in magazine ads. All in the name of 'feminine hygiene.' Diabolical."

"I think I read about it somewhere."

"So getting back to my original point, this new girl shows up today at the Y, thirty-nine weeks in, tiny as a mouse but a bigger bat in the cave than I've got. And I realize I've seen her somewhere before. You know how I'm always saying I think I might be psychic?"

The tale took its sweet time getting out. Elfa made the subliminal effort not to comment on the perfectly obvious: that Danny's supernatural powers of cognition had been enhanced by the new girl's face and name having been all over the local news media a few weeks ago. Josana Briseño, the girl charged with Shaw Jepsen's murder, was apparently out of jail, the charges dropped, and now a student in Danny's Natural Family Planning class.

It was something to think about. Strummer (*Asher*, she reminded herself, uncomfortable as it felt to allow the kid a bona fide given name) claimed in that final, unhinged radiocast that the Border Patrol was on the La Paz bankroll; that he had watched BP agents providing cover and active assistance while Simon's people moved whole platoons of migrants across the *despoblado* or around the Black Mountain. The platoons consisted mainly of teenagers, the majority of those girls. Shaw had a letch for teenage girls, including Elfa herself, as she'd still been a teenager when Sam gave her the disc-jockey slot at XAMO. It was all entirely plausible. *Too bad*—she reminded herself again—*that I don't care about any of it. No shits left to give.*

After departing Trygg's, Elfa drove across the interstate freeway and returned to Nueva Anapra, bound for the racetrack to collect her mother. The Jetta's radio was set to XAMO; she couldn't help it. So okay, alright, maybe she *did* give a shit or two. At any rate, a tape of one of Sammy's afternoon shows, six months old, was playing. Somebody was still flying the plane up there, but it was anyone's guess as to who the pilot was. Would Jaz feel like sticking around with her and Sammy both gone? He cared for the new management even less than she and Sammy did. It occurred to her that Jaz would be someone she'd like to talk to just now, but in the few years that she'd been colleagues with him, she'd never ascertained where his home was—Texas? New Mexico? Old Mexico?—or indeed if he even had one. A phone number? The white pages were a possibility. Maybe she'd take a look after getting home with her mother. Worth a shot. So maybe she gave three shits.

The sky to the south was the color of an underwear skid mark. This was the time of day when a layer of smog parked itself over downtown El Paso and Juárez and hung there in space like a proud stubborn turd. Some said it was the smelter, others the substandard auto-emission regulations in Mexico. Thoughts of the ozone layer, of swollen-bellied children in Africa, and of general human-led planetary cataclysm crowded her mind, and she shoved them all away angrily as she found a parking space near the casino entrance and cut the engine. Really, there were so many perfectly justified reasons to be bitter. Had Julian Lennon actually bought his father's swill about that fucking feather, or had he long since discovered the lies that lay behind pretty much every human utterance? "Imagine" nothing to kill or die for? Sure, but had John the Apostle ever imagined himself being shot in the back for no good reason at all? Suppose it turns out that dying for nothing might just be both the worst *and* the likeliest outcome of any given person's days on earth—even in the best-case scenario?

By the time Elfa reached the racetrack pavilion's brass Moderne grand-entrance doors she was swiping tears from her face yet again. It had occurred a lot in the past few days. Luckily another ecological outrage—the casino's ubiquitous pall of indoor cigarette smoke—hit her in the face immediately. She found her way along the arabesque-carpeted corridor to the restaurant in search of her mother. The staff were busy dismantling the afternoon all-you-can-eat buffet. A couple of women walked by her with trays of uneaten crab legs and garish slabs of prime rib in their hands, much of it destined for the garbage. The restaurant had a strict discard policy.

"*¿Sabes dónde está Delia?*" she asked one of them.

Delia was in the employee break room downstairs, alone. Elfa found her sitting at one of the circular folding tables, her belongings piled neatly on the tabletop before her and hands folded expectantly in her lap. She had emptied her locker.

On the ubiquitous piped-in intercom feed from XAMO, Sammy was reading a promotional spot for the Nueva Anapra racetrack.

"*¿Que es esto, mamá?*"

Delia looked up. Her new sculpted Lady Di hairdo, another of Elfa's inspirations, was presently flattened from the just-removed hairnet. She held out her paycheck envelope, her eyes telegraphing clearly enough what it contained. Elfa pulled out a chair and sat, took the envelope and removed its contents. $1.67 an hour times thirty hours over two weeks—not counting the extra off-the-clock hours—minus taxes. A grand total of $688.50. A short typewritten note was folded into with the paycheck bearing the Scottish serif letterhead of Piper Enterprises LLC.

Helen had also been there at the hospital in Juárez that morning, goddamn her. Had smiled and chatted pleasantly with Elfa. The hard words in her office long forgotten, it seemed, subsumed to Sammy's health emergency—this man whom the both of them loved, if in very different ways. Or maybe not so very different.

Goddamn her.

"*Está bien mamá,*" she told Delia, taking her mother's hand in hers.

The old clay-roofed station building looked homely and desolate, like the final outpost on some forsaken hellish pilgrim's road to the very ass-crack of the earth. Maybe it was only her state of mind. After all, the first time she'd ever laid eyes on it three years ago the place had looked exactly the same. Still a teenager, she'd gunned her new blue

P'up across the lonesome *despoblado* on a wild-hair impulse one August afternoon after leaving work at Sound Warehouse. It was near Manny's death anniversary, and Elfa was again in her throes. XAMO was playing on the dash radio, Sammy doing his show, counting down the week's most requested. Some rancid British synth-pop hit was at the top of the list that day, she remembered. Poser music.

In those days—yes, "those days" were as recent as three years ago—the Radio XAMO open-door policy was still in effect. You walked in, nodded to the receptionist Luz if she wasn't on her *cigarro Tigre* break—and followed the yellow painted footprints on the floor through the tiny entry area, then down the hall to the right, to the broadcast studio. There outside the studio's soundproof window were two vintage chrome soda-counter stools where you could sit and watch the DJ do his show. A two-way intercom allowed you to make in-person song requests. A slender gentleman in an Italian corduroy blazer was perched on one of the stools, languidly smoking a Vogue Menthe. Elfa approached the other stool and sat.

The man behind the window wore a high, haystack-blonde mullet wig and a vintage HELLS ANGELS ENGLAND biker jacket. She'd never seen Hitman Hayes in person. Watching him at work was like watching a samurai Waffle House chef at full tilt breakfast-rush boogie. Twin turntables cued or spinning, phone lights flashing, dozens of scattered Fidelipac commercial tapes, plus the reel-to-reel with prerecorded comedy bits on standby. Maracas and miniature bongos at the ready. Coffee mug and an open bottle of Glenlivet on the soundboard. And those savage, mysterious, intermittent cries of "Sta *ween*-ah!" for which he would lean close into the mike, raise his right hand high over his head and then close it, then pull down in an indefinably lewd gesture.

"You," said the corduroyed gentleman after a few minutes, "look *litost*."

"Pardon me?"

"I say, you look *litost*. And you have the *duende* about you. Are you *litost*? Are you *duende*? Speak, child."

The slender man leaned back and leered at her with moistened, merlot-glossed lips, cigarette poised in one raised indolent hand.

"Are you planning to request something, honey? Or have you come only to admire?"

The man was a drama professor at the local community college, she learned somewhat later on. He too was an admirer, though nothing more. Once Elfa understood who and what Sammy was apart from the on-air persona, she found there was much she didn't know about the world, such as men like Sammy and Abejundio, the drama professor, being perfectly capable of mere friendship. In fact her lifelong attitude toward men like Sammy and Abe up to that point, while not outright hateful, had, to be sure, fallen well short of generous.

Lesson learned.

The front doors were locked. Elfa cupped her hands around her eyes and peered into one of the glass panes. The front entry was deserted, the

322

art-nouveau neon sign dark. She lowered her hands and thought for a moment, then went back to the car.

It was Sammy who'd coaxed Mandy out of her, helped Elfa locate the surly, sexy, self-assured voice of her own conscience. Mandy loved music, sure, but she loved truth more, and that was what Elfa loved about Mandy the most. Beautiful truth. Hideous truth. And Sammy had endowed her with Radio XAMO, which had carried Mandy's voice and her conscience and her truth across the country. Not only could Elfa never have done that on her own; she might never have known she'd *wanted* to do it until Sammy made it possible. And so it was Mandy who propelled her now as she dug her Colt from the glove compartment and returned to the station's entrance.

Clutching the gun behind her back, Elfa rapped loudly on the front doors and waited. Still no movement, no sign of life within. So she pivoted to the bleached Saltillo pavers that led in hopscotch formation around to the side entrance. Off in the distance the La Paz Ministries building looked just as deserted, the lot empty, yet something told her that this too was somebody's wobbly contrivance. The work of posers.

The station's side entrance consisted of a solid pewter door, yet this she found unlocked and standing slightly ajar. The corridor within was strewn with loose assorted documents, as if a file cabinet had exploded. At the corridor's end the soundproof window looking into the broadcast studio was shattered, the floor and windowsill layered with shards. The whole place smelled of smoke and sudden violence. And there in the captain's seat she found Jeremy Santana.

"You," said Elfa.

Jeremy had been chomping down from a bag of pork rinds and watching the soundboard, a library tape of Sam's afternoon show underway on the reel-to-reel behind him. Jeremy froze in mid-crunch as if caught flogging himself.

"Muh?" he ventured, mouth full.

"You. Explain yourself."

The bag crumpled in his hands and he gulped down the mashed remainders in his mouth. Elfa walked around him, shoe soles crunching on glass, and picked some songs from the cart.

"Amscray," she said. "I've got a show to do."

"Simon said you weren't coming back."

Elfa paused. "You talked to Simon La Paz? When?"

21

The Risen Christ, palms down in an attitude of blessing, reigned in His silent stone firmament high above the desert plain. The sculptor had enlarged the Savior's head and face so that the proportions seemed natural from below, similar to Michelangelo's *David*, which Ash had seen once at Movieland Wax Museum.

The Poser Christ, Ash thought. Frozen and ineffectual like Dante's Satan. He felt a touch of pity now for all those who'd ever made the journey up here. It was the eyes that ruined it. *David* was more or less eyeless too, but at least you had the illusion of motion; the dude poised almost casually on one hip moments before lobbing that famous, fatal shot at the tough-talking Goliath. But the Christ, or at least *this* Christ, stared blindly into the ether, mouth slightly agape—a levitating, oblivious zombie…more life in his bare, chipped, dangling toes than in his stupefied face.

Even so, Eulalia, the old-as-Methuselah boxcar-pilfering Bolivian witch, had dispatched him here in search of God, to suss out His will (*la voz*, she'd called it) in some urgent, magical, nonspecific way, despite her own simultaneous caution that Simon's people were still combing the mountain in search of Asher. She'd tutored him in brief about the sculptor's trail—*el rastro del artesano*—a forgotten footpath that cut straight up the mountainside from the abandoned stone hut where the Catalan had lived during the 1940s while constructing the monument. And so Ash, lacking any more practical options at the moment, had entrusted his stolen horse to Lalia's care and made for the mountaintop, semi-camouflaged in a Kangol bucket hat and Benetton rugby shirt hand-picked from her hoarded crates by the good witch herself.

The monument base was forested with spent and blackened devotional candles. La Virgen, San Joseph, Sagrado Corazon Jesus, San Martin Caballero, Los Siete Arcángeles. The whole dismal, crazy menagerie of Mexican Catholic superstition. *Los santos muertos*, Mauricio had often remarked (in those moments of private bitterness he'd shared only with Asher) *son sabios solo porque están muertos.*

Ash retreated from the altar and moved to the peak's unbounded edge, taking in the dusty, smog-tinged Pass of the North as the limestone zombie presumably saw it. Had any of the pilgrims before him ever leaped to their deaths from this mountain on purpose? The drop from here might not have been steep enough, but now he could distinguish several sudden drop-offs on the sacred trail below as it stitched its way up the mountainside, conducting the faithful through the fourteen Stations of the Cross. Maybe *that* was the real test: not making it to the top to honor a stone Christ, but resisting the mad urge to hurl yourself over the side, and perhaps meet the real one a little ahead of schedule, at various points along the way. Is that what he'd ultimately come to Nueva Anapra to do? Having blown up his life on Radio XAMO—that *other* voice of God that had called to him for so long, and from so far away—why not conclude that same life right here, right now?

The roofless stone cottage stood hundreds of feet below, resembling from this vantage point an open grave. On more than one occasion, Dr. Tune had attempted to suss Asher out for any trace of suicidal intent, and on each of those attempts Ash had rebuffed him and meant it. Only posers offed themselves.

A brown four-by-four pickup appeared near one of the trail turns below, cutting an angry wake of lingering dust, then paused, moved on again, then paused again. Searching. He backed away from the peak's edge and found that two teenage girls in jean shorts and colorful batwing blouses had joined him at the monument. They eyed him warily and moved to the altar, where they knelt side-by-side at the concrete prayer bench. The two looked vaguely familiar, and he thought of the girls he'd seen on the bus ride from Juárez to Anapra that first day—the girls whom he now understood worked in the outlying *maquilas* unless (or until) Ministerio La Paz recruited them and smuggled them into the U.S. Ash started for the ramp leading back down to the trailhead to allow the two girls their space, but as he passed them by, his eyes fell upon something at the foot of the monument, something he'd failed to notice earlier, and he stopped short.

But how did it get here? How *could* it...?

The girls were watching him now, chins on their folded hands and widened eyes registering him with plain, escalating alarm.

"*Con permiso*," Ash said brusquely. He darted behind the bench and snatched the item from where it sat among the clutter of candles, then withdrew from the girls' accusing stares to the ramp behind the monument.

It was a yellow Little John portable radio, much like his, though it couldn't possibly be the same one he'd brought from California. Not in a thousand years. Had some nameless nobody, in a zillion-to-one coincidence, actually carried it up here, set it down on the altar, and then forgotten about it? Or had Lalia taken the thing from his bag and placed it here where she could be reasonably confident that he'd discover it? And how could she have gotten here before him? And to what purpose?

He tried the ON switch and Elfa's...*Mandy*'s voice greeted him at once, clear as day and hard as a slap.

"—calling it quits. You heard me, people. The network news just interrupted *General Hospital* with a special bulletin. Those nimrods tried to pull one over on all of us, and they lost, even if they won't honestly admit it because they're still posers, after all. But either way, New Coke is officially a bust!"

Asher knelt on the ramp and sat. His own deeds of the past few days assumed sudden, irreversible weight. High overhead an airliner raked its contrail into the sky. The world went about its dreary, imperative business.

"Anyhey," Mandy continued, "life is lousy with surprises, isn't it? Short ones and tall ones, nice ones and nasty ones. With everything good comes something bad. As some of you might already know, the Hitman is... *un peu patraque*, as the French say. Under the weather. At least that's the tea they're serving in the local news media right now. But then that isn't exactly *all* they're saying, is it? No, what they're saying is that he has...

"Wait for it, now...

"*AIDS.*"

In Ash's mind he as good as saw the tears singe her eyes as she said it. Which meant, of course, that it was indeed true. The verdict was in.

"You know, the gay flu. The 'back from Africa.' Well, friends and neighbors, that's nothing but a wicked, bald-faced lie. I just wanted you to hear it from me. Because there are some important people in this community already turning their backs on him on that account. People who should know better."

There was a long moment of dead air—the deadliest sin in radio. Yet had anyone tuned in to Radio XAMO at that moment, they would surely have grokked Mandy's presence there behind the mike as she struggled to right herself. Grokked *Elfa's* presence. The airwaves, the ionosphere, the very universe shuddered with it, with *her*. The voice of God resonant in her gravid silence. The love for her friend Sammy; the raw stockpiled rage at her father's murder; both powered by a 500,000-watt antique RCA transmitter gone, if only for that lone spare instant, dormant; a heart between beats.

"A lie," Elfa repeated, for Mandy had stepped aside the same way that Strummer, in the end, had given way to Asher. "Aren't you tired of lies, and the lying mouths that spew them? Funny how so many of those mouths are attached to friendly, smiling faces. *En boca del mentiroso, lo cierto se hace dudoso.* Or *Behüte mich Gott vor meinen Freunden, mit den Feinden will ich schon fertig werden.* My *Opa* taught me that one. But the person I'm mainly talking about—and talking *to*—right now doesn't know German, so here's a song by The Clash that maybe best says what I'd like to say to her wicked *mentirosa*'s face. This one's for you, Sammy."

In the studio Elfa thumped the turntable switch releasing "Rudie Can't Fail" from its cue position and pushed away her mike. The presence of daylight in the room, she decided, was handicapping her game. Mandy only came out at night, and Mandy didn't crack up all Tammy Bakker-style on the air. At least there was no runny mascara to see—neither Elfa nor Mandy cared for makeup.

Elfa turned her attention to the swarthy, snazzily-dressed, bald-pated gentleman also in the room with her; like the daylight, he was also an unusual presence in the Radio XAMO studio, if not an altogether unfamiliar one.

"So do you have a name, cousin?" she asked him in Spanish. When he'd first walked in she recognized him immediately as one of Simon's associates. She'd seen that particular pair of Swatch sunglasses perched on that particular head before. But he'd offered no introduction, no word of clarification as to his unannounced visit—not so much as a handshake. Instead he'd silently taken up residence in a plastic chair by the studio door and unfolded a copy of today's *El Diario* that he'd brought tucked away under his arm. Right now he was absorbed in the sports pages.

"Any requests?" Elfa tried when he didn't answer. "Or how about a dedication? What's your wife's favorite song?" This at least seemed to dent the lunk's concentration.

"*A ella le gusta*...," he began, and the man's eyes wandered upwards while he sifted his memory. "'Frankie Say Relax'?" he finished uncertainly.

"Good one," said Elfa. She launched an automated string of commercials on the Fidelipac and pushed away from the sound board. "I'll go dig that up."

Having returned to his newspaper, he hardly seemed to notice Elfa walking out of the room, let alone her pausing to pick up the Colt from the console table. She crossed the (still) trash-strewn hallway and ducked into the restroom. She laid the gun in the empty sink basin and sat down on the toilet with the lid closed, thinking.

Whatever his reason for being here, it was plain enough that the lunk was not much concerned with her, which should have been reassuring. Should have been, but wasn't. Which meant, of course, that her only sane option right at this moment was to get her ass out of here and never look back; get out before the next terrible thing happened, whatever that terrible thing turned out to be. So why was she not doing exactly that right this very minute?

Why stay?

Because she had a show to do, whether the rest of the world cared or not; or rather *two* shows, hers and Sammy's. Because no one from Simon's organization had as yet bothered to tell her that she was indeed fired. And because Helen Piper had first fired her mother for no cause, and then, as was becoming more and more evident, had betrayed and abandoned a mutual friend. Elfa's *best* friend. *You're going to have to be our go-between for now*, Helen had said that day in her executive lair at the racetrack. *I'm doing everything I can for him. I'll have him transferred back over here as soon as it can be arranged and see that he gets the best possible care*, the old bat had promised. And then the news media had gotten wind of Sammy's condition.

Gun in hand, Elfa went out across the hallway again to the library. It took some rooting around, but she ultimately came up with an old twelve-inch maxi-single and returned with it to the broadcast studio, where the lunk remained enthralled in his newspaper. She cued the record and did a quick air-check before launching the eight-minute "Sex Mix" of Frankie Goes to Hollywood's one and only hit, already over a year old. A creaking, cobwebby relic by pop-music standards. But soon the lunk was bobbing his bald head in time with the disco-flavored beat.

Down the mountain he came, no wiser than when he went up. Clutching the little radio in one hand (because it wouldn't fit snug in the waistline of his jeans like his grandfather's .45), which made it harder to manage his footing, but the inconvenience was worth it. The sound of Mandy's voice at his side was worth it.

Keeping a wary eye out for the brown pickup truck, Ash came to the first intersection of the artisan's trail and the pilgrims' trail. Here the twelfth Station of the Cross—signifying the moment of Jesus's death—stood shadowed in a mountainside alcove. On either side of the large marker cross, with its Roman numerals above the transept, two smaller crosses stood in representation of the savior's two thief compadres.

He squatted and allowed himself to scoot-slide the last few feet, landing on the mercifully smooth and level pilgrims' path just ahead of a Pig Pen-like swirl of loose pebbles and dust. He imagined Casey Barefoot sassing him: *Nice work, California. Looks like you're a better horseman than mountaineer. Don't quit your day job.*

No sign or sound of the truck. It was blazing mid-July hot, Ash was tired and thirsty, and now the meandering pilgrims' trail seemed much more inviting than the steep, straight-shot sculptor's trail. The new Nike trainers that Lalia gave him had looked great out of the box but gave crummy traction. He swatted the dirt from himself and started at a tentative pace down the trail in the direction of the eleventh station. If the truck showed up again he could always duck out of sight.

Oddly, Elfa was spinning an extended (i.e. excruciating) dance mix of "Relax" on the radio. He remembered her condemning Frankie Goes to Hollywood as *basura* months ago. Either someone had requested it, or some other someone was there in the studio with her holding a gun to her head. Maybe both. Or maybe it had something to do with Sammy Hayes, whose show she was covering, likely at her own insistence. As the next station neared and the soft-surfaced trail sloped away gently beneath him, tugging him forward, Ash began to imagine himself back at the Rede stables in Visalia, calling Mandy on the XAMO request line like before, and the thought made him smile. As recently as an hour ago the prospect of things going back to exactly what they'd been before his coming to Nueva Anapra would have been like a sucker-punch to his gut; might even have brought him to the depths of paralytic despair. As in Dr.-Tune-was-right-to-worry-about-you-committing-suicide despair. Because it would mean that the mission was a failure, that *he* was a failure. The Rede curse would continue. But now the mission seemed not so awfully urgent and important, the curse itself a less and less substantial thing in Asher's mind. It might even be just another category of dismal, superstitious bullshit. A candle in search of a saint. It came to him now that what he'd really like to do is forget the whole fucking dumb-shit idea and go home.

Cuando desenterras el pasado, todo lo que obtienes está sucio.

Not his *bisabuelos*'s words but his *abuelo*'s. *When you dig up the past, all you get is dirty.* Unlike Mauricio, Ivan had brooked absolutely no use for, or consideration of, the past—maybe because every one of his toes and three fingers of his left hand were themselves nothing but useless memories. Maybe because the war that had claimed them had no legitimate name. Maybe because his mangled body had made him unable to ride or train horses after that nameless war, effectively estranging him from the family business. Maybe because in the chambers of his own broken heart he suspected the Rede curse might be real. Or maybe—just maybe—because he'd had the right idea the entire fucking time.

As the path glided down Ash lost track of the marker numbers. It was a lovingly curated trail, layered in Indian-red chat that no doubt had to be reapplied after each heavy rain, and bounded at the appropriate stress-points by stone safety walls and check dams to protect against runoff. Yes, someone had loved this ugly black mountain, a whole lot of someones in fact, and they continued to love it still. Strange that Mauricio had wed his faithless bride in a place shaped and kept by the stubbornness of faith. Who could blame him for thinking that the succession of women who'd plagued his family ever since then could only be explained by another kind of faith, in the form of a curse?

Then Asher stopped himself short, for he'd come to an honest-to-goodness fork in the road. The trail branched in two before him. Uncomfortable memories of Robert Frost and Mrs. Garvey's junior-high English class flitted across his brain: he had stumbled into a Chihuahuan-desert sendup of "The Road Not Taken," or maybe even "Stopping by Woods on a Snowy Evening," sans the woods and the snow. The right path went in a slight upward grade closer to the mountain, much like the railroad tracks he'd followed when he was being chased on horseback a few nights ago, while the left tracked down into a stand of creosote. Having gone right last time, this time he opted for the left.

335

Beyond the creosote bushes he came to a clearing where seven waist-high stone shrines stood in a semicircle. But these weren't Stations of the Cross; seemed he'd taken an offshoot from the main path. A man in Saint Leo University sweats and canvas fanny pack was kneeling before one of the shrines. He heard the approaching sound of Asher's radio and stood up, his devotion incomplete. It was Padre Snoddy.

"Why, it's Neil Peart, if I'm not mistaken," he said, his guarded expression giving way to a bemused but kindly grin. "I hadn't imagined I would ever run in to you again. Never in a hundred years."

He offered his hand in greeting, and when Asher went to accept it he noticed that the shrine Padre Snoddy had been praying to had been damaged. Where a clay relief of the Pieta should have been there was only a shattered fragment of a man's bare, prone foot and a woman's bent, robed knee.

"Yes, a crying shame, isn't it?" said Padre Snoddy. He held his arm out in a solemn sweeping gesture towards the other stone shrines. All of them bore similarly smashed or missing plaquette icons. Then Padre Snoddy pointed to the Little John radio in Asher's hand, and his smile returned. "Hey, that's a genuine classic novelty item there. I haven't seen one of those in years, except, you know, the one just like it I've got in my apartment."

"What happened to all of them?" Asher asked.

"You mean the Seven Sorrows?" The Padre shrugged. "The work of vandals, sadly. Kids like you, for the most part, but not always. It's a constant battle. This old mountain attracts the righteous and the unrighteous alike, always has." He removed a silver pouch of tropical-flavor Capri-Sun from his fanny pack as he spoke, offering one out to Asher, this one a flavor called Surfer Cooler. Asher accepted it almost unconsciously, his thirst taking over. He pulled the little straw from its adhesive, punctured the bag with it, and drank. The contents were delicious.

"You know," the Padre continued amiably after enjoying a hit from his own straw, "back during the Reformation, protestant mobs used to go through cathedrals smashing statues, ripping the curtains, burning priceless artwork, and even pissing on the altar—because they thought these things all represented violations of the second commandment. I suppose on some level you have to admire that kind of devotion, misguided as it might be, when it's rooted in faith. But I can't help suspecting that the acts of devotion you see here were inspired less by the *Spiritus Sanctus* than a case of Tecate."

"Not Satan?" Asher said.

"I'm not acquainted with that brand of beer."

Ash had finished his drink.

"You've been out here awhile," observed Padre Snoddy. "And how is the mission coming along? Isn't that what you called it—your 'mission'?"

It was Asher's turn to shrug. "Maybe I was wrong to call it that. And a lot has happened since that night. There's no mission anymore. I was just being…stupid."

"I don't think Strummer would see it that way." The Padre was grinning again.

"You were listening?"

"To *The Party Line with Mandy*? Most assuredly. Longtime listener, regular caller. I like to think Mandy and I have one of those special DJ-listener relationships. Marvelously erudite for such a young woman in such a, well, *provincial* media market. She turned me on to The Replacements, and I introduced her to Marshall Crenshaw."

"You're Niles," said Ash.

"At your service. And *you're* Strummer. No need to hide it from me. I remain bound by canon law.

"From what I heard you say on the air the other night," he added, "it seems the mission is alive and well."

"They're looking for me," said Ash.

"You're hiding out here, then."

"Yes."

Padre Snoddy eyed the sun doubtfully, then Asher's clothing. "In plain sight, is that the strategy? You're a bit conspicuous in that trendy garb of yours. Who is 'they,' might I ask?"

"Right now I think they're a brown four-by-four that's been trolling the mountain trail for the last hour or so."

"Art?" Again the young Padre looked bemused—as if it were his default facial expression. "Art Mercado is a volunteer on the trail committee. Has been since before I ever arrived in this humble neck of the woods. He was just here not ten minutes ago. We were kicking around options for restoring these damaged shrines, as a matter of fact."

Asher shrugged again. "If you say so."

"Ah, the voice of doubt. I know it well, believe me. Suppose you walk with me back to Nueva Anapra, then? I'm on foot myself, but once we're back at the church I can offer you sanctuary, both physical and legal, if necessary. No strings attached."

Ash thought it over. Lalia and Asia would be waiting for him, and he owed Lalia proper thanks and an honorable farewell for helping him this far. To say nothing of Asia's rightful owners. To say nothing of Casey Barefoot. But the problem of escaping this predicament and making it back to Visalia without getting his own head blown off remained, and here before him stood the only plausible solution.

"Can I meet you there?" he replied at last. "I have something to do first. A couple of somethings."

The Padre stood silent, studying Asher's face. "All right, then," he said, and then he reached into his fanny pack and removed another silver pouch of liquid heaven. Orange flavor.

"Just in case," he said.

They shook hands and the Padre proceeded back to the main trail alone. Asher stayed behind and watched him leave, afraid to give away the route back to Lalia's hideout by going too soon. "Mad World," a favorite of his, was playing on the Little John.

"That was Tears for Fears," Mandy broke in as the song faded out. "Doing a song from back before most of you ever heard of them, I think. They're all over the MTV now, as you know, and good for them. Don't get me wrong, I love 'Shout' and 'Everybody Wants to Rule the World' just as much as the rest of you. And I love 'Raspberry Beret' by Prince and I love all those nine hundred Phil Collins hits on the charts right now. But do you know what I love more?

"I love diamonds in the rough. I love the kind of beauty that nobody cares about or appreciates. You know what I'm talking about, all of you who hate living here and wish you lived in someplace sexy like Austin or San Antonio or Cancún or, I don't know, goddamn Ibiza. El Paso's ugly, you say. And it's boring. *Es aburrido aquí. No hay nada que hacer.* But the Hitman still tells me this city—*these* cities—are the most beautiful places he's ever seen on Earth. This is a dude who's lived in the Hollywood Hills and on Fifth Avenue, at one time or another, and visited some exotic places I can't even pronounce.

"So here's to diamonds in the rough. I have in hand my last bottle of real Coke, given to me by another good friend back in April when New Coke first hit the stores, and we all thought the 'Real Thing' was going away forever. I don't know when new-old Coke 'Classic' is going to show up, but right now I lift my bottle in toast to my best friend in the world, because he's also the Real Thing, and I know he's going to be back. Here's to the Hitman. And in that same spirit, I'm going to play you more songs by people who everyone loves now but didn't always, which is important to remember. Because some people have conveniently slippery memories. I'm going to play 'Solsbury Hill,' by Phil Collins's old bandmate Peter Gabriel. I'm going to play something from Prince's very first album. Something by that new band that I'm very fond of, R.E.M. But first here's another diamond that the Hitman discovered before anybody else, going all the way back to 1964. Recorded by a kid from east El Paso."

The famous drum-fill by The Bobby Fuller Four led Mandy's next slate of tunes. Satisfied that Padre Snoddy had moved on far enough and been gone long enough, Asher opened the other pouch of Capri-Sun and resumed walking the path, which linked up right away with the main trail again a few yards farther on. Here the fourth Station occupied a ledge of protruding rock facing the lower branch trail to the Seven Sorrows. As Mandy had promised, "I Fought the Law" segued to "Solsbury Hill." And all at once it occurred to Asher that he felt happy.

A peculiar thing to contemplate, this happiness. It wasn't as if anything had worked out as he'd envisioned before he left Visalia. None of it had worked out. So maybe happiness wasn't the word. He felt *better*. Less angry, less frustrated with the world as it had been before all of this. No doubt Dr. Tune could have supplied the right word.

Liberado, that was the word in Spanish. *Released.*

He had come to the artisan's house, a roofless ruin of a stone cottage tucked in a narrow pocket formed by a curve in the main pilgrims' trail. From here, the hidden artisan's trail ran in a straight line up to the mountain peak. Ash left the main trail and began his way down to the ruin and that other path that would return him to Lalia's hideout by the railroad tracks.

Something thumped Ash's left leg just above the ankle as he descended. Thumped it hard, like the force of a BB. When he paused and saw the coiled diamondback there in the loosened dust on the mountain slope, readying for a second strike, he froze, mostly in surprise. The thump was strong but it hadn't hurt. With any luck the bite hadn't made it through his jeans. Slowly he lifted his other foot behind him in an effort to back away, the balancing act made trickier by the Little John radio he stilled clutched in one hand and the drink pouch in the other. He brought the tip of his foot down on that same loose soil behind him, seeking purchase with his eyes fixed on the rattler, and the soil gave way. His foot slid out from underneath him and he fell chin-first into the slope, fresh pain exploding near his eye as the rattler struck the side of his face.

Through the studio window Elfa watched a baby blue Gran Fury pull into the station lot, dealer tags still on display. Simon La Paz emerged from the driver's side and stretched his arms, apropos of nothing, smiling and svelte in a jaunty tennis-wear getup, and then strode out of sight towards the building entrance. The lunk closed his newspaper and got to his feet.

"*Relajete*, Tommy," said Simon in a subdued voice, walking into the studio moments later, a bit breathless. He surveyed the floor debris with the briefest of frowns, then beamed again when he saw Elfa.

"My hero!" he exclaimed, and held his arms out.

"Who, me?" said Elfa.

"Do you know what you've done for this ministry, my dear? You've saved us!"

"That's hard to believe."

"But you have!" He came to her, bent, and hugged her where she sat in the jockey's chair, gathering her up in his arms so that the scent of his pricey cologne—Obsession? Yves Saint Laurent?—filled her nostrils. Not an altogether bad sensation, she conceded inwardly.

"Excuse me," she said, holding a finger up. "Talk about the Passion" was fading on the turntable. Elfa pulled the mike to her and rattled off a quick air-check and weather report, introduced the next song, and pushed the mike away. When she looked again Simon and the lunk were conferring privately in the corridor. The lunk nodded and left.

"I have a message for you, by the way," Simon announced, returning.

"From who, pray tell?"

"Ms. Piper."

Elfa eyed him skeptically. "I'm a wee bit confused about what's going on," she said. "I didn't even think I still had a job here. I came in to cover Sammy's shift because I don't want him to lose *his* job, and when nobody stopped me, I just kept on doing it."

"The confusion still reigns, to be sure," Simon acknowledged with a heavy sigh. "Your friend Strummer stirred up quite the hornets' nest. I've been preoccupied, to put it mildly, with convincing the Mexican authorities of my innocence these last few days. I know Ms. Piper has been coping with similar troubles on the American side, both from the authorities and the press, and she wants you to know that's why she hasn't been available."

"Okay, fair enough. But when she stopped returning my calls I went to her lawyer directly, and he was a lot more generous with me, even though he only had bad news to give me."

"And what did he say?"

"That Sammy renounced his U.S. citizenship ten years ago, and INS isn't letting foreign nationals with HIV into the country right now, no ifs, ands, or buts. He told me that Helen knows this too and she's basically given up."

"Yes, that much is true," Simon replied. "As far as her attorney knows. It is *he* whom she's given up on at this point, not Mr. Hayes. Her message to you is that our mutual friend, Sam, will be moved across the border tonight and, in a few days, taken to Cedars-Sinai in Los Angeles, where she's arranged for him to receive the best medical care available anywhere in the United States."

"Tonight? How is she going to do that?" Even as she asked, Elfa recognized that the answer was obvious. Simon glanced around the room in search of a seat, locating the plastic chair the lunk had been sitting in beside the studio entrance, then fetched it and sat down close beside Elfa.

"Let's suppose," Simon began, "just *suppose*, that there is *some* truth to the allegations that Mr. Strummer—his real name is Asher Rede, as we all now know—made from this very room, indeed from that very chair you're seated in now, over the airwaves that night. That my ministry, like

344

Piper Ministries before it, engages in a variety of humanitarian efforts for the people of Anapra…and that among these efforts is helping those who seek a better life and better wages in the United States to achieve those aspirations."

"'Let's suppose,'" Elfa repeated, watching his face for evidence of duplicity. "Speaking *hypothetically*."

"*Creo que nos entendemos*," he affirmed with a weighty nod. "Such an arrangement, if it existed, would necessitate the desire and consent of all involved in order to work. Crossing the border is not an end in itself; merely surviving the river canals or the treacherous desert, or merely evading capture by La Migra, are not feats worthy of aspiration. *If* I were indeed involved in the kind of 'human smuggling' scheme that Mr. Strummer described, it would only be because I had reasonable assurance from someone on the American side that the men and women, and boys and girls, I was sending their way had somewhere to go and something to do when they arrived. In short, that they had a future. And that future could only exist because someone north of the border saw profit in it."

"But that's just what Asher—what *Strummer*—said," Elfa reminded him. "You smuggle them across, and she employs them at her racetrack-casino, or she farms them out to her rich fat-cat friends."

"Exactly!" Simon's eyebrows jumped and his dimples—Elfa had never guessed he was that young—stood out in sunk relief on either side of his glowing, professionally waxed face as he smiled his approval.

"But you aren't telling me anything that I haven't already heard. I still don't understand *any* of this."

Simon rose and moved the chair away from himself. "No, you *haven't* heard it, because until now you haven't heard it from *me*. Now you know that if I were actually involved in such a compact, then by its very nature it could not be a crime. Your friend Asher witnessed things that he *concluded* to be crimes because he has other, more personal grounds for wishing ill against Ms. Piper. Grounds that have nothing whatsoever to do with you or me."

Troubled, Elfa returned to the soundboard for the next air-check. She read live spots for Cowtown Liquors and the Texas Super Custom Lowrider Car Show '85—hosted by Cheech and Chong! Admission free for children under two!—while Simon waited.

"Bravo," he said when she turned back to face him. "Speaking of the future, I believe you still have one here at Radio XAMO, if that prospect interests you."

A vehicle approaching. He had fetched up against the outer wall of the artisan's house.

Pain. Again.

You're making a damned ass out of yourself, young man, Dr. Tune said.

The distorted wail of guitar, rising and falling like a Klaxon submerged in some pulsing bottomless pool of liquid. A brooding English voice proclaiming himself "son and heir"—of what Ash couldn't make out.

Then he heard the vehicle decelerate to a portentous crawl, tires crunching the trail surface just above his line of sight. Asher reached for the Little John radio to silence it, finding only his hat instead. The radio had landed further down the slope. He managed to get to his feet, keeping his head low, the tingle in his lower leg uncomfortable but not yet crippling. The immediate pain was in the left side of his face, where the rattler had made clean contact. His left eyelid was swelling fast, the vision there narrowing to a red slit of light. He fell to crawling on hands and knees along the sandstone wall. His right hand found the Little John radio lodged on its side near the corner, its yellow faux-toilet lid snapped away. He took the radio in both hands and clicked the volume dial all the way off.

Sensing movement from the truck above him, he scrambled around the little roofless structure's corner to its front, where a skeletal, weather-blighted wooden doorframe remained. Now his leg offered searing jolts of pain at the slightest pressure. He crawled through the doorframe anyway, pushed himself into the adjoining corner, and vomited on the ground.

Next came a man's voice, the squeal of a tailgate being lowered, and then barking.

Willie and Waylon.

Asher lay on his side, head swimming, and drew his legs up towards his chest in an effort to better hide himself behind the inner wall. His gun was still tucked in the waist of his jeans. He pulled it free and released the safety latch.

The barking ceased, but he heard the clatter of long-nailed paws against the rocks and the busy, investigative sniffing of a canine on the other side of the wall. The tiny house was the size of a modest walk-in closet, hardly large enough to accommodate a bedroll and small table, if that. A crumbling fireplace and chimney dominated the wall opposite from where Ash lay on his side in the dirt. He wondered if the artisan who'd lived here decades ago, devoting his whole waking life to that eyeless Christ atop the mountain, had ever for the slightest millisecond doubted his work. Then he turned his one functional eye back to the doorway and raised his gun.

No puedes cubrir el sol con un dedo.

"Shut up," Asher rasped through his teeth.

A dog appeared in the doorway, just one dog. Ash fired the gun. The dog yelped, the bullet missing him by a sliver and exploding against the rock wall, and fled. Then the silhouette of a man appeared in the doorway, hands raised. Ash fired again.

The man lowered his hands. Ash had missed.

"*No tengas miedo,*" said the man.

"*Por qué no?*"

They each held their positions, frozen in fear or futility; it was hard to say which. Sweat stung Ash's remaining good eye. The other was numb and swollen shut.

The man exhaled a callous laugh, his posture easing. "*Porque ya estás muerto.*"

Because you're already dead.

Ash squeezed the trigger again. Nothing happened. The silhouette turned and left. Asher lowered the gun, both hands trembling now, and let it fall. The sun had shifted behind the mountain in its long descent, and the shadows in its wake enfolded him.

22

"Ain't good lookin', but you know I ain't shy," Sammy warbled (with remarkable strength) through his oxygen mask. Elfa clutched his saline bag and tried to steady herself against the edge of the loft bunk where he lay, longing to sit in one of the camper's two crushed-velvet swivel chairs, but the I.V. tube wasn't long enough.

"Bob Seger!" Simon called from the camper's passenger seat below. "'Ramblin' Gamblin' Man.'"

"Jawohl," Sammy replied.

"Would you pretty-please shut your face, you old pain in the ass?" Elfa admonished.

"Ah, *that* I will do soon enough. Never fear, my sweet."

Tommy Cereceres, the lunk, was at the camper's wheel. The lights of civilization beyond the windows had dwindled to near blackness as they edged out of Juárez proper and into the dirt-road shanty-land of Anapra. The Winnebago's headlights, so far as she could tell, revealed only a few

350

scant yards' worth of rutted white caliche at a time. How could he even see well enough to navigate?

"Try this one," Sammy continued, fraying her patience to its last ragged fiber. "*The sweetest woman in the world can be the meanest woman in the world if you make her that way.*" He winked at Elfa.

"*Esos son…*" ventured Tommy after an evidently stumped silence from Simon. The first words he'd uttered since they'd loaded Sammy into the Winnie's loft and departed Hospital Norte Médico in the heart of Juárez.

"The Persuaders," Simon finished for him. Tommy nodded in recognition.

"*Órale, vatos,*" Sammy rasped. And his eyelids drew closed.

"Stay with me," Elfa prodded.

"Maurice Williams and The Zodiacs," he replied at once.

"Wasn't that one by the Four Seasons?" Simon interjected.

"*Shh!*" Elfa hissed. "You two chuckleheads aren't helping! Stop making him talk."

Darkness without. The Carter-era crochet shades over the kitchenette window swung wide as the camper rocked, offering bleak claustrophobic glimpses of moonless velvet black—the kind that seemed to physically press against the outside glass—and nothing more. Fortunately that same rocking motion caused some of Elfa's hair to catch on a brass ceiling fixture that turned out to be a hook, probably for some good ole plant-hanging macramé. She found the notch in the I.V. bag and suspended it from the ceiling hook, then took a moment's rest in the nearest lounger.

Simon and Tommy had fallen to hushed, business-minded small talk in Spanish—a pending mutuel quiniela at the Juárez Turf Club—as if Spanish weren't her own mother tongue. Perhaps because Tommy was plainly more comfortable with it than English. All of it growing more surreal by the second. They might just as well have been plowing through Damnation Alley, Jan-Michael Vincent and George Peppard piloting up front rather than Simon and Tommy, a gauntlet of mutant roaches and scorpions awaiting them out there in the dark. Hell on earth. Or the drive-in-movie version of it, at any rate. How had she gotten herself into this? And why?

Because...Sammy, she reminded herself. Because the prospect of losing him so soon was a kind of hellish specter all its own. She trusted the two shady figures up front about as implicitly as she trusted a mutant scorpion, but they wanted to help Sam as much as she did, of that there was no doubt. And that was kind of touching, albeit weird beyond estimation.

Then she saw it through the windshield, the trick to Tommy's amazing navigational skill. Of course. The XAMO transmitter, its airplane light pulsing alone in the dark. The voice of God, heralded by the torch of God. Gradually the light swung around to the driver's side as Tommy steered the camper north through the open *despoblado* and the unguarded border. Some part of her still expected Shaw and his two dogs to come riding out of the dark and waylay them.

Instead, the handsomely lit form of the Piper mansion came soon into view. Helen was waiting for them outside by the fountain, a cordless phone pressed to her ear. She gestured to the camper and then to the open front door of the house when they got out, hastening them to get on with bringing Sammy inside while she carried on a conversation with one of her attorneys.

Idahly met them in the front foyer and directed them to the great-room, where a fully functional hospital bed, I.V. pole, oxygen tank, and cardiac-event monitor had been set up in the center. A white-haired gentleman in a string tie and lab coat was seated in one of the armchairs perusing an issue of *Us Weekly* with Shirley MacLaine on the cover.

"I see we've arrived in the V.I.P. wing at Piper Towers," Sammy wisecracked from his wheelchair. "Valet doctors, fresh imported oxygen, and chilled champagne in every room. *N'est-ce pas?* And where's the cable TV?"

"I see my new house-guest has arrived," said Helen, coming down the foyer steps. Elfa was positioning Sam beside the bed. "Any problems getting this *enfant terrible* here?"

"Nary a hitch," Simon replied a little too proudly.

Elfa set the wheelchair brake and helped Sammy to his feet. The weight of his almost sixty-year-old body as she pulled him towards her belied the levity in his voice; he felt heavy with illness, slumped and slackened; the faint but unmistakably labored noises from the recesses of his chest telling their own grim story. The man in the lab coat set aside his magazine and rose to collect Sammy's vitals after Elfa had him settled in the bed.

"Sam, this is Dr. Rosoff," Helen said. "Please mind his orders and give him no lip."

"*Yassum*, Miss Scawlett," croaked Sam.

"Would anyone care for a late supper?" she asked, addressing the rest of them.

"Not necessary," Simon replied, though Tommy looked as if he could've leaped at a free meal. "It was our pleasure to help."

"And you, Elfa?"

"Sure. I'm going to need a lift home, though."

"Fair enough," Helen said. "I thought we'd go up to the casino before the restaurant closes. I'll drop you off on the way back."

Sam had already fallen asleep. Elfa followed the others back out through the foyer after sparing him one more worried glance. After exchanging a few pleasantries with Helen, Simon La Paz and Tommy Cereceres returned to the Winnebago and headed out.

"I guess maybe I owe you an apology," Elfa said, accompanying Helen out to the garage wing of the house.

"What on earth for, dear?" She removed a key fob from her purse and pointed it at the garage; one of the four bay doors slid upward to reveal the gleaming chrome grille of her sumptuous Lincoln Town Car.

"I thought you'd given up on Sam. I thought you didn't care."

"And what do you think now?"

They had come to a halt in front of the open garage door. Elfa considered her answer.

"Now I don't know."

"That's rather cagey of you," Helen said, nodding appreciatively. "But you should know, there's no crime in *thinking* badly of someone. I've entertained my share of uncharitable thoughts about a great many people over the years—the overwhelming majority of them entirely justified, mind you. As long as you don't actually *speak* badly of those people, or, you know, take out a full-page ad in *Variety* proclaiming it, then you've nothing to apologize for if it turns out you're wrong."

"That wasn't all of it, though."

A look of impatience darkened Helen's face—the kind that came from enduring the silent opprobrium of others day in and day out, from knowing full well how much they blamed you for their suffering, and how, by the same token, you wished they'd all stick their blame and suffering up their self-righteous, ungrateful, freeloading asses. Elfa thought of Sammy's spot-on observation about the rich: *They believe they're* worse *off than the rest of us. They believe they are* more *abused and pushed-around and exploited than anyone else. Perverse, I know.*

"Listen, I have to ask you for a rather large favor," Helen said then. It was maybe the absolute last thing Elfa would've expected to issue from her mouth under the circumstances, short of a confession of murder.

"Then my answer is no," said Elfa, surprising herself in the same instant.

"There's no call to be ungracious," Helen warned, her head drawing back. "You haven't even heard my request yet. Maybe it involves something, or *someone*, you have good reason to care about."

"More than my own mother?"

Her impatience was threatening to spill over outright, but Helen planted her hands on her hips as if willing it not to. "I'm afraid I don't follow you, kid. I was only going to ask if you'd accompany Sam to Los Angeles until I can make it out there myself. I have business here right now that simply won't wait. I'd put you up in a nice hotel, of course, and compensate you for your time and trouble. Is it so unreasonable of me to suppose you might want to do that? For Sam's sake if not mine?"

"You fired my mother. Don't act like you don't know, or pretend like you didn't do it on purpose. And now you have the nerve to explain to me why I should give two shits about what *you* want? You don't care about Sammy, not really. You don't care about anyone but yourself. If you did, you wouldn't be standing there throwing money at me to handle it for you."

The spillover came. Suddenly Helen Piper was weeping right in front of her. The tears spilled, plentiful and silent, right out of her wide stupefied eyes as if she were an ordinary, mortal human being after all. Still she held Elfa's gaze in something like defiance for a long and excruciating several seconds, until it became too much and she looked away, dropping her car keys onto the glimmering acrylic-sealed driveway pavement and burying her face in her hands. For her own part Elfa could only watch her cry while careening through her own wild salvo of emotions, at the same time stunned and sympathetic and furious at this ridiculous reptilian millionaire spinster with hardened razor icicles coursing through her veins for provoking her, somehow, to genuine pity. So perhaps what happened next was not only inevitable but also serendipitous.

Someone was approaching on horseback. Hooves clopping light and easy on gravel somewhere beyond the water fountain, in the direction of the railroad tracks and the black mountain.

Helen shuddered soundlessly, may even have heaved a dreadful disconsolate sob or two, before lowering her hands and raising those same acid-laced stiletto eyes to meet Elfa's once more before she too recognized the approaching sound. Her face was a smeared and haggard effigy of itself.

A white horse. A rag-robed figure astride it.

"No," Helen rasped.

The white horse reached the fountain, paused and lifted its nostrils as if to sample the air, and then circumnavigated it.

"No," Helen repeated, voice faltering.

The white horse came. The white horse found them. It stopped.

"What?" Helen said, trembling with rekindled anger. "What now, you bitch?"

"*Thta-ween-ah!*" the rider answered.

23

Love. All you need is love. Love will find a way. Love will keep us together. Could it be I'm falling in love? Lawyers in love. I love the nightlife. What's love got to do with it? Love at first sting. I love rock n' roll. Lookin' for love. Hot love. Crazy love. When love comes to town. Feel like makin' love. Love me do. Can't buy me love. Thin line between love and hate. Do you love as good as you look? When a man loves a woman. This ain't the summer of love. My one and only love. You're in love. Will you still love me tomorrow? Let your love flow. Lovers in a dangerous time. Can't help falling in love. Victim of love. It's only love. Words of love. Bye bye love. Need your love. I want to know what love is. Lover's rock. Turn your back on love. Everybody I love you. Modern love. The look of love. I'm not in love. Love child. Love's crashing waves. Tunnel of love. Not enough love in the world. Real love. Love her madly. Love me two times. Hello, I love you. Victim of love. The best of my love. Never my love. Shine a little love. All the girls love Alice. Mama can't buy you love. Love song. What's so funny 'bout peace, love and understanding. Love me tender. I want you,

I need you, I love you. See what love can do. Love is a stranger. When will I be loved? Say you love me. For your love. Modern love is automatic. Space age love song. Love and marriage. Love is alive. I dig love. You're in love, Charlie Brown. The one you love. Lust to love. Method of modern love. Love me like music. What about love? What is love? Do you believe in love? Sea of love. Love stinks. Somebody to love. Plastic fantastic lover. Love potion #9. Oh my love. Every man has a woman who loves him. I need a lover who won't drive me crazy. Give my love to Rose. Stone in love. Send her my love. Shot full of love. What are we doin' in love? Don't call it love. All my love. Whole lotta love. Love is a rose. Endless love. I love you, Suzanne. It must be love. Dedicated to the one I love. Heard it in a love song. My love. Lovely to see you. Only love can break your heart. Don't tell me you love me. I honestly love you. How deep is your love. Your love. I think I love you. We live for love. Love is a battlefield. Silly love songs. Loves me like a rock. 50 ways to leave your lover. Love comes quickly. Baby, I love your way. You can't hurry love. Easy lover. Tattooed love boys. Message of love. International lover. Love my way. Crazy little thing called love. I'm in love with my car. Baby, I love you. I love L.A. Don't renege on our love. Chuck E.'s in love. Lovers in the wind. 4.47 AM (The remains of our love). Love in vain. Pure love. I'll fall in love again. The power of love. Love hurts. Love the world away. True fine love. Jungle love. Love struck baby. Part-time lover. If you love somebody set them free.

24

Helen pushed away her untouched bowl of chop suey and turned her eyes in desolation to the pale bird-and-flower wallpaper to her right. The restaurant was in lunchtime high swing, the busy wait-staff in their black tunics and aprons reminding her, punishingly, of the steadfast wasp-stung butler Seong…and, accordingly, of home.

A baby was squalling in the next booth over.

Back in the car, within a stone's throw of the Visalia city limits, the roadside tents and mattress-laden jalopies crowded out what there was to be seen of the fields and groves. Some of the riffraff took notice of her father's new caramel-colored Imperial as it passed. Their sun-beaten faces and observant, hungry eyes made something inside of her shudder. So many of them, dispossessed and desperate. One of them a pregnant girl about Helen's age. In spite of herself, Helen regarded the budding protuberance underneath the v-shaped lace inset running down the front of her green day-dress, and again she shuddered.

She had irrigated herself with Lysol solution after every encounter, just as all of her favorite monthlies, from *Photoplay* to *Vogue Paris* to *I Confess*, had advised. As Margaret Sanger and the whole of modern science recommended. With Goossens, her first lover, this had proven to be the reliable course. Only now did the possibility occur to her that Goossens might have been defective in more ways than one.

Daddy was behind the Chrysler's wheel in his Cuban jacket and scarf, uncharacteristically pensive for most of the nine-hundred-mile drive. Zerina rode in the back, holding Tavish, her brindle Scottie, in her lap, and musing loudly about Cactus Jack Garner's chances at beating Hoover come the fall. Just imagine! Governor Piper and President Garner! Cactus Jack was a childhood friend of hers from Detroit, Texas, and surely in that spirit he would see fit to honor the Reverend Doctor Governor with a cabinet post! Imagine it! The stars are with us, and the stars never lie!

Until at last they came to a modest bungalow ranch house on a broad, weed-riddled patch of dust outside Tulare. A bent sign reading EVACUATION SALE ALL MUST BE SOLD still waggled against the wire fence facing the highway. A brown-skinned, middle-aged woman in a calico print dress emerged on the front porch as the Chrysler came to a stop. Mauricio soon joined her, hands in his trouser pockets, looking gaunt and sheepish. As Dr. Piper emerged from the vehicle and approached the house, Zerina and Helen on either side of him, the woman came towards him, face wet with soundless tears, threw her arms up, and hugged him to her tightly. At more than six feet, the Reverend Doctor was forced to bend forward to accommodate her small frame, to the point that the both of them were in danger of falling over for a few perilous seconds.

"*¿Puedo confiar en que los arreglos han sido satisfactorios?*" he rasped, still in the woman's hard and joyously tearful grip. She released him, then took his face into both hands and kissed him on the lips. Zerina adjusted her bulky peach-basket hat and raised a hand to her throat.

"My land!" she exclaimed, her east Texas coquette briefly subsuming her affected European vamp. "I do believe my goiter is coming on, Donald. It must have been the Darjeeling oolong I had with lunch at that appalling tea garden in Visalia. The drinking water in California never fails to vex my good health. Isn't it about time we begin the taxing journey home?"

But the Reverend Doctor raised a slender index finger to her in rare shushing mode. "There is business yet to conclude here, lambkin," he said. He touched the finger to his lips and gave her a chastising look over his shoulder.

Mauricio stepped forward. "Yes, and Mother has prepared supper for us."

He didn't lie. Beatriz Rede had made them a savory-sweet *mole poblano* and boiled turkey, served with fresh corn tortillas, rice with peas and diced carrots, and slices of avocado. There was no dining table in the house, only some rusted French garden chairs with rotted-through *chinoiserie* cushions, and a matching tripod table. Aside from a single hobnail milk-glass vase on the mantel and the corduroy-back checkerboard lying on the floor, there was precious little to indicate that the Rede clan had ever resided here.

They ate as the sun set, the light slanting in rose-colored beams through the windows. Helen refused any food, accepting only a dish of almonds and taking them back out onto the front porch.

The dying sun was lighting up an irrigation pond across the highway from the house. Mauricio came outside to find Helen seated on one of the two front stone pedestals, legs crossed, eating her almonds one at a time from a Ritz Blue glass tumbler.

"You father was going to bring Wahnfried."

It was something to say.

"Don't be a loon," Helen said. She flicked away an almond seed that she'd deemed disdainful in some way.

"There is still your training to think about."

She ignored him.

Mauricio moved to the pedestal opposite where she sat and leaned against it, pretending to mind his own business while simultaneously wanting nothing more than to take her into his arms. Just as any young husband had every right to wish for, and reach for, his wife. She was the oddest of creatures, this princess of the pink hacienda, this daughter of the great goat-testicle surgeon. This love of his life. Why she, and why he?

Across the road, two hawks who'd been perched on a fence wire beside the pond launched themselves in sudden pursuit of prey, darting aloft into the crimson light.

"I love you," he said softly.

Helen picked at her almonds, index finger pushing them to and fro inside the blue dish in her hand.

"You never fucked before, did you?" she said then.

Mauricio didn't move, but felt as if he'd been slapped.

"Pardon?" he said.

Helen leapt from her own perch and hurled the Blue Ritz tumbler against the concrete front steps, where it shattered. Almonds rained like hard bullets across the concrete porch.

"You heard me! You never *fucked* anybody before me, did you, you idiot wetneck! You think *love* and *fuck* are the same things, don't you? Answer me! Well I don't love you and I never will!"

And she slapped his face for real.

After sunset, the Doctor and the woman at last emerged from the house to set about the journey home. Helen lay asleep on the Bentwood leather settee in the back bedroom, under the sway of an atropine and phenobarbital admixture from the Doctor's cowhide Emdee bag. The Doctor pulled Mauricio aside near the Chrysler once Zerina and Tavish were safely ensconced in the front passenger seat.

"My daughter," the Doctor declared in confidential and refined Spanish, "suffers from *psychopathia sexualis*, known in the lay tongue as nymphomania. She is acquainted with the physical act of love, yet she does not love, not in the true sense—the platonic sense. She does not know Diotima's ladder, nor, I fear, is she destined to find let alone ascend it. She does not love you, she does not love even me; the manifest truth is that she may indeed never love another living thing apart from herself. For this reason I grieve for my daughter and tremble for her immortal soul. I fear that you too will grieve before long, for the understandable yet still foolish error of loving her. But do not despair. I know your grief. Let us both not condemn but rather pity her in her affliction. Please continue to love her and the child which, soon, she will bear you."

And then the Doctor climbed into his Imperial and drove off, trailed by a Red McKenzie crooner from his own radio station.

She gave birth on a chill November morning, on that same cragged leather settee, Beatriz acting as midwife.

"No," she moaned when Beatriz held the child, a boy, swaddled in a lavender patchwork quilt, to her in offering. "Take it away."

25

Elfa knew the woman seated astride the white horse from Buena Vista Emporium. Even in Elfa's childhood the woman had been a crone, ancient and somehow calamitous, a routine pest. Wafting into the shop on Sunday mornings in her rags and smelling of goat, objects disappearing into the voluminous folds and billowing tentacles of her fragrant shroud.

"That palomino," Helen said, regaining her composure. "Where the devil did you find her?"

The hag lifted her jagged ptotic chin and returned Helen's stare haughtily. Elfa found herself straining against her own eyes in the dark, the shadows playing tricks, as they appeared to suggest that the woman's rags had gone decidedly mod since those old days—were those really fishnet gloves and double-hoop earrings?

"*Encontré máth que un caballo,*" replied the hag. "*Encontré lo que queda de tu thangre fría y conthentida.*"

I found more than a horse; I found what's left of your cold, spoiled blood.

"What's she talking about?" Elfa asked.

"Get off of that horse right now, Eulalia!" Helen barked, ignoring the question. "I'm not going to tell you twice!"

The woman laughed harshly and tugged the palomino's reins to the left, prompting her to turn around. Already she was navigating away in the direction of the black mountain—the same way she'd come.

"*Thta-ween-ah!*" came the reply, this time a shrill taunt.

"You miserable hobo cunt!"

"That's the horse that Strum...that Asher took, isn't it?" Elfa said aloud, though more to herself than anyone else. Again Helen didn't answer; in fact she was no longer standing there. Elfa heard an iron gate squeal on its hinges somewhere. The old woman and the white horse were now nearly out of sight. A freight-train air horn sounded its approach from off the pitch-black desert far beyond the house, and Elfa grasped with sharp appreciation that she was stranded.

But then came the sound of hooves on pavement again, except closer. A bay horse emerged underneath the driveway's floodlights, Helen at the reins and wearing her favorite felt cowgirl hat. Another bay strode obediently beside her own mount, Helen clutching a lead line clipped to its bridle.

"Hop on, kid," Helen said. "We're going after the crazy bitch. It's what she wants us to do."

There was no possibility of argument. Elfa had ridden horseback maybe half a dozen times in her whole life, the thought of which reminded her (with unbidden guilt) of Casey Barefoot. Helen issued a few curt directions (some to Elfa and some to the horse, who was the smaller of the two bays), and soon enough Elfa and she were en route, the young bay complying with Elfa's every tug of the reins and nudge to the hindquarters just as if they were a lifelong pair.

Eulalia and the white palomino had reached the mountain and were just clambering up its bottom slope as the Southern Pacific freight was moving in along the eastbound track. Helen used the interlude while the train passed to remove a large stainless steel revolver from her saddlebag and check the chamber for bullets.

"I really don't like this," Elfa said as Helen tucked the gun back inside her saddlebag.

"Then don't do it," Helen said.

"You just *told* me to."

"I also remember telling you to knock off that Coca-Cola crusade of yours a few months back. You picked a funny time to start doing what I say." She turned her head and nodded towards the house. "Go back and wait with Sammy while I take care of this, then, if that's what you'd rather do. That woman has a stolen horse belonging to some good friends of mine."

"What's the gun for?"

"What do you think? I'm going to kill the old bat."

"No, you're not," Elfa said, alarmed. "You wouldn't!"

Helen bowed her head and chuckled dryly under the brim of her hat. At last the train completed its passage, the telemetry box on the last car winking its strobe light at them as it slid away in the dark. Helen lifted her head.

"And there she is, laying for us." She pointed to a spot further up the mountain where the white palomino stood in profile to them, the figure of the old woman still vaguely discernible astride its back. "Relax, hon," Helen added, returning to Elfa. "I'm not going to shoot anyone if I can help it. But Lalia isn't the only unsavory character who haunts this mountain. The place has kind of a violent history, if you didn't know. Better safe than sorry."

"Yes," Elfa answered softly. "I know."

"Come on, then, if you're coming," said Helen, oblivious to the irony. Naturally she had no way of knowing about Manny Schultz's murder or its connection to Elfa. "And if you are, then I can use your help getting that palomino back down here after we get her away from Lalia."

High above them, the white horse stirred to life again in the same instant as they. The old woman was without a doubt coaxing them on toward some inexplicable somewhere for some inexplicable reason. When they came to the westbound railroad tracks Helen stopped her horse and produced an angle-head flashlight, also from the saddlebag, and swept its beam over the mountain slope, revealing only jagged black-tinged layers of rock and ugly skeletal clutches of weeds, made all the more garish in the flashlight's merciless monochrome glare.

"Do you do this a lot?" Elfa asked.

"Hush," said Helen. She ran the beam once more over the mountainside before them, gave an unexpectedly daunted sigh, then killed the flashlight. "I can't begin to think how that freak of nature got that horse all the way up there so fast," Helen then admitted. "We're just going to have to keep following the train tracks as far as we can without losing her."

"There doesn't seem to be much danger of that," said Elfa. "She obviously wants us to follow her."

True enough, the white horse had halted yet again, its coat the only thing that stood out—even as a distant smudge—in the dark, which had thickened noticeably the further they moved away from the surrounding city lights. The mountain seemed to hug the darkness to itself like a blanket.

Andale," said Helen.

I'm really doing this, thought Elfa. What would Mandy think?

What would Strummer think?

Sometimes during the *Party Line* show he'd disappear into the XAMO library and reappear bearing some forgotten hit or, just as likely, some tasteless trinket-trash novelty—Weird Al Yankovic, Stars on 45, Rick Dees. One night he'd returned with an LP sporting a fuzzy green puppet character on the cover, an agitated expression on his face; not at all what she'd come to expect from Strummer. Those other picks had been snarky tongue-in-cheek wind-ups, chosen for their irony; this one was sincere.

"What's this?"

"No," he said, shushing her with his hands. "Just play it."

Of course she recognized the cover. *Sesame Street*, The Muppets. That wasn't the point. The dopey punch-drunk look on his face was the point.

"Ash…no. Jesus, come on. No way."

He lowered the record in his hands.

"What'd you just call me?"

And of course she'd also known his real name all along too, but *knowing* and *caring* were two different beasts altogether. At that moment she *cared* about his real name just about as much as she cared to hear "Mah Nà Mah Nà." Her face flushed and she'd shooed him away, instructing him to fetch Depeche Mode instead.

The white horse flitted in and out of sight. Helen and Elfa followed. The lights of west El Paso slid into view as they rounded the mountain's curve, a welcome sign of civilization in Elfa's judgment. One by one the television and radio towers arrayed along the southern tip of Mount Franklin winked into view, all of them juvenile cousins to the much older Radio XAMO tower on the opposite side of the river plain. When Helen paused again to run her flashlight over the mountain slope, the beam touched on a green miniature cross with a Roman-numeral seven at its center. Eulalia had led them onto the pilgrim trail not far from the place where Manny Schultz had been found shot dead five years ago.

"I'm liking this less and less," she said.

"What would you like me to do about it, sugar?" Helen snapped in reply. "You had your chance to go back to the house and wait there with Sammy."

"My father died on this mountain. I don't expect you to understand."

Helen killed the flashlight and returned it to her saddlebag. "Yes, I believe Sammy mentioned that to me once," she remarked, her tone softening just a little. "But I think we're probably close to whatever it is the old hag wants us to find, if only because I don't see her anywhere. Let's give it a few more minutes, then I promise we'll head back with or without the horse."

At that moment the palomino reappeared just ahead, this time riderless. She crossed the trail from behind a knot of creosote and paused, nose up, to test the air.

"Where's the old woman?" Elfa asked.

"She's right here." If that was a joke Helen gave no sign. She held out a gloved hand in a signal to keep still, lest the palomino take fright at their presence. The palomino bent her neck and touched her nose to the ground, lifted one hoof, and stretched her neck forward as if longing to move in that direction but wary of the first step.

"Somebody's coming," whispered Elfa. The sound of an engine had arisen somewhere below, moving closer. Then a set of headlights splashed against the mountainside up ahead and turned towards them. Meanwhile the palomino had found the nerve to pick her way down the slope, and disappeared from the trail.

"Dammit," said Helen. "Let's go before she wanders any further. I'm going to have to climb down there and lead her back up onto the trail on foot. I swear to Christ, the next time I see that mountaineering old harpy I'm liable to murder her with my bare hands."

They came to the place where the palomino had wandered off of the trail just as the vehicle, a brown Silverado with twin flood lamps hoop-mounted over the cab, came to a stop in front of them. The driver killed the engine but not the lights, then climbed out. It was Art Mercado, in jeans and cowboy hat.

"Señora Piper?" he asked, hitching up the waist of his jeans and pivoting his head in bafflement between the two horsewomen before him. He'd developed quite the beer belly since Elfa had seen him last. "Elfa?"

"Arturo," said Helen, curt to the point of bloodless. "You might have just scared off the filly we're trying to recapture. Did you not have anything better to do in the dead of night?"

"Yes, I saw her too," said Art, removing his hat in respect. His eyes shifted to Elfa in search of safety. "I was going to catch her and take her to Lou Barefoot myself before I found you. I thought it must be the palomino taken by the…that boy from the radio station."

"Art, you don't live in Nueva Anapra anymore," Elfa interrupted, denying him the comfort he sought. "What are you doing up here this time of night?"

"Never mind that," Helen said impatiently, dismounting her horse and snatching the lariat from her saddle horn. "At least there are three of us now, which should make things easier. Come with me, both of you."

"*Bleib!*" Art called towards the truck, raising his palm in a halting gesture. It was a German dog command that Elfa could recall hearing from only one other person in her life, ever. He helped her climb down from her horse, catching her by the arm as she freed herself of the stubborn remaining stirrup.

"I honestly don't know what *I'm* doing here," she huffed, more to herself than to Art, after finding terra firma again.

Helen was scoping the incline below the path's edge with her flashlight. "There she is, standing beside the old stone hut," she said. "Let's get this over with. Come on." She started down the slope, lariat in one hand, just as sure-footed as if she were clad in hiking boots rather than ostrich pumps.

Elfa moved to follow, but Art still had her by the arm. "No, *mija*," he said quietly in her ear, his grip tightening.

"What? Let go of me."

"You should stay here. This place...it's not for you. This is the place where Manny..." He longed not to finish his sentence; his face made that much clear.

"I know where we are," Elfa answered. "You have no idea. I've been back here to see it plenty of times since it happened. More times than you think."

He released her, his eyes suddenly unreadable. *Bleib*—it meant "stay" in German. Was he commanding her as well as the dog? That dog—

"Where did the dog come from, Art?" she said out loud.

"¿*Mande?*" It sounded like a play on his own name, coming from his lips. The English equivalent was *I beg your pardon?* He was looking more and more the way he had that day at Buena Vista Emporium. The day he'd come to tell her the news.

"The dog in the bed of your truck."

"Hello? Why am I all alone down here?" Helen yelled from below. "Are you two going to help me with this mess or not?"

Something had changed. Elfa felt as if she'd crossed some threshold, stumbled over some thin but bottomless crack in the fabric of everything from which there was no about-turn, and all before she'd had the chance to contemplate whether doing so was worth her while or not. The world was the same yet completely different. Art's face, which she'd known from earliest childhood, was also the same yet different. And once again, as when her father had died—or rather, when he was *murdered,* was *cut down,* was *shot dead,* was *blown away,* was *rubbed out*; pick the winning catch phrase, Jiminy Cricket!—nobody had extended her the common rudimentary human politesse of even seeking her consent.

Art offered no reply. Elfa left him there and started down the rocky slope. The palomino was standing idle, just as Helen had said, beside the ruined stone shell where the man who'd shaped the Christ monument from the dust of the ground—so to speak—had lived during the early thirties. Much later, and to far less public notoriety, the man now apparently struck still as a salt-pillar atop the trail behind her had discovered her father's body inside the same hut, face down in the dust, a single bullet wound between his shoulder blades and a black stain on the ground beneath him from where the bullet had exited his chest. Art had gone back into town for beer and burritos while Manny stayed to watch the Bobcat. The rains the night before had washed out more of the trail than both men had anticipated, and the morning's work had turned into a full day's work. Eventually, Elfa supposed, the work had been finished.

Helen had moved around to the palomino's left, then raised her arms out to both sides with the coiled lariat in one hand and began making kissing sounds. The horse answered her with a momentary turn of her head, then snorted and approached the doorway of the stone hut.

"Hold your arms out like I'm doing," Helen said to Elfa in slow, soft tones, as if she were speaking to someone whom she gave a damn about. It was obviously meant to sooth the horse. "Get ready to wave her down if she bolts."

Elfa obliged, but it was so dark, if the palomino had opted to run she would likely have been on top of her before she could even react. Helen segued from kissing noises to clucks to whistles and back to kisses again, tossing out a dizzying spectrum of horsey argot, but the palomino seemed to grow more defiant, lifting her nose, snorting, and pawing at the dirt just outside the hut's doorway. At last Helen dropped her arms to her sides, simply walked up to the horse, and slipped the lariat's noose end up over her head and past her ears.

"I don't know what this little Miss Priss is so agitated about," she said, cinching the noose, "but I'm not about to wait around here all—"

The palomino's head moved suddenly, and Helen screamed. Shrieked, in fact. No horsey talk was this. Elfa ran towards her in the dark, nearly falling over a bump of rock herself. She found Helen collapsed in the hut's doorway holding her left hand in her right, and the warmth of fresh blood touched her own hands when she tried to help Helen up again.

"My finger!" Helen cried. "God help me! She took my goddamn finger!"

"Art, come down here!" Elfa yelled over her shoulder. The palomino remained where she stood, even bending to sniff Elfa's hair as she fought to pull Helen upright against the doorframe and get control of the blood flow. The palomino bent again and nudged at Elfa's neck and shoulder.

"Stop that!" Elfa said, swatting her away. She got up and found Helen's flashlight in the other horse's saddlebag, then returned to Helen, bent, and shone the light on her left hand. The ring finger was nearly gone, the torn stump bleeding steadily. Art arrived and held out a cotton hankie, which Elfa took in exchange for the flashlight and wrapped quickly over the stump and around Helen's hand, drawing vaguely on her Indian Princess days at the Y. Again the palomino moved in and pressed her nose into Elfa's neck, snorted, and stamped her hoof on the ground. Startled, Art dropped the flashlight.

"I'll get it," Elfa told him, though Art scrambled for it anyway.

"Get my finger while you're at it, will you, babe?" Helen added, having recovered something of her old sass. "It must be lying around here someplace."

Elfa's hand found the flashlight first, the beam still lit and pointing at a slant toward the hut's opposite wall. As she picked it up the lamp also revealed something—*someone*—in the far corner. In the same instant Art seized the flashlight from her hand.

"*Rápidamente, mija*," he told her. "We must get her to the hospital." But Elfa snatched the flashlight back and shoved him away. When she raised the beam again some long-entombed yet elemental stratum of her soul leapt high into her beating chest, for it actually thought to find her own dead father lying there. Instead the light revealed a dirty green-and-white rugby shirt attached to a tangled shock of black hair.

"Strummer?"

The shape in the rugby shirt twitched. Now her heart froze with dread. Clutching the flashlight in both hands, she approached the shape cautiously and knelt, her brain at stubborn odds with what her eyes were seeing. An arm hooked over a knee clad in begrimed denim. The heel of a loose Avia high-top sneaker. Only the hair was familiar. She stretched out a hand to touch it, the sweat-slick roughness like animal fur. Her fingers traced an ear, the nape of a neck, all reassuringly human. The skin warm and clammy but alive. The smell of blood—was it his or Helen's? She drew her hand away.

"Asher, is that you? Talk to me."

"What the? For f-fuck's s-sake," Helen began, the beginnings of shock impeding her voice. "Wh-who are you...t-talking to?"

Asher groaned. At least Elfa had become reasonably certain that it was Asher/Strummer even though, impossible as it seemed, he appeared to have no face. Where was his face? Only a veiny, purple-black protrusion of tissue on one side of his head, as if part of his scalp had been torn off. Then the tissue blinked at her. Two swollen, deformed eyes all but buried in their sockets, yet open and conscious. She'd been looking him in the face all along.

Ash had been lost in a dream, was dreaming still for all the difference it made. A harsh light had pierced his dream. Shapes behind the light, one of them the shape of Mandy/Elfa, the wine-stained girl who'd inhabited so many of his dreams for so very long. One of them the shape of the man who'd come to kill him and then thought better of it. And one more, the shape of everything wrong and unjust and out of joint in the world. The shape of Timera Rede, Catherine Rede, Helen Rede. All of the wives and mothers who'd left him and his family. The shape of betrayal, of broken dreams, of love promised and withheld.

"*Mi novia infiel*," he whispered.

"What's that he's saying?" Helen asked. She had somehow gotten to her feet and joined Elfa and Arturo inside the hut.

"'My faithless bride,'" Elfa translated.

The eyes closed and opened again slowly in acknowledgment. Elfa found a hand, the one not swollen and blackened, and enclosed it in her own.

"I'm sorry, Asher," she said.

The eyes closed.

26

"Yes, my brother in Christ?" said the blue-suited man in Spanish. "Do you have testimony to share?"

Jared reached behind himself and pulled Asher and Lex close on either side.

"Yes, brother," he replied, leaning once more into the mike. "As a matter of fact, I do."

The room seemed to hold its breath. Asher looked up at his dad, sensing something off kilter, and he was right. Jared had gone dumb, mouth ajar and eyes shifting this way and that in stumped agitation, as if his brain were trying to summon words that simply didn't exist. Ash raised up on his tiptoes and leaned into the mike.

"Sta-*ween*-ah!"

A collective chuckle swept the room. That seemed to stir Jared out of his paralysis. He grinned and ruffled Ash's hair.

"We used to say that a lot in our house," he said. "My sons grew up hearing it, and so did I."

He released the two boys and approached the microphone with sudden confidence.

"Wolfman Jack had 'Squeeze my knobs,' Alan Freed had 'Moon doggin',' and Hitman Hayes had his *Krazy Kat* version of '*esta buena*'. When I was cruising Visalia in my Ford pickup as a teenager, I thought 'sta-*ween*-ah' was The Hitman's invention, until the day my *abuelo* set me straight on that subject.

"See, my grandfather was...*is* a *mesteñero*, the son of California mustangers. Our family line first came up from Trincheras, in Sonora, before the war between the United States and Mexico, and stayed after the treaty of Guadalupe Hidalgo made all of us Americans. We managed to keep some of our land after the Greaser Act, only to lose it all, much later, to the Great Depression." He pointed to the buddy-painting of Dr. Piper and Jesus. "And then a miracle happened. Dr. Piper bought our land back from the bank and returned it to us."

That brought on a spate of applause, some of it authentic, some of it tentative and confused. Jared held his hands up in polite interposition.

"But then that isn't the story I came to tell you today."

The paper streamers fluttered softly from the saucer-shaped air ducts in the cloistered heat. There was the abrupt sense that the funeral service had exceeded its rightful hour, that the late, great Reverend Doctor's memory had been duly honored, thank you very much; and now enough was enough. Asher looked to Timera, who sat with her chin on her shoulder, her disdain and cringing embarrassment at the whole pointless affair—or had her disdain now settled on Jared exclusively?—writ large in her body language.

For his own part, Jared looked suddenly youthful, Asher thought, in his long wavy hair and David Crosby walrus mustache. But had it really been his hairstyle that impressed Asher just then? In a sense, it was Jared alone versus the whole room now; Timera had already abandoned him— had already abandoned *them*. Jared had probably known it even then. Later Ash would come to realize that the right word for Jared's face that day wasn't *youthful* but rather *vulnerable*.

"I came to tell you about a man named Ivan Rede," Jared went on. "He was my father, and *abuelo* to these two boys. He helped my *Lito* to build our horse stables into a prospering business before he was sent to serve his country in Korea. Lost three fingers to frostbite while holding off a hundred thousand Red Chinese in the Chosin Valley in the winter of 1950—the Frozen Chosin, they called it. When my father came home, he could no longer ride or train horses, not as well as he used to, at any rate. Then my mother, who never liked being a housewife, decided she liked being housewife to a crippled war-vet horseman even less and left us. I still don't know if it was only my dad's missing fingers that sent her packing; maybe his disfigurement was only an excuse.

"I grew up fighting with my father a lot and listening to Radio XAMO a lot. There were other border blasters around in those days, mind you, but they didn't have Hitman Hayes. Sometimes my fights with Papa were about the music I was listening to. He hated that new rock 'n' roll stuff, and the more he hated it, the more I rubbed his ears in it at every opportunity. He did not know what to make of the Hitman, with his character voices and telephone pranks and 'sta-*ween*-ah'. Everybody else in Visalia thought Hitman Hayes was black, which was why so many parents hated him, but Papa said he sounded more like a white man trying to be Mexican. '*Sta buena* is what we used to say to a beautiful woman walking past,' Papa said. 'That joker on the radio, either he doesn't know Spanish or he doesn't like women.'

"Papa still had his machismo, his masculine pride, so long hair on a man was also effeminate in his eyes, as contemptible to him as it was to most Americans of his generation. So you can imagine his anger when I grew a thick Beatles mop-top in junior high, then wore my hair down to my shoulders all through high school. I was a garden-variety hippie, and yes, like a lot of hippies, I had a grudge against my parents. I especially began to blame Papa for my mother leaving us. He'd become a drinker, opening his first beer around ten in the morning and moving on to Cuervo around sundown, leaving it to me and *Lito* to keep the stables going. As much as Papa hated weakness, in the end he became the weakest man I ever knew."

He paused.

"But then...*that* isn't the story I came here to tell you, either."

"Please, brother, *do* tell us your story quickly," the blue-suited man prodded him from the stage, his smile straining.

"Right," Jared said, recovering once more. "Papa died three years ago. By then I had my own wife and children, as I think you can see. His funeral was nothing like this, of course. We buried him at the national cemetery in Bakersfield, beautiful bronze-plaque headstone. Which brings me back to my original point. After the funeral we were driving back to Visalia, and Hitman Hayes was on the radio. All of us in the car were silent. *Lito* was in the front seat with me, my wife and the boys in the back. I had just buried my father, *Lito* had just buried his son. What do you talk about at the end of a day like that? So I just let the radio play while we rolled through the California desert. Then the Hitman screeches out 'Sta-*ween*-ah!' while introducing the next song. And my *Lito* leaned forward in his seat and snapped the radio off.

"Well, I assumed it was the same thing as my Papa—*Lito* didn't like the Hitman's tacky, Frito Bandito fake-Mexican act, and I wasn't going to argue with him under the circumstances. But then both of my boys piped up from the backseat. 'We want to hear the Hitman! Bring back the Hitman!'"

Jared turned aside, smiling, to the bench where Mr. Famous and the redheaded woman were seated.

"I asked *Lito* why he turned the radio off. He was quiet for a long moment or two, and then instead of answering the question, he began telling a story. The same story that I want to tell you. The story of a rich doctor and his beautiful but spoiled daughter. The story of a famous radio station. The story of..."

The redheaded woman had shot abruptly to her feet, clutching her burgundy handbag to her chest, and started for the exit.

"...of the rich doctor's grandchild, who is sadly buried now in that grave in Bakersfield, and his great-grandchild, and his great-grandchildren, all of whom are fortunately standing here before you. It's a tragic story, but it has some beautiful moments. Don't you want to hear it?" He was addressing the redheaded woman directly, his voice rising—or rather strengthening, gathering unexpected force—with each of the last six words.

"I'm afraid that's all the time we—"

"*Abuela!*" Jared shouted into the microphone.

The woman halted. Mr. Famous had risen from his seat too and approached her, speaking softly, and she held up a palm in an at-ease gesture. She turned around and marched up to the microphone stand, laid a hand over the mike, and smiled down at Ash and Lex, a smile as leaden and false as a career politician's.

"Sugar, if that's true," she said in a barely contained snarl, turning that smile on Jared, "then you know that your family and mine have an agreement going back some fifty years, and the terms of that agreement haven't changed. I advise you to go back where you came from and never return, not if you'd like to hold onto that beloved hacienda of yours."

"Your son is dead," Jared replied. "I just thought...you might like to know that."

"Well, I sure do appreciate the courtesy," the woman said. She cast one more glance at Ash and Lex, as if marking their faces for some future unwelcome encounter like this one. "Thanks for thinking of me. You all have a nice day, now." She removed her hand from the microphone and proceeded again for the building exit.

"*Lito* always said you were a cold-hearted snake," Jared told her back as she strode away once more, Mr. Famous taking her arm. "But I didn't want to believe it."

"That, ah, concludes our service, everyone," the blue-suited man proclaimed from the stage in Spanish, and he motioned to the man in the black cowboy hat holding the *vihuela*. He resumed strumming and the two boys resumed singing. The crowd rose to their feet, united in one final reprise of "Don't Fence Me In" before filing out through the front entrance, where the ushers had swung the hangar doors wide, flooding the room with a rude blast of sunlight. Jared remained at the mike, looking first desolate, then angry. Livid, in fact.

He did it so fast that Asher didn't even comprehend that it was his father on the stage overturning the casket. He did register, as did everybody else, the corpse spilling like a rag doll from the satin-lined interior. Jared had moved on to the velvet painting, yanking it from the easel and smashing it in two over his knee, before they tackled him—the man in the blue suit and the *vihuela* player, his cowboy hat spilling from his head and tumbling from the pallets, where one of the boy singers rescued it from the dirty concrete floor, not far from where the Reverend Doctor Piper's final bodily remains had landed. The boy backed away from them, clutching what was probably his own father's hat in both hands. Then he met eyes with Asher, the whole abominable scene reflected in his face. A universe of inexplicable circumstantial misery, one pointless generation begetting another, pointlessness upon pointlessness. Why any of it? And who to blame?

Except there had been hope in this place. Only moments before, hope. That's what he glimpsed in the other boy's face: hope extinguished.

27

Elfa had been dreaming of a crystal teardrop falling from the sky, descending in a graceful arc, the weight of its rotund belly guiding its plunge and its translucent surface dancing with a prismatic range of colors in the sunlight. Then the plaintive tinging of her bedside phone woke her before the teardrop of her mind's eye could touch the earth.

The time on the Pioneer's flip-card clock display read 1:55 PM. The avocado Trimline's cradle tumbled to the carpet as she lifted the handset and tugged it towards her face, its coil-cord knotted inward upon itself like some contorted, self-devouring snake.

"My love, I speak to you from within smoggy view of the HOLLYWOOD sign," Sammy's voice greeted her from eight hundred miles away. "I can think of no better metaphor for my current predicament. *This* is where they've deposited me in the name of restoring my good health—in the bowels of a poison cloud."

"Do you have a private room, at least?" Elfa asked, sitting up in bed.

"Sadly, no," Sammy replied, although there was humor in his voice. "I am blessed with a roommate. Did I ever tell you about my brief, wretched career as a Presbyterian?"

He explained that the man lying a few feet away was a hairdresser-cum-producer who'd conceived *Hully Gully*, a TV dance show that Sammy had hosted for a while in the mid-sixties. *Hully Gully* had aired on Saturday afternoons on a UHF station whose owners also happened to be deacons at Presbyterian Church of Pasadena.

"At their urging, we both joined the church to show the station management our literal good faith," said Sammy. "Suffice to say that my relationship with them didn't work out, and I left the station and the show within a year. But it turned out that Gene was a more convincing holy-roller. He went into the tele-Jesus business after that, had quite the profitable run, from what I gather."

"Your roommate is Gene Lufkin, the preacher?" Elfa sometimes saw him on late-night TV, broadcasting from an old hotel in downtown Los Angeles. "You mean he's got...?"

"So it would seem," Sammy finished for her. "The coma precludes any chance of conversation." He paused to cough; a wet, congested hacking that sounded so close it made the phone handset twitch against her cheek. *Amazing long-distance service, Ma Bell*, Elfa thought ruefully.

"On the lighter side of the news, the cheery atmosphere here has done me wonders," Sammy resumed at last. "You really must venture out here and see it for yourself. Everybody dressed up like astronauts, every object dropped into biohazard bags on first use. They practically shove our food under the door. I can only hope they'll separate me from my bedsheets before burning them."

"You sound better," Elfa lied.

"Eh," he responded mildly. "*Lo que será, será*. I understand there's been some additional...I don't mean to make light of it...*drama* out there since I left you."

"Yes, you could say that. I don't even know where to start."

"No need. Helen told me some of it, and what she didn't tell me I can probably guess at. This young man threw one hell of a Molotov cocktail into her life for the foreseeable future."

"You mean it's all true? Those things he said about her?"

"Very likely. I don't know about the family history part, but the business part is all too plausible, and Helen knows it. She is clearly frightened. In high dudgeon at the boy's impertinence, too, of course; but frightened nonetheless. After all these years, it's almost endearing to see."

"Strummer is dead." Painful even to utter it. Painful and dreamlike, akin to her imaginary teardrop.

"I know," said Sammy after a respectful pause. "And that's also why Helen is afraid now, much more so than she was after that radio broadcast. Before the boy's death, I think she would have been able to finesse her way out of those claims he made about her on Mandy's show with relative ease; but now there will be far greater legal scrutiny of her life and her dealings with Simon. Oh, I'm still confident that she and the Piper financial empire will come out the other end of it all more-or-less intact. But it's an intriguing question to ponder—for whom, exactly, would she be preserving that empire? She's nearly seventy years old now, and even Helen knows she can't take it with her. She has no heirs to speak of, the poor woman. My poor, dear Helen."

Back down the narrow road leading off the hill, then underneath the highway overpass. The white-hot westering sun was just touching the Christ monument high in the near distance. After hanging up with Sammy and going into the kitchen to fix herself a grilled-cheese, it had come to Elfa—as if pressing her sandwich in the scratched-up old Teflon Toastmaster and waiting for it to cook had somehow wrung it from her memory—why she had dreamed of the teardrop. Not imaginary after all: indeed, far from it.

On the roadside just beyond the overpass someone had parked an unmarked police cruiser, a Crown Victoria with its A-pillar-mounted spotlight still intact and a generic FOR SALE sign taped inside the windshield. It was technically parked on the Schultz property, and at a rather slipshod angle at that. She walked around it and made a mental note to have it towed. She reached the backdoor and pulled the Sky Chief fob from underneath the paver, then let herself into the shop.

The skunky fragrance of Mexican brick in the air, too fresh to be the same remnant as last time. Elfa came into the cash register area, what had once been the original service-station's sales room. Where Marty Robbins had supposedly sat with his band and shared a six-pack after returning from his adventure on the Black Mountain, an improbable but enduring yarn about love and murder incubating in his head. Except the yarn *behind* that yarn was even more improbable—was in fact a preposterous, inexcusable lie. Marty Robbins had never once set foot in this place, nor been anywhere near it.

Elfa unshouldered her purse, squatted behind the sales counter and poked at the row of vegetable crates that Manny had always used for unsorted merchandise. It wasn't hard to locate, having lain undisturbed in the exact spot where she remembered discarding it after Manny's funeral five years ago (tucked in the back corner of a Donnatex orange crate). Which meant she'd only discarded it in a pitifully childish sense, not quite permitting herself to throw it in the trash.

A diamond earring!

That's right, mija! *Find the other one and you'll be the richest little girl in Buena Vista! Keep looking!*

The day she'd discovered it, in this very room, while exploring some just-delivered boxes from an estate sale—the "estate" being the one-bedroom home of a widowed neighbor, her husband another *esmeltiano* taken early by lung cancer—Manny was in the other room and Art Mercado was in here, thumbing through the *Herald-Post* while waiting on Manny to join him for another afternoon's upkeep-work on the mountain trail.

She stood up and held the earring now in her palm, or rather, held the thing that first Art and then her father had encouraged her that day to believe was a diamond earring. Later, in junior high school, she had come across the correct word for it in the encyclopedia during a library scavenger hunt: a pendalogue, it was called. A worthless, tear-shaped crystal pendant, probably knocked loose from the deceased widow's humble dining room chandelier by some careless rummager.

Something—or someone—made an abrupt shuffling noise in the other room. Elfa let the teardrop fall on the sales counter in fright and reached for her purse, removing her pistol.

"*¿Quién está ahí?*" she demanded loudly, approaching the doorway to the old service garage.

"*Yolki-palki!*" came the reply. Elfa lowered the gun and turned the corner into the larger room. There was Jaz, lying in a sleeping bag on the floor beside the pup tent.

"How long have you been here? Are you the one who's been breaking in?"

"I didn't break into anywhere," Jaz protested groggily, trying to free himself from the sleeping bag. It seemed he'd been sleeping fully dressed, in a Billabong jacket, T-shirt and corduroy shorts, his Birkenstocks placed neatly beside the ugly chocolate-slag ashtray. "You keep a key outside underneath the paver."

"Everyone's been looking for you. Have you been hiding out here the whole time since…?" She stopped herself, uncertain as to whether he knew about Strummer's death.

"Since what? Oh." At last he managed to sit up and peer around the room in both directions until his eyes located her. "Like I told you, Lori kicked me out of my own house a couple of months ago."

"So you're *living* here. Without asking."

"Am I?" He seemed to consider it a question, and a novel one at that. "Okay. I guess so. I didn't mean to."

"Jaz," said Elfa, coming further into the orbit of his makeshift campsite, "how much do you know about what's been going on? About Strummer and Sammy and…everything?"

He scratched his unshaven chin. "How much do I know?" he said, again as if it were the most amazing, confounding question ever put to him. "Don't know much, never have," he said, shaking his head slowly. "Don't know much about history. Don't know much geology. But I do know that my ass is grass if I leave here."

She wanted to scold him but couldn't. He was being funny, but at the same time he wasn't. He looked frazzled and frightened, which Elfa could more than understand in her current frame of mind.

"Are you hiding from someone?"

Jaz got to his feet in no particular hurry and went to his Birkenstocks, slipping first one foot into a sandal, struggling somewhat to find home, and then the other.

"I fixed the inlet holes in that old toilet with some hot vinegar," he said. "You've also got frayed wiring in your weather-head that makes the lights flicker when it's windy outside. I found a couple of hacksaw blades in those boxes over there and clamped them to your down-pipe, but you'll need to call in EP Electric at some point to replace the whole thing."

"Jaz," said Elfa, exasperated. "Talk to me. What's the last thing at the station that you remember?"

He gave her a disheveled yet purposeful look that reminded her of Peter Falk in *Columbo*.

"Let me ask you something," Jaz said. "How much do *you* know?"

Coda

The desiccated, slack-chinned man lying in the open casket wore an extraordinarily feathery, flamboyant head of hair, something akin to a finely layered icing or cotton candy. Lex had never seen anything like it on a man before, let alone the wine-colored blazer and charmeuse cravat. He found himself reaching out with his index finger to press that hair, fascinated by its sculpted texture and its unnatural blondness, which reminded him a little of He-Man; but Lex's father laid a corrective hand on his at the last second, redirecting it.

"No," Jared warned in a tight, hushed voice.

"Why?" Lex asked. "You let me touch Ash's hair."

"Because Ash was your brother. This man is not family. Don't embarrass us."

A perplexing statement coming from someone who'd violently overturned the casket at the last funeral they'd attended in this place, but Lex dismissed that from his mind as Jared gripped his shoulder, steering him away from the casket and down the shiny maple stage-steps, towards the rows of handsome, upholstered white pews. The whole interior of the place was transformed from what it had been in 1980, the roof beams painted beau blue and festive red chile *ristras* ornamenting the walls. Renee, his new stepmother, was already ahead of them both, having quitted the viewing line in haste to find a seat. Lex turned his eyes once more to the stage, where two teenage boys, each comparable in age to Lex and Asher (or the age that Ash would be now) belted out *"La Golondrina"* ("The Swallow") into a microphone stand while an elderly gentleman in a black cowboy hat accompanied them from a nearby folding chair, strumming a Mexican-style *vihuela*.

Renee had located a pew in the fifth row. She hurried over to it as if in fear of it floating away and sat, scooted close to the far endcap, and crossed her legs with observable effort. Her plump stockingless thighs tested the limits of her tulip skirt. Then she motioned commandingly for Jared and Lex to join her. Lex liked Renee, but sometimes it was as if she'd married Lex's father more than vice-versa—as if *she'd* selected *him*, whether Dad liked it or not. The savings-and-loan branch that she managed in Visalia figured prominently in their lives now—Lex understood that much.

The song ended, and just as Jared and Lex had seated themselves beside Renee, the whole room rose to attention. The other man onstage approached the podium, unmistakably the man who'd wrestled Jared to the floor six years ago and thrust him (holding Jared's left wrist up against the small of his back and driving him forward by the back of his head, gripping him by a snatch of that long hippie-esque hair) out through the

398

building's side door as Lex, Asher, and Timera had followed in horror. Now he pulled the front of his bespoke pinstripe suit snug and nodded in cordial acknowledgment to the pair of women, each strikingly attractive and strikingly different from one another, entering the room, one slightly ahead of the other.

The lady walking in front was the same handsome, redheaded *grande dame* with whom Jared had exchanged such harsh words years ago. She wore a black belted skirt-suit and veiled hat, but something in her stride and carriage, and the red-gray hair tied up in a smartly compressed bun at the back of her head, proclaimed her identity to the crowd. But it was the girl a few paces behind her who drew the gasps and whispers. Also clad in black, her crimped hair and fingerless lace gloves still gave her away. Lex's favorite song just lately was "I Wanna Be a Cowboy," and here was the girl who introduced it every week on *Dial MTV*: Mandy Strummer, in person. Of all the dumb, fantastic luck! And to think that Lex, with help from Renee, had given his father a hard time about coming back to Anapra for yet another funeral.

"*Bienvenido al servicio,*" said the man standing onstage once everyone was seated again, raising his arms. "*Oremos juntos.*" Lex was still standing in amazement, and this time it was Renee who corrected him, tugging the hem of his T-shirt to get him to sit down.

At the foot of the stage was a table decked with electronic consoles, from which emanated numerous cables running in all directions. A lean, goateed technician with half-moon glasses on the end of his nose and wearing big orange-foam headphones sat overlooking the consoles, occasionally adjusting a knob or lever while a toothpick migrated between the corners of his mouth. He sported an ashy braided ponytail, tie-dyed T-shirt, Bermuda shorts, and bare-toed sandals.

"How are our levels, Jaz?" Lex heard the pinstripe-suited man say in English after the opening prayer.

Reverting again to Spanish, he told the audience that they would soon be on the air and admonished them to, at all times, heed the rules of radio etiquette while also remembering they were in a house of worship, however humble. Then he motioned to Mandy, who'd taken a momentary seat in the front row beside the veiled lady.

Mandy rose, came up onstage and took the podium. She looked to Jaz, who made a few more adjustments on his consoles, then gave her a thumbs-up.

"This is Mandy Strummer coming to you live on Radio XAMO, Anapra, Mexico," she said into the microphone, paused, and then added after a long, preparatory deep breath, "Sta-*ween*-ah!"

The audience chuckled, and Lex looked around the room at them all, confused.

"Well, I knew I could never do it like Sammy," Mandy said. "He tried teaching it to me, but it was his catch-phrase, not mine."

The service was concluded. Mandy had eulogized Hitman Hayes for nearly half an hour (in a disappointingly serious, adult, and non-MTV way), and then Simon La Paz had preached and led hymns. At some point Lex had dozed off. Then, suddenly, the large hangar doors in the back were thrown open, and the people of Anapra were shuffling out as respectfully and peaceably as they'd shuffled in.

Renee stood up and retrieved the keys to their rental car from her purse and held them out to Jared. And then the veiled redheaded woman appeared at the end of their pew and approached him. Lex felt his father tense up, surely recalling—just as Lex did—what had occurred between them the last time.

"So you came," she said.

Jared gazed at her for a long moment in stolid silence, still clutching the car keys in one hand.

"You didn't have to," she continued. "But I'm so glad you did."

"You invited us," he replied evenly. "And you came to Ash's funeral, so…"

He seemed unable to finish. The woman nodded in apparent understanding. Then she looked down at Lex. "Is this your other son?"

"Mrs. Piper, what a pleasure to finally meet you!" Renee interjected, holding out a hand in greeting. "We talk about you in our Women's Chamber of Commerce meetings all the time! You're such a true inspiration!"

"That's *Ms.*, honey," the woman corrected her, still offering her hand in greeting. Then Lexed noticed the odd plastic device attached to her wrist and extending out to the place where her ring finger should have been, and yet wasn't. "I was never a Mrs."

"Yes, of course," Renee said, faltering.

"Well," the woman said, returning her attention to Jared. "I do hope you'll come on back to the house with us for some refreshment."

Ms. Piper led them over an unmarked, unpaved artery of desert road in her tan Mercedes Roadster, waving out her side window at a pair of Border Patrol agents observing them from a parked truck on a nearby ridge. The agents waved back.

The Mercedes made a left onto another road lined with railroad cross-ties, and then its taillights flashed as they came to a momentary stop before a pair of iron gates, each bearing the shape of a rearing stallion. Then the gates swung inward, and the Mercedes proceeded up a long curving driveway, Jared following it at a respectful distance from behind the rental's wheel. The house slid into full view, resembling something out of the movies, or maybe out of the more decadent rock videos—the ones that also featured beautiful girls with big hair and skimpy bikinis. Soaring pink stucco walls, Spanish-tile roof, balcony windows with flowering vines climbing through the grillwork.

"And so this woman is actually your grandmother?" Renee exclaimed in wonder.

"Technically," Jared replied. "Only if you think sharing blood cells with someone counts as 'related.'"

"Well, my word, that seems a little harsh," Renee said. "All this wealth she obviously has...and there you are in Visalia—there *we* are—paying a third mortgage on the house and stables and barely making ends meet. I would think she'd be in a perfect position to help if you asked her. Have you ever tried asking?"

Jared cast an uncomfortable glance at the backseat, where Lex was sitting in his Ocean Pacific windsurfer shirt (both he and Renee had balked at wearing hot funeral clothing), having shifted his eyes to the ash-colored mountain adjacent to the house. *The* mountain. Where Asher had died almost a year ago.

"Let's not talk about that right now," Jared said to Renee.

The driveway wound its way around the house to a red-chat courtyard in the back, where the Mercedes came to a final stop beside a Spanish-tile water fountain. The old woman who was missing a finger climbed out of the driver's side, and Mandy, who'd been riding shotgun, got out on the passenger side.

After parking, Jared, Renee, and Lex entered the house, where Helen and Mandy awaited them in the main foyer. Lex marveled at the grand staircase and iron chandelier. The house was like no private home he'd ever seen.

"It's a spooky-looking old dump, isn't it?" Ms. Piper said to him, registering his amazement. "But it keeps the rain off my head, at least."

When they entered the great-room a teenage Latina girl in a white tuxedo shirt, white gloves, and pleated skirt approached them with a tray of Coca-Cola juleps in small silver cups. Another was serving sweet and spicy Coca-Cola shredded pork bites on tomàquet toast.

"They're alcohol-free, don't worry," Mandy assured Jared when he told Lex to put his julep back. "Everything's made with Coke Classic, even the desserts. Helen likes to spoil me whenever I come visit." She winked at Lex. "What do you think?"

Up close, she was beautiful. Something in her green eyes and delicate peach-undertone skin, which included a faint port-wine stain on her left cheek that Lex had never noticed when she was on TV, made him nervous as he tried his drink. And something in the way she looked at Jared as she found them a vacant sofa and led them to it made Lex think that she and his father were already acquainted. Mandy withdrew to speak with Simon La Paz, who had also just arrived from the church across the desert, and Helen. Then another wan-faced serving girl approached with a tray of chicken-bacon bites barbecued in strawberry-Coke jam. A man on an adjacent sofa interceded to collect two chicken bites for himself. He was already holding a saucer loaded down with pork bites, zucchini-and-pepper gratin with herbs and cheese, and smoked tri-tip on blue-corn tortilla pinwheels.

"Daddy, please control yourself," said a young redheaded woman whom Lex recognized from Asher's funeral. She rose to shake Jared's hand.

"Hello, Mr. Rede. Hello there, Lex."

"Hello, Casey," Jared replied. "It's good to see you again."

"Did you know Mr. Hayes before he died?"

"Only from the radio, like everyone else. Helen invited us to his funeral, but I'm not altogether clear about why."

"That comes as no surprise," Casey said, lowering her voice. She smoothed her skirt and sat back down beside her father. "I've never known Helen to be clear about her true motives in just about any situation."

"I see no call to insult the lady in her own home," Renee remarked then. "Especially when she's being such a gracious host."

"Er...sorry, this is my wife, Renee," Jared explained, his own mouth full of gratin and cheese. "We were married in December. I had to refinance our land after everything that happened last year, and Renee's S&L branch took a special interest in our case. And then *she* took a special interest in *me*, though I'm damned if I know why."

The hors d'oeuvres and small-talk with Casey and Lou Barefoot seemingly exhausted, Helen came back into the great-room as if on cue and asked Jared to follow her to the upstairs study. Renee immediately rose with her saucer in hand, eager to follow, but Helen made a shooing gesture to her with that maimed hand.

"Oh, you can keep your seat, honey," Helen told her. "I'm just going to show your husband some old horse-riding books I thought he might like to have. Try the banana pudding pastry cups."

The study was in a sun-filled room just off the grand staircase's top landing. Only one wall held a bookcase; the others were dominated by arched windows, an adobe fireplace, and on the wall opposite the doorway, a mural depicting a cattle stampede (led by a maddened, blood-eyed black bull) underneath a lightning storm. A hapless lone cowboy, toppled from his horse, was in the process of falling headfirst into an arroyo, no doubt to his death.

"You're still welcome to spend the night here at the house, I just want to remind you," Helen told him, walking around the ornate writing desk. "That Motel 6 out on the highway has a reputation for bedbugs."

"No, thanks. What is this supposed to be?" He approached the mural, hands on the hips of his slacks, drawn to it despite his better sense.

Helen glanced up from the paperwork she was gathering together on the desktop. "Tom Lea painted that," she answered, seating herself at the desk and producing a pair of bifocals. "A late friend of the family. It's from 'Little Joe the Wrangler,' that old folk song."

Jared let it go, turning to face the desk. There really was a small stack of antique books on the desktop, he noticed. The top title, bound in indigo cloth with gold inlay, was *The Blood of the Arab: The World's Greatest War Horse*, by Albert W. Harris.

"So what am I doing here?"

Casey had excused herself from the gathering downstairs to roam Helen's art collection again, a ritual indulgence of hers that she liked to squeeze in during every visit to the Pink Piper hacienda, preferably alone. But really, it was the house itself that she admired. A conscious, ancient, living thing, vibrant with unexpected light and wisdom that amounted to more than its gorgeous old hardwoods, wrought iron, and ceramic tiles. Shadows and secrets as well. Coldness and warmth alike pervaded the rose-tinged adobe walls. The millions of hairline cracks in the plaster, the nicks and blemishes on the baseboards, and the tiny, decades-old scuffs in the wainscoting all contributed as much beauty as age lines in a loved-one's face. The soft groans and creaks in the wooden joints, the sighs of drafty air suggested the textures of sound in an old grandmother's voice. Oh yes, this hacienda was a woman.

Then she came out onto the back terrace, entertaining thoughts of setting up camp there to watch the sunset, except that it was much too early in the afternoon for that. Instead she found Elfa Schultz seated by herself, a single lace-gloved hand over her mouth, weeping silently.

"Want some company?" Casey asked. "No one should cry alone."

Elfa seemed to flinch ever so slightly in startlement, then lowered her hand from her face.

"Sure," she said.

"Here." Casey held out the folded cocktail napkin she'd been carrying in case her summer hay fever started to act up. "Long time, no see," she added, taking the Adirondack chair beside Elfa's.

"I know, right?" Elfa daubed her eyes with the napkin and offered Casey a thin smile. "The last year has been pretty wild. It never rains, but it pours."

"Well, congratulations on your career, anyway," said Casey. "I saw your interview with Julian Lennon the other day. Like I needed another reason to be jealous of you."

"Thanks. But it's all happening a little too fast lately. Sometimes I wonder how much more I can take. All the good stuff seems to come with just as much bad."

"You'll get through it," Casey said. "I'm really sorry about that other stuff, about your father's friend, you know...that he was the one who did it. And the drug-running on the mountain. Dad and I followed it pretty closely in the news, we couldn't help it. And when I heard them say that Shaw Jepsen was involved in it, too, well...I didn't date him for very long, but just knowing that's the kind of person he really was...." Elfa had looked away, so Casey decided to change the subject. "Anyway, you must be looking forward to getting back to New York."

"It was Helen," Elfa said softly. "Helen got me the job. I didn't do anything to deserve it. Nothing except lie about—"

"Don't," Casey said, taking her hand. "Don't do that to yourself."

They sat there together in silence for a while.

"He loved you, you know," Casey said then.

"Who? Oh. Yes, I know."

"Did you love him back at all? Even a little?"

Elfa shrugged. "I loved Strummer. I never knew that other person. The person he really was. Asher."

"Yeah, me neither."

After a while Casey rose and left Elfa to her solitude and mourning. Somewhere along the way to becoming famous as Mandy Strummer, Elfa had found time to return to Nueva Anapra and testify against Art Mercado for murdering her father. Manny Schultz had discovered Art's part in a drug-smuggling ring on the Black Mountain six years ago and threatened to turn Art in to the authorities. After Asher's death on the mountain, Elfa, troubled that Art had somehow ended up in possession of one of Shaw's service dogs, had gone to Art and confronted him wearing a wire placed on her by the county attorney. Art confessed to her. Upon his arrest, Art had then implicated Shaw Jepsen and Tommy Cereceres. An additional witness, Tolf Denetclaw, had further implicated Simon La Paz and Helen Piper. Strangely, Tolf had been found shot dead in his van, parked near the river bank, shortly thereafter.

No way those other two weren't in on it, Lou had groused during a nightly news segment on Art Mercado's trial. *Helen and Simon must have been cleaning house.* Casey had told him to shut his mouth, thinking of Tolf's fate.

She spared one last look at Elfa before going back inside. Sunset was still hours away, but the light had shifted such that it glinted against her eyes in profile. Those eyes were dry now, dry and hardening like calluses over a wound. Yes, Mandy was going to be all right. But Elfa Schultz was no longer there.

When Casey re-entered the house through the terrace doors, a pair of voices came from just beyond an open door down the hallway, growing louder as she neared the stairway landing. She slowed, unable to help herself, as she recognized one voice as belonging to Jared Rede, Asher's father.

"—want nothing of yours, so just put your checkbook away."

"Not even for your other son?" came the voice of Helen Piper. "You can put it in a college fund. Or you can donate it to charity in Asher's name, I really don't care."

"Yes, I think that was the original problem all along. You didn't care then, and you're only pretending to care now. What is it you're after, anyway, a tax deduction? Trying to buy yourself some peace of mind, maybe?"

"There's no call for insults. I only want to acknowledge what happened to Asher, to acknowledge the connection between my family and yours, just like I told you a year ago after his funeral. And it's still the way that I feel. I suppose that I thought you might feel a little differently now that some time has passed. Don't you think your son must have wanted that? Isn't that the only reasonable explanation for his coming here in the first place?"

"No, in fact, I honestly believe he came here originally to kill you," Jared replied, closer now to the open door. "I know my *abuelo* filled his head with some nonsense about you cursing us. Ash was close to my *abuelo*, and I think now that I didn't do enough to warn Ash about my grandfather's anger against you; how it poisoned his heart over the years after you jilted him. But I also think that Asher must have changed his mind at some point, probably when he found out the truth behind your power and wealth. He realized that there was a better way to avenge his grandfather, by exposing you to the whole world for what you are. Not that his doing that really even hurt you at all. You're obviously still...*you*."

"And what am I, exactly?" Helen answered, plainly exasperated. "Go on and finish hurting me, if it makes you feel better, if that's what it will take to lay this whole sordid business to rest for the both of us. Maybe you're more like your grandfather than you think."

"I think," Jared replied after a long silence, "no, I *know*—now more than ever—that you're satisfied being whatever you are, whatever the right word for it is. And that makes me feel sorry for you, which is something my *abuelo* could never have done himself. Now that I know you, I pity you. I think *you're* the one who's cursed. As for my family, I think if there was ever any curse on us, it started when my *abuelo* accepted your father's dirty money. So that ends right here. Goodbye."

His shadow fell on the door, meaning he was about to step out into the hallway and catch Casey eavesdropping. She hurried away towards the stairs.

"Take the dad-gum horse books, at least!" she heard Helen call out after him. "So you're wife doesn't think you're a complete fool!"

"She'll think that anyway," Jared deadpanned, coming out into the hall. Casey stopped at the top of the stairs and turned back to face him.

"That sounded a little heated back there," she told him, feeling sheepish. "Sorry, I couldn't help overhearing some of it."

"No worries," Jared replied, though his face was still flushed with anger. "It was nice to see you again, Casey. And if I never thanked you for all the kindness you showed Asher, then I'm thanking you now."

"You're welcome," she replied.

He turned and hooked a thumb back at the open door to the study. "Maybe you should peek in on her while she's in a check-writing mood. I thinks she's still itching to give some money away to *somebody*."

Casey laughed nervously, and Jared moved on and headed down the stairway. Deciding that now was probably a good time to excuse herself and her father for the day and head home, she approached the door and tapped it lightly with one knuckle.

"Come in," said Helen.

Her voice sounded as if she'd already recovered from whatever rattling that Jared had given her, so Casey proceeded into the room, mouth open to say a quick thank-you and goodbye, and then she stopped short.

A woman was seated at the large writing table in front of the row of windows, but it wasn't Helen. This woman, much older, wore a dirty indigo *rebozo* and some kind of black bowler hat. In one hand she clutched a mummified animal fetus, shriveled and also black. She smiled at Casey, her mouth toothless and beset on all sides by hundreds of wrinkles, a strand of wiry white hair falling over one hoary leather cheek.

Seeing no one else in the room, Casey backed away in confusion and returned downstairs to her father.

Acknowledgments

The author wishes to thank the following for their generous guidance and support: Joy Baggett, Thomas Collette, Gyneth Garrison, Heidi McConnell, Dr. Alisia Muir, and Dr. Bruce Louden.